NECROLOGUE

THE DIVA BOOK OF THE DEAD
AND THE UNDEAD

EDITED BY HELEN SANDLER

DIVA

In the same series:

The Diva Book of Short Stories

Groundswell: The Diva Book of Short Stories 2

First published 2003 by Diva Books,
an imprint of Millivres Prowler Limited,
part of the Millivres Prowler Group,
Unit M, Spectrum House, 32–34 Gordon House Road,
London NW5 1LP UK

www.divamag.co.uk
www.divamailorder.com

'Ladies' Fingers' by Stella Duffy is adapted from a shorter piece
originally written for *The Hand*, Gay Sweatshop, 1995.
'The Book Club' by Ali Smith is taken from her collection,
The Whole Story and Other Stories (Hamish Hamilton, London, 2003),
copyright © Ali Smith 2003, reproduced by kind permission
of Penguin Books Ltd. and the author.

A CIP catalogue record for this book is available from the British Library

ISBN 1-873741-87-1

Printed and bound in Finland by WS Bookwell

Distributed in the UK and Europe by Airlift Book Company,
8 The Arena, Mollison Avenue,
Enfield, Middlesex EN3 7NJ
Telephone: 020 8804 0400
Distributed in North America by Consortium,
1045 Westgate Drive, St Paul, MN 55114-1065
Telephone: 1 800 283 3572
Distributed in Australia by Bulldog Books,
PO Box 300, Beaconsfield, NSW 2014

Contents

Acknowledgements

Thanks to everyone who has been involved with this book, including Kathleen for bringing it out, Raj Rai for publicising it, our mystery man for the cover, Sue Harper for proofing it, my partner Jane Hoy and other friends and colleagues for encouragement and wise words, the writers who are in here and the ones whose stories didn't quite fit this time.

Introduction

When I was putting together the 2002 anthology *Groundswell*, I found myself with a dilemma. There were twice as many good stories as I could use in a single collection. But it slowly dawned on me that about half of them were, in some way, about death, grief, memory, the occult and the spirit. It was a loose connection but one that gelled when I took a second look at Susan Em's story 'Necrologue', a strange and disturbing piece whose title was begging to be the title of a book – more precisely, the title of a book of the dead.

As I ran the words through my head, with all the stories about ghouls and murders, hauntings and grieving and noises in the woodshed, the rest of the subtitle clicked into place and the project was a goer.

Admittedly not everyone has been excited by the idea of a book of the dead and the undead – some thought it rather morbid, which it undoubtedly is – but those who liked the idea *really* liked it. This was encouraging because the last two anthologies were hard acts to follow. With this book I have kept the most important ingredients from the earlier anthologies: a mixture of established and newer writers, including first-timers; a focus on writing from the UK (but this time with a few more Americans in the mix); some humour and some darkness... Actually, this book is by far the darkest of the three, but that's probably what you were expecting.

It opens with Carolyn Finlay's sad and atmospheric story, 'Zoom', in which a teenage girl drives around thinking about her lost friend; then continues the journey with Ali Smith's 'The Book Club', in which the narrator is in a taxi thinking about a missing girl from her childhood and her own dead mother. How do we make sense of our identities when those who shaped us have left us? Rose Collis explores this question further in 'Proof of Identity', with an array of gory corpses and a mother with some skeletons in the cupboard. Then Kathi Kosmider, in 'Baking Bread', makes use of brutal and poetic language on her 'road for the dead'.

Robyn Vinten lightens the tone (sort of!) as a group of friends compare funeral stories at a party in 'Whatever Gets You Through'. There's another group of friends in 'Glowing' by Elizabeth Woodcraft, who strays from her usual crime writing with this tale of making a connection before it's too late.

For the mother in Frances Gapper's 'There Was an Old Woman', it's almost too late already, whereas the senior citizen who goes 'Shopping' without taking the trouble to pay, in Caril Behr's story, is determined that it's never too late.

The thread of conversations with the dead is taken up by Frances Bingham in 'Call Me by My Name', in which a woman visits a medium, desperate for contact with a certain lady; then Bryony Weaver's narrator gets more contact than she bargained for in 'Ashes'.

There are ghosts you're glad to see and ghosts you hoped were gone forever. Cara Bruce shows us a date with one of the latter in 'What She Left Behind'. This is a turning-point in the book, introducing a world of people who live beyond normal morality and pay a high price. But it's hard to stay with them for long at a time so Ellen Galford (yes, she's back!) brings us up for air in 'Daddy's Girls' before the fantasy turns dark again in the title story, Susan Em's dystopic tale of the clerk who writes the names of the dead in the Necrologue. Susan Em, Fiona Zedde, it's an alphabet out there. The latter author drags us back down to the underworld in 'Nightshade' and Julie Travis explores another kind of hell in 'Owl-blasted'.

But what is hell? And what is heaven? In 'Terminus' by Rosie Lugosi and 'Little Ironies' by Linda Innes, we see two possibilities, while 'Your Ghost' by Kim Watson seems to leave its narrator in limbo.

One of the themes of the book is clearly ghosts. It's hard to read this far without making a case for their existence, whether they are formed from our own imaginations or whether they are 'real' separate entities.

But in 'They Flee from Me that Sometime Did Me Seek', which takes its title from a poem by Thomas Wyatt about the effects of one's ageing on one's suitors, it is the spectre of the future that haunts the protagonists. In this, the third episode in the adventures of Androula and her lover, Cherry Smyth paints a tragicomic portrait of the middle-aged butch who models herself on a teenage boy. At the end, she's seeing coloured lights; at the beginning of 'The Auto-cannibal' by Kathleen Kiirik Bryson, there is bright light again but a dark future for characters living in a post-apocalyptic world without food. What do they do? The title, alas, is the answer.

The 'Ladies' Fingers' of Stella Duffy's story are not for eating, while a lady's feet in 'Dirty Cow' by Fi Benson give the game away. Another foot kicks off Ann Rower's story about a woman who can't stop collecting souvenirs of other people's deaths. She is strangely drawn to the cemetery; so too is the narrator of 'The Passing Guest' by V.G. Lee, who goes one further when she seems set on causing a couple of deaths. That story ends with a difficult phone call and the next, 'Justin Thomas Is Dead' by Georgina McIntosh, opens with one, before sitting us round a Ouija board with a collection of workmates who are not exactly a help in a crisis. The narrator's mother is dying; perhaps that is why she is 'chosen' by the spirit of the seance. If so, is she perhaps doleurvoyant?

What's that? In Cecilia Tan's haunting story 'Touch Pain', we find out. Both this story and 'Switch' by Shireen Sharif share a disturbing feeling that reality is shifting, that cause and effect are far from straightforward. Similarly, but more optimistically, Charlotte Cooper's 'When the Car Slammed into Me' takes us in and out of 'reality' and up, up and away with a much-missed brother.

For my own story, I had ghosts to visit too, but then 'I Saw God'. I've become fascinated lately by how we see 'spirit' or 'soul', and the more I ask around, the more answers I get. Perhaps it's the theme for another book, but Tenea D. Johnson explores it beautifully in the final story in this collection, 'Deep Night', through three generations of African-American women in the southern states. As with Shireen's story, splitting and madness are the results of being pulled between one's heritage, one's individual path, and the drive to assimilate or gain the approval of family or the mainstream. They are themes that many lesbians will recognise.

I am writing this at midnight on a day when the temperature in London topped a hundred degrees. Through the branches of the tree outside my window, a full and yellowish moon emerges from spooky black and white clouds. The house is still sweltering. All the ghosts of the book are clamouring around me. Take them away! But beware, they will haunt you too.

Helen Sandler, August 2003

Zoom
Carolyn Finlay

Zoom
Carolyn Finlay

Dark water, dusty trees, a knife of sunlight. Your body a creamy line on grey rocks. The scene in black and white. Rewind.

Wasn't this in colour? Weren't there browns, greens? When I passed you at the window wasn't there the usual sky? Didn't your eyes change, didn't they always change?

Hot town, window down. Bubbled tarmac. Edges potholed like a ribbon of film. Of all the times we met, how many can you remember? How many can I? Five million, maybe. All through school, same class, same row. Or ten, the ones that mattered. Just the last ten times, just the last term before we finished. Just last year.

At school they used to say I couldn't concentrate. Couldn't remember things. There one minute, gone the next. Changeable. But now I know what concentrating is, remembering. Keeping it still in your mind, even if it bounces around like a car over country roads. Even if it keeps changing.

Even if you can't tell it's there any more. Even if the dust settles down all thick on top of it, the way it does on the quicksand down at Fowlers Marsh late on a summer evening.

Over by the ghost gums out there on a hot night the lagoon shines black through the white branches. It's hot again now. From the Rosny turn-off I can see Mum's washing line. Good drying day, she'd say.

Good driving day, I'd say. Funny to see our underwear from the other side of town. Jim's drainpipe Wranglers full of wind. Better than his bandy ankles sticking out of them. He's nicer to me now though, anyroad. Well, not so much as brotherly. Just, like careful. Eyeing me out of the corner of his. Like he's trying to understand something.

I just keep watching the TV. Not the news. *Sea Hunt*, *The Mouseketeers*. Juvenile stuff. Too young for a sixteen-year-old. Keep a low profile. Don't want them sending me to the Convent up on Mt Nelson. But they won't. That's a home for naughty girls. What that means is girls with babies, only no one says.

So you and me must have been good girls, eh? Not what old Gus Watkins said when he wandered past us in the sand dunes that time. I was only feeding you sherbet swirls. He didn't like us laughing. So they keep asking me stuff. Keep on and on asking me. Like when did I last see you, where? What did we do, who with? On and on.

Best thing is, keep out of the way. Don't pout you don't get a clout, Dad used to say. Put up or shut up, Mum says. What she's good at. Even when Dad went off, even the last time. There one minute, gone the next. See, I can remember when I need to. Round the school gate there was a great big nothing. Like on my reports. Don't have to care about that now. Or snarky teachers. Can't you remember *anything*, Doran Taylor? I could concentrate hard enough for the driving test though.

I knew it would be better once you get the licence. I take Jim's Falcon when he's at work. He says, what's he need it for at the garage, he can walk home down the block. I just drive around. Fast, slow, take photographs. Zoom. Stop. Zoom. Close-up. Not too close up though. That's when everything goes out of focus.

Last summer. I remember that. When you were here. Like when we all went along wallaby shooting even though Mum yelled at Jim not to take us? All crammed in the back of Billy Reid's ute. Jim boiled it up on the fire after, made wallaby-tail stew. In between him looking you up and down. But you gotta catch your wallaby first. That's what he kept saying. Thought it was so funny, he nearly choked laughing.

Past Sullivan's Point, the light hits down the side of each wave. I keep the camera on the floor in the back, just in case something happens. Where'd you get that? Jim asks. I told him you lent it to me. Before you went away. He gives me that look again. My cheek's a pale slice in the rear-view mirror. You should always check who's behind you.

Why didn't you believe me when I told you everything would be all right? How many times did I say it? Ten times? Or was it five million? You just kept staring out to sea. Do you remember me telling you the turning? You said the track was too narrow. You said the light was too bright in your eyes.

But your eyes changed, they always changed. Like when you fell out with Diane. Best friends for two years, then one day you reckon she's boring. I should have known. Should have remembered.

It's supposed to be me who forgets things. Wouldn't forget a friend though. Forget them like they didn't exist. Well, I never had that many to forget. Annette Funicello on *Mouseketeers*, she's really popular. She's the Pineapple Princess. If someone's got that many friends, it must be easy to get bored with one or two of them. Not notice if you haven't seen them in a while.

Like when all us final-year class had to go to the film festival. Mr Clark made us go, went on how it would be good for our English. He just wanted to get in free. A whole day we had off school. Two films before lunch, three after. Rubbish, I thought. Stupid rubbish. But it wasn't. It was the best thing ever. Afterwards I remembered everything. Gave Mr Clark a big surprise when he read my essay, even though he said the spelling was bad.

But right at the end there, that was the trouble. When the lights come on and everybody stands up. You were there. Not sick in bed at home. You stood up, laughing, holding hands. The lights were too bright to see your eyes. You didn't check who was behind you. Didn't care. Didn't remember to care. It was supposed to be me who forgets things.

I should tell them now, how I spend the whole time driving around, just remembering. But I can't tell them. Can't tell them anything. The road's melting. February's the hottest.

Jim used to skive off most days, do wheelies round the block listening to 'Hey Paula'. Not any more. Since you disappeared, he works all day and nights down the garage. I'm going to save up. Go to film school. I'm going to photograph the wind, the metal leaves. A whole film of the wind in leaves.

Or a picnic. Jim goes, 'Life's no picnic.' But mine will be. I'll make it one. The film of the picnic of my life. Black and white. First scene with you on the rocks lit all from one side, looking out over the dark water. Last scene a pile of leaves, all dead. Just the lens of my camera sticking out the top.

There's always a film going on. Inside my head. Images. I think of your mouth, filled up with red dust. With sweets. Your eyes, blue, or green, reflecting clouds. The ghost gums, the black water. The school gate, empty. A knife of sunlight. And me driving. Driving down the melting roads.

The Book Club
Ali Smith

The Book Club
Ali Smith

The girl who went missing was the same age as I was. Her school photograph was in the papers and on the Scottish news on television, which I found very exciting at the time since nothing about where we lived was ever on television, not even Scottish television. I was ten. I spent the long light nights that summer playing by myself in and out of the greenhouse my father was putting up in our back garden. It had no plants or glass in it yet, just the concrete floor, the frame of its sides and roof and the new door stiff in its runners. I could put my arm through glass that wasn't there and imagine it passing through solid wall, like in The Bionic Woman. I could lean out of the top half of the door like it was a stable door, or crouch down under the metal bar across its middle and walk through the bottom half of it without opening it.

I heard my father over the fence talking to someone by the garages. He called me out of our garden. She loves books, he was saying to the man. Here, he said to me, this man says he'll let you choose any book you like out of his van, then when you've read it you can give it back to him and get another one.

The man's name was Stephen; he sold books round the Highlands and Islands. The inside of his van was all books. It had folding steps at the back doors; it was all right to go in because my father had said it was. It wasn't a library, they weren't for borrowing, they were for selling. They had titles like Papillon and Shogun. I chose one about someone looking for someone, with the actress I now know to be Diane Keaton on the cover smiling and smoking a cigarette; I chose it because she was pretty.

If you're careful with it, the man from the van said, I'll be able to sell it on.

He showed me how to hold it and bend it gently so the spine wouldn't crease and so I wouldn't smear the page-edge with dirty hands. I read it in bed. It was about sex, then somebody killed her. Each night I held the book like he'd shown me because of the person who would be reading it after me, maybe someone who lived out on one of the islands. Someone up there would buy it from the van and would have it in their house and I had to make sure they would never know I had read it before them. There was a girl from the Outer Hebrides at my school. She spoke like her words had extra sounds to them, fussy-edged like the lace things my mother stuck with long pins on to the backs and arms of the new three-piece suite in the front room.

My mother, eyeing me blank and steady over the breakfast plates.

Iona, you're looking a bit pale, she said. Come here.

She felt my head. I had been awake long after everybody else, reading and rereading the bits about sex and the part at the end where the man did it, holding the book as hardly open as possible with my head at an angle to try to make out the words at the hidden inside ends of the lines.

I was up late reading, I said.

She pushed the butter into her toast, hard and spare with the knife. Neither of my parents read books. If you worked you had no time for it. My mother especially had no time for it, she saw no point in it, which is why it's still surprising to me that one of the very few things I have of hers now, ten years after her death, is a book. Rip Van Winkle and other stories by Washington Irving. She gave it to me one afternoon when I was in my twenties, home from college for the summer; you can have this, she said. God knows where she'd kept it, I'd never seen it before and I knew every book in the house. It was a school book. It has her maiden name and the name of her school written in neat handwriting inside a printed shield saying This Book Belongs To, and her name scrawled in blotted blue capitals all along the page edge in messy different-sized letters. Its date of publication is 1938, the year her father died and she had to leave school. She was fourteen. Now I have the book, her grey leather driving gloves and her wedding ring.

I am thinking about all this between the airport and home, in a black cab crossing the south-east of England. The driver is keen to talk to me, I can sense it. I take a book out of my bag and hold it ready, though I know if I do actually try to read it I will get motion sickness. It's a book that was on a lot of shortlists last year. It's written by a man and the trick of it is that it's written as if a woman were writing it. Everybody says it's good. I turn it over in my hand. It smells of my father's tomatoes. I hold it to my nose and fan its pages. My bag is full of tomatoes, some near-ripe, some still green. I am supposed to put them on my windowsill when I get home.

The driver half turns towards me. I open the book in the middle. I glance at it, then out of the window. The grass on the road verges is high again, the fields the gold colour they go at this time of year. I press a button by my armrest and the glass to my right slides down. Summer air comes in. The summers go round and round, they seem not to get any older at all, they seem smooth, repetitive, summer back again, but really they date as hopelessly as if you put an old 45 on a turntable, or maybe took an old 45 off a turntable and skimmed it into a canal on a still day like today then stood staring at the surface where there's nothing to say anything ever skimmed across it or sank below it or happened at all.

Now the driver is asking me something. Excuse me, he is saying from behind his divide. Where do you want?

His voice sounds amplified but far away. I've already told him where we're meant to be going. What if we're going the wrong way? I don't have that much cash on me and already the animated circle on his meter which lights a new piece of itself every three or four seconds and means ten pence each time the circle completes itself has completed itself an alarming number of times and we're only just on the outskirts of Luton.

I tell him the name of the town again.

No, but where? he says.

Near the centre, I'll tell you when we get there, I shout at the divide.

But where exactly? he says. The street you live in. How is it spelled?

You won't know it, I shout. It's very small.

You don't need to speak so loud, he says. I can hear you.

Without taking his eyes off the road he points to a sign above the back of his head. When the light is on, the sign says, you may speak to your driver.

Oh, right, I shout. Then I speak more normally. The street I live in is very small, I say, but when we get there I'll tell you which way to go.

No, he says. Because look.

He has a screen stuck to his dashboard about the size of a paperback. He flips its insides down and open. He punches some buttons.

I just told it the city we're going to, he says.

A voice comes out of the screen, the voice of a middle-class English lady. She says: *at the next roundabout, continue straight ahead.* Words appear on the screen at the same time saying the same thing.

We come to a roundabout. We continue straight ahead.

So where do you live exactly? the driver says.

He enters the name of my street into his machine. Several maps flash up. That's where you live, isn't it? Is that where you live? he is saying. There? He swivels his head from me to the road ahead and then back to me then to the road again. The cab swerves as he turns. I slide about in the seat.

Yes, I say.

See? he says. It's good, isn't it? It can tell you anything about anywhere. Anywhere you ask it. Anywhere at all. It sends a signal to the satellite and the satellite sends a signal back.

He points at a small dark box fitted on to the other side of his cab.

And you can have the voice on to tell you, or just the words on here if you don't want to listen to the voice, or both, if you want both, or neither, if you don't want a voice or the information, he says.

He switches the voice on and off to show me. He turns the volume up and down. He is a lot younger than me. It's a new cab. Everything metal about it is reflecting light and its grey insides are new. It says on a sticker by my hand on the door the words Made In Coventry With Pride.

It cost eighteen hundred, he says, and that's not all it does. It tells you, look, it tells you all these things.

At the next roundabout, the lady's voice says, *continue straight ahead.*

He presses a series of buttons one after another.

It tells me the fastest route, he says. And the route that is quietest. It tells me exactly how many miles till I have to turn left or right. It tells me about roadworks. It tells me how many miles it is to your house, not just to the city but right to your house. And look, it can tell me the route that saves me petrol, and when we get to town it will tell me exactly which way to go to get to your house and exactly how many yards before I have to turn left or right to get there. See that roadsign? What does it say?

Bedford 15 miles, I say.

Look on here, look, what does it say?

Bedford 15 miles, I say.

Exactly, he says. Exactly. So if we wanted to go to Bedford, we would know for certain without needing a roadsign that it's only fifteen miles away. Did you ever travel in a cab like this before?

No, I say, this is my first.

I wonder to myself if it is an elaborate chat-up technique. Do you want to go to Bedford. He tells me that soon all cabs and probably all cars will have navigation systems like his.

My name is Wasim, he says. I'll give you my mobile number and whenever you need a cab from Luton you can call me and I'll always fetch you from the airport.

What? he says when I tell him my name. How is it spelled?

He tries to make sense of it.

It sounds like three words, not one, he says.

It's the name of an island, I say. It's a place. You could type it into your machine and find me on it.

Ha ha, he says. But where are you from, if it is OK to ask?

I point to the screen. You know exactly, I say.

Ah, he says. No, before that. You're from somewhere else. I can tell by the way you speak.

At the next junction, the middle-class lady's voice says, *turn left.*

He tells me he has a cousin who works in Glasgow. I tell him

Glasgow's not really near where I'm from.

I visited, he says. It rained.

He lifts both hands off the wheel in a shrug which takes in the whole country round us, deep in its afternoon sun.

I nod and smile. I sit back.

Are you too hot? Do you need air-conditioning? Tell me if you need anything, he says.

I'm fine, I say. Thank you.

If you want to go to sleep, go ahead, he says. I'll wake you when you're near home.

He flicks a switch on the dashboard. The little red light above his head goes out.

Her name was Carolyn Fergusson, she lived down the Ferry, it was before the new bridge and I can remember the posters stuck on the shop windows with her school photograph on them, she looked sad. They found her in her uncle's house up in Kinmylies hidden all over the place in supermarket bags in cupboards, I remember a friend of my parents going round to the house and telling them; he knew because he worked at the police labs, and that the smell when they went in was really terrible even though the summer hadn't been nearly as hot as the one the year before; they were in the kitchen talking about it and I was listening through the door and when they heard me there my mother shouted at me to go out in the back garden and bring the washing in. That summer I Feel Love by Donna Summer was number one for weeks and after it the Brotherhood of Man. Running away together, running away for ever, Angelo. Whenever I hear those songs now I think of then. We weren't supposed to leave our gardens; we were supposed to stay where our parents could see us at all times. The following summer we could go where we liked again and I can't remember what was number one.

Next to the tomatoes in the bag is the lump of defrosting soup in its Tupperware container; he wrapped it in newspaper to keep it cool. He is refusing to take any of the pills his doctor told him to take. He was proud about it. You're being stupid, I said. Rubbish, he said, they do you more harm than good. He took me out into his garden and pointed at some huge concrete slabs by the greenhouse and said, as soon as you've gone I'm going to take those seven slabs up and put them back down on the other side of the garden and then I can swing the caravan round on to them, and then there's the fridge-freezer in the garage I'm going to move into the house later today if I can get it through the door. You are joking, aren't you, I said. But he's a bit deaf in one ear and he was looking away from me with the wrong ear turned towards me, he didn't answer.

I feel the cab turn left. The soup is wrapped in newspaper covered with the story of the missing schoolgirls, which is why, I suppose, I'm even thinking of Carolyn Fergusson. It's pushed the build-up of war on to the second and third and international pages. It's always in the summer they go missing, as if it's the right season for it, as if the people who take them have been waiting, like farmers or fruit pickers or tabloid editors, for the right weather to kick in for it. When I was about twelve and got home late one summer night, when they'd been calling me and calling me all round the neighbourhood to come in and I hadn't heard, they were so angry that they threw me round the kitchen, my father grabbing one arm as my mother let go of the other. I bounced off the units. I was bruised all over. She was particularly good at being furious, slamming the prongs of her fork into a piece of potato at the dinner table, warningly looking away from me and saying nothing, and because the saying nothing was so much worse than the saying something I remember her saying:

I swear Iona, in a minute it'll be the back of my hand.

You'll be the death of me, girl.

You'll be sorry when I'm gone.

Then I remember something I haven't thought about for years. She was standing at the table flicking through a magazine and she held the magazine up and looked at me across the room. It was summer. I was sitting on the couch watching anything on TV. I was seventeen and sullen. She flapped the magazine in the air.

I think we should join this, she said.

It would be something about sewing or Catholicism or being more like a girl was supposed to be. I watched the TV as if something very important was on.

For only a penny each, she said, if you send to these people, you can get four books. A penny each. There are all these books you can choose from on this page. All you have to do is buy their Book of the Month. And then what they do, after that, they send you their Book of the Month every month for a year and you don't have to buy it if you don't want it. They have all these things you can choose from for a penny. The Collected Works of William Shakespeare. That would be a useful book for you to have.

What? I said, because I had been fighting for nearly a year to be allowed to do English at university, not law or languages but something that meant I would never have a proper job. I can see myself now coming across the room, my eyes wide, my face like a child's, or like someone whose hopelessly foreign language has suddenly been understood, and my mother pleased with herself, holding out the open page to me.

We ordered the Shakespeare collection and a dictionary and a thesaurus and a book of quotations. Four weeks later they came all together in a box through the post and with them was the hardback Book Club Book of the Month which was called Princess Anne and her Horses and was full of colour photographs of Princess Anne and horses. My mother laughed and laughed. Then she saw the price of the book.

The following month the Book of the Month was a book about royal palaces. The month after that it was about the life of an English Edwardian lady. The month after that it was about the history of fox-hunting. They came every month, about gardens and the stately homes of members of royalty, always glossy with colour plates, expensive unwieldy hardbacks and my mother, who kept forgetting to send them back before the crucial eight days' return time, kept having to pay for them. They were stacked in the back room on the floor under the coffee table and there were more each time I came home at the end of a term.

I am wondering where all those useless books ended up, where they are now, whether they are still piled up unread somewhere in my father's house, when I hear the taxi driver speak. I open my eyes. The red light above his head is lit.

See how close we are, he says.

At the back of his voice the middle-class lady's voice is telling him to turn left in twenty yards.

Nearly home, he says.

Nearly home, I say.

He edges his cab between the cars parked on either side of the narrow roads before my own narrow road. He drives well.

You laughed in your sleep, he says. It must have been a good sleep.

He pulls up outside my house. It isn't as much on the meter as I thought it would be. I get the money out and count it and try to scrape together a good enough tip and I want to ask him, who called you Wasim? was it your mother or your father? is it after someone? does it mean something? what does it mean? I want to say, are you married? have you any children? are your parents still living? are they old enough to be supposed to be taking medication for anything and are they refusing to? did you grow up in Luton? what was it like to? what's it like there since Vauxhall closed and so many people lost their jobs? can we not just drive somewhere else, choose a place at random? could we go somewhere and not know where we're going till we got there? could we leave the navigation system off and just see where we ended up?

I get out of the cab and give him the money.

Thank you, I say.

Your book, he says. Don't forget.

I reach back in and pick it up off the seat.

He is looking at his watch now. Look, he says. We made good time. We took good roads. We were lucky.

He writes his number on the back of a receipt and I tell him I'll call him next time I need to come home. He drives up to the end of the road and round the corner, out of sight. I find my keys, unlock my front door, go in and close it behind me.

Proof of Identity
Rose Collis

Proof of Identity
Rose Collis

*'Identity': who or what a person or thing is; 'identity crisis':
a period of uncertainty and confusion in which a person's
sense of identity becomes insecure, typically due to a
change in their expected aims or role in society.*

I must confess to you: I cannot take my eyes off the maggot-ridden
corpse in front of me that, ten years ago, was a pretty young
woman. I know who she is. I know what she was. I know what she
did when she lived, and now I can see what she has become after
death. She is being offered up as evidence – as Exhibit A, clear and
uncontested proof.

This year's Brighton Festival offered up a sumptuous feast of
Japanese opera, Russian ballet and German theatre to slake
anyone's thirst for culture. Yet here I am, in a community hall
festooned with posters advertising yoga classes, diet clubs and over-
sixties whist drives, for this talk on murder cases and forensic
evidence. It has attracted a large, cross-sectional audience: retirees,
students, crusties – and, if the criminal statistics are accurate, at
least one dormant psychopath.

And then there's me.

With whom in this crowd do I identify now?

In this kind of identity parade, it is easier to pick out certain
'criminal' types than others. I can identify some as those who have
had their more morbid appetites whetted watching Inspectors
Morse, Wexford and Frost solving homogenised TV murders – the
perfect accompaniment to homogenised TV dinners – and would
like to have a crack at picking over the bones themselves.

Tonight's speaker is a former Chief Superintendent, with

twenty-two years in the CID under his belt. His record reads: thirty-one murders solved, one unsolved.

He's a real old-school copper: 'He coughed for that one,' he says when describing how a suspect confessed to a murder. 'The foxes have had a go,' he says, while dispassionately discussing a photograph showing the young woman's decaying body which had sustained grisly post-mortem injuries. It's not the usual slide-show image and some of the audience are looking a little green around the gills. But, like the other victims on show tonight, this body is telling us what happened, who was responsible – and how to catch that person (or persons) unknown. They were, in death, bodies of evidence.

French scientist Dr Edmond Locard coined the phrase upon which modern forensic science is based, Locard's Principle: 'Every contact leaves a trace.' The ex–Chief Super explains this theory in layman's terms: 'If we touch, we'll leave a part of each other *on* each other.'

In criminal law, there are seven main categories of admissible evidence: testimony, circumstantial, documentary, hearsay, real, presumptions, and presumption of legitimacy. In a criminal investigation, these are all sought after, as well as witnesses and physical evidence.

Officers at a murder scene search for evidence that may tell them exactly when the crime took place. Have post or newspapers been gathering for several days? Are any domestic appliances switched on? Is there evidence of a meal – leftover food, dirty dishes and glasses?

Then they have to look deeper. What is at the scene? What is there that *shouldn't* be there? What *isn't* there that should be?

The police search in drawers, on tables, in cupboards, under beds, in bags, in pockets, in rubbish bins. In these circumstances, someone's harmless detritus can change identity and become real evidence. It can hold identities. That of the victim – and of the crime's perpetrator.

The Chief Super explains how DNA evidence is gathered from a murder victim: first, the body is vacuumed for forensic evidence. A leg is removed and the marrow examined to see if it has crystallised – if a body was found in water, this reveals whether the person was dead before or after submersion.

Foul play or not, this ex-copper is adamant: 'No matter where you put a body, somebody, or an animal, will find it – even at sea... People are afraid to point the finger – but somebody always knows the truth.'

Someone *always* knows.

What identifies us, when we're alive and when we're dead? Many of the traits are common to both conditions.

Dead or alive, we generate paperwork, official numbers, statistics, physical evidence. It proves we were here, and who we were, and where we were. Doesn't it?

Anyone can have an identity crisis – dead or alive. I have proof of this now. Forensic science would allow my body to be correctly identified, but it might not identify *me*. My obituary would say 'she never married'; it would be legally correct, but far, far from the truth. My birth certificate bears the names of two parents, but it doesn't mean they were both mine. My mother swore on a stack of bibles that they were, but it doesn't mean she was telling the gospel truth.

I have the death certificate for one of those parents – 'bronchio-pneumonia' is stated as the cause of death. But that doesn't explain what caused someone to give up on life.

People are afraid to point the finger, but someone always knows the truth.

Establishing one identity is hard enough – it can take a lifetime. So why take the time and effort to establish more than one version of yourself?

Because it's much easier than you might think, that's why.

I bear a name, but who's to say whether it's my 'real' name? £97.50 and an online application allows me to change my name by deed poll, as many times as I like, and you would be none the wiser. Or I could take your name, your identity, your life. All I need is your National Insurance number and your home address, and, open sesame: I have access to loans, credit cards, bank account, even a passport. I could commit crimes in your name.

There are thousands of 'impostors', the 'masqueraders', who go through the world bearing more than one name, one identity, living more than one life. They can all produce evidence to prove that they are, indeed, who they claim to be. But it really proves nothing.

Charismatic psychopaths are charming people, and accomplished liars; they usually have some talent or propensity, and often use this to manipulate others – especially if the talent or propensity is for deceit. They are persuasive and able to convince people – including themselves – of anything. They come to believe the fiction they create: fictional lives, relationships, identities.

But there will always be something that marks a stranger out from familiar faces. It might be the way they look, or what they buy, or even the questions they ask. There will be evidence: hearsay, presumption, documentary, circumstantial. There will always be a trace.

Someone always knows. Someone always remembers.

My mother had a wonderful memory, but she often forgot things.

She remembered to tell me that I got all my brains from her: that she got into trouble with my primary school because I could read, write and spell before I was five, and they didn't know what class to put me in or what work to set me, since I would get through a week's worth of reading in a single day.

She could remember falling down a set of escalators, from top to bottom, at the tube station when she was fourteen.

She remembered to tell me how to choose a good cauliflower from a bad one (plenty of white in the middle, and lots of green on the outside) and how to paint a wall – 'Fill your brush!'

She even remembered to point out that the two rather drab-looking women we often saw while out shopping, trundling their trolley the way we did, were 'lesbians'. She forgot to tell me what that actually *meant*, but somehow I was supposed to know (someone always knows).

She forgot to tell me what periods were or what they entailed.

She forgot to tell me why my oldest brother lived with my aunt. Or why we never saw them.

Or, in fact, who my father was.

There were two secrets I knew my mother would take to her grave: one was her legendary pickled onion recipe; the other, the identity of my real father. Everyone in the family was always more concerned with learning the former than the latter. In the end, I was only able to get her to 'cough' for one of them – unfortunately, not the one that would have solved my identity crisis.

I was always the family queer: my birth virtually ensured that. It was so secret, only my mother knew it was going to happen and I was delivered without the benefit of doctor, midwife, nurse, clock or weighing scales. All that was missing to complete the scene was a group of farmyard animals and a manger. And a father: not The Father – *the* father. Any father, really.

Mum told me later, 'Babies look exactly like their fathers when they're born.' No one could tell me whether I looked like mine. All she remembered to say was, 'If a woman has a child because she loves a man, then that is a wanted child.'

When Mum became a widow, I thought my father was dead. I'd never met him, but I thought I should feel sad about it. I piped a tear or two but it didn't feel convincing. It didn't convince my brother, who rounded on me and spat out, 'I don't know what *you're* crying for – he wasn't your father!'

On the day of the funeral, I wasn't allowed to attend – a peculiar decision. When my headmaster died five years before, not only was I taken to the funeral but I was taken right to the graveside by my weeping mother. But this time, I wasn't even kept home from school. It must have been 'family only'. Suspicious behaviour, certainly, but not incontrovertible proof.

My 'otherness' was confirmed when I became the only one in the clan to show a pronounced interest in books. Along came this strange little girl with wispy blonde hair, who for Christmas and birthdays wanted only books and more books. Their reactions to the stranger in their midst could be creatively sadistic: before I'd reached double figures, one favourite family game was to pull out a gardening encyclopaedia and ask me to read out the plant names – in Latin. Eventually, I could trot out *Rosmarinus officinalis* as easily as my own name – and would sign that name repeatedly on anything that would take ink, as if I needed proof of who I was.

I also had an unfathomable fear of water being anywhere near my face – admittedly, a trait not uncommon in tomboys, but not one I grew out of. Nobody could offer an explanation as to why a wet flannel on my face would trigger a fit of the screaming ab-dabs. It was just accepted as one of those things – another little bit of queerness.

I always felt short-changed in the adult relation department: I'd only ever known one parent, one grandparent and one aunt. Why did my family tree look as if it had been pruned by Lizzie Borden? I knew there were three uncles knocking about somewhere. One of them, I was told, went to Kingston College of Art and did an especially memorable painting of the life-class model. 'It looked like a man and a woman,' my mother recalled. She remembered this only after the model's face and name became familiar to the world as Quentin Crisp.

Was the painter Uncle Jim, suspected of being a deserter during World War II?

Was it Uncle Fred, suspected of being a bit bonkers, because he refused to pay his rates in protest against some unknown grievance with the local authority?

Or was it Uncle George, suspected of screaming around the gay pubs of wartime Soho in make-up, whilst still in his teens?

Every year, sixty thousand people in Britain are reported as 'missing'. My uncles never featured amongst these figures, but they disappeared from the family line-up – two of them, forever – just as if someone had disposed of them and all traces of their physical presence.

Murderers believe they can do this. But it's harder than you'd think to make someone disappear completely; destroying a human body takes skill and planning. Victims are often dismembered – murderers believe it facilitates easy disposal of a body, but it's messy and difficult. It is one thing to destroy a person, but to destroy their body in this way reveals real determination and callousness.

My youngest brother told me once he was going to make our mother disappear: he boasted he had a gun hidden in the house and was going to use it to kill her. And, afterwards, during all the time it took him to calm me down from my hysterical, fearful sobbing, I never got to ask him why he wanted to do it.

Our family weren't dirt poor; we were respectable poor – clean and well-behaved, but with limited prospects. As well as growing up afraid of water, one of my biggest fears was… The Light Bill. Every three months, the terror of its arrival was palpable in our house and, prior to this, we were always being urged to 'switch that light off!' or 'turn that fire down'. If anything was going to cripple our fragile economy, it was *The Light Bill* – Hammer Horror couldn't have conspired to provide anything more terrifying.

My mother's cleaning and catering jobs allowed us the occasional treat, like a pint of unpeeled prawns or a quarter of smoked salmon offcuts from the delicatessen counter at Safeway, but not usually enough for our summer holiday.

A week or fortnight in a seaside holiday camp or on a caravan site was Mum's idea of a perfect holiday: she got waited on, she didn't have to do any cooking, cleaning, bed-making, washing-up or washing. What's more, she could play endless rounds of prize bingo and enter the weekly talent contest.

I never liked the camps that much myself: I was fussy over my food, so picking over my plate in front of a dining-room of strangers imbued me with an awkwardness about eating in public that hasn't entirely left me. I was embarrassed by her singing, too, but as long as I got to go horse-riding at least once and peer into rock-pools at unidentified wiggly creatures, I was reasonably content.

The money for this annual respite came from her weekend job: she did the catering for an amateur sports ground. Or, rather, *we* did. At ten years old, I was a cheap and compliant workforce, even if I couldn't see over the counter for the first year. My arm muscles, much admired since, are the impressive by-products of five years of lugging gallon aluminium teapots around every weekend. And I picked up an unusual and little-known skill, too: I can manually mass-produce sausage rolls. It may not be the sort of skill that would be especially useful in an emergency castaway situation, but it has come in handy occasionally as a conversation ice-breaker.

Football in the winter meant half-pint mugs of tea, hunks of bread pudding, meat pies, pasties and sausage rolls – all home-made. Cricket in the summer was cups and saucers, sandwiches, cakes, crisps and biscuits – *not* all home-made. The scones came from fourteen-pound catering packs, while the dainty slices of moist Madeira and Jamaican ginger cake were carefully hewn out of two-pound slabs from the cash-and-carry. Everything came in bulk in our house – for years, I didn't know what an individually wrapped cake or pie looked like, and could only roll out and cut pastry a yard at a time.

Mum had managed to wangle herself a cash-and-carry trade card so, once a month or so, she and I would trundle our respective trolley and basket for a good mile, over the disused railway lines that ran alongside the industrial estate and past the Beverley Brook. Since most of the warehouse customers had cars and vans, we cut an odd sight with our trolleys – we probably looked just like 'those lesbians'.

On Friday evenings, the heat from the oven and the smell of hot pastry would hit me when I arrived home from school. Mum had already made a start, on the outsize chest freezer in the living room, its lid doubling as a worktop, and in the kitchen, on the not-quite-square, fifteen-inch-wide block of wood topped with red Formica, both smeared with ice-skater streaks of flour and dappled with blobs of uncooked pastry. In summertime, when the living was not easy, seven loaves of Mother's Pride would sit on the freezer, waiting to be spread by me ('Fill your knife!') from the huge tub of greasy margarine manqué and filled with slices of processed cheese or ham.

*

My Uncle George, it transpired, (after his screaming excursions in the West End) had also become a caterer, but not for the masses. He worked for an exclusive clientele of the very wealthy and, in many cases, the very closeted. Shortly before his sudden death – officially, of that all-encompassing, euphemistic 'broncho-pneumonia' – I finally visited him at his Brighton home, where his beloved partner, Norman, had died five years previously. I went there out of curiosity, but also in the hope of finding some admissible evidence.

George's testimony was full of hearsay and presumptions, but he had never presumed legitimacy. He couldn't tell me who my father was, but he was able to tell me who it wasn't.

'You were always such a strange child. No one really knew what to do with you,' he testified. 'You were always asking questions, and nobody knew the answers. You had trouble getting your words out sometimes – I think your brain worked quicker than your mouth – and they treated you a bit like a village idiot.

'I used to look after you sometimes while your mum was at work. One summer day, I took you for a walk on Wimbledon Common. We stopped at one of the ponds so you could peer in and look for fish and tadpoles. And then you fell in, head first. You couldn't swim – and nor could I, but somehow I fished you out. You were all right, but you were soaking wet.'

George was terrified of my mum finding out what had happened – he knew, as I would grow to know, what her temper was like – so he kept me walking around and around in the sun until I'd dried out, eliminating all the incriminating evidence before he took me home. He never said a word to anyone about it, and nor did I.

I hadn't remembered it. I hadn't remembered him.

I've always had a wonderful memory.

I remember she was discovered lying in a ditch on Wimbledon Common, filled with winter rain. A man out walking his dog found her.

Actually, it was the dog; it always is. Animals know where the bodies are buried, in water or earth – rats, foxes, insects – they know where to go. And the dogs – *especially* the dogs. This one happened to find her on Boxing Day, 1976.

Halfway through the most miserable Christmas of my life, I was in a car, travelling along Kingston Road, the A3 that borders the Putney/Roehampton side of Wimbledon Common. I looked to my left and noticed, at the top of the grassy bank, a lilac tape cordoning off an area of the common. I knew what it meant: the police had found a body there – possibly in suspicious circumstances.

> *Wimbledon News, 31 December 1976*
> *DECOMPOSED BODY FOUND ON COMMON*
> *The remains are thought to be of a Wimbledon woman missing from home for a month… police said there was nothing suspicious about the cause of death… she was said to have been depressed… a note at her flat made it clear she was intending to take her own life.*

'The remains' – that's what she had become. No longer Gillian, not my best friend's mother. The remains.

I was shocked to find that she was only forty-six when she died – eight years younger than my mother. But I wasn't surprised that she'd been depressed; whenever I remember her, it's never as happy.

> *… was said to have been depressed at the time of her death and had failed to keep a hospital appointment… the Battersea coroner said a note made it clear she was intending to take her own life.*
> *Cause of death: Drowning. Took her own life as a result of her illness.*

What goes through the mind of someone who decides to drown themselves in a ditch full of water? Perhaps it was a spur of the moment impulse: she had gone for a walk, looked in the water, saw the reflection of her own misery and drowned in her own sorrows. But why had no one found her sooner? Perhaps someone had, and walked away from what they saw. The physical evidence would have been even worse than that in the images shown to us by the Chief Super.

Body decomposition begins about forty-eight hours after death. First the abdomen turns a greenish colour, then the neck, shoulders and thighs become reddish. The veins become prominent, the effect known as 'marbling'. After three weeks, the body is grossly disfigured – features become swollen and unrecognisable. First go the soft tissues. A body will be reduced to bones within a year in outdoor conditions. If the body is immersed in water, the process is delayed.

'It didn't look like her,' said her daughter, my best friend, matter-of-factly. It shocked me that a child could be so apparently unemotional about viewing her mother's half-rotted corpse. It shocked my mother. But she was always like that – business-like, unsentimental. I wasn't at all sure that I could have been so calm if I had been unable to recognise my own mother.

I knew it would happen quickly. I knew it would come with a phone call. I knew the call would come in the middle of the night. And those calls that come in the middle of the night, they're never good news.

It took less than thirty seconds for my mother to go from 'your mother' to 'the body'. Less than half a minute for a living, breathing entity to become a nameless object. That's all it takes – the biggest change in the briefest possible moment.

Hours after the call came, I went to her flat, in search of all types of admissible evidence – proof of my identity and evidence that substantiated my suspicions: she had known she was going to die. It was a trait that seemed to run in the family: someone always knows.

There was my aunt, my mother's sister, walking into her doctor's surgery for a routine appointment, clutching the door and exclaiming, 'My God, I'm going to die!' and then doing precisely that.

There was my grandmother, lying in the same hospital where her husband had died and where her youngest daughter would die – the place where she swore she would die if we ever sent her there

– clutching my arm as I said goodbye and whispering in my ear, 'I don't want to die.' I left that ward – and she died.

Now I found myself walking into that same ward, knowing the threat my brother made almost thirty years ago had been carried out. No gun had been fired, no trigger pulled, but her heart had been torn apart, dismembered, destroyed. It revealed real determination and callousness – a real killer's touch.

I gazed upon my mother and failed to recognise her. She had an identity bracelet on one wrist; at the bottom of the bed was a medical chart with her name on. Apart from this, there was nothing to tell me it was her. She hadn't been found in a ditch, but she was almost beyond recognition, and certainly beyond recognising me. We had both lost our identity.

I knew how much she would hate being there, furious that it had come to this. And now it *had* come to this; *we* had come to this. One look at the evidence before me provided ample proof: she was not responding to any of the treatment; her blood pressure was falling even as I sat there watching the nurses gauge it while they tried to hide the concern on their faces.

'It's all right,' I told them. 'I know what's happening. I know what's going to happen.' Someone always knows.

She wasn't there any more and she wasn't coming back. Who would I be left with?

I was left with my theory, one that I kept to myself as I sat there, watching this shrunken, fading, diminished figure refusing to fight for the first time in her life, and trying to connect her with all the strength, determination and passion that I hoped was my legacy.

Circumstantial evidence gave my theory some weight but I had to find real evidence to back it up. So, when all the fighting was over, I made a thorough search: I looked in drawers, on tables, in cupboards, under beds, in bags, in pockets, in rubbish bins.

What was there that shouldn't be? What *wasn't* there that should be?

In these circumstances, someone's harmless detritus can become real evidence. It could hold clues to identities – hers and mine.

The dried blood I found down the front of her nightdress – which had been removed from her by hospital staff and replaced with a flimsy garment almost transparent from numerous visits to the hospital laundry – was evidence of a struggle. When I stripped the clothes off her bed, the stain on the bottom sheet and the layers of dead skin, shed as quickly as her identity, further substantiated this.

The room itself contained items that I expected to find: bulbs of garlic tied to the door handle; palm crosses pinned near her bed, on the chair and the window; a gold crucifix in her purse. More than twenty-five years before, when she was left at home alone, living with a queer child growing into an even queerer teenager, she would stock up on palm crosses from church each Easter. One would be pinned on every door, over every mantelpiece and even under my bed, to 'stop evil getting in'.

None of it had worked for her.

Then I found items that I didn't expect to find – that really shouldn't have been there. The most curious was a packet of disposable razors: it had been a pack of ten, but only eight were left. Why would she have worried about removing body hair so late in life?

I found the answer when I talked to someone who had witnessed what these items were actually used for. For weeks, in line with her lifelong mistrust of doctors and hospitals, she had refused to have the ulcer on her left leg treated, until it turned into a red, raw hole that gushed at the slightest touch. Before it reached that stage again, she decided to apply her own method of treatment. And so she would take a disposable razor to the ulcer and carefully slice off the top layer, as if it was an overlapping lip of pastry round the edge of a pie.

I found the best evidence to support my theory in the drawer of her bedside cabinet: her rings. She never parted with them or removed them, no matter how dirty the work. Yet here they were, all of them. Witness testimony told me no one had taken them off her before she left home. It proved beyond reasonable doubt that she knew she wasn't coming back, especially as she'd left them in the first place I would look for clues. They were there, but they shouldn't have been.

Then I looked for what wasn't there. It was late September; months before this, she would have started shopping around for bargains in preparation for Christmas. Cards, presents... even last year's wrapping paper would have been carefully stashed away to re-use. But none of these was here. Instead, I found a selection of presents given to her last Christmas – all unopened, unworn, unused.

As far as I was concerned, that wrapped up the case. I had found evidence from all of the recognised categories: real, circumstantial, documentary, testimony, hearsay, presumptions – even presumption of legitimacy.

I had never presumed my legitimacy, and nor had anyone else, even though I had evidence of it. While trying to prove one theory, I had also searched for the evidence that would solve another: a newspaper cutting, a letter, maybe even a photograph that she had kept hidden. I would look at the photo and see my own eyes gazing back at me from an unfamiliar face. But this evidence, if it had ever existed, remained undetected.

There had only been one key witness, and she took her testimony with her. I didn't have enough evidence – from any category – that pointed to a prime suspect; the case would probably remain unsolved.

Yet someone always knows. Every contact leaves a trace.

Baking Bread
Kathi Kosmider

Baking Bread
Kathi Kosmider

Today was the last day you would be able to find me. Not that you even know I've disappeared, but I have. I lost the way last year, around this time. We had a deal. You've forgotten I'm sure. But it has been a year.

This city is turning. I've been travelling along this road, a sacred road. I guess I'm doing a sacred act, walking on this road. Because this is a road for the dead, which leads to a place of interment. Not anymore, but some time long ago. Somewhere along here I'll come to a centre where maybe there will be a well and I'll feel the energy laying itself down as I walk. This is what she told me. I'm not so sure that's true, but for now I just walk and hope that there's something good in this. I just want to walk and hopefully someday someone will find me. Because I know I'm lost by now. That's for sure.

This is the place where one is forced to turn back. But I'm not sure that's what I want to do. Further and beyond this place they tell me I cannot venture. If I do, I won't come back. This is what they keep telling me. I think it's bullshit. So I'm going. I'm going past this place to the next.

Don't ask me where I am right now. I've come to the other side. It's a slippage. Falling through a worm hole on this earth. On the other side I can tell you what I see. I see the following:

A man I met the other day bought a lamb to use as a lawnmower. He said it cost him so little. With Mad Cow Disease it's difficult to slaughter because you have to remove the spinal cord and that is too costly. They used to use the blood and gallbladder for ink, but not anymore. One sheep costs less than a packet of crisps.

The man near the canal held his bag tightly and the police thought drugs was his thing but he was selling worms from a bag.

Thousands of little ones sprinkled with curry for the culinary appetites of the fish. This was his gold for the day.

I'm watching her. I watch her from this vantage point. A spasm of a shroud. Her dress of lightning bugs crawling on leftover silk.

I can fist a ghost and rim a phantom.

I can.

She says:

Today I am a daddy to a boy. Just don't follow me too closely. You'll see what you like and it will turn you. Turn you like this city.

This will be the last you'll see me.

We couple in the most unreliable places. You can never tell who will see us, but I see her and that's all I care about. It's so rare that she'll reveal herself to me. Down in the Brighton toilets and the Regent's Canal, these are the best places to find me. Come see if you can find me.

That's where she would tell me to go to find her.

Decode me. I'm artificial intelligence. Here is what I became.

I'm a girl, but I'm a daddy to a boy's ass. I can't stop what I do. It's part of that wheel turning down the Thames. That is what I smell now, while I cut the excess skin off my soles. The smell of the Thames and a boy. Well, really a girl, but I treat her like a boy. She is in me. He is part of me. We keep walking, all of us and that wears the soles down. I take a scalpel and cut through the brittle bottom. My methods aren't always exact. Trust me, sometimes I miss and blood gets on the carpet, but it's got to be done. Don't you think? Cleaning those stains is hell. But I catch it fast so it doesn't grind the carpet down with all that rubbing. I have a very good rug cleaner. It gets the hardest stains out, even oil. Good Virgin Olive Oil. That's much worse than blood.

The possibilities are shifting.

I lean against the car and she brings her leather glove inside to steal me.

What a dimension I evolved into.

This is the end of summer pain and this is where you could always find me replaying the scene over and over.

Conjure me again. Go ahead. Make visible something that cannot be seen and does not exist in visible form. Try it. The eyes in your body want to see. The head filled with pictures, memories, fantasies, hopes, daydreams and nightmares. I am your phantasm.

Sometimes she tells me to go look for her. Other times she asks me to stay. She had given me instructions to come find her if she didn't show up after five days. She drew me a map of London and a line of all the places she stopped and flashed. In a treasure hunt, she coaxed me into following her and figuring out the clues that would lead me to her. I had one clear sign to go on and that was her smell. The smell of someone who wanted to still be alive. The smell came from her stomach, which was hollowed out and stuffed with cottonwool and a blend of myrrh and frankincense. Also this slight taste of yeast, bread turning blue. In that place her need was rancid. I could see it. At each opportunity I would simply ask her to come to the women's room with me and in a stall I could rehearse the loss that was to come. In that rehearsal I tried to make an outline of her body after the disappearance. The hollow of the outline held her and myself leaning into a frozen sink. Pressing into her and forcing myself to remember the fact that she was only a ghost and no matter how hard my arm reached into the hollow of her, I could never be enough. This was at the penetrative moment of vanishing.

When you fuck a ghost you have to dream carefully of how.

It was a time of high visibility yet I was unrecognizable in my lurking about. I was ready to create a new name, an identity, a new physical embodiment, a structure in which to dwell, interact, create a dialogue, and the connection to the network was linking me up.

Yet I still couldn't find her.

When she was alone she would not open her eyes. She kept them closed, as a boy would appear to her. She didn't want her boy to show her what she really was; to desecrate and speak the other voices she contained. There were many within yet the boy spoke loudest and she wrestled hard to kill the sound in him.

So the father showed him his fatherliness.

Fisting a ghost, rimming a shroud, it's what you could love about the invisibility of not knowing what is and is not.

Bloated and blissed out, I didn't need your approval. But I knew that you were there waiting for me to find you. I saw you wink at me once in Soho, turning around, swept up in the theatre crowd, churning my stomach like blades weed-whacking the last of the summer crops to prepare for the fires of fall. Always August. Always August you have to come back.

I'm not here to supply you with reality. I am something conceived which cannot be presented. Something perceived but cannot be seen. Only at certain times in my manifestation will you believe how real I am.

Between that last inch of moisture trapped inside the burnt yellow room and between the parched jaundice of my hand where death suits you more than life, there must be an impostor between the two of us. You will tell me that you are real. I push in further into the yellow room, with a little trim of blood pounding against the walls. In between the walls you rise from time to time. Fucking death is a glorious thing.

This is the form I have taken. This is what happens when you spit life into me as such. You can't really scorn me, you see. I'm yours. I wish I could be a grown slender angel with a fourteen-foot wing span. I wish I could lick my soul so I too could see how black my tongue is. Black you know is the new brown. Demons are the new 'angels'. But I'm neither of these and I have no color. So who am I to you?

Envision the invisible. Unpresentable in this place of the unreal. Nothing at this moment is part of this plane. We move into a video game realm. She is one massive somnambulist wandering the streets of London. Haunting every crevice and corner. I'm telling you, she is there and she will take you any which way she wants.

Wide awake in the middle of the night. I'm in a landscape of Half Life, Resident Evil and Silent Hill. The background of my existence is pixelated. I have no limits, no guidelines, no cheat sheet on how to move around the territory. I can no longer sleep because I am waiting for her to appear around the next corner and I need to be prepared like any survivalist, like Snake in Metal Gear Solid. I've come to see her as my opposition, yet the predator in me just wants to take her by any means necessary and with all my weapons intact. I know this is what will be required of me.

Sometimes I think it is her smell that follows me down into the tube station at midnight. The smell is the taste of sugared chestnuts chewed on Christmas Day. That dreaded confection tastes like the endpoint. That is how sweet she is.

She says:

I've been lonely for ten centuries of undoing and unfurling in the grave. Try to untwist my rigor mortis, it's such a bitch.

From the age of ten I had the sense of someone pressing me. Someone lying on top of me and ironing me out. I could always sense this out-of-focus face with a smirk around the edge of what seemed like a mouth. But her face was always lost in a kind of computerized shadow. I felt at that age she was sent to me by some sort of Star Trekian malfunction of an image generator. Yet even through the machinery, I always felt the dampness in the background and a smell of mildew, of an animal smell that later I realized was something like an 'interrupted' sex smell. She was a body of lead dripping with mercury. All the time the weight never moved as I thrashed. As the damp fell along my neck, covering my face, draping my arms, my chest was exposed to the breeze of her move rhythmically taking me with no member, just her ghost body rocking me like sound waves off a radio frequency. The bandwidth of her was multiple, information travelling on light circuits beyond the visible spectrum. She was pure fiber optics and there was absolutely nothing to see, rather smell, taste and believe, have a faith in this concrete weight.

So, once a year she marked her arrival. On my way to a client, I smelt the shock, like burning hair. I walked into a Mayfair hotel lobby and stood near a stairwell banister of marble and gold and there she exposed herself to me. The glimpse was a little pause that brought my body to bend down at the knees because of the volume and velocity of memory and brushing against my leg was that moth-eaten silk dress catching the edges of a door, ripping through and the charcoal smudge of a woman who erases herself as quickly as she comes and this started the routine again. The dress pieces falling off, the ripped skin of soles, the smell of burnt sugar, the pressure before sleep marking her routine of visitation and beginning my desperation to lurk.

I scoured books, computers, archives, to find her name, to know her story and it was a man with broken teeth and a houndstooth suit that looked like a hologram who found me in the British Library who said, 'Follow her scent forever, she is all of them triple squared. Smear the blood on your face with the end of the paw and stripe each cheek and one on the forehead and then keep the paw as a souvenir. She would love that.' He cackled with that last word. She was an amalgamation of disgraced women and a boy and a girl and now an animal and I'm supposed to hunt her down.

I walk the canal in the underneath of night. My clients are on hold, I don't answer my phone for weeks. August in London when everyone disappears to swallow the sun and drink salt-water. My shirt is full of sweat and peach silk and strawberry stains and it is only the beginning of my own freeze. I know she is closing in. When I see her near the arches it begins from the damp of the puddle of rainwater, swirling, centrifugal forcing up in a charcoal smudge of smoke then neon, waxy and arresting the spin in my head. I had taken half a Valium and the down was sweet and warm. I was about to fall on my knees out of sickness. I had been following her for one year, unexpected sightings of ripped pieces of dresses, fingernail parings, hair rolled into tiny gumballs bowling across my floor. She left herself behind for me to find the evidence and I was failing, drowning in the fog of my hunger to touch her, to eat the damp, to burn more hair, to roll myself into her ghost.

Last year I didn't fail. I reigned supreme in my sighting, in my occupation of her. Already I knew as her legs leaned into my lower half, her hands grabbed my head and my neck raising straight up to her with no face, just more dust and musty grit of a stunning video image. Thousands of atoms bombarding her face, squinting my eyes to find eyes. I recognized the outline of gravel, worms and millions upon millions of tiny particles thrashing and whipping around her. She bent down behind me, still holding my neck straight up, pulling me out of my skin almost with an anger and a need to stretch me like long strands of licorice. She was ready to rip me apart from my head to my knees like skinning a rabbit.

She touched with a smell of something gone off. And after touch, this smell was imprinted on the top layer of my skin. She rolled herself over me, trying to dig at me. She was like a wolf trying to mate me but at the same time like a blind human pawing me to find what I am. With her paws she pressed every inch of my body pushing and pressing trying to find entry, as if my body held a secret door into a yellow room where she could actualize her being and make herself appear. She was invisible in this moment yet at a certain point I could glimpse pieces of her and shreds of skin formulating a photo of her now and in the past. A rosy boy with jet-black curls, the red-haired girl furious and bleeding, the animal cut with a paw trapped in rusted metal. This image began to look like a Niepce photo from the first days of a Paris discovery, capturing images in a magic box.

In her animal state she kept rolling me flat like dough, pressing and rolling, as if gathering me into sausage meat to be stuffed into a skin. She would then try to shuck me like peas, tearing a seam down my body with her nails, trying to make the incision to get me out of my container. Her hands were like two falcons' beaks spearing a heron's neck. I could feel her energy running through the top epidermal layer of my skin. She could rip my entire lining with the strength of an executioner. I was left with bruises around my neck for weeks and strange formulations around my skin as if she had injected a fungus. A horrible despair and dankness spread over me after this.

And there was nothing but the thought of vermin and basements unopened for ten years excavating the hope of some light and a wall that kept crumbling and peeling layer after layer of plaster, always with a slight thread of blood framing an outline.

She was asking me to break into her. To do a thief-like thing. When the damp rises from off the canal, that is when you end up on your knees. That is when the crave stings, when the children are sleeping, when Sheep Lane is slow, when the worms in the bag stop slithering, when you stop asking me for favors on the banks of the canal. I would do anything for you, because I know when you leave tonight it will be again one year before the next sighting of you. That is when at daybreak my arms plow into you like into a field and your voice reaches a pitch that is unattainable during the banality of the day. Only now, in the magic time between day and night, do you groan, a sound of your dead animal coming alive, awakening, even growling a smile of sarcasm as your body lies in the bushes of the Regent's Canal. It's the slyness and the fury that you will never really feel what I'm doing to you, in the flesh, but rather now only in your shroud and death dress. I hope the stain never comes out of you. Don't ask me to follow you again.

Your thighs are like custard, thick and wet. I can't cling to you, grasp you and hold on to you. You're slithering, a lizard in water, a puddle left behind of rain you made.

You're not really here are you?

Crows cawing and baby bats calling out as two women face each other in almost skinless suits of clear. There are days that seem to end before they begin. And you look at me like Vermeer's girl. You look like you know. But there is nothing, absolutely nothing to know. This is not about knowledge but about the least amount of light that can be detected. I like small things and I'm learning to like the dark.

Can I name you now? Can I intend you? Yeast rising on the canal. Steam, legs buckling, the smell of bread. She was making me, rolling me like her father did, like her brother did. I watch the water conduct the recollection. The maiden and the cutting down for the field, for the earth to rise again from its burnt-out wasteland. We are watching you now. Your growing in the earth, your dead body has bored its way from under the Hackney street skin into me and you are animating me.

I was thirteen when my dress was black and torn from their doings. This was where they filled me with bread and cackled and chopped me into pieces and planted me mixed with the baker's yeast and flour and sugar and summer berries. I was never touched before that day. I was whole, I was intact and beginning to crave. The harvest was abundant that year and every year. I had fertilized their lives so well and now you can take me. You can make me whole. You can conjure me. Each year, each harvest you can do with me what you want. You can tear me apart, you can spit into me, you can couple with me, you can be my daddy, you can make bread out of me.

I began to fall slowly into the canal. Each piece of my body convulsing and electric. The shock of the body coming out of my body was voluptuous. Her creep, her chill, her gnawing crawl took me under as I fell slowly into the canal. I woke to see the haze of the black dress tearing itself out, the body of a naked woman levitating slowly down the water. No longer boy, no longer girl but a great grand woman. And for a moment I heard her laugh. Something she had never done. She never made a sound of pleasure, only pain, and suddenly I felt like the joke was on me. She never came back after that. I only heard her giggling. The child giggling. She was only twelve when it was all done to her. When she rose up to meet the sickle.

Several years later I will see you fall into the earth and there will be nothing for me to do but call your arms around me and in my arms I will hold your fall. This will remind me of a stunned child running in a circle with nowhere left to run to and earth will be a Martini shaken not stirred and in the ferment of the alcohol we will dance as the earth begins to taste how delicate we really are.

'I want to see her face before they cover her up,' the father says after the Armenian earthquake, as a child looks for its mother.

To travel along the sacred road is a sacred act. In the ninth century I found you walking. Still you walk down those ley lines on Curtain Road leading to the well that now is Old Street. Trying to find a drink of water to soothe the dread of wandering. Magic tracks running across the city. Your dress was stained. Your smile was still curved in a slick. Little tears of blood followed along the ends of your shattered blouse, and again you were faceless and nameless.

I'm enacting the disappearance by calling her toward me and watching erosion. I'm a realist.

Beyond this place I cannot venture. If I do, I won't come back. This is what they tell me, as I go to soak myself in the canal's last embrace of her visitation, breathing in the spores of a bread that has been rotting for centuries in my brain.

What a dimension I evolved into.

This is the end of summer pain and this is where you will always find me replaying the scene over and over in the mind of the wandering lady off the Regent's Canal.

Whatever Gets You Through
Robyn Vinten

Whatever Gets You Through
Robyn Vinten

'Have I told you the one about my mother?' Bridget asked, leaning close, drunk but still able to string a coherent sentence together.

'No.' She was at her most entertaining like this. To be encouraged.

'About the time she got into the freezer.'

She had told me but it was a good story and the party was beginning to get on my nerves. 'Yes, but go on.'

She took a swig from her bottle of beer and a drag of her cigarette. 'It was one of those big chest freezers, you know the sort.'

I did, we had one when I was a child, for the sides of lamb people sometimes left on our doorstep. (We being the minister's family and therefore poor.) I remember having to nearly climb in to find the ice cream under the frozen mixed veggies and the meat.

'Well...' Another swig of beer. 'This one day, I was home from school. Must have been the summer holidays. It was hot, I remember, and we were watching TV. Me, Dad and my sister. Don't remember which one.' She paused and took a drag on her cigarette, apparently trying to remember which sister. Bridget's stories were always long and involved many diversions, often funnier than the main thread, so it was best to let her go off on any tangent she chose.

'Benny Hill, it was. God, I loved him.' She sighed and went silent again. I thought I had lost her completely.

'Really?' I said. I hated Benny Hill. I wondered if I should get another drink but decided it would make me maudlin.

'Anyway.' Bridget seemed to come back from wherever the memory of Benny Hill had taken her. 'I went to get a drink from the kitchen and there she was. My mother,' she added as if I might have forgotten whom the story was about – or maybe to remind herself, 'climbing into the freezer.'

She said it as if it were the punchline of the story, as if there wasn't any more story. I knew there was.

'What did you do?' I asked.

'Well...' She stubbed her cigarette out in the already overflowing ashtray and lit another one. 'I went running back to my father and said –' She put on a childish voice and her face softened into the concerned look of a child '– Father, Father, Mother is climbing into the freezer.'

I had never met her mother but I could picture her so clearly in the kitchen standing on a carefully placed stool, climbing into the freezer. Dressed in a pastel-coloured twinset and pearls. Grey skirt, tan tights. Neat, sensible shoes, her hair permed in tidy curls around her expressionless face.

Bridget was looking around at what was left of the party. Looking for another beer. I didn't want her to lose the thread of the story. 'What did your father do?' I asked.

'Oh, he just said...' And she seemed to remember this was the punchline. She put on a thick Dublin accent. 'Leave her be, she's only attention-seeking. So she is.'

That was where the story usually ended, but tonight I wanted to know more. Tonight I was left with the image of her mother frozen solid, curled up with her arms outstretched as if trying to push the freezer lid open. I was left with the image of Bridget, pigtailed, sitting on the freezer licking a giant ice lolly, kicking her heels against the side of it in time to her mother's muffled cries.

It was late and I was a little drunk myself.

Bridget got up and wandered into the kitchen for another beer. I followed her.

'Did she get out?' I asked, although I knew that she must have for she was alive and well and living in the Home Counties.

'Yeah.' Bridget had found a beer and was looking around for a bottle opener. When none was immediately apparent she tried to open it with her teeth. I took it off her and unscrewed the cap.

'Screw-capped beer!' she said in amazement. 'Whatever next?' She drank a mouthful. 'I imagine she got bored,' she added in answer to my question, looking suddenly bored herself.

'Or cold?' I suggested.

'Yeah, cold.' She took a crumpled packet of cigarettes out of her jeans pocket and tried to knock a cigarette out by flicking the bottom. Several flew out and landed on the beer-splattered floor. 'It would be cold in the freezer.'

'Why did she get in there?' I hadn't really thought of that before. A mother driven to such desperate lengths, even if it was only to get attention.

Bridget shrugged. 'It was hot.'

'She could have been looking for something,' I suggested, 'and just fallen in.'

'Nah. She was attention-seeking, she always was.'

She bent to pick up the fallen cigarettes. 'And,' she popped one in her mouth, 'shutting yourself in the freezer is very dangerous.' She wagged her finger at me as if I had just suggested we should do it for a lark. 'The son of a friend of one of my sisters, don't remember which one, but the son of one of their friends died shutting himself in a freezer. It wasn't on or anything so he didn't freeze to death, he suffocated.' She tried to light her cigarette but it was wet from where it had landed in a puddle on the floor.

'I went to the funeral with my sister, whichever one it was, whose friend's son had died. It was awful.'

I drifted back into the lounge; I didn't want to hear any more funeral stories. It seemed like I had heard nothing but stories about funerals all night. Funny stories, most of them, but funeral stories all the same.

There was Shirley, who had told me about when her difficult, bed-ridden mother had died just hours after her sister left to go on holiday for the first time ever. 'Selfish bitch,' Shirley had screamed at the still warm corpse. When her sister arrived back, very upset, after spending the night at Athens airport, Shirley showed her in to see the body laid out. She tried to be comforting, saying, 'She looks at peace now.' Her sister took one look at the body and said, 'No, she looks fucking dead.' They laughed then, laughed so hard they cried. Holding on to the sides of the coffin to stop themselves falling over.

And Kate had talked about being forced as a child to see her grandfather's body. How she had been terrified of seeing any dead bodies ever since because she thought that death transformed people into terrible ghouls so that they looked like something out of a horror film. (Only she said 'filim' like they do in Wales.) She only learned much later that the nuns who had attended him put powder on his face and lipstick on his lips to pretty him up.

I'd laughed at the stories. I'd even told some of my own, like going to see the body before they nailed the coffin shut. How her teeth weren't right and her hair wasn't done. And how the teddy bear my niece had given her in hospital was tucked into her hand and when we tried to pull it free, it wouldn't come. 'Come on, Mum,' I said. 'Milly wants it back.' But she wouldn't give it up. Not till Dad came in and pulled it free in one rough tug which had me worried that her hand would come away with it.

They'd laughed at that one, Shirley, Kate and Bridget.

'Did I tell you the one about the dog?' Bridget had followed me back into the lounge. She dragged me down to sit with her on the sofa.

'The one your mother killed.'

'With the bread knife.'

'That they still use to this day.' I had heard the story several times before.

'To cut the bread with,' she concluded.

'Did I tell you the one...' I asked, 'about when my mother was at home after being in hospital and had fallen over...' I knew she hadn't heard the story. I hadn't told anyone. 'My father and brother were there, but even between them they couldn't pick her up, so they rang the police.'

'The police?' She didn't seem to believe me.

'It's what the hospital told them to do. This is small-town New Zealand, they've got nothing better to do.'

'Oh.' After all her tall tales, I thought it was a bit rich for her to question my story. 'Go on,' she said. 'Go on, go on, go on.' Lapsing once more into her Irish accent.

'And when the police arrived...' I remembered Mum telling me this story on the phone and then my brother telling it at the funeral and giving away the punchline before he got to the end. I reminded myself not to do that. 'She was on the floor and the young policeman asked her how she was. And she said, "Flat out."'

'Flat out,' Bridget said as though she didn't quite get it. Maybe it was the way I told it. It got a laugh at the funeral.

'Flat out,' Bridget repeated again. 'Like she meant she was busy when she was actually just flat out on the floor.' She laughed then, but it was too late.

'Did I tell you the one...' she started, as if these stories were some sort of competition, 'about when my mother offered to pay...'

'For a sex-change operation,' I finished for her.

'She seemed to think...'

'You've told me,' I said, sharper than I meant to. Bridget didn't seem to notice.

'I'm seeing them next weekend.' She pulled a face. 'I'd rather not but, hey...' She shrugged. 'One's got to do what one's got to do.' She stood up rather unsteadily. 'To stay in the will.' She tapped the side of her nose as if it was a secret and winked before wandering off towards the loo.

I stayed where I was and wished everyone would go home so I could go to bed. Kate flopped down on the sofa, not as drunk as Bridget but well on the way.

'Have I told you about my grandfather's funeral?'

I shook my head, suddenly very tired.

'He hated his sister. He used to hide when she came to visit, I remember being there as a child when he did it. He made a game of it. I had to hide behind the sofa and keep very quiet. It was great fun.' She looked around for the ashtray to flick off the ash from her rather long cigarette. 'Anyway, when he died, his sister took over all the funeral arrangements, wouldn't let my mother do anything.' I watched as the ash got longer until it was in danger of falling off onto the sofa. 'She arranged for him to be cremated and the ashes were to go to the family plot, when he wanted to be buried in the churchyard.'

My mother had been cremated, her ashes were in a jar somewhere at the funeral director's while we decided what we wanted to do with them. I tried to picture them in some sort of Egyptian urn, but all I could see was a jam jar with a handwritten label. Her handwriting, like the jars in the pantry we cleaned out after the funeral. 'Semolina' one label said, but it hadn't had semolina in it for years. I don't think it had had anything in it for years. It was just there for show, to fill up the pantry. That was before the pantry was full of the special protein meals Dad bought to tempt her to eat something, which she never even tried. They all went to the church fair along with the jars, which we washed and removed the labels from.

My sister had wanted to take some of the ashes back to the States with her. We joked about what US customs would make of them, given their heightened state of paranoia. Would human ashes look like anthrax? We laughed but I was glad she didn't take any. I wouldn't like to think of Mum broken up, it didn't seem to be her style. I'm not even sure she's the scattering kind.

'Well, after the funeral, my mother grabbed the urn...' Kate was still telling her story. I hoped I hadn't missed too much. I would need to be able to laugh at the end of it. It was clearly going to be a funny story. '... ran out of the church, took the lid off and just scattered the ashes right there in the churchyard.'

That was obviously the punchline.

'Good for her,' I said, but without much enthusiasm. I picked up the ashtray and held it under her cigarette just as the ash fell.

I remembered my sister telling me a story about working in a vet's. If an animal died there, they sent it down to the city incinerator. One day, a couple asked what had been done with their dead dog, and she said they'd cremated it. A sort of half-truth. Well, this couple then asked for the ashes, so they could scatter them in their garden, so, my sister went around the staff room and emptied all the ashtrays into a jar and gave it to them. They were quite happy with this, apparently.

My sister's husband had the ashes of his cat on the mantelpiece. He talked to them when he was sad. I guess it's whatever gets you through the day.

'Our taxi's here,' Shirley said. I stood up. The hostess should see her guests out.

'Thank you for a lovely party.' A kiss to each cheek. 'And we're sorry about your mother.'

'That's OK,' I said airily, as if it was my birthday and they had forgotten to buy me a present. Which it was and they had.

'Give us a ring if you need to talk.' More kisses and they were gone. Suddenly the house was quiet, just Bridget and a few others left. I went back into the lounge.

'Did I tell you the one...' Bridget seemed to have sobered up – or maybe there was something going on in the bathroom that I was better not knowing about.

'... about my sister and the hospital porter?'

'No,' I said. A new story and one not about mothers or funerals.

'Well...' Bridget settled herself on the sofa, cigarette and beer bottle in hand. 'My sister, I don't remember which one. The one that's the nurse.' She looked at me as if I should know which one that was. 'That one, anyway, she's married and works at the hospital. Well, she was having an affair with one of the hospital porters.' She paused to drink some of her beer.

'One day the porter doesn't come into work and she goes around to his flat, because she has keys on account of them having the affair, and she finds him dead.'

So it *was* a story about a funeral. I must have groaned, because Bridget said, 'It was just natural causes, nothing fishy. Heart attack or something. Anyway...' Another swig of her beer. 'My sister, the one that's having the affair with him... Actually, they're both nurses, but one's got kids – she wouldn't be having an affair, would she?' She looked at me as if I should know that too. I shrugged.

'Well, whichever one it was, she had to call the police and let the hospital know and she even ended up organising the funeral.'

I put my head in my hands, I didn't want to hear any more funeral stories but nothing stops Bridget once she's in full flow.

'Now my mother thought this was all very strange.' She put on a serious face and an Irish accent. '"It's all very strange, you doing this," she said to my sister, and my sister finally had to admit that she'd been having an affair with him. And do you know what my mother said?' Bridget looked at me as if she expected an answer. I shook my head but only a little – too much and I thought I might fall over.

'She said...' Again the Dublin accent, full of scorn and disapproval. '"A hospital porter, you were having an affair with a *hospital porter?*"'

I smiled; laughter seemed beyond me.

'You see, if it had been a doctor, my mother wouldn't have minded, but a porter...' She leaned back on the sofa. 'A hospital porter,' she said again in her Irish accent. She shook her head. 'Honestly, mothers!' She sighed. 'Who'd have them, huh?' Then she looked at me. 'Oh, sorry.' She put her hand on my arm. 'Jesus, sorry.' She stood up and then sat down again and started picking at the label of her beer bottle. 'Sorry,' she said again, not looking at me.

'That's OK,' I said lightly, like it was my birthday party and she had stayed later than she should. Which of course it was, and she had.

Glowing
Elizabeth Woodcraft

Glowing
Elizabeth Woodcraft

One of Dee's concerns was that she wouldn't have sex again before she died.

She was thirty-six. She was an actor, she'd had roles in two films – one with Judi Dench; she'd had lovers, she'd left them. She was five-foot-eight, with brown wavy hair, American-style good teeth and large breasts. I only know that last part because she complained now they were so small; I don't notice people's breasts.

I didn't really know her before her illness. She was a friend of someone in my women's reading group. I knew she was meant to be really funny. Someone once said, 'She's the wittiest woman I know,' and that was quite scary. I'd say hello to her at parties, if we were both, say, standing by the food table, and she'd make a joke. I'd say, 'Is this hummus?' And she'd say, 'It must be, this is a feminist's party.' I've never understood the connection between feminists and hummus, but sometimes I think there's a lot I don't understand.

I don't work at the moment. I'm a teacher by profession, I teach primary, but our school was closed down, merged with another bigger one, and I took redundancy. It was just at that time it became obvious that Dee's illness wasn't going to disappear, so when the rota of carers was drawn up, it was natural for me to put myself forward as part of the team.

She didn't want to talk or anything, she just wanted someone there for emergencies. I would arrive with a pile of books and sit in the kitchen area of the living room, reading, and every half hour or so I'd ask her if she wanted a drink. If the phone rang I'd answer it and mouth to her who it was. If it was her sister she'd say, 'No,' and I'd say, 'I'm sorry, she's asleep at the moment, can I take a message?' (Apparently her sister just cried all the time.) If it was someone from work she'd whisper 'F— off!' which of course I wouldn't say. And I'd do washing up or put fresh water in the flowers. She loved flowers. I went to Chapel Market and chose big white lilies, branches with dark red berries, eucalyptus leaves, and she arranged them. I've never known anyone who had so many vases. She'd say, 'Jenny, these are lovely. You always choose such nice ones.' But she'd throw the lilies away as soon as they started to smell. 'Funereal,' she said. 'The one good thing about all this is I won't have to go to my own funeral.'

'Wouldn't you like to?' I asked. 'See what everyone says about you?'

'I know what they'll say about me,' she sighed. 'They'll say she was great in life and great in bed. But she was a pain to work with.'

'Well, I wouldn't say that,' I said.

'You could if you wanted.' She looked at me and laughed at my expression. I was shocked. She had cancer. She was dying. It was three o'clock in the afternoon.

'I meant,' I said slowly, 'that I would say you had lovely long fingers that could make the most wonderful bouquet out of a pathetic bunch of flowers.'

'Oh, Jenny,' she said.

'I'll make a cup of tea. I've brought some ginger biscuits today.' Ginger's good for nausea. I put three on one of her delicate china plates and made the tea in the matching cups and carried them through. The tray looked pretty, the spoons tinkled in the saucers.

'You're a peach, Jenny,' she said. She was sitting up in bed, wearing a shirt with a scarf tied round her head, writing letters to all the people who kept sending her cards. 'What else would you say about me?' she asked.

'I don't know.' I put the tray next to her on the bed.

'How about, the first time you saw me? That's always a good one.' She'd been interviewed by journalists, had her picture in a feature about Shakespeare in *Hello!*

I honestly couldn't remember the first time I'd seen her and I looked at her blankly.

'I remember the first time I saw you,' she said.

'Do you?'

'It was at a show at the Drill Hall, that American woman, comedian, what's her name, May Aculpa.'

My heart sank. I'd had a marked ticket. May Aculpa had called for the person with the marked ticket to come up on stage. She'd made a fool of me; she told me what to sing and then she changed the tune as I started singing.

'You were looking so neat in some fabulous jacket you had on, didn't it have big checks?'

'Yes,' I said miserably.

'And you just did what she said, and you laughed when everyone laughed, and you didn't try to tell jokes. I was really impressed with that.'

'That's nice.'

'No, honestly, I mean it. I thought, that's the way you should deal with situations like that, just go with it and let the star shine.' Dee was dipping the ginger biscuits in her tea, nibbling them carefully. 'These biscuits are great,' she said. 'Thanks.' The phone rang.

As I went to answer it I wondered if she got fed up with being so grateful all the time.

It was Amanda. She always wanted to speak to Amanda, who was her oldest and best friend. 'Hello, Mand,' she began and I went into the kitchen to wash the cups. I could hear her voice but not the words, but I knew from the tone that she was telling Amanda about her pain and the nausea and vomiting. Which she never mentioned to me.

I heard the phone ting as she replaced the receiver and I walked back into the room with a bowl of grapes. 'Sex! Sex! That's what I need,' she wailed. 'What do you do for sex, Jenny?'

'Not a lot,' I said, putting the bowl on her bedside table. 'Not at the moment.' I hovered at the end of the bed, looking down at the snowy white duvet cover. 'I read books, I suppose.'

'You mean you get your kicks from *The Mayor of Casterbridge* or *Our Mutual Friend*?' She followed my choice of reading.

'Oh no,' I said, 'You know, books, Anaïs Nin, Nancy Friday, Robbi Sommers.'

'You old dog, Jenny.' She coughed on a laugh. 'I'd never have thought it of you.'

'I don't normally talk about it,' I said primly.

'But as I'm dying, I can take your secret to my grave.' She gazed at me with her big blue eyes.

'I suppose so, yes.' My cheeks burned.

'You know what I want, I want that glow that you get the first time you do it with someone you really fancy. When other people say to you, "You're looking well." And I want to give someone else that glow. Jenny, I think you're my only hope.' I looked at her. 'Let's make a deal, you bring in your books, and I won't tell anyone. I'll give it a glow.' She snorted. 'You glow your way and I'll glow mine.'

'Coming and glowing,' I added, then realised what I'd said.

Dee laughed. 'Oh, glow on,' she coughed.

I'm a dutiful girl, I was a Brownie, I promised to help other people every day especially those at home. I was on the rota in three days' time. I took my small package of books with me.

She had just come back from the hospital. She was dopey with drugs. 'The bastards,' she muttered, 'they couldn't do the chemo, my platelets are down.' She stomped into the bathroom and stayed there for twenty minutes. 'I'm going to bed,' she announced, coming out in her blue towelling dressing gown, her ankles thin in big slippers. 'I don't want to talk to anyone. Oh, thanks for the flowers, put them in a vase, will you?'

I picked up the slim bunch of irises and went into the kitchen. She was still asleep when my relief, Amanda, turned up. The books stayed in my bag.

The next week I had a cold and it was felt by Amanda, who was in charge of the rota, that I should swap turns with someone else, till I was as free as possible of germs. I covered the books with brown paper and wrote different titles on the front, 'Glow in the Dark, light up your life,' 'Day Glow – try it sometime,' 'Way to Glow, a travel guide for the modern woman.' I knocked on the door of the flat and left them with the rota person, a thin woman with long straight hair who I didn't know.

Dee left a message on my answerphone, her husky voice soft down the phone. 'Jenny, you are such a peach. I asked Lesley to leave me alone for an hour. I wasn't in to anyone, even Amanda. Now I'm feeling flushed and relaxed. I've had a lovely afternoon. Looking forward to seeing you soon.'

Then I remembered where I had first seen her. It was at a party. I was just going home and I walked into the bedroom for my coat. Dee was lying on the bed, wrestling and laughing with another woman. She spurted with badly disguised amusement as I groped for my coat. I had hated her for her opulent body and easy way of being, she wasn't even embarrassed, with her shirt undone, someone's mouth on her dark nipple. I felt prim and breathless at the same time.

So I had seen her breasts.

My cold got better, Dee's condition got worse. Her skin was flaking badly and she had difficulty eating solids.

Amanda gave me an overnight turn on the rota – 8 p.m. to 8 a.m. She stayed to show me how to put out the sofa bed, take the duvet from the cupboard and put on new pillowcases. Everything smelt fresh, Dee couldn't bear the smell of hospitals and the washing machine was rarely still. Amanda fussed, reluctant to leave me with her precious charge. Dee was dozing in her room.

'If her temperature goes up, call me, whatever time it is.'

'I will,' I promised.

'Don't close the living-room door, you've got to be able to hear if she calls for you.'

'I won't.'

'You've got all my numbers?'

'I have.' I knew the drill, what I wasn't sure about was whether I would be able to cope, alone with her all night.

Amanda left and I washed the remains of soup and mashed potato from Dee's mugs. I hesitated over whether to throw away the bendy straws.

It was nine-thirty and I went into Dee's room. She was still asleep. Two small nightlights flickered on a chest of drawers. I picked up a copy of the *Guardian* at the foot of the bed and put it in a pile with her shoe box of writing utensils. I sniffed the water in a vase of cornflowers, then went to the edge of the bed and gently pulled the duvet cover straight. Her left hand lay on top of the covers. Her fingers were long and thin, the nails neat and short, and her skin was dry. I picked up her hand to tuck it in to the warmth of the duvet. Her fingers curled round mine and a lazy smile crossed her face. Without opening her eyes she said, 'Alone at last. I can't tell you how difficult it was to get you on this shift.'

I stood uncertainly, her hand still holding mine, willing her to keep her eyes closed.

'Jenny, this may not be the most elegant proposal that I've ever made or that you've ever had, but I'm dying so I don't have much time. Would you like to slip all your clothes off and gently, very gently, get into bed with me? I want you to make love to me, very delicately. And have done ever since I saw you standing on that stage singing "You are my Sunshine".'

I laid her hand back on to the duvet cover and looked at her. How could this happen? I hardly knew her. How had we got to this point? Was it the books? Had they put ideas about me into her head? Why had I brought them? Because she asked me. Because I thought she was lovely with her smile that made you feel warm and included, and the way she shouted at the TV when the news was on and the way she said, 'Oh, Jenny.' This was just what I had wanted. It's what I'd intended. I began to take off my sweatshirt.

'Oh.' She smiled. 'You're going to do it.'

I froze with my sweatshirt over my head. 'Are you joking?'

'Lovely creature, I am not joking.' Her voice was a sigh.

As I pulled off my jeans she said, 'What a pretty little body you have. And you haven't shared it with anyone for how long did you say?'

'Two years.'

'Come here quick then,' she said and moved the duvet to one side.

With all my clothes off I slid onto the bed. I could feel her heat before I felt her body. I edged gently towards her. The light from the lamppost in the street filtered through the Venetian blind. Her large white cotton shirt gleamed. Her face was pale; her eyes watched me as slowly I moved over to her.

'Oh God, I don't know what we can do,' she said. 'I hurt everywhere.'

I put my index finger up to my mouth and rubbed it on the inside of my lower lip. I knew the inside of her mouth was raw. I brushed her lips with my wet finger.

'That's a kiss,' I said.

'I don't hurt that much,' she murmured.

I leaned over her and licked her mouth.

'That's nice,' she said, and my tongue slipped inside. 'Ow, ow,' she whispered.

I moved back in dismay.

'It's hopeless,' she moaned. 'We can't even kiss.'

'Do you want me to stop?'

'No,' she said.

I leaned on one elbow and slowly began to undo the buttons of her shirt. I looked down at her small breasts, then up to her face and smiled.

'You are an old dog,' she said, as I bent over her right breast and put my lips around the nipple.

'Ow, ow, ow,' she said.

I lifted my head. 'No?'

'I don't think so.'

I pursed my lips and blew on her breast. Then I opened my mouth and breathed out warm air. Her nipple rose in pleasure. 'Oh fuck,' she said, 'ow, ow, go on, go on.'

I blew and breathed till both nipples were erect. I dripped saliva on them.

'Oh,' she moaned.

I looked over at the glass of water by her bed. Carefully I leaned across and dipped my hand in, then trailed cold drops of water onto her chest.

'Ow. No, that's a different kind of ow,' she said as I hesitated. I went back to the glass, and dripped water onto her nipples.

'Ooh. Ooh. You're very good,' she said. 'This is not what you led me to expect. People are so different in bed, aren't they? You think they're going to be quiet and passive.'

'Perhaps you should be quiet and passive for a bit,' I said. 'Just enjoy it. You are enjoying it, aren't you?'

'Well, that's hard to say, but I don't want you to stop.'

I put out my tongue and tentatively licked her nipple.

'Oh, how lovely,' she said in surprise. 'So this is how it's done.'

'What?'

'Love on a deathbed.'

'Don't say that.' I looked up at her. 'Dee, don't you dare die on me. I'm serious. What would I say?'

'Well, you could say, she died a happy woman. Ow, ow, I don't think you can go further than that using that method.'

I was trying to lick the bony part between her breasts. The skin was paper thin.

'It's a bit like rice paper,' I said, hauling myself up so that my head was level with hers. 'Like eating the outside of a bar of nougat.'

'I broke a tooth on some nougat, when I was nine,' she said, arching her neck as I blew gently on her face. 'We went to Cyprus on holiday. It was in, mmm, it was in Paphos. Well, just outside Paphos. My mum bought it for me for being good going round the mosaics.'

'The mosaics in Paphos!' I exclaimed. 'I went there two years ago. I took reels of photos. And they all came out blurred.' She was looking at me. 'I bought some nougat there, too.'

There was a pause. 'I hate nougat,' we said together.

I ran a finger across her thin hair.

'I don't know what to say, Jenny.' She put her hand flat on my shoulder and moved it down until it cupped my breast. 'I don't think there's anything I can do for you.'

'You could talk dirty.'

'After all that sweet talk, you mean? The terrible thing is I'm really tired. But I so wanted to do this. It's been lovely.'

'Shall I go now?'

'Yes, no, yes. I can't take the physical contact.'

'Oh.'

'I suppose I'm just afraid of intimacy.'

'I could lie really still on the far side of the bed,' I suggested. I moved across the sheet. 'Apart from the palms of your hands, is there anywhere your skin's not dropping off?'

'The soles of my feet.'

Hesitantly I moved my foot towards the bottom of the bed. She groaned with pain as I touched her shin. I inched down and brought my foot round, so that the arch slipped into the curve of her instep. I rocked my foot gently back and forth. 'You feel like velvet,' I said.

'You are such a surprise, Jenny,' Dee said, sleepily. With her instep, she stroked the arch of my foot. Her breathing grew deeper and slower.

She woke me at three in the morning. I knew she woke at night. Amanda had told me to listen out for her because of her nightmares. I turned my head. 'I'm feeling a bit more perky now,' she said.

'Oh?'

She ran her fingernail down my back. 'I can't believe I have a naked woman lying beside me. Touch me,' she whispered.

I rolled over and felt tentatively under the duvet. I brushed against her pubic hair. She moaned. My hand crept down between her legs and the back of my nails rolled over her vagina. She sucked air in between her teeth.

'There's some KY in the drawer on your side,' she said. As I groped in the drawer, she murmured, 'This may not work. It may just be all talk.'

'Let's see.'

I touched her with my fingers slipping with the greasy jelly. I stroked her gently at first and then more insistently. A sweet, musky perfume rose from her thighs. Together we moaned in pleasure.

'You're glowing,' I whispered.

'So are you,' she replied.

Her breathing was heavier and faster. 'Oh God, I'm coming, oh God, oh God, I can't believe it, oh God.' She exploded in a howl of triumph and lay panting and coughing. 'Oh Jenny, we did it.' She laughed with difficulty. 'I don't think my body knows what's hit it.'

'You may have to take it easy tomorrow.'

'I think I took it fairly easy tonight,' she said. She picked up my hand, still warm and sticky, and contentedly rubbed her finger in my palm. Her eyelids drooped. 'Where's your foot?' she asked.

Carefully we moved our legs. The arch of my foot nestled in her instep and she fell asleep.

The next day I got a tickle in my throat. Before my next turn on the rota my cold had come back with a vengeance. It was in my voice, making me sound nasal and throaty. Dee's condition was deteriorating, Amanda told me on the phone, her skin was flaking badly and she had difficulty eating solids. 'Don't come,' she said. After that I rang once and asked to speak to Dee but the woman who answered the phone said sorry, but she was asleep. I was disappointed, but she was probably thinking that my germs would wriggle down the phone to lodge themselves in Dee's ear. Or Dee had said, 'F— off.' So after that I just rang in for bulletins, and I didn't ask to speak to Dee.

The week before Christmas, Dee went back into hospital. I still had my cold. I drove down to the hospital and sat in the road outside, wrapped up in my coat, sucking cough sweets, looking at the fairy lights in the trees, thinking about her. I got a ticket for having no road tax.

Two days later Amanda rang. 'It's looking pretty final,' she said. 'If you want to come and say goodbye, I don't think a few cold germs are going to make any difference now.'

The hospital staff were used to Dee's support team. Amanda had arranged for a room, where six women now sat talking quietly. One or two of them I knew slightly – one was Lesley with the long straight hair – and we greeted each other uneasily and talked about the coffee machine and hospital food.

When Amanda walked into the room we all fell silent and looked at her. Her face was tired and her eyes were puffy. She said, 'They've given her a load of morphine and she's more comfortable. She's dozing on and off. Oh, Jenny.' She noticed me in the corner.

'Can we have a word?'

We moved into the corridor. Nurses strolled to and fro, smiling kindly at Amanda, asking, 'How is she?'

'I think she wants to see you,' Amanda said. 'She's been saying your name.'

We walked into Dee's room. It was silent, full of chrome and steel machinery. Dee stirred in the wide white bed. The flesh had fallen from her cheeks, her face was skull-like.

Amanda bent over her and spoke softly. 'Jenny's here.'

Dee's eyes remained closed, but her face cracked into a smile.

'Jenny,' she whispered. 'Jenny, Jenny.' Amanda moved away, and I stood beside her pillow. 'Where've you been? I wanted to give you your books back.' She coughed.

'I had a cold,' I said, leaning towards her. I stroked her face with the back of my finger. 'You're looking well.'

'I don't think so,' she murmured, her mouth moving painfully, her eyes still closed, 'but I have fond memories. How about you?'

'Yes, yes, I do.'

A small smile came to her lips. Slowly she drew her hand out from under the sheet. Amanda moved forward, saying 'Dee?' but Dee waved her away. Stiffly she turned the cupped palm of her hand upwards. 'Do your stuff,' she breathed to me.

'Here?' I said. I looked anxiously at Amanda.

'I'm not going anywhere,' Dee said.

Amanda pushed a chair towards me and I sank into it. I leaned over Dee and slid my hand over her hair, picking pieces of the damp fringe from her forehead.

'Tease,' she sighed.

I dipped one hand into the glass on her bedside table and trailed drops of water along her arm. Dee moaned. My other hand slid past her curled fingers and began to circle her cool dry palm.

'Yessss,' she said.

My fingers moved in her palm until her breathing deepened and her chest rose and fell regularly.

'The morphine's just kicking in,' Amanda said. She stood up and we walked into the corridor. 'What did she say to you?' she asked.

I laughed. 'We talked about books.'

Amanda looked at me. 'Didn't she say thanks? She said thanks to the others. I'm sure she meant to.'

'It's OK,' I said.

It was snowing on the day of the funeral. Everyone sent flowers. Waxy white lilies, rich rusty chrysanthemums, purple irises. Dee had said, 'I don't want any of this no-flowers-please nonsense. I want a profusion, I want a riot of colour.'

I said to the florist, 'Dark green leaves, and six red roses.'

I put them in the allotted area; they stood out like a heap of ruby velvet against the damp black concrete and the white snow. She'd have liked that effect. I didn't sign the card, because everybody reads them. I just wrote, 'Where are you glowing now?'

There Was an Old Woman
Frances Gapper

There Was an Old Woman
Frances Gapper

A song keeps going through my head, the one, you probably know it, about the old woman. *There was an old woman who swallowed a fly, I don't know why she swallowed a fly. Perhaps she'll die.*

Perhaps she'll die. The headmaster of my primary school, Mr William MacGregor, used to sing this, accompanying himself on the guitar. He'd go round all the classrooms. The other song in his repertoire was 'There's a Hole in My Bucket'. *Then mend it, dear Henry, dear Henry, dear Henry...* But anyway, the old woman song. At first I can only remember the first and last verses, but then they all come back to me.

There was an old woman who swallowed a spider
That wriggled and jiggled and tickled inside her.
She swallowed the spider to catch the fly, (we all sang the chorus)
I don't know why she swallowed the fly. Perhaps she'll die.

She swallowed a dog (what a hog!) to catch the cat, she swallowed a cat (fancy that!) to catch the bird, she swallowed a bird (how absurd!) to catch the spider, that wriggled and tickled... She kept on swallowing bigger and bigger creatures, until she died, no 'perhaps'. It was the horse (of course) that did for her.

The song keeps repeating itself in my mind. I wonder if the phrase *She'll swallow anything* could be rooted in history, i.e. were there once people – women – who really could and would swallow anything?

Swallow, I think. Swallow, swallow, little swallow. I swallow. I look up swallow in the *Shorter Oxford*, which I haven't yet packed. Gulf, abyss, corresp. to MLG *swelch* (also *swalh*) throat, whirlpool. A deep hole or opening in the earth. A swallower is a certain deep-sea fish with an immensely distensible stomach which enables it to swallow fishes larger than itself. Appearances of the word in modern literature: He swallowed it in three gulps. They made him swallow... the tablets. He kept swallowing as if he felt... a lump in the throat. Thick forests seemed... about to swallow them up. The beloved machine has 'swallowed' your card. He swallowed all Anna's savings fixing up this house. Every moment swallowed up and forgotten. Franz's interest in socialism... was... swallowed up by his terrible anxiety. She'd done her best to swallow her anger and be nice to Ruth. I must swallow my pride, and overcome my fear.

It's those bug-eating people, on that TV programme. That's it, I think. The poor grubs and larvae and pupae and beetles being eaten by minor celebrities. I'm an insect, get me out of here. I don't even have a TV, but it's in all the newspapers. Phil Tufnell, hailed as a new British hero – and as 'delightfully self-effacing' – for chomping five plates of ants, et cetera. After being sick, Tuffers went on to bite the body off a large maggot. His catchphrase: 'If you can't do it, you can't do it. If you can, happy days!' And he crunched a moth pupa (pictured) that was just getting ready to unfurl into a beautiful moth. All very one-sided and no protests from the insect rights organisations which don't exist. Now if it had been kittens... just as I'm thinking this, lying on a mattress in what will soon be my ex-bedroom, for I no longer have a bed or any other furniture, I'm starting again, shedding, discarding things like old bits of skin and hoping to be reborn, or simply for my life to change – just then, my own young cat jumps up to the window, kills a fly with a single blow of her paw and eats it.

She looks pleased with herself. It's the first thing I've ever seen her kill. Just like that. Happy days. Well done, I tell her. And I feel no compassion for the fly, no, none at all. The fly had to die. The fly is dead, eaten. The cat ate it. She has not (yet) been sick. And greater triumphs lie ahead – mice, birds, God help us.

There was an old woman who swallowed a fly, I don't know why she... I should ring my mother, to check up on her. She's been very ill. In fact, I think I'll ring her now. She's bound to be at home. She used always to be out, walking in parks or visiting friends, but now she's in. She has Meals on Wheels – these are stodgy, she says, with too much Bird's Custard. But she eats them. I think she does.

I ring her. Guess who's here, she says. Louise!

Oh, I say, is it a surprise visit?

Silence.

Just a moment, Mum says. In the background she asks, Is this a surprise visit?

No, my sister says, I phoned you yesterday.

Mum comes back on. No, she phoned me yesterday.

The cat burps, or hiccups. My mother was in hospital last month, for blood transfusions and tests. She was sedated before the tests, but not anaesthetised. They put a camera down her throat – uncomfortable, she said – and one up her anal passage, for a colonoscopy. Then she had a barium meal, which I'd heard was horrific. Mum drank the barium like a cup of tea. They X-rayed her, tracking its progress through her body. But the end result of all these tests was, they found nothing.

How are you getting on with the meals on wheels? I ask.

I don't think they're really necessary, my mother says. I had plenty to eat before. Lots of salad. And watercress sandwiches. But we'll see how it goes, she says – one of her little phrases, to pretend she's still independent and not under anyone's control.

Her fridge, when I last looked inside, was full of eyedrops and packets of watercress long past their sell-by dates. Been up to your old tricks again, the young doctor asked her at the West Middlesex. My mother looked alarmed. Sorry, he said, and giggled. It's Friday afternoon. I'll prescribe you some more iron tablets – Here she interrupted, Now what about my eyedrops?

All right, sweetheart, the doctor said, irritated. But you'll get me in trouble. It's not really up to us. Which kind do you have? he asked. We brandished a bag of them, which Mum had insisted on bringing along. Three different sorts. And how many times a day do you put them in? She was uncertain. Once a day, she said. OK, he said.

The hospital pharmacists (women) called us back to the hatch and back again. They rewrote the prescription. Twice a day for these, they said, I'll write that down for you, and use these ones as necessary to relieve dryness. And we're giving you a month's supply of iron tablets, not fourteen days.

While we were waiting for the pharmacists to call us back to the hatch, so the prescription could be freshly puzzled over, other people kept coming along. They'd look up at the number in a box on the wall – it was 93, lit in red against black, like at a supermarket cheese counter – then they'd look at the hatch, then at the number again, then finally uneasily at me. Excuse me, they'd say, where do I get a number? I'd say, you have to ring that little bell, then someone will come to the hatch and take your prescription, and then they'll give you a number. Thanks, the person would say.

All afternoon, Mum and I had been standing in the wrong queues or waiting in the wrong seats and now the moment I'd grasped one tiny little bit of the system, it was my job to explain it to everyone else. It reminded me of when I worked in an office in High Holborn and used to spend all my lunch break, and my popping-out times, directing tourists to the British Museum. Go along that road, I'd say, until you get to Museum Street. Oh, Museum Street, they'd cry in delight. Yes, I'd say, turn right along Museum Street and carry on to the end. Then you'll see the British Museum, the main entrance gates are just across the zebra crossing. I would see the roast-chestnut sellers in my mind, but these I never mentioned. I kept to the point. My directions were clear and succinct. And the tourists were so grateful and I'd feel so much more useful than I ever did at work, I used to daydream about being retired and making myself a little placard with a map on it, so I could parade up and down High Holborn all day, directing people to the British Museum.

That's because he's not French at all, he's from Dagenham. I can hear our next-door neighbour saying this, forty years ago. In between directing people, memory keeps thrusting images and voices at me. A weak wall has broken and the past is rushing back, in mirror-pieces. Mum is there too, of course. Maybe it's the effect of us sitting so close. She's in a quiet dream. I'm thinking of the onion man, with his striped jersey and beret, pushing his black bicycle. The tightly plaited string of onions, hanging on our cupboard door. Very advanced for the 1960s, the French country kitchen look. Only it kept being spoilt by me, rubbing the brown crackly skins off the onions, to reveal their young shiny selves. Rustle, rustle – a thrill like biting my nails. Rustle, crackle. And my mum like a trapdoor spider, emerging from the back kitchen to slap my hands away.

The spider – I was collecting rose petals, a delicacy my rabbit seemed to appreciate, a change from grass and dandelion leaves. I was only allowed to pick up the fallen petals. Sometimes these were fresh, but more often brown-spotted and wrinkled like old skin. When I thought my mother wasn't overseeing me from the kitchen window, I'd pull loose petals, or fixed ones, from the heads of Peace and Fragrant Cloud. One day, one bad day, I pulled a whole rose. Then I looked down at my dress. There sat a huge spider...

I'm trying to get to sleep, but I keep waking up. There's a fly in the room. It's buzzing. *I don't know why. Perhaps she'll die.* I put my earplugs in, the ones I keep for defence against next door's TV and radio. He's ninety years old, next door. I seal my ears and now I can only hear the ringing inside my own head, like a burglar alarm when the owners have gone abroad and the other people in the street lie awake, disturbed and made helpless. An alarm that can never be turned off, that's always ringing behind and beyond all the world's other sounds. Although it's mine and personal to me, I don't think it'll stop when I die, no, it will go on forever, ringing and ringing in the silence of eternity. I remember the haunted holiday flat in Portugal, right by the cemetery, and Helen doing the washing-up, she was just thinking it's a pity there's no plug for this sink when a plug came flying through the air and hit her on the cheek. The fly is still annoying me. It keeps settling on me, on my face, my arm.

I get up. The moonlight is very strong, it's lighting up this room and the hallway. A floodlight, a searchlight. I open the bedroom door and the fly flies out. Then I open the kitchen door, feeling somehow the fly wants me to, and the door to the back garden. Out goes the fly. My mother is there, in the garden. She's lying in a sort of hammock, all made of spider silk, in a web between the trees. And there's the spider, a very large one, it's right on top of her, spinning her into a cocoon. And the most peculiar thing is, I can see all this very well, without my glasses. My mother looks intrigued by what's going on, not frightened. All around the garden, things are hatching. Pupae are pupating, throbbing. Even the moon is like an egg, distended, bulging at one end. New things, hungry new things, are being born.

Shopping
Caril Behr

Shopping
Caril Behr

Dora's card table stands under the window, set with her best lace cloth and two glasses of sherry. The green oval platter is precisely where it should be, in the middle of the table, filled with Rich Tea biscuits. Only Rich Tea will do. Anything else is too common, the wrong texture or the wrong shape. Lavinia is very particular about which biscuits she dips into her drink. She likes to down her sherry in a single gulp.

She's late, but then her timekeeping was never anything you could rely on. She turns up when she feels like it, breezing through the door without knocking. Lately, though, she's taken to using the window. You feel the curtains flutter and there she is, chattering away about this and that, pouring scorn on everyone they know.

After drinks they go to bed, Dora on the left, Lavinia on the right, lying face to face, hip to hip, the way they always did. Lavinia's touch is as deft and thrilling as if she were still made of flesh and blood. Her skin is softer than ever, her need more urgent. By morning she'll be gone, just as it was when they were young. She never was one to stay the night. It's always been a matter of principle with her.

Dora dozes in her chair, wakes with a start, checks her calendar. Yes, it's Sunday. Lavinia always comes on a Sunday. So why isn't she here now? At midnight Dora downs both sherries, retires to bed. She's puzzled. Lavinia often turns up in the week as the fancy takes her but she's never missed a Sunday before.

Mind you, she's had a bee in her bonnet lately. Dora remembers lunch just three days ago when Lavinia comes floating down through the ceiling and kicks the water jug off the table. Just as well the others can't see her. There's enough fuss as it is with staff rushing to mop up the ladies and rescue the gravy.

'No point in waiting for your ageing daughters to offer you a few crumbs,' Lavinia screams. 'It's up to you old bags to do something before you die.'

'They're deaf, Lavinia,' Dora reminds her.

'Deaf my arse! They're bloody lazy.'

'What do you want them to do?'

Just then a rock-hard roast potato pings off Dora's fork.

'No point in talking.' Lavinia disappears as the words issue from her lips, leaving Dora staring stupidly at the vacant space.

That night she's back again at the foot of Dora's bed.

'One must take something big every day,' she says, 'something that will be missed. Remove it from where it is to somewhere else.'

'Why bother?' Dora snorts.

'People shouldn't be allowed to get used to things being in the same place. It makes them tiresome and lazy.'

'Tireless, busy people are just as boring in their own way, if you ask me,' Dora replies.

Lavinia slips into bed beside Dora. Night air rushes through the open window. An owl hoots. Lavinia's fingers trace shivery patterns along the soft hollows of Dora's spider-thin inner arms. They lie in peaceful contemplation of the ceiling.

'Shall we discuss gardening or philosophy?' Dora asks.

'The cemetery is full of oddballs.' Lavinia is working herself up to something. Dora can feel it coming.

'No point in being choosy out there, you know! Some of my best friends are criminals. Thieves are full of imagination and invention but the respectable never stop complaining.'

'Well, that's hardly surprising, is it?'

'Make me proud of you,' Lavinia demands. 'Do something terrible for once.'

'I'm too old for that.'

'Age has nothing to do with it. You're alive, that's all that matters.'

'It's too late. You should have come up with this years ago.'

'You could have come up with something yourself! Why didn't you?' Lavinia asks.

'You never listened to a word I said. You always had to be right.'

'You should have made me listen.'

'There was nothing I could have said that would have convinced you,' Dora insists.

'How do you know? You never tried.'

'I'm tired. My eyesight's not what it used to be.' Dora clings to Lavinia's arm. By morning Lavinia's vanished. There's not a single trace of her, not even a lingering whiff of the lavender cologne she usually leaves behind.

Monday morning and Dora wakes up troubled. She puts on clean underwear, the black velvet skirt Lavinia has left her, the blouse with a button missing, her good coat and walking shoes. The brown brogues will do. She wears two hats one on top of the other to stop the thoughts from flying out of her head. Setting off before breakfast, Dora walks down the hill and through the town. She crosses the motorway bridge, trudges through fields to the churchyard. Hands on hips, she faces Lavinia's grave.

'Where the hell are you?'

The rippling grass and creaking trees talk to her. There's a breathless whispering but she can't make out what's being said. She's waiting for a sign, something tangible. She's been waiting for a long time. The dead have a way of hiding when you need them most. Surely there's nobody else? Why would a dead person want to be unfaithful? Why would a living person want to be unfaithful, for that matter? There's no knowing what goes on in another person's mind, living or dead, Dora thinks. Anyway, it couldn't be that old bugger Hugh. Lavinia finished with him when they were all still alive.

'Why won't you answer me?'

A wave of silence washes over the graves.

'That's what comes of reasoning with the unreasonable.' Dora argues with herself, gesticulating wildly. She retraces her steps, gets home in the middle of pudding.

'We've been worried sick. Just look at you, covered in mud. Dear oh dear! We'll have to keep an eye on you!'

'No dinner, thank you,' Dora waves an imperious arm. 'Just tea. Put a dash of brandy in it.'

At bedtime she thinks, perhaps it's time. Perhaps this is all there is from now on. Oh how paltry and tedious, surely not! One shouldn't depend on others so much. One shouldn't be thrown into a tizzy by their comings and goings. Dora sleeps for an unusually long time. When she awakes, a new day is well under way.

'Can't pretend to be dead when I'm not.' She puts on her dressing gown and marches down the corridor.

The two remaining gentlemen are smoking in an alcove by the front door.

'Got a fag?'

She blows smoke against the windowpane. Is it Tuesday or Wednesday, she wonders? 'Surely it hardly matters what names the days have.' Dora notices that one of the gentlemen is beginning to nod off. She takes the cigarette from between his fingers and puts it out.

'If the days could choose their own names, they might want a change. Nobody ever asks them what they want to be called.'

'It's Tuesday, dear.' The other gentleman offers his arm with as courtly a bow as his stiff limbs will permit. 'You're a fine gal!' His dentures make small clicks as he speaks. 'In time for tea, what's more!'

'Don't talk to me about time,' Dora scowls. 'Something so dependent on clocks is not be trusted.'

Dora returns to her room to dress for a suitable occasion. She finds the white angora v-necked sweater she used to wear to bridge parties and that beige skirt with the pleat at the back. The one that always made her look like a vicar's wife. Not her favourite but it'll have to do for the moment. One simply cannot start looking for things that might be long gone or might never have existed in the first place. How is one to know what is real and what is not, and does it matter? She wears her pearls, puts the tortoiseshell comb in her hair, takes her handbag and marches to the television lounge.

'My, don't we look smart!'

'If one has to dwell in the past, one might just as well look one's best,' Dora retorts coldly.

She settles into her favourite chair, glaring at the gathered company. 'Bloody fools! Who told you to come here?'

A shaft of sunlight streams through the window. Late afternoon shadows do a slow dance across the wall, their elongated shapes dissolving with the fading light. Darkness brings smells of cooking, the flushing of toilets, running of baths. After ten there are hours of fitful sleep and waking dreams. Then dawn, a patch of grey light through her curtain.

'How is one to manage another day? What a pity one sees it all but is too blind to read.' Dora talks to the birds on the grass. 'How the decades pass! We take ourselves so seriously in our forties. Our fifties are beset with symptoms. There's a brief moment of joy and then it's downhill all the way. If I could have it over again I'd make the same mistakes and revel in them this time!'

Moments swell into hours. Dora marks the rotating periods of light and dark. Sunday comes and goes. 'Bollocks to Lavinia!' she says.

Dora leaves the lace cloth in the drawer, throws the biscuits in the bin, drinks the sherry by herself, goes to bed. She's drifting into the mist when Lavinia wafts through the window.

'Sulking, are we?'

'Where've you been?'

'Shopping,' Lavinia replies.

'What could you possibly want?'

'Everything! The world's full of desirable objects. All one has to do is remove them.'

'That's not shopping, that's stealing.'

'It's shopping if you take them from shops.'

Lavinia slides under the covers, takes Dora in her arms. 'You're cold enough to be in the cemetery.'

'It's your fault. You left me!'

'I'm back now. I had research to do.'

'Of what?'

'Shopping. I've a list of things.'

'There's nothing I need.'

'Never mind need. One must want. One must take. If you don't have anything, you can't give anything away.'

'And since when have you been philanthropically inclined? You've never given anything away in your life.' Dora's eyes glint in the darkness. There's a chink of white light from a street lamp showing through the gap in the parted curtains.

'People change.' Lavinia embraces the sharp angles of Dora's body, fingers the few remaining strands of fine silvery hair. Mermaid silk.

'You're as beautiful as ever.'

'Stop flattering.'

'Come shopping with me?'

'No!'

'Come on. It'll be like the old days again.'

'I don't want to.'

'Be reasonable, Dora, for heaven's sake! It's not as if you've got anything better to do.'

It is just like the old days again. They go out in the morning, down the hill to the high street.

'I'm here beside you,' Lavinia says. 'Don't be frightened. Take what you want.'

They go to the newsagent's, the chemist's. Dora takes a newspaper, a box of crayons, a nailbrush, bars of soap.

'I don't want any of it,' she says.

'Then throw them away and take things you do want. Good heavens, Dora, you were always such a goose!'

Into the supermarket to face a dizzying array of things, fairy cakes in transparent boxes, foreign biscuits in fancy tins. A punnet of strawberries gets squashed in Dora's bag.

'It's heavy. My feet hurt.'

'Let's rest.'

They sit on a bench in the bus shelter, eat the fairy cakes.

By afternoon, Dora's exhausted. They go to bed, Lavinia's cheek soft as a living child's on Dora's papery skin. Dora sleeps through dinner, refuses tea. Lavinia stays the night.

'Today we take something big,' Lavinia says after breakfast.

'How big?'

'Big enough.'

Into Pearsons on the high street and up the escalator to the third floor. Household goods. Dora puts a teapot into her shopping bag.

'Leave it on the low wall by the library,' Lavinia says. 'People should get used to finding things in the street.'

There are glittering things made of stainless steel, towels, curtains, cushions.

'Take one of those there.' Lavinia points to plump embroidered cushions piled together in an enormous wire basket. They shimmer with gold thread and fragments of mirror glass sewn into the patchwork velvet.

'It looks dear.'

'All the more reason to take it.'

'Too big to carry.'

'It's only a cushion, just walk off with it.'

'If you want it so much, why don't you walk off with it?'

'If I could I would,' says Lavinia, 'but it's too late for me now.'

Dora's brow furrows as if she is solving a difficult problem. Then suddenly she becomes angry. 'You don't love me at all,' she shouts. 'You're just using me for sport because you're bored lying in that grave year in year out.'

'Nothing could be further from the truth.' There is a look of infinite sadness in Lavinia's dark eyes. 'I would have taken the earth and given it to you. Lord only knows I used to dream about decking you in finery, but when the moment came to act, I lost my nerve. I tried and failed.'

'All mouth and no trousers,' says Dora. 'I wish you'd been more consistent. I would have been satisfied with that.'

'Do you need help, madam?' A shop assistant interrupts Dora's flow of speech.

'Good heavens, no!' says Dora peevishly. 'How on earth could you possibly help me?'

After some hesitation Dora takes the cushion under her arm. 'Do you want it or not?' She speaks irritably into thin air.

'I want you to have what you want,' Lavinia says humbly. 'This is for you from me.'

Dora examines the cushion's delicately patterned glittery surface. It is extremely pretty. 'Oh bugger, why not?' she says, her face breaking into a grin. The cushion has an unwieldy triangular shape causing her to stagger. She musters resolve, heads for the escalator, hesitating before the cascade of rolling metal. She never liked the blasted things at the best of times. Which foot is one to put forward first? It would be easier to dive into a waterfall. Suddenly there's a hand on her shoulder.

'Excuse me, madam.'

'Lavinia!' Dora screams. 'Lavinia, where are you?'

They've caught everything on video, both thefts, the furtive looking, the hesitating before and after. Such an old lady though, they're ever so kind.

'Where do you live, love?'

'Damn you, Lavinia! You can't rely on her. You simply can't!' Dora informs the store detective, a pleasant young woman dressed in uniform like a policeman, rather mannish. 'I shall never listen to her ever again.'

At home they keep an eye on her.

'Can't have you wandering off any more. Heaven knows what you'll get up to next.'

Confounded nuisance. Of course Lavinia evaporates into thin air, just when she's most needed.

There's a meeting in Matron's office with the doctor. Dora's son Rupert and his wife come too. How tiresome! Rupert has turned into his father, same weak chin, watery eyes.

'Have you got false teeth yet?' Dora demands.

He smiles at her.

'He pretends to be nicer than he is,' Dora says to no one in particular. What about his poor wife? Look at her, only in her sixties and so feeble already. Dora reaches over, pats her knee.

'Mother, you do know you've done something wrong, don't you?' Rupert clears his throat. Matron serves tea. They talk over her head.

Dora looks out of the window. The garden is so beautiful in autumn, her favourite season.

'It's hot in here!'

They've put her next to the radiator. Central heating dulls the brain. No wonder the younger generation are so stupid. Their voices buzz irritatingly. She nearly dozes off, when Lavinia appears, clear as day, taking up her usual stance, feet planted firmly apart, hands on hips.

'What do you think you're playing at?' Dora yells. 'Getting me into trouble, then turning up when it's too late!'

'It's never too late.' Lavinia touches her with a cool dry hand. 'I've been thinking,' she says. 'It's high time I moved in with you. It's what you've always wanted, isn't it?'

'You always said you'd never be seen dead in a place like this.'

'I've been dead so long now, nothing matters any more. Besides, you're here and the way you keep going, you'll be here forever.'

'Thanks to you, they're keeping me under lock and key,' Dora rages. 'Can't even collect my own pension from the post office.'

'I shouldn't listen to them,' says Lavinia. 'There're possibilities you haven't dreamt of yet.'

'Mother, please don't shout. Come and sit down.' Rupert tries to take Dora's arm but she pushes him away.

'Leave her be,' Matron says soothingly. 'Most of them rant in here. We're used to it. We'll look after her for you, won't we, dear?'

'I'm not your dear!' Dora takes a turn around the room, then confronts the gathering with folded arms. 'Dears are for letters and regrets. Don't think you can get around me so easily.' She wags a finger at Matron, who smiles tolerantly.

With a withering look, Dora leaves the room, her back impressively straight, head held high. She sweeps along the corridor. Lavinia floats after her.

The meeting plods its earnest course into the gathering shadows. A spider spins industriously in a corner. They talk, repeating themselves until they run out of things to say. And not one of them notices that Matron's small gold clock has disappeared from the mantelpiece.

Call Me by My Name
Frances Bingham

Call Me by My Name
Frances Bingham

The woman who destroyed my peace was not so out of the
ordinary. At that time, in those days of mass bereavement, all kinds
came to me for help. It made no difference to me whether they
were Eton-cropped or cloche-hatted, in bow-ties or chiffon scarves.
Help is what I gave them, unstintingly. Sometimes I was so tired at
the end of a session that my assistant Vera would bring me a little
brandy, instead of my usual cup of tea, to calm my nerves. It was
draining work, and of course I had to charge; I had to live on
something if I was to go on with it. Some financial investment
helps people concentrate, anyway. This woman came to me for
help, like the rest of them, having lost a loved one. Vera said she'd
mistaken her at first for a man, and a nice-looking one, too, but
that was Vera's usual wishful thinking. (She pretended to have an
eye for the gentlemen, but it was just to tease me, really. For my gift
to thrive I needed peace, quiet, a tranquil atmosphere, as she well
knew. Vera could make a drama out of any client.) To me, the
woman looked more like one of those female pilots or racing
drivers who were always in the newspapers then. I could see at
once that she was grieving; she had that look of being lost inside a
glass paperweight, hopelessly entrapped in her sorrow. Yet there
was something else – my work has made me sensitive to these
things – if she *had* been a man, I'd have said she was having an
affair without the wife knowing. So I suppose there was something
odd, even at the beginning.

My consulting rooms were in Mecklenburgh Square in those
days, on the first floor. I was preparing for the session, dimming the
lamps, spreading the table with its baize and the paisley cloth. At
the window, I paused with my hand on the thick curtain's fringe of
braid bobbles. It was misty in the square, the trees were still in leaf,

but brown and dripping with melancholy. I saw her striding along through the garden, in a long driving coat with an astrakhan collar, and I stepped quickly back from the tall windows as though I knew already what she was bringing me.

The woman was brisk, businesslike, not nervous, with a strong handshake and a direct look. I knew the type, but had nothing against them as long as they paid. Also, she was obviously wealthy; nothing ostentatious, but I saw it in the well-kept teeth, the cut of her cloth. Quickly then, we got down to business. The afternoon is not my best time, evening is preferable, and it was a sluggish, sunless day. We held hands unenthusiastically, and I felt my sitter's warmth, dry-palmed, strong-fingered; noted a big gold signet ring like a man's, no wedding ring. This is a good way to start. As soon as I closed my eyes, expecting nothing much, the crowd of khaki came shuffling in, overflowing the mind, too many figures to identify.

So I began, 'Someone in uniform, a youngish man.' The hands stayed slack. The images drifted past me, nameless, unknown. 'A soldier,' I confirmed, 'with a name like Harry.' (This was simply a try.) Barrie, Freddy, Laurie? One of them floated towards me, almost self-effacingly, hovered like a child on the outskirts of an adult conversation.

'I think he wants to speak with you.'

'No!' Her voice was surprisingly firm, but a little petulant. 'I know nothing about any soldiers. Send him away, please.'

The only woman in London without an army ghost, and she had to come to me! That immunity was something no one could have guessed at that time, in that place. It was inconvenient.

Resolutely, I dismissed my regiments. The flu epidemic had been my other great source, recently, so the odds were good here, too. I concentrated on her hands again, cleared my mental picture board, waited. Probably it was her mother.

'Now I see a woman.' There was a tension in her silence. 'She is older than you.' Her hands tightened, involuntarily. 'A beautiful lady.' (This is always a safe one, and quite truthful, for beauty is in the eye of the beholder.)

My sitter sighed, very faintly, but I caught it. She was squeezing my hands now, quite firmly. I saw the lady now, her mother, behind my closed eyes, bowing graciously.

'She is smiling. She wants us to know she is happy.'

'But what does she look like? What is her name?'

'Wait,' I admonished her (though her impatience pleased me). 'She is quite a tall lady, majestic, with her hair up in the old-fashioned way, and a beautiful gown, with lace on the breast, and a high collar.'

I could visualise her quite clearly now, a well-built dowager of the old school.

'Is she dark or fair?'

I concentrated. 'Brunette. With a lovely complexion.'

'*Yes.*'

We sat in silence, the gas hissing its ostler's whistle of warmth, the trees clicking their leaves. I saw the lady smell a rose self-consciously, with the exaggerated mimicry of a movie.

'But what is her name?'

I tried again, but to no avail. Perhaps the room was stuffy.

'I am not – told that. All I can receive is that she is a lady. What is the name of your loved one? I will ask if it is her name.'

'No,' she said hoarsely. 'You have remarkable powers, Miss Elland, you have it already. That lady was known, by her intimates, just as "Lady".'

The sitting was over, the woman withdrew her hands from mine and stood up. I drooped in my chair, my nerves raw, my vision departed.

'Are you unwell?' she asked gruffly.

'No – it is just tiredness – would you be so kind as to ring the bell?'

She pulled the cord abruptly, and then took out a slim wallet from her breast pocket. Inside it was a photograph, carefully fitted to the small frame set aside for boys boastfully to show off their sweethearts.

'Is that the lady you saw?'

'Yes,' I said, trying to conceal my astonishment. I rarely saw anything as vividly as I'd seen her, even down to the full figure, the lace-trimmed bosom.

Vera came in with the tea, and I was surprised to see the woman smile at her as she put the tray down. This was not what I expected.

She drank her tea thirstily, trying to conceal emotion.

'So next time, will you try to speak with Lady?' she asked, breathlessly.

'Perhaps. It is hard to know what will happen at each session. As you know, usually it is easier when we have a circle.'

'But you can speak directly to the departed at a private session?'

'Oh, yes. Sometimes nothing happens, as I told you, or it is difficult. Today everything came easily.'

She smiled at me then, almost grinned. It was quite alarming.

Before the next session Vera found out all we needed to know, simply by consulting the newspaper library. I was glad I had not said anything definite about 'your mother'. People of their sort have so many details of their lives recorded – places, other people, interests, family events – which give me a starting point. The name is what they always ask for first. Yet how can you summon up a spirit without knowing its name? So in her next visits, we were able to see her Lady singing, remembering their seaside holidays, talking with friends who had passed on. I worked the watch in, though it was a risk, but it would have been a waste not to use the advertisement, which sharp Vera spotted by chance.

'She is showing me a wristwatch,' I said neutrally. I could visualise it very clearly. I described it: the rectangular face, the diamond winder, the initials on the back. My client's hands pulsed lightly where they clasped mine, the oval watch on her wrist whispered on. 'She says that where she is now all lost things are found.'

When I opened my eyes I saw that she was crying – big, bright tears.

I was cautious when she told me she wanted to speak to Lady directly, herself, instead of constantly saying 'ask her, tell her' and hearing always 'she says'. I explained that it would require that I surrender my body to the spirit's use, a dangerous and exhausting situation. She offered me more money, which I accepted. (The woman always paid in mint guineas; she seemed to think a session quite on a par with consulting a physician in Harley Street.) I stipulated that we would need a circle, and it was agreed that Vera would come in, for the sake of privacy and convenience, and the woman would bring her companion, Mrs Anstruther. As soon as I saw *her* I understood the hangdog swagger, the adulterous husband manner. Mrs Anstruther was a voluptuous woman of fashion, extremely desirable, obviously devoted to her. Probably their affair began while Lady was still supposedly the wife; thus the guilt, thus the repentance. Now I knew what she really wanted Lady to say.

It was an evening session. I had rested all afternoon, and taken my brandy, and my tablets. Vera had made the room warm, and dimmed the lamps. We held hands around the table, with Vera's familiar hand rough-palmed to one side of me. I had asked for a piece of Lady's clothing which I could touch, so I was wearing a silk scarf of hers across my shoulders, pink. I closed my eyes. Vera was there, solid. My sitter was rigid with her locked emotion. Mrs Anstruther was not inimical, as I had expected, but willing something fervently. She could not tell me what. I summoned up the picture of Lady quickly enough, in her usual regal style. I tried to imagine her way of speaking, her elocution, what she could possibly have said to these two women. A long time passed. I tried to prepare to speak in a voice like hers. What would she want to say now?

'Darling.' I spoke. My voice was thick and muffled, indistinct as a stroke victim's, but decipherable. I was very frightened, because I had not meant to speak, not this, not yet. 'Darling.' The voice spoke on, telling my sitter how handsome she was, how well-dressed, how charming. My hand broke the circle and stroked her cropped hair, her sleek head. It caressed her face, hard with violent unshed tears. I was aware of Vera staring at me, warily, of Mrs Anstruther watching her lover with tender anxiety. But I could not reach them. I could only croak endearments to my client. She stood up (I had forbidden them to move) and half-lifted me out of the chair, holding me so fiercely I was afraid of her strength in the midst of my other fear.

'Is that you?' she shouted, but not to me.

'Yes, yes,' my voice babbled. 'Here I am.'

Shouting at me, through me, to that other one she could see so clearly, my sitter brought her head close to mine, so that I could see her wild and desperate face, her widened eyes. She clasped me as passionately as any lover.

'If it is you – if you forgive me – Lady, for God's sake, *call me by my name.*'

And before my inert brain could remember the name on her visiting cards, her notes, her monogrammed cigarette case, the initialled watch, my altered voice answered promptly, crazily, surely wrong.

'Jack,' I said.

*

I had expected the medium to be unprepossessing; the President of the Society for Psychical Research had warned me that the most gifted women are often unattractive and not of our class. So I was envisaging a plain woman of no taste, a boarding-house matron, and was greeted by a Vermeer virgin, a Quaker lily. She spoke to me like a nun at the supper-hour, excitedly but low, in brief words, and refused the cigarette I offered her as though it were poison. I was on my guard, of course, as they had warned me about the tricks these people can play on the unwary. I was armed with my full panoply of scientific observation: logbook, stopwatch, cold eye. But my emotion got the better of me as soon as she said 'Lady'. I left there thinking, 'There are more things in heaven and earth...'

When I reread my notebook, I was convinced. For how could she have known about the fine complexion? And in later visits the singing, the beach at Filey, *my wristwatch*? My anxiety was, naturally, whether Lady would be discreet. What if the messages turned from those of love and friendship to others of a more intimate nature? Once or twice, in the automatic writing, I thought she came close to saying something; there was the word 'lips' repeated, and then 'your hands'. But nothing she saw or wrote seemed to disturb Miss Elland. As my visits became a regular thing, like a routine trip to the doctor, although I depended on them absolutely, I also yearned for more. I had visions of abducting Miss Elland, and forcing her to hold sessions for me twice a day. I seriously considered asking her to be my exclusive medium, for a generous fee, to bring Lady to me on my whim.

It gave me a curious sense of bigamy, almost, a frisson of unfaithfulness at least, to let myself into the house and find my lover waiting for me, the voluptuous mistress. And yet – it was as though she were the beautiful wife, waiting at home for my pleasure, and Lady was the inexplicable, unattainable mistress to whom court must be paid patiently, with ritual and repetition, without consummation. In my mind, I was wooing the old, dead one for even a word, coming to me second-hand through a girl like a telegraph-operator. In my body, I was physically enjoying my lithe, arousing lover, there in the flesh. I felt my duality. I wanted to give myself solely to my new love, my true love. My pursuit of Lady was a search for absolution, benediction, redemption.

After so many meetings, so much time spent waiting, holding the seer's cool, passionless hands, I had brought myself to trust her. (Yet there was – and is – a part of me which still doubted. Do the dead wait all around us, trying to make themselves heard? If so, why are we not all comforted thus by our dear ones? Do we need a stranger, a nonentity, to bring us the words of a departed lover? I sometimes wondered if Miss Elland was merely a mind-reader, plucking pictures of Lady from my disordered brain.) My need had overcome my disbelief at first, and then credulity fed need. It was no longer enough to pass messages to each other, like a pair of children parted in the classroom. I frantically desired the actual presence of Lady. I longed to hear that voice again, for her to hear me speak, and ask her forgiveness. I forced Miss Elland, despite her reservations, to agree.

When she began to speak, it nearly killed me. The voice so slurred and muffled was how I had imagined she might sound, during the long vigil when I waited by the bed. During that terrible time – those hours more vividly recalled than any moment of pleasure – I willed her to open her eyes, to speak to me. I prayed, I offered my soul, I begged whatever gods might hear. If violence of longing could have any impact on the physical world, she would have lived to forgive me. It was not so much the affair – that, she was worldly enough to understand, indulgent enough to permit. (Although, I admit now with gall in my mouth, she cannot have liked it.) No, worse was the fact – no secret – that I killed her. My temper was a joke between us, the dark side of my passion, but I turned it against her when she tried to upbraid me. We argued, viciously. I spoke to her roughly; she was contemptuous. At last, she heaved herself out of the bed, with her vast dignity gathered about her. It was outside the door that her heart failed her and she fell, speaking my name. I ran to her, too late to know if it was a curse, an absolution, a request. She never uttered again, but slipped from sleep to death. I waited beside her all that week, listening, entreating the silence. Surely, if ever someone needed to speak again, it was she?

I heard the voice now, fondling me as she used to do, as she would have done then if she could. (For what was her life but love for me?) The pain – or was it joy – was so extreme that I was driven half-mad. It was overpoweringly urgent that I should understand, beyond doubt, that she had absolved me. I seized Miss Elland like the ventriloquist's puppet she was and demanded to know if it was Lady. She – or they – answered yes. I asked my deplorable question. I begged her by all she held holy to grant me forgiveness, to call me by my own name again, that I might hear it once more in this world.

And then she said it.

*

'Jack,' I said.

Vera swallowed a laugh. Mrs Anstruther cried out sharply, like a clock striking once. My sitter gave a sort of groan, the coarse sound of release, and her wild eyes closed for a moment. Then she kissed me. My mouth kissed her in return, my body told me that if she had taken me there and then, it would not have resisted. But she set me back gently in my chair, and knelt beside her new lover, who embraced her as a mother comforts her headstrong child. I regained myself, abruptly, and knew myself deserted. I saw my sitter reprieved, restored, but I was sentenced to perpetual anguish – for I was not the woman she had called and kissed, and I did not know how I had spoken her true name.

Ashes
Bryony Weaver

Ashes
Bryony Weaver

I come out of the kitchen and cross the dining room. Checking. Rechecking. Everything turned off, plugs out, windows closed and locked. Yes, for a third time. The house is secure. Safe. Walk through into the sitting room and check the same. All OK, all tidy, all quiet. Satisfied, I stand for a moment and listen to the silence.

And I hear her breathing again, rasping and jagged in, sibilant and soft on the way out, like the sea across shingle.

'I want to see the sea again,' she said.

You will today, I hope, my love.

The silence hurts my ears. But so did the full house, two weeks ago – is it only two weeks ago? The friends we hadn't seen for ages – years, in some cases (where had they been?) – came and devoured food. Some, like Jane and Terri, consumed a piece of my grief through their genuine sadness at losing Charlie; some, like Kate, added to my burden with a pinch of platitude. Too late now to say how sorry, ladies. I guess they just hadn't wanted to see what she'd become. I couldn't blame them, really.

Like a carrion eater, Kate arrived early, first-footing it across the threshold into my midnight, carrying a home-made cheesecake rather than a lump of coal – but it tasted just the same, as it turned out. Officiously, she helped out in the kitchen, tidying up the leftovers, kicking out the stragglers. Charlie had known her from schooldays, but said she was more a hanger-on than a true friend: someone who, both jealous of and intrigued by Charlie's difference, hoped, by association, to make herself more interesting. And Charlie, though aware of the falseness, had been flattered. Now, it appeared, the vampire Kate would make a friend of me by default.

She offered to make the journey with me: 'Amanda, darling, you can't drive all that way on your own. You should have some company. I thought you said Jim was going with you?'

'Not now.' I kept to the other side of the kitchen, hands itching. Had the art of being a good hostess allowed for shows of eccentricity to keep one's guests amused, I would have made a cross with my fingers to ward her off. That, or kept a knife handy. That would have been more appropriate.

'Little bugger! When did he cry off?'

'Yesterday.'

'Some damn nephew!' She bunched the clean knives and, with an air of ownership, put them away in the cutlery drawer. 'You should have told me, honey, I can easily get the day off.' She smoothed the hair out of my eyes, with owning fingers, taking hands.

Leave me alone, I thought. You need warm blood, not a frozen heart.

'No, I'm glad,' I said. 'I didn't really want his company, anyway. I always knew he was only coming out of duty – and what he thinks she's left him in the will.'

'Oh, she didn't, did she?' Hypocritical indignation. 'The little sod visited her *once*, all the time you were together.'

I smiled, arms across my chest, thinking of Charlie's revenge on him and hugging it to me. 'No. She knew he wanted her car, but she's left it to Jane and Terri. They came around a lot, and she wanted them to have something they needed.'

'Hah!' Kate hugged me closer for longer, neither soothing nor respectful. She looked into my eyes and I shrugged out of the embrace, thinking, *She hasn't left you me.*

I shudder in remembrance, put my hands in my pockets and hunch my shoulders. Head down, I listen to the real sounds grief makes. No wailing and gnashing of teeth (teeth don't gnash in East Dulwich; dentists are expensive), just a whole lot of quiet indifference. Cars still pass by outside. No one knocks on the door, or stops by with a 'We just heard – couldn't believe it…' Why hasn't everything stopped?

Carefully picking up the backpack from the corner chair, I take one last look around, sweeping up the ghosts of memories so they won't be there when I get back. Taking the past, leaving the future for later.

I walk out into the hallway, put the envelope with the cleaner's money on the hall table, set the alarm (1812, Charlie's birthday – make a mental note to change it), swing the pack up onto one shoulder, open the front door and step out, shutting it behind me. Every movement a conscious act, everything significant; a dream ballet. Pausing momentarily, heavy with reluctance, I take a ragged, deep breath, huffing it out. *OK, I've got this far, outside the front door, at least.* Only two hundred and forty miles more to go.

I get into my own car. Charlie's Celica, proud and polished, is in the garage, unaware of new ownership. I begin the comfort rituals of pre-ignition checks: keys into lock, radio on and tune to something soothing, anything to get through town traffic, adjust mirrors (almost twenty minutes of painstaking angling before I am certain of all-round visibility). Chewing gum and mints on dashboard, bottle of water in the well behind the gear stick, open packet of tissues in the well under the stereo. A quick prayer to the gods of the road: please let me get there in one piece; please just let me get there. Shaking, I ease out of the driveway into the street, and head off down the road.

Charlie was always the driver; I hated the responsibility. Against all expectation, however, traffic is OK through Tulse Hill, Clapham, Wandsworth and Sheen. Most people out of town for the weekend? Or a new theory: the Law of London Traffic – the greater the fear of arriving, the less anxious the journey.

The route to the M4 and down to Wales is another ghost to lay, a blessing and a curse: her last trip back home, all over again…

Charlie was on a mission, to say goodbye to old friends and places. Friends were stunned and tearful; places in the town were stone-faced and unmoving. Unmoved. All except the outside of her grandmother's house, the one face she wanted to find unchanged. Once a grand old Victorian lady with graceful bay windows, like graceful skirts billowing out towards the shingle and sand beach, it had been stripped and covered in a tawdry slip of white concrete.

Her grandmother used to run it as a guesthouse, and had some seasonal regulars who came to the Gower coast for the short laverbread-and-cockle summer. Like a Spanish tart it was now – rooms for rent by the hour, perhaps, not the season – sashaying on the promenade of the quiet Welsh seaside town, blowsy, dirty and cheap. We were appalled. And I heard the strongest echo:

The 70s, our younger selves on our first date. Having walked out along the front, past the dinghies with sheets tinking against masts and pennants flickering in the wind like lizards' tongues, as far as the ice-cream kiosk shaped like an apple, we'd strolled back, tongues practising licking on melting ice-cream cones, and stopped outside the house. Charlie had been out to impress: 'That's my grandmother's old place. She ran a guesthouse. Don't remember much about it... or her, except she always wore a floral pinny; can't remember her in anything else. And she stood up at the table to have her breakfast: piece of paper-thin bread and butter and one apple, always just one. She'd give the peel to my sister and me to throw on the table and see the initial of the man we were going to marry.'

'Did you ever get an A?' I blushed. Girls still did then.

'No. I knew there was a reason I should never have asked you out.'

We laughed and that had been it – bargain sealed – and we had walked on, Charlie humming, 'Oh, I do like to be beside the seaside,' with a smile in her voice...

The rape of architectural style was one thing, but the rape of memory was worse, and I took Charlie back to the car and held her while she cried.

The drive up through the Mayals and over Clyne Common produced rich pickings for her, glad to be away from the town.

'Look! That's Mr Jones's old house!' Her favourite teacher at the local school. 'Ah.' She closed her eyes and recited: '*Timothy Winters comes to school, With eyes as wide as a football pool...* Oh... bugger, what was it?' She coughed raggedly, tired eyes blinking as she struggled, with depleted energy reserves, to recall. 'No, can't remember the rest. He was such a clever man, Mr Jones. He told stories about when he was a boy at the school. The class swot was a prissy little blonde piece called... oh, what was she called, now?'

She smoothed her hand across her forehead, dragging the past back with it. 'Gloria! That was it, Gloria. And Miss Witherspoon, his teacher, who had a thing, you know, about Gloria – God, definitely a candidate, now I think about it, Miss Witherspoon. The innocence of youth; I never spotted it. The way he told those stories, we were convinced Timothy Winters was really a classmate of his. A clever, lovely man he was.' She rarely paused for breath when she spoke, but latterly, it had begun to shorten. I had tried to stem the ebb tide by becoming more talkative myself, against natural inclination.

Around past Bishopston (my home for a while), and up the long curve of Kittle Hill. 'How green was our valley,' I thought, with a wry smile.

Charlie insisted, despite the pain, on going down to see Three Cliffs Bay. She had forgotten how weak she was; I wanted her to have what she wanted, too weak to say no. The tramp down across the links to the great stretch of sand took more than we knew she had. Inquisitive ponies, part of the straggling herds that roamed freely among the gorse and bracken on the headland, stopped their grazing to watch. Limpid eyes followed us: me carrying Charlie piggyback, we must have looked a very strange two-legged horse and rider. Their warm grass-breath caught the scent of our futility, and they bowed their heads once more, in silent prayer for all creatures who bear burdens. As we walked across the rippled beach, its rocky cliffs and sea-carved caves looking more Neolithic than city-adjusted eyes remembered, she breathed in energy for a while. She sang, laughing and kicking water at me.

I watched the grey in her face become more pronounced, the thief of precious minutes. She got cold suddenly, quickly, as exhaustion caught up with her, sucking at her breath. After almost three agonising hours of scrambling, stopping, sometimes crawling and hauling to get her back to the car, she insisted on driving to the cliffs overlooking the sea at Pennard Point, in order to show me the exact spot where she wanted to be.

'You expect me to come all the way down here?' I turned into the seaward gusts so my tears would look wind-born. 'I can't do that.'

Her desperation made her rough. 'Tough shit! I want to be out in the gorse, or for a pony to come and eat the grass I'm on so I become horse crap. I want little pieces of me everywhere – anywhere but in here.' She thumped her chest hard, which brought on a coughing fit. I piggybacked her to the car.

I slam my hand on the horn. 'Damn well learn to drive, can't you! Bloody hell!' I really, really hate driving. Having Charlie beside me always calmed the collywobbles; somehow, her own skill behind the wheel seeped into me when I did the driving, and I coped. Now, especially now, I am not sure why I don't drive off at the next exit and turn for home. The more motorway that passes, the more time that ticks away – without her tuneless whistle as she tuned in the radio, without the noisy sucking of travel sweets, or her ebullience at being on the road (but, thankfully, without the incessant smoking) – the more nervous I become. *I don't think I can do this, love.* Talking to her, imagining her here, smiling at me lopsidedly in thanks for this one last act... it may not be enough to get me there.

There is a bit of a wind up; it nudges the car every now and then, like a cat nudging its owner's leg at teatime. Annoying, it makes me more tense. The wipers, swiping away the curtain of rain that now runs down the windscreen, breathe in and out. And I hear her rasping breath again, the bellows hopelessly fanning the dying life, the waves coming in and out. I rub the past out of my own tired eyes, and look at the dashboard clock. 10 a.m. Time for a break. Where am I? Near the Membury Services, the one with the bird – The Welcome Beak, Charlie used to call it. I decide to stop for a bit.

I turn off the ignition and pause, taking a deep breath. Don't like services, but now that I've stopped, realise I do need to pee. I walk up the steps, backpack over shoulder. Won't leave her – the pot – in the car to get lonely.

Predictably, the place is heaving. Coachloads of geriatrics, off for their weekly glimpse of the outside world, quietly menacing in obstructive, beige huddles around the entrances to the loos, tutting over the rising costs of spending a penny. I navigate the rock of indecision and make it to the safe harbour of the toilets. There are other dangers on the way to the cafe: I skilfully steer past family groups, killer whales on a mission to devour whole schools of Filet of Fish. Their kids, pale and blinking mole-like at the light, mither and pull towards the games arcade, hoping to relieve their Playstation withdrawal symptoms with a quick fix.

Exposure to the public en masse brings out the Hyacinth Bouquet in me.

I hear Charlie's voice: *'That's your mother's influence. She encouraged you to watch the damn programme. I always said she was a sadistic snob. It's her fault you're a dyke, too. Making you watch* Blue Peter, *it really marked you… years of watching Valerie Singleton moulding sticky-back plastic with those strong fingers…'*

I smile at the memory of the love–hate relationship she had with my mother and, joining the queue for drinks, take two cups and saucers and shuffle along obediently to the tea station. I suffer the delights of indifferent service, then the checkout:

'That's £2.80, please.'

'Sorry?'

'£2.80 please, madam.'

'For one pot of tea?'

'You've got a pot of tea for two there, madam. That's £2.80.'

'What? Oh… no… I only want tea for one.' How long is it going to be before I forget to live as two?

'Well, I've rung up a pot for two now, madam. It's in the till,' she sneers at me, putting me down as an escapee from one of the OAP coach tours, and/or a dangerous loony. Upset, and wanting to save myself any more embarrassment, I pay it and hurry away as quickly as a backpack slipping down one arm and a laden tray will allow. I search wildly across the crowded cafe to find as inconspicuous a spot as possible. I find a two-seater table, rare as real wood in this place, and, sinking down into one of the non-adjustable seats, try to get comfortable as I settle my debris and shaken nerves around me.

The pot leaks over the table as I pour mauve effluent into the cup and take a sip. Not enough caffeine to keep a mosquito awake. The caffeine must be extra.

There is no space left now in the crowded eating hall. Large people with large Family Sunday faces, large voices and loud clothes fill up every space, except the one opposite. I take a sip of tea, close my eyes and escape into the smell.

An afternoon in early May. I carried two mugs of tea out, so we could catch the last of the day's warmth together. I pushed through the bushes that separated the garden into the cultivated and the wild, moving from mundane into mysterious, like a doomed mortal finding the door into Tir nan Og – where Charlie would be, forever young. She was weeding at the back of the garden, digging with grim intensity, as if doing penance for the sins of the world and flagellating her body. I watched her attack the intruders with aggressive fervour, ripping them from unseasonably dry earth with evil delight and a triumphant 'hah!' at every little death. I stood for a moment, drinking her in.

'Darling, teatime.'

She turned with a warm smile. 'Say not the struggle naught availeth. We're gaining on the little buggers.' The sunlight through the leaves dappled her, and she looked yellow and green and powder-grey all at once. Portents.

I handed her a mug as she rose – either one was fine; neither of us took sugar, both liked it strong. She smiled into my eyes as she drank, her wheezing more pronounced after her exertions and, leaning over, kissed the tea off my lips.

'Taste nice?'

'Mmm. You look tired, Mand. Early night?'

I smiled back and kissed her. Gently, exploring the texture, remembering when her lips were smoother but less sure of us, kisses more passionate but less deep. Age has its benefits.

I sip my tea, drinking in the taste and the memory of the taste. Well, enough reflection. I want to hear her voice again. In my mind, she is, as then, pale, drawn, grey face pinched with pain. I imagine her contrite:

'Look, darling, I know this is hard for you –'

'No, you don't – all I've had of you in the last year is a skeleton and a cough. Keeping the ashes… you'll always be there… and quiet again –'

'And always dead. Darling, I know you've been living with having to do this since long before now. I told you everything they told me would happen: all the breathing difficulties, what the gasps would mean, so you wouldn't go running off for the doctor every two minutes. It was selfish, I suppose –' her smile would be weak but brave – 'but it was for you, too, because I thought you'd want to know what to expect…'

'Yes, and I expected everything except this moment. You have you… wherever you are… For all my trying to convince myself that you'd be around somehow, now it comes down to it, there's nothing else but the pot and the ashes. I won't get rid of them. I can't do it. I'm finishing my tea, and going back, and you're coming with me!'

My mind made up to leave, I gather all my bits together, go to get up… and look up into her eyes. Charlie's eyes. Charlie. There. Sitting in the spare seat in front of me, which is, surprisingly, still vacant – except for Charlie. In full technicolour.

She grins.

That's it: I have gone mad. And I know I've gone mad – apart from the obvious – because she is eighteen again, the Charlie I knew at uni, all angular face, long, wavy hair, wide forehead, large eyes and too-big mouth, pink fake-fur bolero jacket, red tie-dye top and wide-bottom jeans. If I look, she'll have the Led Zeppelin cheesecloth bag at her side. I look. She does.

'Oh shit!' I sit down again with a thump, pour what's left in the pot into my cup, gulp it down, and stare at her.

Her grin widens, exposing tombstone teeth; she laughs. That is, her mouth opens, and her body shakes, but there is no sound. I stare, stunned, for a long, long while. Charlie – the spitting image of Charlie – there. It can't – she can't…

'Oh damn!' I put my head down as a sudden dizziness overtakes me. I take a few deep breaths, trying to clear away the vision. Through my stunned haze, I become aware that the people at the table beside me are silent. They must have heard me because all of them are silent, listening intently. The older boy, peaked cap pulled down, is snorting, trying not to laugh; the parents, concentrating on their coffee, are wound up tight like springs, ready to drag their kids away should the batty old lady get louder and intrude upon their personal space.

Their little girl, however, has it sussed. 'You said a rude word to your friend,' she pipes up, cracking through the moment like a starter's gun.

Her mother leaps up out of the starting blocks, grabs her daughter, whips in her husband and disappointed son with a curt 'Come on, we'll be late for grandma', and hurries off.

I look up. Charlie – the picture of Charlie – is laughing uproariously, silently; a film with the sound turned down. I look around guiltily. I have a larger audience. Beleaguered nerves snapping, I also leap up, gather my bits again and this time successfully head off, as quickly as the packed aisles will allow, out of the eating area – 'restaurant' is too grand a description – to the exit.

Gulping for breath, and fighting off tears, I reach the car, unlock the driver's door with shaking hands, get in, dump the bag in the back and, closing my eyes, subside. She was there! My Charlie!

I feel the air shift. She is there in the passenger's seat, nearly shocking me also into an early grave. I burst into tears, shut my eyes and open them again. She is still there, through the blur. She takes out a lighter, her old T Rex lighter, and – I can't believe it! – languidly and disdainfully lights up a cigarette.

Suddenly, she speaks, the sound more shocking than the dumb show of earlier.

'What's wrong, Ms Thou-Shalt-Not?' Her lip curls around the old nickname. 'It's not like it's going to kill me now, is it? – or you, for God's sake.' The smoke moves to the edge of her image (just to the edge, as if she were encased in glass) until she is wreathed in a dirty, translucent halo that moves and shifts, like oil on water, in the shafts of sunlight that lance in through the window.

'This –' she gestures to the parameters of her shape, which wavers for a moment as if it were a projection on the air, and then the backpack '– is the pot and you.' She smiles languidly, the old, sly smile.

'Me?' I find my voice. I have been holding my breath, I realise, expecting to inhale her smoke if I speak.

'Yes, my love. The pot contains me, and the cosy "chats" you've been having with me, the pale *Dame aux Camélias* gardener, the trip down Memory Lane to Grandmama's. Your Emily Dickinson imagination has trapped me in this... shell-hell.'

Sarcasm in her voice. I feel cold. She may look like her younger, scatty, hopeful self, but the sentiment is all later Charlie. Sarcasm! Not today! I stare at her, at her smug, hard face.

The long-forgotten anger – God, through her illness, I thought I'd buried it – surges up. I start up the car, slam into reverse, and nearly knock over a young lad, who swears at me as I steam out of the car park and along the exit onto the motorway. Anger makes me forget my sentimental resolve of a short while ago and I turn the car south, on course once more for Wales. This time, no reluctance worries my driving and I put my foot down, eager now to get there.

With a sensation that causes a tightness in my chest, and a sound like a soft *phuh*, she disappears.

The traffic, which has finally remembered it is Sunday, thankfully eases and, gradually, so does my abuse of the accelerator. Just as well; she materialises again just as I get onto the Severn Bridge and am filtering into the inside lane. I swerve, narrowly missing the side barrier.

'Strewth!' I regain control, heart hammering.

'Glad to see you've decided to do the right thing – finally. At long fucking last.'

'What... I... what do you mean? What are...'

'It's me, love, it is me, promise. Full-strength, no low-tar or medium shit here.' The swirling eddies move around her like the shroud she never had, but an ironic reminder of her cremation.

I am too stunned to be anything but prosaic. 'You're not here. I'm upset... I... what do you mean, I've trapped you? I don't understand.'

'Love, you... are holding onto me –'

'Of course I bloody am! I loved you, for God's sake –'

'You're holding, as always, onto nothing. You created, for thirty goddamn years, an image of me that wasn't me. I was never sugar. I was gravel and stupidity. I didn't want to be dependable or enjoy shopping and nesting. That was you, love.'

She begins counting off points, one nicotine-stained forefinger tapping against the other.

'Look, we came down to Mumbles that last time to get my brother to co-sign the Enduring Power of Attorney with you, so you wouldn't get turfed out of the house when I snuffed it. The only reason we went down to Three Cliffs was 'cos I'd had enough of the bloody family wailing all over the place, and needed a place to smoke in peace – which was why it took yonks to get back to the car; the wind burned my cigs away too quickly and I had to keep lighting fresh, remember, hmm? Your self-delusion is more fanciful than old Jonesy's Gloria stories – you got those right, at least.' She pauses, then says quietly, 'Let me go, please.'

'I...'

'You did *know* about me and Kate, didn't you?' Her flippancy and lazy cruelty lash me. I keep my eyes fixed on the road ahead, but see instead the imprint of the two of them: she and Kate caught in a moment, through a partly open kitchen door (had they deliberately left it open?). She in Kate's arms, stroking her face – taking hands, owning fingers – and leaning in to kiss her deeply. More deeply than she had kissed me in years. The pit of my stomach folds in upon itself at the realisation of the casual, deliberate brutality of it.

'You bitch! You and that bloody woman! You bitch!'

'That's the spirit! That's better!' She sighs deeply. 'Couldn't leave you with memories of things as they weren't, love. The weird thing is, I always thought, deep down... you must have been OK with it to put up with everything. I *did* know you knew about Kate. Think I was giving you an opportunity to go if you wanted, or stay and...'

She pauses, and her external appearance gathers itself together, like a prism being turned suddenly from the fractal spectrum to shine a hard, white light. The smoke around her clears instantly, as if someone has turned on a fan and blown it away. 'I guess I hoped you'd love me enough to want to put up a fight for me.'

She is silent finally, spent, dimming, like a candle slowly going out. I fall into the hole she left in the conversation, tumbling down a deep mine shaft, sin-black, falling interminably into a place that contains long-buried, unresolved lies. Scarlet-like, I will think about them tomorrow. I have held on for what I hoped she'd want to be, but never did. Today, at least, I am travelling in the right direction. After all these years.

The day is clearing, the clouds ragged and wisped at the edges as high winds take them. The car is buffeted again, but this time I shrug it off. I drive through Swansea and ease onto the long approach road to the peninsula. Pass the old swimming pool, and hug the curve of the bay, holding it close as the past rushes by. We pass the bay gardens and the statue in honour of the little dog that rescued drowning sailors – *rescue this drowning sailor* – pass the reaches of the bay and its sands, formerly cockle-rich. My eye follows the line of the headland as it curves round, its finger pointing into the Channel, where the Mumbles lifeboat station safeguards the little town, but turns blind sea-eyes to me.

We walk across the gravel road – the pot, Charlie and myself – along the verge to the place. Sea shushing on the hidden rocks of Foxhole Bay sounds loud. Beside me, as we stride across the headland, I hear her breathing getting louder. I listen, as I did at the end, to it getting caught and ragged and loud. I listen to Charlie beside me fight and struggle for the truth of her own life. The wind pushes me from behind, hurrying me along. I push back, dragging out the last few steps – the last few breaths of the past – and reach the spot.

The slope of the grass running away down to the cliff edge whipples in the breeze, like mice under a carpet. I smile bleakly, noting the horse droppings scattering among the tufts and tummocks. I look up at her as she stands opposite me. She is licking an ice-cream cone. She smiles at me.

I take the lid off the pot, hand shaking, more than cold, and tilt it.

The air, laughing, takes Charlie's outstretched hand, swirling the ashes up and out onto the wind. I hear the sound of her very last breath wash out and spread, dissolving into tiny pieces. I take in a long breath, let it go, and stand listening for a moment to the wind humming with a smile in its voice.

What She Left Behind
Cara Bruce

What She Left Behind
Cara Bruce

They say you always remember your first time, and I guess that's true. I can vividly recall the first time I watched a snuff film. I knew it wasn't real but I was still sitting on the edge of my seat, hiding my eyes. I was dating this guy who fancied himself a Satanist. I thought he was so cool. Looking back I realize what a poseur he was. He's now a stockbroker and drives a Subaru.

So we were in the room that he rented in the Lower East Side. He had painted it black, much to the chagrin of his square roommates.

The snuff film consisted of a woman sitting in a chair giving a blow job then getting shot. It turned me on so much it was scary. I started collecting the films. It got so when someone would come across one they would immediately call me. Some films were real. I even watched a few get made. For years none of it bothered me. But everyone has limits and finally mine was reached.

A woman came in. She had heard that the 'company' would pay a lot of money for someone to agree to be in a film. She wanted to do it. The money was to go to her young daughter. She got half up front and half after. It became one of the most infamous underground films of all times. She made me promise to get her daughter the other half of the money. And I did.

Fifteen years later I had outgrown my Goth phase and was working odd jobs – some voiceover work, a few X-rated CDs, bartending, that sort of thing. I had stopped actively collecting the films when one of my boyfriends overdosed and my snuff-making buddy filmed him dying, never even trying CPR or calling 911. But I still had the tapes. I kept them locked in a safe in a storage unit because one of the guys had gotten popped on an illegal porn distribution charge and was serving time in Rikers. You never know.

So the snuff was in the back of my mind when Lanka came to

see me. She looked fourteen years old, pretty. A sharp girl who wasn't afraid to look you in the eye and speak her mind. I was working in an editing booth at NYU. I often snuck in there to save some money.

'Tammy?' she asked, cracking open the door.

'I'm working,' I snarled. 'I still have forty minutes of my session left.'

She opened the door and slid in. 'I'm Lanka Barrow. You knew my mother. You gave me her money.'

For a second I didn't remember. Then it came flooding back. Lanka was an odd name. I can almost hear her mother saying, 'Lanka, as in Sri Lanka. It's where she was conceived.'

I didn't know what to say so I sat there staring at the two editing monitors. I was doing a commercial for a chain of appliance stores in Brooklyn and Queens. A man swinging a crowbar was frozen on one monitor while a TV was caught on mid-shatter on the other. I wondered why violence was used as a selling tool.

Lanka sighed. 'This is weird, I know. I just want to ask you some questions.' She paused and I looked up at her. I wasn't sure if I should play sad, sorry, angry or crazy. Her blank face gave me no help. I shrugged. 'I don't know...'

'Oh, don't even,' Lanka cut me off. 'I know almost everything. My mom left me a note. I don't blame you. She knew what she was doing. She was dying anyway, she had at most three months to live. She did it for me – to leave me something.'

I didn't know what to say. In a way I felt cheated. She was dying already? I had always thought it was a stupid idea, having someone volunteer to be killed. What was the fun in that? The best part of the film was the surprise. I really didn't want to deal with this girl. I wasn't really happy with my life. It was fifteen years since I had last seen her mother. I felt ashamed, like I should have done something with my life by now. Lanka gave me an annoyed sigh as if to say, 'Come on, you dumb bitch, I know.'

'What do you want to know?' I asked her.

'I want to see the tape,' she said.

'What?' Her statement was like a smack in the face. 'No, you don't,' I asserted, turning back to my editing board.

'Yes, I do.' Her voice never wavered.

'I don't have it.'

'Bullshit. I know you have it.' She changed her tone and raised her eyebrows. This girl had already learned the art of manipulation. Her voice became sweet and innocent, a hint of tears on the edge. 'It's my mother. I don't even have a picture of her. Besides, she did it for me. She left me your name and said you would have it.'

I shook my head in disbelief. Lanka's mom was pretty presumptuous. But you have to be bold or fucking crazy to be in a snuff film in the first place.

'What the hell.' I shrugged again. 'If she wanted you to see it and you want to, then what do I care. Now go outside so I can finish, you're wasting my editing time. I'll take you when I'm done.'

I sat and stared at the stupid man with stupid crowbar, thinking back to Lanka's mother. Remembering the smile that hid gritted teeth. The glaze of fear in her eyes. I could see her knuckles holding the arms of the chair, the man jerking off next to her as he raised the gun, aiming it at her head. I could hear the shot; my ears rang for hours. The second he pulled the trigger I had closed my eyes. When I opened them her blood covered the wall and pieces of her skull were scattered over the floor. Now that I was sober the image was disturbing. I didn't think Lanka understood.

I couldn't work anymore so I gathered my things, hoping she would be gone, but knowing she wouldn't. I didn't say a word to her. We walked silently out of the building.

Once we were outside she began asking me questions. Why I liked snuff films, if they were always real, that sort of thing. She told me she read a lot about serial killers and wanted to be a forensic investigator.

'How old are you now?' I asked her.

'I'll be twenty next month. Why?'

'I was trying to remember when the film was made,' I said. 'I was eighteen when it was made. Now I'm thirty-three.'

'You don't look that old,' said Lanka. 'You're prettier than I thought you'd be. I pictured you as some stupid Goth chick with blue-black hair and a big silver crucifix necklace and the type of dress Russian grandmothers wear to funerals.'

I laughed. 'That was me fifteen years ago.'

She smiled. She was a very pretty girl. She looked younger than twenty herself.

We reached my studio apartment. Lanka stood in the doorway surveying the room. A double bed, dresser, TV, a loveseat with clothes draped on it, a kitchen area with a few plates stacked in the sink, and tons of books everywhere. Not messy, but definitely not neat.

'You live alone.' It was more a statement than a question.

'Yup,' I nodded, picking a bra up off the edge of the couch. 'Sit down but don't get too comfortable, we're only here for a minute.'

'What about the tape?' she whined.

'Relax,' I cooed. I could feel the power shifting. I could sense her nervousness. She was alone in a strange, older woman's apartment. A woman who had watched her mother die and gotten off on it. 'I don't keep the tapes here, it's too risky. We just came to get the key.'

I pulled my faux-Japanese screens between us so I could get the key without her watching me. I could see her reflection in my dresser mirror. She was perched on the edge of the couch, her hands planted on either side, ready to spring up in an instant. She was chewing on her lower lip and I knew if I was closer that I would see a bead of sweat on her forehead.

I both admired and felt sorry for her. It took balls to come here and demand to see the tape. Fuck, it took balls to watch the thing. At the same time the situation was sad. After all, it was her mother.

For all I knew she had been raised in an orphanage or a convent. I got the key and grabbed my jacket.

'Ready?' I asked, striding toward the door.

She was immediately beside me. 'Yes,' she answered, using her strong voice again.

We took the N train to my storage locker. My collection of tapes was buried in a box in the back. She helped me move stuff to uncover them. She watched in horror and awe as I dug through close to fifty tapes.

'Are those…' she started to ask.

'Yup,' I replied grimly. I was enjoying the power but also felt a twinge of disgust at myself. I must look so fucked up to her.

I got the tape and we left. Walking to the train she took my hand and squeezed it.

I liked the way her hand felt in mine.

By the time we had reached my apartment I had fallen in love with her. I didn't want her to see the tape. I stood by the couch, the tape in my hand.

'Lanka,' I said. 'I don't want to show you this.'

She sat down on the couch and cried. She put her head in her hands and I held her. She sobbed for a long time, then stopped.

'I have to,' she said.

I handed her the tape and went down to the store. The tape was eight minutes. I was gone nine. When I got back Lanka was in the bathroom throwing up.

I felt horrible. I sat on my bed and waited for her to come out.

'I'm sorry,' I said, as she walked toward me.

She nodded then came into my arms. We kissed. She was all over me, pushing her tongue down my throat, squeezing my tits.

'Fuck me,' she snarled. She scared me. I wanted her but didn't. 'You owe me that much,' she hissed, sensing my hesitation.

I threw her on the bed and ripped her clothes off. I rammed one finger, then three, and finally my whole fist up her. I punch-fucked her as she screamed, not letting up until she came.

After it was over she lay on my bed panting. I sat with my back to her. She stroked right above my jeans with her big toe. 'Tammy,' she purred, saccharine as strawberry milk. 'Thank you.'

'You liked that?' I asked in my best I-don't-care voice.

'Sure, whatever. Thanks for everything.' She stood up and dressed. Before I could stop her she ejected the tape and was at the door. As soon as she turned the knob, my heart sank.

Four cops came in, one of them bending down to kiss Lanka on the lips.

'Let's go,' another said, motioning for me to stand. A third cop handed me my shirt before they cuffed me.

I looked at Lanka and shook my head. 'Yeah, Lanka, thanks a lot.'

'Lanka?' laughed one of the cops. 'What kind of name is that?'

'It's the name of the girl whose mother is on this tape,' she said. 'You know, the OD that came in two nights ago.'

My jaw dropped. For Lanka to have turned me in as an act of revenge would have been one thing, but to just get busted by a cop after fifteen years, fuck, that sucked.

'I knew her,' she said. 'We were roommates in a boarding school in eighth grade. That kid was screwed up good. In and out of institutions, junkie, part-time whore, but her mom was killed in a snuff film, she didn't have a chance. Plain-looking girl too, and a lesbian. Just having a name like Lanka has to make shit hard.'

The cops snorted in agreement. Two went to my storage locker while the other two searched my apartment before taking me in. Before she left she leaned in close, her breath hitting my face.

'Lanka was a great fuck. You don't even come close.' She gave me a quick pat on the ass. 'Don't worry,' she winked, 'you'll get better in jail.'

I shook my head. She was really a bitch.

'See you in court, Tammy,' she called out. 'Try not to miss me too much.'

The story hit all the papers. A film crew came to visit me in jail. They were making a documentary. It was my first time in front of the camera instead of behind. As soon as I get out, I'll try acting again, but only if I have a gun.

Daddy's Girls
Ellen Galford

Daddy's Girls
Ellen Galford

My mother likes nothing better than raising the dead. Once in a while she even does it for free. But in the normal run of things she charges plenty.

She is, or so she claims, directly descended via the female line from the biblical Witch of Endor, who brought the prophet Samuel back from beyond the grave. I don't imagine many of her customers have ever heard of the lady. But my mother likes to think this connection gives her the edge over her professional rivals.

And when she started up, back in the late 1970s (before I was born) there was more competition around than you might suppose. At that time there must have been at least a dozen mediums working that odd urban-suburban strip of north London that lies between Wood Green and Enfield. They operated out of redundant churches, curtained shopfronts, or – in my mother's case – the Joyous Reunion Tabernacle of Palmer's Green.

Anyway that's the official name. Among ourselves we call it Seances 'R' Us. It consists of two rooms over a monumental-sculpture workshop just off the North Circular Road. From the ground floor rises the tap-tapping of the stonemason's tools, inscribing death dates and the usual repertoire of valedictory one-liners: Sadly Missed, Fallen Asleep, Gone Home, and so forth. And down from above, as if in response, comes the repeated thump of a heavy table, lifted up and dropped from a great height by various visitors from The Other Side.

Relations between the two businesses are more than merely neighbourly. The stonemason – unusually, for that line of work – is a woman. She's also my other mother.

And perish the thought that anyone should use such an ideologically unsound phrase, but Mum's and Maggie's is definitely a marriage made in heaven. Like most long-term partnerships, theirs has its own sacred origin myth.

They met for the first time on the day my mother set up shop. As she stood on the pavement, watching the joiner hang her sign above the door, her new downstairs neighbour came out to see what was going on.

This was Maggie, coated in marble dust from her red bandanna to her purple Doc Martens. She studied the faux-gothic lettering.

'The Joyous-Reunion-what-the-fuck-you-must-be-joking-lady-Tabernacle!? Sorry, but I just don't buy the life after death thing. Once they have one of my gravestones on top of them, believe me, they stay put.'

My mother laughed this off, looked Mags up and down, and said that it was a pity she was so dusty, since she'd be glad to have her up for coffee and a little tour right there and then, except to be honest she couldn't bear the thought of footprints on her perfectly pristine new carpet.

'Maybe another time.'

For a few months after that it was just nods in passing, exchanges of wrongly delivered post, the usual moans about the weather. Even so, any bystander could have told in a flash that there was more than a tiny bit of noticing going on.

Then one night Maggie turned up at the Tabernacle door. My mother noted that she'd left her dusty workboots at the bottom of the stairs. Staring down at the holes in her socks, Maggie confessed to a little bit of a problem.

Well, maybe not so little. A grieving widow had placed an order for her husband's gravestone, to be ready in three months when she returned from visiting relatives back home in Cyprus. It was a top of the range job, polished black marble, with an incised Greek Orthodox cross, an inset frame to hold a photograph of the departed, and several lines of verse composed by the bereaved wife herself. When Maggie got round to carrying out the commission she discovered that one item on the instruction sheet was illegible. Unfortunately, it happened to be the dead man's Christian name.

'Why don't you ring the wife?'

'I told you, she went to Cyprus.'

'But she must have given you her address. You could check the phone book, see if the listing has his full name...'

'I did. Ex-directory.'

'Did she pay by cheque? Maybe both names are still on the account...'

'Cash.'

'So what are you going to do?'

'I wondered if maybe you could, you know... make contact. Get the info from the horse's mouth, so to speak.'

'I thought you thought my work was all a load of...'

'This could be a professional disaster for me if word got round... failure to meet promised completion date... send my business down the Swanee... oh God...'

'Only problem, lovey,' said Mum, putting an arm round Mags's shoulder and ushering her in, 'is that we usually summon the Departed by pronouncing their full name. Catch-22. You ain't got it.'

'Couldn't you just ask for Mr Kyprianou, formerly of Green Lanes?'

'Get real. They don't call this part of London Greek City for nothing. Can you imagine how many different Mr Kyprianous from Green Lanes have passed through those old Pearly Gates? We'd have a traffic jam of ghosts, be here all night. I'd run out of ectoplasm, not to mention energy. Can't you give me anything more specific?'

'How about the exact date of death?'

'Well, that might do it...' She thought for a minute. 'If so, we should be able to sort it out, spelling and all, as a straight table job.'

'A what?'

'You know, tap-tap-tap... yes or no answers... Otherwise, we might need to stretch to an actual three-dimensional corporeal Summoning. And that would take all night. I'd like to be neighbourly and do it for nothing, but it's a massive job. I'd have to charge you...'

'Look, I'll pay whatever you ask – as long as you don't tell anybody!'

She led Maggie into the sanctuary.

'We must first sit down and join hands across the table...'

So they did. My mother doused the lights and got right down to it.

It took only four wrong numbers, so to speak, before she called up the right Mr Kyprianou. He was not only charmed to be of assistance, but delighted to hear of his wife's plans for his memorial.

The next morning Maggie arrived at the Tabernacle door with a fat envelope full of twenty-pound notes and a dozen perfect roses. It was only when my mum tried to sniff them that she realised they'd been sculpted out of delicately veined pink marble.

'Wow!'

Mags told her it had taken all night. 'I couldn't sleep anyway.'

'Funny,' said Mum, 'neither could I.'

So that's how they got together. They soon discovered they had a lot of things in common, starting with a shared interest in dead people.

This fascination went far beyond the purely professional. Their first actual date was a rainswept walk through the old part of Highgate Cemetery. Their first kiss took place in the shadow of draped urns and angels at Abney Park. Their first dirty weekend consisted of a trip to Glasgow, to admire the Victorian gothic glories of the Necropolis.

A few months later they gave up their separate flats and moved into a maisonette above a shabby shopping parade full of strange or struggling enterprises. These included a dolls' hospital lined with half-naked catatonic Barbies, a shoe shop that stocked only teetery, fuck-me stilettos in curiously unladylike sizes, and a kebab place that didn't open till 3 a.m. It was the sort of neighbourhood where nobody asked questions. This was probably a good thing, especially when the two of them suddenly appeared on the street together, wearing identical besotted smiles and pushing a pram.

We weren't the only lesbian family in the district. At primary school the bane of my life was Alice Bee Toklas Boudicca Frauenhaus. She had three co-mothers – one Irish, one Danish, one Australian – instead of merely two.

Little Alice Bee Etcetera was famous in our class for criticising everybody else's lunches. Tuna sandwiches tortured dolphins.

White bread was rubbish. Eggs exploited chickens. Good people ate only tofu, organic grains, and carob instead of chocolate – which was, as any idiot knows, a deadly poison.

One lunchtime I decided I'd had enough.

'Everybody doesn't have to like what you like, tofu-face,' I am reported to have said to her. 'You suck.'

This was overheard by a teacher and communicated home, and oh did I ever get a talking-to. Not because I'd stood up to her sweeping generalisations – which, my mother granted, was the right thing to do – but because 'you suck' as a term of abuse was both phallocentric and heterosexist. And no, nobody was going to start explaining those words when it was already half an hour past my bedtime. When I was old enough to understand I'd find out what they meant.

However, to teach me a lesson about reconciliation and negotiation, Mags and Evie decided to invite little Alice and all her mums to our place for a gala gourmet-vegan tea party.

'I bet she says nasty things about your cakes,' I sulked.

Mags said that if she did, she'd shove those butterless, eggless blueberry muffins right down the little darling's throat. My mother said this wouldn't happen, and that we'd all have a perfectly lovely afternoon.

Which we did. Probably because while Alice and I spent it silently perusing my collection of multi-cultural, non-sexist picture books, our five mummies hit the homemade organic elderberry wine. Soon they were all laughing and shrieking and getting along like the proverbial house on fire, only they were having such a good time that if our place had been ablaze, I doubt they'd have noticed. By the time they polished off the third bottle, they were all best friends.

I'm not sure how much of their conversation I absorbed on the spot, and how much came from my mothers' reminiscences years later.

Anyway, the gist of it was – interestingly enough – about their chosen methods of conception.

Little Alice, typically for that era, had arrived thanks to a simple domestic implement available at any cookware shop and a sperm donation from a politically evolved and carefully health-checked gay man who wished to support his lesbian sisters-in-struggle (though not their offspring) and was emigrating to New Zealand.

My mother said, 'Well, we decided not to go down that route.'

'So what did you do – pick up a stranger, lure him home, close your eyes and think of No Man's Land?'

'Puh-lease,' said my mother.

'So how…?'

'Just used my professional skills, didn't I?'

This took a minute to swallow.

For most people, my mother's profession was a definite no-go area, except when they were talking about her behind her back. There were two schools of thought in the north London lesbian-feminist community: according to one, she was the victim of some bizarre but harmless mental aberration, and had therefore to be indulged and supported. According to the other, she was probably a con woman and a crook. But this was OK if you interpreted her activities as a radical guerilla action to expropriate the wealth of the heterosexual capitalist Thatcher-loving WASP patriarchy.

'Are you saying you did it with a dead person?'

My mother sighed and, for the ninety-millionth time in her career, repeated her favourite mantra: 'I wish people would realise. There's no such thing as dead. We just make a transition. It's like moving house, only without the estate agents…'

'Oh come on, stop pissing us about…'

'It's my iron-clad rule not to waste energy arguing with unbelievers.'

'But how…?'

'I'm not going to bore you with the technicalities. Just take it from me, darling, DNA goes on forever. Coffee?'

Next they started wanting to know who my father was… On reflection I think this was just a tiny bit pushy, since I'd never – up until that point and not for several years thereafter – thought to wonder about that for myself.

Maggie said they wouldn't have gone for just any Tom, Dick, or Harry. It had to be someone with creative talent, intelligence, an open and inquiring mind, a healthy lifestyle ('Wait a minute, don't you mean deathstyle?') and a progressive attitude.

'So,' said my mum, 'we drew up a list of preferred candidates, held a few exploratory interviews...'

'Interviews?'

'Well, not all the possibles wanted to play ball... Leonardo da Vinci, for instance, got very twitchy about the whole thing... And King Solomon was a big disappointment. I was sure he'd have been up for it, what with those seven hundred and something wives and concubines and all, but unfortunately... Anyway, we finally got our man.'

'Who was...?' They were on the edge of their seats... or, in this case, on the edge of their floor-cushions.

'We promised we'd keep it confidential. Somebody's reputation is at stake here. These guys are very protective about their places in history.'

Alice Bee's three mothers exchanged meaningful looks, then went into a huddle.

'You know,' they said, after a while, 'we've been thinking that it's time our Alice had a little sibling...'

There was a short and mutually satisfactory discussion about an appropriate fee for my mother's services, and then they got down to the much tastier topic of possible papas.

'Personally,' said my mum, 'I'd recommend one of the ancient Greek philosophers. A nicer, brighter, more sociable bunch of boys you couldn't hope to find... good at dinner parties, delightful conversationalists, and, as a bonus, most of them are gay.'

I can't say for sure what happened next. My mother, as she said, is a bit of a stickler about confidentiality.

But less than a year after that famous tea party, Alice Etcetera did acquire a little sibling named Sappho. She turned out to be a lot more fun than Alice herself. We got on very well. In fact, I used to babysit for her after Alice left home to become a Buddhist nun.

As it happens, little Sapph eventually followed me to university. She studied with the same tutors, read the same subjects

(Philosophy and Maths) and, coincidentally, also earned the same Double First.

Now, strangely enough, we're both writing doctoral dissertations on Pythagoras. You might think that, some 2600 years after his death, there'd be nothing new left to say about his fusion of mysticism and mathematics. But Sapph and I are equally convinced that we have a unique understanding of the way his mind worked. Unfortunately, our researches have led us to completely contradictory conclusions. But this doesn't stop us from loving each other to bits.

People sometimes say we look so alike we could be sisters. I don't see it for myself – but then you never do.

Necrologue
Susan Em

Necrologue
Susan Em

Someone is waiting for me to die. Me. Maybe. The priest's vestments are thick again, they abandoned the modern materials when the modern ceased to be. It's linen now, thick linen, thick like it was quilted. Though my eyes are half shut I can see the seams. It looks grey. It reminds me of something. A picture. Only it was a woman in it. Not a man. This priest is a man. Bastard.

They are snuffling at the end of my bed, snuffling like pigs, their eyes full of truffles and tears. They are looking for some sign from me. A raised hand to show that I want his blessing. All I want is to pick my nose but a raised finger would make them pounce. The gods have spoken, I can hear the squawking cry, anoint him. Anoint him.

Anoint me arse. Fuck off.

The priest moves closer. I can feel his hot breath on my cheek, his stubble brushes my cheek. He moves away and I see that a flake of my flesh has scraped away and dangles from the black hair. He has murmured something to me and his eye flicks sideways, I am half dead but I see the rhomboid reflection of the faraway window in his eye, a pane of white over the blackness of his pupil. He glances at me and I know he doesn't like me. I am an awkward bugger, he knows that, he knows I will hold out and that there will be nothing in it for him, not even a shilling at the gate of heaven.

It is that that does it for me. Knowing the priest doesn't like me, I mean. I am too happy to die now. Fuck the lot of them. I think I will not be able to do it, and that I will die trying. Which is why I do it, really. I raise myself first up onto my elbows, the joints snapping and popping moistly.

'Has he seen a vision? Is it a vision?'

Some old bitch is bundled up in the corner, some ancient old slag who can function as nothing any longer except as a prayer-raiser, earning a miserable existence at the foot of deathbeds.

'*No*,' says the priest sharply. No one as bedevilled as me would have a vision. The angels did not descend from the seventh sphere for cussed bastards like me. No, they didn't.

I can't speak, my throat is parched and full of painful cracks that throb beautifully when a meagre stream of water covers them. My lips are swollen. The insides, now brightly pink and slick, puff out over the thin, stretched band of the outer lip. Minute flakes of skin cling and fall, and the corners are blocked with a shockingly white scurf.

I don't know who it is, in their wisdom, who has strategically placed the mirror so that anyone pushing themselves upwards with their hands and glancing, as we do instinctively, towards the window, towards a means of egress, can see themselves. Perhaps they feared I might start to struggle back from the gateway of the Valley of Death, and they thought to scare me into the arms of the Prime Mover by letting me see the sight of myself. I have tramped the world over and dragged my banded rags through every city and hellhole, I have slept nights in sewers and at the last rattle of brutal sicknesses, and they thought to scare me into faith by my reflection in a polished glass.

Mind you, I look at myself now and I think perhaps they had a point.

The mirror is badly polished, at that, but I see clearly what it is that they have had to look at this last week and for a nanosecond I feel a fleeting pity for them. They don't know what to say. I brought back my own sickness from the filthy heathen countries I chose to visit, so they should be able to happily wash their hands of me and leave me to die, and to descend, as they believe I should, to the First Sphere. But I stomped from country to country, growling and shouting, for what they also believe is a noble cause. I had the Necrologue.

The realisation of their discomfort at that particular cleft stick pleases me and gives me enough strength to continue my journey into the vertical.

The greatest distance I travelled was into the East, out where the Crusades had been fought millennia ago. It would hardly be the death of me to run out into the garden but the fact of the matter is that I hoped it would. I wanted them to have to chase my corpse. Dead man running.

I was used to running. I had lived my life almost always in sewers, that is how I got from country to country. The whole world was reduced to that but we didn't say so. No, we pretended. And that was how I survived. Night after black night, cities full of people all staring at the stars – *what are they saying now? Are we safe yet?* They lay on the mountains, on the hills and on the turrets. I sneaked below them, gathering the names and adding them to my list.

Now any of you lazy bastards who have bothered to read any of your recent history, any of you who have the faintest interest in why it is the world seems to be going down the sink hole and doing its best to turn itself into an arsehole will not have missed reading about the disappearance of the Emperor of Never. The blistering heat flashing like the wrath of the Angel from the helmets of the men, the swirling clouds of red dust in the brittle desert heat and the impatient hooves of the stallions, not a cliché left unchewed by every hack journalist around and many of the serious faces from the quality newspapers, the kind of newspapers that your budgie wouldn't be ashamed to see on the floor of his cage. The battle, the steel, the shouts of the fighters and the screams of frightened horses and then, abruptly, the end. They were gone. The journalists stood, puzzled, on the ends of phones in their sweating hotels, looking into the old-fashioned receivers as though the smooth metal would tell them something. Bar owners and taxi drivers, leaning their elbows on their counters or glancing in the rear-view mirror at their trapped audience, choking off into silence, predictions left unmade, crafty interpretations exposed and naked and false. People stood in the streets looking at each other, at the white walls, then up at the shield-blue sky like it would tell them something. There was a second in the whole world into which anything could have fallen. And the fucking Angels got there first, fuck them from a height. Into the pre-natal silence from which anything could have come – a symphony, Venus rising, a magical tree – a caterwaul went up and the bastard Angelites claimed this moment of birth for themselves. This was proof, they said, of what they had always maintained, that the ancient bands round the earth were true, spirits and humours and ideals and what-have-you floating serenely between them, and a deputation of Angels to make sure each band was ticking over. All as you might imagine, these Angels, dream-coloured wings and long dresses and smug smiles you want to smack off their faces. After everything else they'd all been through it was not surprising that people flocked to this. My grandfather had been in the desert at that battle. Being low scum that we were, he wasn't on a shining stallion or encased in silver armour. He had not come of the right stock for that bright history. He was on the ground dodging and running and shitting himself, stabbing here, biting there, hoping he didn't maim or kill the wrong person. When he didn't come back to his factory-work lifestyle, my grandmother's grief drove her into the ethereal wings of the angels and we became the most viciously Angelite family for miles.

That priest waving angrily out the window at me is tired, the old prick. He can't give up. He has to be the stony face that does not hear the insult or feel the missile. (They could have run away, of course. Some did – savage priests, now on the streets among the greasy urchins. But some – stupid, stubborn – stayed; grimy hands washing the heavy grey skirts, ironing the length of surplice in shabby rooms.) Bastard. Everywhere you go now you cannot escape the afterlife, the pride in the faces of people who have winkled the reality out from behind the merely manifest, you can dispute it and you will hear happy talk of wheels and everything being one but you see a glitter in an eye, a hidden eye where before it had only been a dark corner, a sideways movement away in a tavern.

I went to the desert. I went where he disappeared. The last sight of my grandfather. You'd disappear too, if the place was rotten with vast underground caverns, big tunnels joining them up. I don't know what they were. They used to say there were trains that ran in tunnels, but who knows what that looked like? I did. I saw maps, you see. No one else was allowed to see maps, but a Necrologue, that was different, I had to see them, see? Mincy old fuckers couldn't not let such a holy one see where to hell they were going. I saw the maps from years ago and the straight lines and the projections. That would have explained the iron stairs. I knew what would happen if I said anything about it. Some years ago, some poor bollocks was digging up his land, whether he expected to find a mine of gold or he was just wanting to plant one bastard of a crop, he dug and dug and his sons dug and his neighbours dug and they found just such a stairs. He, having some shred of sense left despite the unveiled sun and thunderous past, bethought himself of these shreds of history, but no. These were, it was announced, a sign that arrogant ancestors had tried to build a stairway through the Angelic Spheres. I haven't heard anything that stupid since the Tower of Babel. Anyway, they invented a whole story about it, the civilisation, what it looked like, what those hubristic forebears had looked like and their long fanatical eyes yearning to see the faces of the Angels. And the poor dick with the shovel? Well. One of life's little mysteries, what happened to him. But sitting in the desert I knew what I was looking at. I took my own little shovel, with a cherry-wood handle, and I dug. There was no one to see me but vultures. Just enough to let me in and to see the irregular serrated iron step, a tattered remnant of bridle, the moonlight gleam of the first skull. Collapse and landslide. Angels, my arse.

There is sand under my feet now. It is a dark night and very very cool, almost solid, cool and reassuring. There are no clouds. The moon is stripped and shadowless, the stars like perfect thoughts. There is a garden, a little border garden. It has cool leafed flowers with petals with colours like jellybeans. Jellybean. Now there's a word. I've never eaten a jellybean – though I have eaten flowers, when things got rough – but I know what they look like. The house is a shadow behind me, blurred edges, cloth-filtered lights. My knees are shaking, they look enormous in my scrawny legs. The skin is so dry and lined I look like a fossil. A dreadful cackle emerges from my lips and I realise I have laughed. That thought makes me laugh again. A legend will start if I don't stop. I am sick with tiredness. I wonder will I break anything if I sit down. Fuck it, I'm practically dead, what can happen? I creak down and sit. The grass is cold under me but it instantly warms to me. Feebly my toes flick the sand.

I had to stay a while in a monastery on my way back from the desert. It was like a different world, high wet wind and cliffs safe from landslide because they had been so stripped to the heart rock there was nothing left to fall. The men and women in their black gowns with the strange little coloured beads around their wrists. They had a huge dinner when I was there and they were very polite about not letting me near the table until I had washed. For fuck sake, I had had to crawl through a sewer on three occasions on the way back and even without the shite of a city clinging to me, walking and sweating and never being able to wipe my arse would make anyone smell. But they chucked me into a big ceramic bath that was full of red water and leaves, and enough foam to cover my modesty as well as wash me, and this bustly woman monk gave me a good scrubbing. I grinned up at her and she just rolled her eyes, she'd probably seen better and been getting it oftener than me. She kept her beads about her wrist. They were a furry sort of red colour, and they smelled sweet. I caught her wrist and grabbed the beads and sniffed them. I looked at her.

'Rosewood,' she said.

A little band of the beautiful beads like a bracelet on her wrist.

'And you'll pray for the people who can't eat,' I said, in a singsong voice, 'on your little rosewood beads.'

'Fuck you,' said the monk and shoved my head under the water to apply the scrubbing brush to my hair. When I was out of the bath and drying on the mat she looked quite surprised, as though she hadn't expected under all the shite and the clothes so old they had to be peeled off me like paper that there would be anything worth looking at. Mind you, she scrubbed so hard she could have brought a diamond out of granite. She smiled at me, and I flashed her but she just went pink and raised her eyebrows nonchalantly.

The dining hall was a marvel to behold, with a vaulted ceiling and tall windows with narrow panes of glass. There were tables all along the sides and sloped black shapes ducking towards their plates, leaning back to spit out gristle, standing up to grab the salt or punch their neighbour. At the far end was the nobs' table, a gem-eyed man with a beard, a boy with a face like thin alabaster. Here, I ate. We didn't speak, I just ate for all the days to come when I would find no food. And afterwards I had to earn my keep. Everyone was silent. I walked into the sunken bit of the floor, shaped like a horseshoe only without the bits of shit and people's bones stuck on. I dragged my bag behind me as though it weighed like the world, which it did, it was full of dead people.

I looked round me solemnly, trying to keep with the mood, but I was reckless and that alarmed me, something was running through me like a narcotic and I feared it was the desire to shock. I unfurled my life's work, paper ran on for miles. I looked round and everyone was silent.

The gem-eyed man said, 'We have heard until June 7th of last year.'

Hmm, I wondered, who told them that much? Fuckers.

I filled my belly with wind and my voice blew out like a trumpet.

'Manger Dorset,' I bellowed, 'Trampled.

'Ram Dolly. Appendicitis.

'Nory Pepper. Choked on vomit. His own.

'Ittie Lamplaz. Died of being aged 102.

'Felly Rubble. Blood poisoning.'

There was a rustle of arses in seats and the breathing changed. They were getting sucked in by the words and waited, in hope with a tiny crumb of watered-out fear, that they would hear a name they knew.

'Yelk Mann. Drowned.

'Payta Mann. Also Drowned.

'Lackey Pard. Crushed by landslide.

'Edoll Tayama. Committed suicide by means of hanging.

'Says Timmer. Bled to death after amputation of leg.'

Usually I stood in one place when I read the chosen section of the Necrologue. That way if anyone couldn't hear me they just had to shout and I would know where to move. But that fuck-you-all feeling was rippling under my skin and there was nothing I could do but scratch it. I walked towards the pit.

'*Tarette June. Stillborn.*'

They thought they were hearing the population of heaven. This was a personal introduction to the choirs of Angels – *Archangel Gabriel, this is the Abbot Smalls. Pleased to meet you. Likewise, I'm sure.*

'*Garganta Smalls. Kicked by his horse.*'

I was viewed as a sort of escort agency of the afterlife. They heard the names, they suddenly knew the Spheres of the Immortals, did they, and the names gave them protection from being the next one like poor *Raman Korik Influenza*. They made me laugh and made me so angry I could have killed them all, with one great roar, one great thunderous explosion of vengeance. There was nothing in this except the poor sons of whores who had died. That was the only reason I did this insane job. There would be these irrefutable double-facts; these people had lived, these people had died. The world would not whirl on into a tangled future without there being the reminder that *Bail Newfork* lived and died from *Eating fermented berries*. Poor little cow. She'd only been three. That is what eventually did for me. Not the realisation that I did not believe in the Spheres, in the Gods of the Spheres, to which I had been taught to refer for all of my life. It was the realisation that I did not believe that what I did had any point. *Where are these names going to go?* I had not realised that I needed eternity.

They said that thousands and thousands of years ago there lived people who were giants and strong, and who had been born from the heads of eagles. They had circular cities and they travelled all around the world and when they died they became petrified, their apotheosis the transformation into huge statues made of polished marble. Now and then, as the countries of the world tossed and split and fell in upon themselves, parts of this ancient life were revealed back to us. An upraised arm here, a hand modestly covering an impossible nipple, the foundations of a building to give guidance to our modern fools trying to raise a building that won't fall down at the first fart.

The monastery where I was staying had grabbed one such place. The bit they got, though useful, was not what the abbot might have chosen. History had eroded the marble city but left the dark pits below, so the monks had built their Aula Maxima over the channels and the semi-circle of stone seating that had, in the past, tidied away the effluvia of the citizens. Dark arches and gargoyles loomed over the neighbouring seats. Baked under a remembered sun, they were dusty and crumbling – the monks would get up with grit and buttons of stone embedded in their bare arses. A little step for your feet and a bottomless pit where you could sit and chat while you strained.

'Paritty Gull,' I intoned, pacing slowly forward, 'Alcohol poisoning.

'Nate Bloogar. Choked on a fishbone.'

I stepped down into the sunken arena and I could hear them shifting in their seats, some unable to hear, some being put in mind by my position of the turmoil in their guts, clamouring to get out.

'Avvid Lore. Car crash.

'Weston Fish. Leukaemia.'

My flesh thrilled to the unmistakable gasp that sounded; it slipped out through unprepared throats. Now that the rosy-titted monk had scrubbed away the clothes that had been growing on me the last years, the robe, butter yellow, slid briskly up my legs and I bunched it, like a wedding train you see in ancient old paintings of certain ceremonies, over my arm.

'Dassy Roy. Race attack – kicked to death.

'Juntie Kracker. AIDS.'

The abbot, gem-eyes gaping and his dark cheek lumpy with blood, was facing the smooth moon of my arse, then the dark curled silk in front, atop my long brown legs, as I turned, very slowly, reading.

'Tamede Almata. Dehydration in a detention centre.

'Dot Commis. Lung Canker.'

I sat down and wriggled to settle myself in. No one on the list yet died of having a shit in public, so I settled in and let rip.

I didn't really think I'd last the night and I was right. The monk who washed me brought me to the square white room they had set aside for me, washed and aired as soon as they knew that the Necrologue would be coming their way. They had to add their names to my list, so the abbot, killing himself to pretend he couldn't see me wiping my arse with my free hand, read out the names and the causes of death for me to scratch on to the paper after poor *Halana Pae* who had been snuffed out by making too many shoes.

'*Brother Carmatel*,' said the abbot through gritted teeth, '*Drug overdose.*'

I knew, I could see in his eyes, he was struggling with an ultimatum he did not dare to give to God. *Strike this cunt, this son of a bitch dead or I will never believe again.*

'*Sister Latam. Pernicious Anaemia.*'

Give me another Necrologue that I may be spared entrusting the brethren's names to this.

I smirked as I left the room but I already had an eye to the narrow chute down to the kitchens where I knew I could land back into a midden heap, a favourite haunt of mine. The monk with the rosewood beads showed me the room and shut the window while I slithered out of the yellow robe and sat cross-legged and titty naked on the bed. She laughed, and I looked at my watch.

'I washed my hands and everything,' I said. 'And I have probably half an hour before they come to boot my well-observed arse out of the window.'

It only took twenty minutes and she seemed pleased and I was nicely set up to go creeping around the intestines of the monastery, to go crawling out of the cloaca of the abbot's home. Well fed, well watered and well laid. What more was there to want?

I can't remember her face now. All I can remember is the raspberry shade of her mouth and the way she laughed. Her hair was like silk.

I can see them in the lighted window. They are debating whether they should come down for me. Even at this distance I can see the look of horror on the face of the old bitch the prayer raiser, the resentment on the face of the priest. He no more wants to come anywhere near me, wouldn't piss on me if he could avoid it. The old biddy is terrified and frosts it with sanctimonious rolling of the eye. The others, the washers, the carriers, the lifters, they are weak in expression and they look mulish. They think the priest has to be immune, *no better than them fuckers the Angelites if he's not immune.* But the poor bollocks doesn't know what it is I have. The whites of his eyes show at the possibility that he might have to die of the breath of a shitty rag like me. He would have been astounded, I was astounded, to know of the sumptuous, satin-lined place in which I contracted it. Whatever the fuck it is.

It isn't what they had in the court, that's for sure. The prince was flailing; his father was failing upstairs, his life seeping away, pushed out by the hardened residue of a life spent fucking the parlour maids; the prince was in charge. Powerful and stupid, his weak head grew merely hot and full of wind when faced with any problem, and faced with an epidemic he could hardly stand up. He stayed in his breakfast room all day eating peaches and only sometimes he had the courage, silk wrapped over his face, to flee across the courtyard to the stables where his chestnut would bear him away and the stable hands might or might not be alive when they got back. The prince had screamed for blessings from the abbey, and the abbot, who did not like the earthly princes at all, slyly kneaded his hands and mournfully told the prince that there was at least a Necrologue in the vicinity, if not a cure.

So I was dragged in from the highway, stumbling and hurrying with a tattered yellow gown and the bones of the dead on my back. I scribbled the names on the paper as fast as could be but I became impatient with the *'cause of death unknown'*. It should bloody be known. It's the only thing we do. So I went and had a look at them. It was not often I had occasion to praise the country of my birth but somehow this court had managed to contract a virus common where I was brought up. They'd never seen it before and had no clue what they should do about it. The fever, the delirium, the skin colour, all left the doctors scratching their scabby heads and lost ones wailing at the back walls near the pits. It was really quite easy.

'A little of this,' I said, 'and a little of this, a pinch of that, a spoonful of that one over there and a few drops of the hard stuff to make it less revolting – for fuck sake, don't spit it out, you stupid wanker.'

The prince was instantly in love with me. The king, when he heard, was so grateful he would have let me suck him but I said I could only chew so we left it at that. The communal fevers dissipated, the heat of fear and sickness had gone. I was allowed to stay.

She was curled up by the redcurrant bushes when I saw her. A comma of a woman in a swathe of tangerine silk, her bare feet turned towards me, her face turned east. The sun fell in little drops on her jewellery. She was not doing anything, just looking. In front of her were patterns that even I saw instantly. The rounded phlox of darkness in the centre of the bushes, the stark sap-green leaves, the perfect, luminescent red globes hanging perfectly still from the brown stems. She was being perfect, doing nothing. I stood still, looking at her, watching the way the cloth and her skin and her jewellery absorbed the light and the sun and made the air look richer for it. I knew, or at least I guessed, that she was one of the king's concubines, but she turned around and looked at me and smiled and I knew instantly that she might have been procured for that reason but that the king had never laid a hand on her. With an elegance that made me want to dance, she turned around so she was still coiled but facing me. The king's cock would have fallen off in terror if he had tried to make it stand up to her. I knew it for a fact. Mine nearly did and I didn't even have one. She was the blackest person I had ever seen, so black she was almost violet, so black her white teeth, her tawny palms came as a shock, and she was a giant, she must have been over seven feet tall. But it was neither her colour in a milky, pink-and-yellow country nor her size that made her so terrifying. It was her eyes. She looked at you and you wanted to roll over to her like a croquet ball. Wrap yourself up in pretty paper with a bow in her favourite colour and hope she would unwrap you. Put your viscera on a plate and see if it entertained her. She smiled at me and I subsided like a ghost when the child runs out from under the sheet.

I could never do it with her. I was certain of that. I helped her pick flowers for the staff quarters, and I helped her clean the swans' lake and I helped her wash the dogs and groom the horses. I sat with her once while she bathed. The bath was big and square, a ceramic bath, white, with little flattened bits for the honey soap. The tiles around it were also square and white but they had red splashes on them, like a curl of red smoke in hardened glass. She spoke to me gently and easily. She spoke everyone's language, seven or ten languages and people came to her to translate and she would do it, always the same with everyone. Letters of diplomacy for the ministers, letters from their mothers to the ten-year-old apprentice gardeners, reread in their language by her gentle, easy voice. The water in her bath was green from the scented pellets she put in it, and white petals floated. She talked to me and I said something that made her laugh, she lay back and laughed a chuckly sort of delighted laugh and lifted her legs up, paddling her feet on the surface of the water like she was walking on it. She kicked her feet up and I wanted nothing more, ever, not a single other thing in the world but her clean legs with rivulets of water running down and the plashing noise of her feet, and the shapes she made on the tiles and the water.

But then of course I got sick and I had to go. Whatever my country gave them that they could not cure, they had their own medical peculiarities. They had germs of their own, the bastards, at the mention of which everyone looked wide-eyed and innocent. They had been immune to it for so long that no one got ill any more. Even if I had given it to her she would not have noticed. And they were all very sorry but they couldn't fucking cure me when I started to die.

'Why do you not believe in the Angels, the Gods of the Spheres?' she asked. I never asked her name because I never wanted to add it to the Necrologue.

I told her. I have never told anyone else.

I had been brought up from a child with one of those fucking angels hovering at my shoulder. I couldn't piss without them knowing about it. But I believed and I said what I was told to say and I believed what I was told to believe. We no longer had any reasons for anything, no coherence against the chaos, no thread to bring us from the monster's cave into the light of civilisation. We deduced, from what we had experienced, the real causes for things and believed in what seemed apparent and the strength of our emotions and what seemed to keep us safe. It was less that I believed, and more that I did not *not believe,* until when I was eleven, I was struck by lightning. And I survived, but nothing else did. The jolt did not shatter me or snap my bones apart but when we were certain I was still alive and when that apocalyptic intrusion from the Spheres into my world became part of my history, rather than I part of its, everything had snapped apart. What had happened to me had not killed me, as I would have expected. I was not different as a result of it, as I had expected. It had happened for its own reason and it had nothing to do with the mysterious and esoteric lines and tangled threads with which we had attempted to map the idea of it before it had even happened. It was a different colour, when it happened, a different smell, a different everything. Like the first time you drink or get high or make love. Never what you imagine, good, bad or ugly, but never what you thought it would be and never, ever, conceivably, any other way. So don't tell me about angels. Even if they existed we would know nothing of them. Wouldn't recognise them. Cocooned by the timorous pictures we would draw and the protective mesh of notion, expectation that would rip apart at the first brush of the actual. Don't fucking tell me about fucking angels.

I had meant to tell her quietly and gently as she spoke to me but I was pacing up and down over the stone by the time I had finished. I knew I was sick then, too, and that I would have to go, so I cared even less than I did by the time I was twelve. We were in what I knew had been an old church, a mega church, high almost as the sky, because the spire was left and, though bits of the walls had fallen out, the coloured glass was still there. Thin, impossibly thin columns swooped into arches and clustered together like pagan fists in the centre. There was a raised table with steps up to it, and a stone, a big stone slab. From there we could see right back into the back of the church, past the sapling forest of columns, to the four tall windows with tiny rectangles of coloured glass. I paced as I spoke and I felt as full of electricity as if I had been struck again. She was sitting on the white slab. She was wearing green and on her arms she wore bands of jade and silver. I stared at her and I can recall very little else. Not because I don't remember what happened, but because I never really knew. I was enveloped by her. Green silk and gold thread that straggled from the edge of the cloth, bloomy grape skin, her white teeth, her eyes that could redirect towards her everything about another person, her hands with the most delicate, elegant bones, the tawny palms, irrefutable woman, unquestionable solidity, flashes of copper, of apricot, of coral and shell pink when she smiled (and made me fall to pieces), of rose and poppies with dark hearts. And somewhere in all of this bobbed I, ginger-topped snuff-coloured streak, and there was not a single fucker in the world better than me because I made her smile and she had wanted me.

The night is very dark now. I had always said my last act would be to write my own name in the Necrologue. I am not going to. I do not, now, know, whether to scream till I bleed, or just sit, quietly, looking at the petals that are turning black with night, becoming secrets that I might have unfurled but have not.

Like scabs they all fall away. The spheres of heaven, the circles of hell, the world ceiling and wall in symbol. We stand in a carnival hall, trick mirrors and sly hands tilting them this way and that. Words writ large, the whole bag of bones and knives rattled in our ears so we can't hear and can barely tell where we stop and that which we fear begins. I do not know how many years I have lived. Thirty? Forty? And in all that time I have never seen eternity. I yelled in triumph that I have not been fooled, I see the warp in the glass, the fake limb hidden in the jacket, marked cards, loaded dice, lies, innocent faces, fucking lies. I stagger under the silence.

The sky is black and full of stars. If I close my eyes I can hear the sea, the memory of the sea. Shells. Fossils in a grey mountain. I will die here, and for the first time that I recall, I do this not because *they don't want me to*. Because I want to. I sit in eternity and am briefly a god. For me to go to my grave with my knowledge of the cracks beneath the plaster has not been enough, and it is too late, now, to go with anything else. The dark is smooth like a jelly, her touch, my life, distilled into one breath. And I am about to die. *Fuck.*

Nightshade
Fiona Zedde

Nightshade
Fiona Zedde

Tonight, it would rain blood. For now, the smell of damp earth and rain-battered flowers rose up from the garden below to sink into the stone and steel of the large circular balcony where I stood. Alone. From behind, the sound of laughter lifted suddenly above the sensuous bass pounding from various hidden speakers. The women looked exquisite tonight, moist and hard in leathers, soft and feminine in silks, or dark and inviting in velvets. They could fulfill any fantasy, any decadent wish. For a price. Celeste's women. Only the very wealthy could afford them, and only the desperate – and in some cases, the desperately bored – became one of them. My sister planned it that way: an exclusive supply to meet any demand. Celeste was an enterprising woman, but I knew only too well that she was deadly. A trickster in the clothing of a benevolent.

At midnight the place already reeked of bartered sex and hashish. I hoped that she would come soon. It was getting cold and crowded. A woman stumbled out from the party, laughing at the serving girl she pulled roughly along with her. The girl seemed delicate and vulnerable with her violet dress and soft mouth. Her bare arms were bruised, but she didn't protest. This was just another game to her. I couldn't fight the nausea that I felt; once, I was that woman. My legs took me inside, beyond the French doors and into the belly of the house. The room's brightness momentarily stunned the eye. Black-clad women were not enough to subdue the gold tapestry and chaises longues; or the opulent banquet set in the middle of the room, surrounded by lightning-bright silverware. Only the rooms beyond were darkly lit, staged scenes for numerous trysts or merely quiet time with your drug of choice. Celeste provided for everything.

Crystal chandeliers with their daggers of light illuminated the scene, which was too much like a scene from Edgar Allan Poe.

157

Women. Every color, every shape, in masks and with bare faces; with stilettos strapped to their thighs or dressed as reluctant nuns with their habits ripped from their cool but inviting bodies. Nothing here was real. Except *her*.

She slid easily through the crowd, touching those who unintentionally paused to block her way, then moved on. The dim light revealed her to be a full-lipped spectre of crippling sensuality. Delicious. At least that's what I thought when I saw her for the first time. The poetry was unexpected, but other than that, no warning bells rang for me. Only the body's urge – a powerful tightening below – that impelled me forward. No one impeded my progress across the room. Few here acknowledged my presence, preferring instead to turn away from me, glad that I was here in search of someone else. If she chose to come home with me (would I give her a choice?), there would be no one to question it. I stopped when she was within whispering distance. But, as I stepped closer, people who I assumed were friends of Jenna's suddenly surrounded her. They touched her without asking.

I leaned my shoulder against a column and admired the cobalt blue velvet of her dress and the smooth length of bare back that it revealed. Her skin wasn't perfect. I could see a small network of scars that ran from her left shoulder blade down to the small of her back; they were slightly lighter than the rest of her skin and could only be seen from a certain angle. They made me want her even more.

'Champagne, Madame?'

A soft, feminine voice whispered the invitation in my ear as I felt the crush of firm breasts against my back. The girl looked little more than sixteen in her Catholic school uniform and pigtails, but her dark eyes spoke of an experience far beyond those years. As she held out the tray of amber wine, the wide bronze circlet on her arm gleamed in the light from the swaying chandelier. Her smile was intimate, but a hint of mischief tugged at the curving bottom lip.

'Not tonight, darling.'

I took a glass from her tray and discreetly tucked a fifty-dollar bill inside the ridiculously prim collar of her blouse. The girl's look was knowing, but she accepted my answer, shrugged and moved on. I was only one of forty or so women in the room. The others would be more interested than I.

There was once a time when I would have found women of her kind exciting, more appealing than getting involved with women with lives outside the Society; women who could be whatever I wanted, whenever I wanted them. But not any more. I had already served my time inside the Bronze Circle. There was only one thing I wanted from this party tonight, and I was looking right at her.

The crowd still surrounded her, but it had shifted, grown closer, almost cutting her off from the rest of the room. She spoke with someone with his back to me, a beautiful man in something very tight and very yellow. Her lips – with their full, inviting curve and the animal sheen of teeth beyond – fascinated me. She laughed, arching her neck, and I could see the soft pink lining of her mouth. The intensity of my gaze drew her eyes to mine and with a slow smile, I told her of my desire. I lifted the glass to my lips before putting it aside and walking to her.

'Hello, Jenna.'

Her name came easily to my tongue. It didn't seem to surprise her that I knew it. She smiled into my eyes and we touched. Palm to palm, eye to eye, and the brief touch of cheeks.

'I thought you'd be here long before now.'

Smoky wet heat, that voice. And she knew I'd been watching.

'You were occupied,' I said, laying the blame for our delayed meeting squarely at her feet.

'And what if I still am?'

'Are you?' A look passed between us.

My hand slid up her arm of its own volition, the fingers curling around the firm bicep and pressing gently against the artery. The skin was so fragile. She didn't shake me off or cause a scene. Instead, she took her time looking me up and down, as if assessing the worth of the silver dress that hugged my body, the diamond studs in my ears and the short, neat cut of my hair.

'Come home with me,' I whispered as my hand tightened on

Fiona Zedde

her arm. It was a command. Before she answered, I motioned to a passing serving woman, scribbled a message on her embossed note pad, and sent her to Celeste.

She slid into my car as if she'd been there before, immediately marking the upholstery with her heady, yet subtle, perfume. My hand on the wheel trembled when the scent reached me. I started the car.

'Where do you live?' she asked.

'Close by.'

I didn't feel like talking, but I wanted to hear the sound of her voice, to feel her breath against my ear. I turned my eyes from the road to glance at her.

'Talk to me.'

Jenna smiled, revealing again the delicate pink of her mouth. When she spoke, it was in a low, confident voice, easing the tension of what would otherwise have been a silent ride.

'How long have you known Celeste?' Her bare fingers moved over the armrest, stroking the supple black leather.

'Not long,' I said, without stumbling over the lie. 'How about you?'

Jenna looked at me a long time before she answered, as if weighing the words that were already on her tongue to see how much she could trust me. *If* she could.

'We worked in the Circle together until a few years ago,' she murmured and slid off her shoes to curl up against the seat. 'We were good friends in high school, so after she heard that I was having a bad time in the real world, Celeste offered me a job as one of her women. That lasted for about three years, maybe more. I didn't find what I needed, so I left. She didn't mind.'

It didn't surprise me that she had been one of Celeste's women. She had that air of chameleon-like sophistication Celeste demanded of her highly paid 'consultants'. I recalled a particularly cold Welsh afternoon in December a few years ago. The assignment had been an easy one, but I couldn't bring myself to go through with the contract. I called Celeste, and a few minutes later there was a woman at my door, smelling of the ocean and Ysatis perfume. All we did was talk, but even at that she had been extremely skilled. My sister kept only the very best women in her employ.

Perhaps it was because of her scars that Celeste let Jenna go. But that certainly wouldn't spoil her appeal. I knew quite a few women, as well as men, who would have paid well for her favor. Celeste was a woman who expected perfection in all things, especially women. That was one thing we did not share. I'd had enough experience to know that if something seemed perfect, then it was likely to be an illusion. A betrayal waiting to come to fruit.

'Did you enjoy it?' I changed gears to push the car uphill, brushing her knee in the process. 'The life, I mean.'

Jenna laughed, a low hungry sound that made a mockery of our conversation.

'I did, actually.'

She touched the loose curls at her temple and tilted her mouth in a sad-sexy smile.

'The money, the women. Who wouldn't? Celeste encouraged us all to be a family to each other so that it wouldn't seem like such a lonely life. At first it seemed like a dream come true. A paradise. But I didn't know anyone or anything else. All my lovers were disposable and so was I, for the right price. Do you know what I was doing on my twenty-first birthday?' She looked past me to the blur of trees and dark sky outside the car window.

'I was in Switzerland, on my knees in front of some woman whose name I didn't even know. She gave me a five-hundred-dollar tip and a mouth full of bleached blonde hair, but she never said a word.' A shudder tightened the muscles of her neck. 'I bet you didn't want to know all that.' She laughed uneasily and shifted against the leather.

'Yes, I did.' I put out an arm to still her movements. 'Tell me, why did you come to the party tonight?'

Jenna shook her head and laughed again, this time with genuine humor. The diamond teardrop in her ear winked in the passing light.

'Normalcy gets boring after a while. I missed the girls, the extravagance, and the unreality of it. There's nothing like the Society in the real world.'

'That's a fortunate thing for some,' I said. 'Celeste's is a dangerous place to get trapped in.'

I pulled into the underground garage, brought the car to a halt, then slid out to open her door. Smiling slightly, I stood aside for her to step out.

'The elevators are this way.'

Our heels tapped a single rhythm as we made our way across the deserted garage toward the elevator. Once inside, she stood against one wall and I another. My eyes drank their fill of her, moving slowly over the cap of tight hair that danced above arching eyebrows to the high forehead, glowing with a layer of sweat. Her eyes closed to put some temporary distance between us, but the tiniest flicker of her lashes betrayed the effort. Fine brown skin plumped over well-made cheekbones, framing a nose that was too low for some, but perfect for her. The pulse beat steadily at her throat.

'What did Celeste say when you told her you wanted to leave?' I asked.

Jenna's eyes slowly opened. 'She didn't say anything.'

I watched her, looking for any trace of a lie, but I found none. Celeste *had* led her to believe that she was free.

The elevator stopped its ascent, and sighed to a halt, opening into my sitting room.

'Come.'

We walked in together, with my hand nestled in the small of her back. Behind us, the elevator doors slid closed. The dull metallic sound of my purse hitting the glass surface of a nearby coffee table seemed to startle her. She stepped away from me and moved across the carpeted floor.

'Where's your bedroom?' she asked. Her bravado couldn't quite hide the faint tremor in her voice. Here, in the dark seclusion of my apartment, everything changed. The romance of the evening was over.

'This way.' The prepared room was at the north end of the hall, as far from the elevators as possible. The window took up an entire wall and the curtains were parted to let in the moonlight which ribboned across the expanse of burgundy carpet to the white satin of the bed. The door closed with a soft click behind us.

With the darkness and moonlight enfolding us, I brought her hand to my mouth and kissed her fingers, one by one, stroking the tip of each with my tongue and inhaling the slight scent of champagne and sweat that they carried.

'Did you ever think that she would come back for you?' I asked. A brush of my hands pulled the dress from her shoulders where it pooled at her waist, accentuating her slight breasts and the dark tips that trembled with each breath she took.

'I thought she might try and find me, but I had hoped...' Her voice trembled again.

'Foolishly.'

'Yes, foolishly. But I'm glad it's you.' She put her arms around my neck and kissed my throat. 'I'm glad it's you.'

I bent my head to hers. On the bed, our bodies flowed into each other. We found a rhythm, natural and sweet, that brought me pleasure and made her cry out against my shoulder. Jenna never felt the blade that pierced her damp flesh, found her racing heart and stopped it. She gasped her last breath into my mouth as her body trembled in orgasm, then was still. Her hands slid from around my neck as her head fell back, baring the moist, fragrant skin of her throat. As her cheek touched the white satin, a line of crimson slipped from her mouth.

'That was beautifully done,' said a voice just beyond the bedroom door.

I didn't bother to look up. With a hand beneath her shoulders and another against the cool sheets, I lowered Jenna's body to the bed and pulled the coverlet over her. Then I turned around to speak to Celeste. She came further into the room and held out a well-padded envelope. I had told her that I don't work for free, not even for family.

'Thank you. I enjoyed it.' My voice didn't rise above a whisper, so she had no choice but to come closer to the bed. When she stepped fully into the light, a dark Madonna in a simple blue sheath and diamonds, I saw that she was smiling. The envelope fell into my hands.

'I thought you might.'

'You know my tastes well. She was perfect.'

My sister nodded and turned to go. She never once looked at Jenna.

'We should do this again soon.' Her dreadlocks swayed with each sinewy movement of her back, brushing against the curves of her hips and buttocks.

'You know where to find me.'

The diamond circlet imprisoning the rich darkness of her hair winked as she disappeared beyond the doors. A moment later, three women came in and went to Jenna. I watched with faint regret as they left together, cradling her body against their dark breasts, heads down as if whispering low something only she could hear.

Owl-blasted
Julie Travis

Owl-blasted
Julie Travis

1

They were lost.

They were right in the middle of London – Alice's home town – and she didn't know where they were. Harry sipped his drink and gave her his best reassuring smile, but it was weak and unconvincing. After dinner by the river they had wandered into the City, zig-zagging down passages and alleyways as the fancy took them, until they ended up outside a dingy old pub. It had made for an atmospheric walk, but the deserted streets spooked them and the pub seemed to offer refuge. Alice was surprised to see it – she thought the City was full of wine bars and bistros these days, that something this old, this genuine, didn't exist here any more. And she was sure no City pub opened this late – the area closed down when the workers went home.

Through the murky lighting she could see figures on bar stools turning to glare at them: strangers were not welcome here. She had wanted to leave straight away but Harry had herded her to a corner table. A burned-down candle sat in the centre, giving a dribble of light. 'One drink,' he'd said, 'then we'll go.' The place was almost gothic. Alice glanced at the drinkers around the bar, trying to see if they were just grumpy old regulars or hostile younger men, but they were no more than shapes in the shadows. They were watching, paying particular attention to Harry. Alice couldn't tell if they had realised he was queer; if so, there would be trouble. She was often mistaken for his girlfriend and it had saved him from more than one beating, but she got the feeling it would not save him tonight.

Still, Harry seemed determined to stay put and, when the door opened again, the attention was diverted from them and Alice started to relax. An argument began at the bar in slurring voices and they looked up to see a man pushing a woman away from him. The woman turned around and caught Alice's eye, staggered over and sat next to her.

'Wassyername?' She was young, twenty-five or so, but her face looked aged. It was round and red, bloated and weathered by drink. She became suddenly aggressive and shook her fist at some unseen enemy. Harry finished his drink and nodded towards the door but the woman grabbed Alice's arm before she could get up.

'I seen things. *Bad things.* I drink to forget them but I could remember them for you if you like.'

The man she had been arguing with glared at them and took a step forward. The candle on a nearby table threw light and shadows up at him, giving him a demonic expression. Alice guessed his age at about forty. He was short and stocky and looked as if he had been carved from stone.

Alice removed the woman's hand from her arm, shook her head and dodged around her. They went outside and tried to get their bearings. As they each pointed in different directions, a commotion began in the alleyway alongside the pub. It was the couple from the bar: the man was dragging the woman out of a side exit. He threw her to the ground.

'What did you tell them? You stupid bitch, what did you say?' He was raging.

Before she could answer he began punching her. His solid fist rammed into her face and head like a hammer. For a few moments Alice and Harry just stood there and Alice knew he was weighing up the situation, thinking exactly what she herself (to her shame) was thinking: Was the woman worth it? The pair of them were probably no match for such a thug, who would be even more dangerous in his drunken state than sober. Alice was still finding excuses not to intervene when the man stopped and disappeared back through the door.

He had left the woman for dead. Alice approached the prone body. She couldn't find a pulse but it looked as if her chest was rising and falling. They needed to find help.

Harry grabbed her hand. 'This way,' he said softly, and pulled Alice along with him.

The streets were silent except for their footsteps, which ricocheted around the walls. Alice wanted more than anything to see a main road, the bright lights and noise of Liverpool Street Station, but there were only more side streets and the feeling of being *under observation*. And then they were in a courtyard. Crumbling blocks of flats rose up on three sides and the ground beneath was uneven, slimy with things Alice didn't want to imagine. The place smelt of neglect and ruin. They turned to go and there, by the rotten wooden gates, the only exit, stood the man who had just beaten a woman unconscious, or possibly to death. He was holding something in his arms. A baby, of all things. It boded well. Harry relaxed and sauntered towards them.

'Took a wrong turning, mate. Can you point us in the direction of Bishopsgate?'

The man stared at Harry. 'You fucking faggot.' He stood there, unblinking, and Alice felt her mouth go dry with fear. The man spat on the ground as if he knew this and wanted to show how brave he was in comparison.

He spoke again. 'What did she say to you?'

Alice shrugged. 'She wanted a drink. I said no.'

'I told you, Caleb,' said another voice. 'She said nothing. You beat her to a pulp for nothing. You worry too much.'

Someone else was there, hiding in the courtyard. Harry looked anxiously around. As the gentle, high-pitched voice continued, they saw movement in the man's arms. It was the baby. The baby, no more than eight months old, was speaking.

'But what does it matter, Caleb? They wouldn't have believed a drunk, no one believes a drunk. And nobody would believe them.' The baby pushed the cradling arms aside, jumped down to the floor and paced up and down as if it were thinking. These were no toddling steps. It walked like an adult. A tiny adult in a baby-gro. It was horrible, frightening, but in a different situation it would have been comical.

The man – Caleb – spoke again. 'You fucking disgusting poof! I'm going to beat your slack arse.' He began undoing his belt.

The baby stopped pacing and looked up at him, its expression one of amusement. 'Do you want to hit him? It seems to me you'd rather fuck him.' It climbed back into his arms and put its tiny face right up against Caleb's. 'After all you've seen, you're still frightened by a homosexual. You really are as stupid as you look.'

The baby fell silent and Alice heard Harry murmur, *'What? What has he seen?'*

The baby showed no indication of having heard him. It sat back in Caleb's arms and addressed them. 'A loyal subject but a dim-witted one. His lack of imagination will be his undoing.' It shrugged, dismissing the problem. 'Go out of here and turn left. Keep going and you will find the main road.'

As they fled towards safety they heard Caleb calling, spurring them on. 'Run as fast as you like, you're both damned anyway.'

2

A month later, Harry turned up at Alice's house in a state of panic, claiming to have seen Caleb in a club. It was the first time either of them had spoken of that night. They had walked in on something unexplainable, too strange to bring up in any kind of conversation, although Alice had privately scoured the local newspapers in a vain search for news of the woman Caleb had attacked. Now Harry told her how he had hidden in the club and watched Caleb systematically trawl its four bars. He was sure the man was looking for him. He had asked around – Caleb was a new face and had been noticed in several bars.

Alice was not surprised. 'He was obviously a closet case. Thugs can be gay too, you know. Or are you believing your own stereotypes now?'

But Harry was not comforted and was too frightened to go home. He spent the night on Alice's sofa. The next morning, over breakfast, they talked again.

'OK, let's suppose that he is just a frustrated, fucked-up closet case,' said Harry. 'I don't want him on the scene. Sooner or later he'll pick someone up. Then what will he do? Take him home to meet the woman he battered – if she's still alive, that is – and that weird baby thing?'

'Look,' said Alice. 'You're a familiar face. The barmen, the doormen – they all know you. Talk to them. You can find out if he's been asking after you and you can tell *them* he's a psycho. Then keep away from the scene for a couple of weeks. They can deal with him, or maybe he'll just move on.'

Harry agreed to her plan, but later, after he'd gone, she thought about the situation. It was making less sense to her now: Caleb had had his chance to do Harry damage when they first met; and he didn't strike Alice as the type who would ever be able to handle being surrounded by queens, however far out of the closet he might come. So she could see Harry's point. Caleb belonged to another world, a scary place neither of them understood or ever wanted to see again. He would be as uncomfortable in their world as they were in his.

And then Harry disappeared. He was supposed to meet Alice for a drink one Saturday night, and when he didn't show up she assumed he'd met some guy and was spending the weekend in bed, but when he didn't call to give her the gory details she began to worry. She went to his flat and he wasn't there. There was mail piled up outside his room. If he'd gone away, then he hadn't told anyone. His flatmates hadn't seen him for ten days, when he'd gone out on a date. Alice rang his parents and a few friends, but no one had heard from him and no one knew whom he'd been going to meet. She thought about calling the police. But there was one more chance: she went to the club where Harry had seen Caleb. One of the barmen remembered Caleb, but hadn't seen him in over a week. The coincidence was too strong to ignore. She reported Harry to the police as a missing person. Of Caleb and their strange experience in the City, she told them as much as she thought they'd believe. And then she waited.

3

When a person goes missing, there is always the hope that they are alive, somewhere, but not knowing keeps their loved ones in limbo. It leaves family and friends unable to grieve, for there is nothing to grieve for, but unable to move on, forever waiting.

A year passed and Alice had not seen or heard from Harry. She felt time drag by, more than once spending the whole day watching the hands of a clock make their way around the dial; but then she would suddenly realise that months had passed. A lot can happen in a year: a relationship began and then ended, a friend went overseas to work and travel, and a young uncle died; but Alice had no best friend to tell. Part of her, the optimistic part, imagined that Harry had met the man of his dreams that night and been whisked off to a wonderful new life, but mostly she was realistic. And eventually she wished for the news that he was dead, just so that it would be over and she could begin to live again.

Then one day Alice walked through Liverpool Street Station and found herself at the spot where fourteen months ago Harry had hugged her in relief and celebration at finding their way back to safety. She thought about Harry all the time, but now instead of sadness she felt anger. She had a huge sense of guilt for not preventing his disappearance. The possibility that Caleb might have been on the prowl for her best friend had been too awful for her to take as seriously as she should have done. Guilt had hung around her neck for more than a year, and she was tired of it. Alice didn't know if the police had questioned Caleb or had even found the pub where she and Harry first saw him. It occurred to her now to look for it herself. It was midweek, lunchtime, the day bright and sunny. The City was busy, alive with people going about their business. If she was to try to find the pub – get its name, its location, something to badger the police with – then today would be as good and safe a time as any. She had to do something. To show Harry she hadn't forgotten him. So she went.

She turned west off Bishopsgate, wanting to search the area between there and Moorgate systematically, but the cartography was so haphazard it was impossible, and she was soon lost. She wandered on, turned a corner, and was suddenly standing in front of the pub. It looked smaller, as if cowering from the sunlight. She took in the split timber beams, the chipped lead window seals, the peeling paint. It was decrepit, crumbling under its own weight and age. Even the pub's name, The Old Familiar, and signpost, showing a medieval woodcut of a man dressed in a black smock leading a goat, seemed to acknowledge that the building's time was in the past. Alice shivered; the temperature had dropped a few degrees, the light had dimmed a little.

She assumed the sun had gone behind a cloud but, when she looked up, the sky was completely clear. Except for the sun. The midday sun was setting. It was racing across the sky as if in a desperate hurry to be gone. The light faded fast, late afternoon and twilight passing in a matter of minutes, and she was left, on what had been a summer's day, with the cold and dark of a winter's night.

In the distance was a sound. It had been there all the time, but now Alice focused on it. It was not machinery, as she had first thought, but a wailing voice, a mournful, despairing sound. A warning, perhaps, to leave now, while she was still able. Alice realised how foolish it had been to come back, but she felt stubborn, unwilling to run away, although she was close to panic. Instead she did either the bravest or the most stupid thing of her life and walked into the pub, knowing Caleb would be there. And he was there, sitting at the bar – and next to him was Harry.

4

They were all there. In a corner sat the woman whom Caleb had nearly killed. She looked bruised and scarred, even beneath the puffiness caused by drink. On her lap sat a baby. When Alice's eyes had adjusted to the light in the bar she looked at it properly. Recognition registered on its rounded face. It gave her a curious look before returning to suckle milk from the woman's breast. That it was the baby who had spoken in the courtyard, Alice had no doubt. It had not grown, or changed, in all of that time. None of them had.

It was a macabre gathering. There was her friend – whom she'd given up for dead – alive and apparently well. Alice had dreamt of seeing Harry again, of his emotional return. But it was never supposed to be like this. His eyes barely moved from the spot on the floor that he was staring at. There was no joy, no surprise, at seeing her. No expression at all. He was sitting with Caleb like they were old friends. At least, that's how it appeared at first. Then Caleb got up. He held a dog leash. The thick chrome chain led up towards Harry's head and as Harry turned around Alice saw that it disappeared into the flesh at the back of his neck. The chain had been implanted, the last link closing around the top of the vertebrae.

The baby stopped guzzling milk. 'He is Caleb's pet now,' it explained. 'He's very obedient. He doesn't need a leash, not really, but Caleb gets so insecure. He needed a sign of… *commitment.*' The baby smiled, and for one moment Alice thought it was going to gurgle. 'You also needed a sign. As you can see, your friend is alive, and it is not your fault he is here. So now you can go.'

'Just what is going on?' Alice demanded of the babe.

'This is our own little piece of Hell. It's not much, but we call it home.' The baby's tone was sarcastic. It looked up at the woman.

'Yes, Jarmara, my little master,' said the woman, getting up and carrying him towards Alice. Her breast flopped out of her shirt. She seemed unaware of it.

'This is a house of lost souls,' continued the infant. 'They have been here always, and they will be here forever.'

Alice looked at the woman. 'Why don't you just go?'

Jarmara laughed. 'All roads lead back here, one way or another. Look at her – is she chained, is she fettered? No. She is free to leave whenever she chooses. Though she could walk and walk, she would still return here. Caleb is another matter. He can be a law unto himself, or so I let him believe occasionally. Your friend made him restless. So I thought Caleb should go and get him. But he was happy to come back. After all, where else would you find all *this*?'

The baby held his palms up to the air. Tiny beads of light

appeared from his pudgy skin and began to rotate, as if juggling themselves. The lights grew to the size of tennis balls. One darted out of the circle and rolled past Alice. She caught a glimpse of a grinning face staring out, before the light sped back to the circle, which spun faster and faster until it fused together and then burst. Alice felt drenched but warm, as if she had been caught in a summer shower. Around her the pub exploded into life. Blue tobacco smoke rolled in the air, seats that had been vacant a moment earlier were now occupied by drunken men and women. Through the raucous laughter and the smoke haze Alice could see Caleb, young and smiling, happy, with a group of men at the bar.

The door banged open and entertainers walked in: a court jester, a dwarf, a puppeteer. They mingled with the crowd. The puppeteer opened his bag and out jumped a miniature Wolf, Red Riding Hood and Grandma. They chased each other around, dodging stools and people's legs, until Grandma jumped onto a drinker's foot and climbed deftly up his leg and stomach to reach the table. The Wolf pursued her, with Red Riding Hood close behind. The people at the table laughed, delighted at the show. Grandma ran towards the far side of the table, but the Wolf was quick. It bounded across, caught her in its mouth and shook her, then dropped her onto the tabletop and tore into her. Bright red blood squirted across the table. Red Riding Hood dropped to her knees and howled with grief and Alice, in horror, realised that these were not wooden puppets after all, but real miniature creatures.

The jester and the dwarf were holding their own performance. The jester took a powder from his pocket and tipped it into a man's tankard. It fizzed and bubbled and sparks flew into the air like fireworks. He gestured for the man to drink. The man laughed and shook his head. The jester grabbed him by the hair, forced open his mouth, and the dwarf tipped the liquid down his throat. He coughed and spluttered, then held his stomach in pain. His friends leaned away from him at the sound and smell of his bowels emptying. He vomited and, exhausted, fell face first into it. Everyone began to laugh and cheer again. The man sat back up and joined in the laughter, despite the vomit splattered over his face and chin and the stench of his soiling. The three entertainers bowed and, as they stood up again, Alice saw the jester smiling, but the expression on his face was more like contempt, his lips pulled back over his gums like a dog about to attack.

Alice was suddenly aware that he was looking at her. 'You see?' he said, his voice clear despite the hubbub of people drinking. 'This is a wonderful place to be. There is so much more to the world, you just cannot imagine. New landscapes, new horizons. Cities of blood. Blood and piss and shit – the fundamental elements of life and the fundamental elements of death. Dark kingdoms where the sun never shines, where you dare not sleep for dreaming, or waking to find the devil feasting on your heart.' He swept his arm around the room. 'These people here are happy. There is entertainment, the drink flows without end. They think they've found utopia, ultimate wisdom. They believe they're the lucky ones, that these crumbling walls are made of gold and the smell of shit is the scent of a bloom from paradise. And why not? They are not fit for anything else.' The jester walked out of the door with his fellow entertainers. Flashes of light passed through Alice again and the pub was back to normal. Jarmara's arms rested by his sides, the last beads of light disappearing into his skin.

The performance – whatever magic the baby had produced – was over. Alice looked around. Harry was on his knees, lapping water from a bowl, with Caleb looking on like a proud pedigree owner.

Then Jarmara indicated for the woman to take him back to their gloomy corner, and there was a look of pride on her face as she walked away. Released, Alice stepped out of the damp, dark building to warmth and dazzling brightness, desperately grateful to be outside again. She made her way to the main road, then called the police and told them where Harry was. She didn't tell them the condition he was in; she didn't have the words to explain it.

She went home and paced her room for hours, as long as she could stand, then rang the City police station. Harry was there. He was free.

Alice wanted to cry, cheer, ring everyone he'd ever met to tell them the news. She knew she should at least tell his parents, but she wanted to see him first, hug him, be sure he was real. So she drank coffee and smoked her first cigarette in a long time. And then she went to bring Harry home.

5

The police station was quiet when Alice walked in. Momentarily. Then the appalling smell of burning flesh settled on her like a blanket, and the noise: a mixture of people screaming and a screeching so powerful that it felt like a physical assault on her ears. A shape appeared and flung itself at her. Alice instinctively ducked down and the figure jumped over her and ran full pelt into the door. It collapsed by her side and Alice rolled away.

It was a policeman. His head was bleeding and his nose looked broken. This chaos could only mean one thing: Jarmara was here.

Alice knew Harry might already be dead. Although it was pointless heroics to press on, she could not leave him here. She found her way to the cells, where the screeching was even louder. A policeman stood in a cell doorway. He was saying something, but she couldn't make out what, then he fell forward. Something had been holding him up by his head – Alice saw a long, thin appendage disappearing into the cell and, as the man hit the ground, a charred hole in the back of his head, smoke rising from the wound.

Alice stepped forward and looked through the doorway. The woman from the pub was in there, hanging, levitating it seemed, in midair. Then the sunlight glinted on taut steel wires, running from the ceiling to a chrome frame like a skeletal hand with its fingers buried in the woman's skull. A figure sat on the bunk behind her. It was brown like overcooked meat, and humanoid, with a long neck and a face that projected forward, like a trumpet. It bared pure white teeth at her and as it opened its mouth a little more, so the unbearable noise moved up a notch. The frame tightened, the hand increasing its grip. The woman was being punished. She was alive, conscious, sobered by pain to a state of complete clarity.

There was movement in the corridor. Alice forced her gaze from the horrors of the cell. It was Harry. He stood just a few yards from her, with his arms outstretched, pleading to be taken away. Alice reached out towards him, feeling, for a moment, that she could close the gap between them, and then Harry staggered backwards. He dropped to his knees; standing behind him was Caleb, holding the leash, a sneering laugh on his face. He jerked the chain violently and walked away with Harry on all fours struggling to keep up.

The noise stopped. The sudden silence was a shock. Alice turned back to the cell. Something was happening to the creature; it was shrinking. Its skin became pale, its teeth moved up into its gums. The trumpet face pulled back, the long neck shrank down. And there sat the baby, Jarmara. Naked, for a moment looking like any other infant. The woman's body moved, the muscles in spasm. Soon she would be beyond help, without Alice ever having known her name or anything about her.

'Don't fret so,' said Jarmara to Alice. 'I'm only doing it because I love her.' He began to laugh, a baby's giggle.

Caleb came in carrying a towel, which he wrapped carefully around the baby. 'More are coming,' he said to Jarmara. He sounded nervous.

Jarmara lifted his arms and Caleb picked him up. The baby reached out and closed his fist, as if gripping the air. Then he pulled, and the facade of the room tore away like a piece of thin material. In the middle of the room stood a stone archway, an entrance. Dust billowed out of the darkness, catching on thick cobwebs before settling. Caleb whistled as you would for a dog and Harry ran in, carrying the end of the leash in his mouth. Caleb grabbed it, pulled Jarmara protectively against his chest and walked through.

Alice stared at the hole. A breeze was picking up. Torn strips of the room – her reality – trailed across the entrance. The wind was getting stronger, coming from the hole and returning into it. The woman on the steel frame swung on the wires, her body pulled straight – straining against its bonds – by the sucking air. And Alice felt the wind taking her, at first suggesting, then insisting, that she go through the arch, arms flailing, grabbing wildly and missing anything that could have stopped her, until she was through and the light of the police cell was a million miles away.

6

She stopped moving and took in her surroundings. She was in a street. The light was murky, although whether it was dawn or dusk she couldn't tell. There were cobbles underfoot, the building European, medieval. There was no sign of Harry and the others, or of anyone else. She began to walk and saw light in one of the windows. She went to look, creeping across the street so that the occupants would not see her. She moved up to the window. Inside, a family was sitting down for dinner. It looked normal, happy, the people enjoying being together. Then a diabolical scene unfolded. The girl sitting at the far end of the table leaned over and, using a steak knife, cut a chunk of flesh from her mother's arm and put it on her plate before helping herself to vegetables and gravy. The woman did not cry out or flinch, or even pause from the conversation she was having with her husband, who got up and walked around the table to the seat nearest the window, where a small boy sat. He slit the boy's shirt open at the shoulder and began carving slices from his back, then carried the pieces on the end of his knife back to his plate. And so it went on, the family devouring one another.

Alice leaned over to be sick. She put her hand on the wall to balance but at its touch jumped away. It was wet, the wood warm, saturated. She lifted her hand to her face and watched blood drip from her fingers. She looked around. Blood ran down the walls of all the houses, dripped off the roofs and door frames, into the gutters along the street. A stream of blood bubbled over her feet and away, like the aftermath of a torrential downpour. This was the place the jester had spoken of. *One of the places*, she remembered.

She was with the lost souls, as Jarmara had called them; the people who walked on streets covered in their own dirt and waste and thought it was gold. A city of blood, draining the life from its people. Alice ran to a door and began hammering on it.

'Get out, you've got to get out of here!' She was screaming, trying to drown out a voice, a memory of something someone had said to her a lifetime ago.

Doors were opening in the street. People, curious and startled, were coming out to see what the noise was. Even the family Alice had seen were leaving their meal. Alice was babbling now, desperate for someone to understand. She tried to explain and they listened, but only with the pitying ear that anyone gives the insane. Leave? Why should they leave? This was paradise, after all.

Eventually she saw that it was useless. She would not save even one of these people. She pushed past them and ran, looking for a way out, a way back, but knowing it was hopeless. Caleb's voice rang out in her head, telling her she was damned, and she wondered, had he cursed them then, all that time ago? Just when had they been doomed, she and Harry? When they walked into the old pub? Was it later, when they laid eyes on Jarmara for the first time? Or had it always been awaiting them, their fate, since the day they were born?

Alice ran and when she tired she walked, through street after street after street, the stench and the sight and the steam rising from the blood, all filling her senses to overflowing as she made her way through the endless city.

Terminus
Rosie Lugosi

Terminus
Rosie Lugosi

The day I died, you were the first to notice. I would say you were the one to find me, but I wasn't lost. I was on the bus, on my way into town. Knew exactly where I was going; meeting Pat for lunch and discussing the second scene. The lighting wasn't right. Still isn't. Idiots. And you were going to sort out your bank loan. We were passing through Brook's Bar, past the bookies, but before Loreto College. Just at those traffic lights, as they were turning to green, the bus turned left and I passed on.

It was extremely gentle. I barely noticed and neither did you, not until the right turn onto Bonsall Street. The bus took it a bit sharpish, I slumped sideways and ended up with my face in your lap. Not a bad place to be. My place of choice whenever I had the time. I always had the inclination. I felt my cheeks flush.

Its timing was very inconvenient, death. I had a lot of things I wanted to do. Sticking my face into your lap was one of them, but it was down the list. This was 10.30 in the morning. Your lap, inviting as it is, was more 10.30 at night. There were things I had in mind to fill the space in between.

You looked down at me where I'd settled like a sack of carrots. You were blushing: ashamed of me. Admit it, it's OK. I know I was always one to be easily offended, but considering how things are with me now, taking offence is the last thing on my mind. I saw you flick your head nervously to the right, trying to work out who might have noticed my sidelong collapse.

You jabbed at my shoulder, grunted my name quietly so no one could overhear. That's when I realised you had no idea I was dead. And if I'm being honest, that's when it sunk in for me, too. I was dead. And what on earth was I going to do about it?

You jiggled my shoulder again. Here I was, Going Too Far as

usual, falling against you on the bend like a big kid. You hissed my name, more irritated now you'd got over your initial surprise. *Will you stop it now.* You didn't have to say a word; I knew that's what you were thinking. Death does that; makes it possible to read thoughts. But the phrase *reading thoughts* is a cliché, and I'll bet not one coined by someone possessed of telepathic skills. It's not so much reading as feeling, like a faint electrical current, subtle as putting your tongue on the end of a torch battery. So, I felt what you were thinking.

Needless to say, I didn't budge. No stifled giggle of oh-what-a-naughty-girl, twisting my head round to look up at you sheepishly. I was lying doggo. Playing dead. Or so you thought. You paused, and I felt the beginnings of anxiety stirring. Your next shove was more exploratory; I felt your thoughts pick up speed. You were wondering, Has she fainted? Is she going to be sick? How am I going to clean it off my trousers? They're good ones, got them from the Karen Millar sale, and they were still pricey even then.

This rankled, your wondering a shade too much about your trousers and a shade too little about my state of health. It was a new side of you, one I resolved to talk to you about – not that I'd lose my temper, you understand – when I remembered I wasn't going to be talking to you about anything, ever again.

I was thinking about how sad this was and how lonely I was going to be when I was shaken once more, both physically and by the force of your emotions. You'd decided I'd fainted, and were trying to wake me up. I was pleased to notice that you'd stopped worrying about your trousers. You'd also stopped feeling embarrassed. Now that I was clearly sick (ill) rather than sick (perverted) you could relax and face the others on the bus with confidence. Call for help, ask if there was a doctor on board. This bothered me too. As if you'd rather I was stricken with disease than stricken with playfulness. I let it pass.

'My friend's ill,' you said to the woman on your right. She'd been staring at us for the past five minutes and her feelings were a bubbling pan of nosiness. 'Can you help?'

Now that I have a lot of time for reflection, I fail to understand those among the ranks of the dead who insist on hanging around the living. It's the onslaught of their interminably boring thoughts. Not only was I exposed to every quiver of your feelings, but also this woman's and those of every single person on the bus, like an emotional Doppler effect, fainter and fainter the further they sat from me. I couldn't shut it out either, still can't. It's like driving past a freshly manured field. You can wind the window up as fast as you like but the stink gets in somehow.

'Can you help?'

You said it again, with more of a squeak in your voice. But your fellow passenger was only geared up for curiosity, not community support. She blinked at you a few times, looked at my back (as that's all that was visible) and staggered to her feet, pressing the bell and muttering that This Was Her Stop. She couldn't get down the stairs fast enough. And she was lying. She hung around downstairs for the next three stops, and I could hear every internal bleat of her attempts to justify her arseholeness to herself. *I would have helped, honestly, but I've got so much to do.*

You swivelled round on the seat, trying not to tip me off your knee. Bloody right too. Have you ever had your nose pressed into the floor of a bus? It's disgusting, and being dead didn't make me care any the less.

As our collective crap luck would have it, the top deck of the bus was almost empty, and the moment you turned round, those few who were there stuck their faces deep into their free morning papers, or gazed determinedly out of the window. The bloke on the back seat even pretended to be asleep, but his thoughts reached me loud and clear: *Don'tbothermedon'tbotherme.*

'Can't anyone help?'

Shuffle shuffle. Bloody hell, I thought. Why did you bother feeling so self-conscious, you silly woman? Look at them all. Cringing into their seats.

I knew you were close to tears now, and trying hard to hold it together. I wanted to tell you *It's all right*, but it was all wrong and I was the cause of it. I was also getting distracted by a new sensation. Heat. I was feeling hot, and getting hotter. At first I had thought it was lying so close to your thighs that was making me steam up. Now it was dawning on me that the longer I was dead, the hotter I was getting. From the first blush when I keeled over, to this.

It was torment. You try lying in a bloody uncomfortable position, boiling hot and unable to move an inch. I was sweating heavily, could feel it collecting between my legs and under my arms. Surely this had to be uncomfortable for you. It's one thing having a dead girlfriend sprawled over your lap, it's another having a hot sweaty dead girlfriend. You had to notice soon, and I wanted you to shift me into a more comfortable position. So the dead are selfish. So get over it.

You were smoothing my hair in a preoccupied way. From the tumble of your thoughts, I'd guess it was to comfort yourself rather than me, but it was nice anyway. It distracted me from the furnace I was in, and I wasn't about to start complaining. The living don't stroke corpses so affectionately as a rule. Then your hand stopped in mid-caress. Became an exploratory grope. Fingers laid flat on my forehead. At last, I thought, you've noticed.

'Oh my God, she's *cold*.'

No, I'm not, you pillock, I wanted to shout, I'm bloody melting my arse off here. Open a window, will you, someone?

'Oh shit. Oh fuck.'

And that was when it hit you. The whole damn thing. Like a kung-fu movie slow-motion punch that connects with the jaw, *crash*, the head swings up, *bang*, and then the arms go flying out, *wallop*, and then it all speeds up to normal time. *Oh. My. God. Ohmygodohmygod.* Dead.

'Jesus, no. No.'

Oh Jesus yes, yes. You were a mess of fear, confusion, remorse, guilt, anger, shame. And I was hot. What had I got to complain about? You started shaking; tears or terror I never found out. Maybe I should have guessed the truth then. It's too late now.

Finally, finally we got to the bus station at Piccadilly Gardens and finally, finally someone took some notice. Not the passengers; they fell over themselves to get off, couldn't get away fast enough from this off-her-head woman with the terrified eyes, cradling the body that had muff-dived into her crotch. I heard them scramble on to the pavement outside, their sighs of *God, why do they let nutters onto buses*, one of the more public-spirited muttering to the driver about two drunks upstairs. Thanks a bunch, mate.

The bus driver stumped up the stairs, bad mood radiating before him.

'Get off now, love.'

Pause.

'Come on now, get off, you and your friend.'

You looked at him with those big panicky eyes.

'It's... it's...'

Your hand hovered over my spine, pointing at me. I felt him roll his eyes. *What now: why bleeding well me? Another drunk on the bloody bus and it's not even lunchtime.* Eventually he registered the rabbit-in-headlights-equals-not-pissed look on your face.

'I think she's... she's... so cold,' you peeped.

Once and for all, no I am flaming well not, I screamed at the top of my thoughts. No sound, of course. Oh, what was the point? The driver leaned over me, reeking of tobacco. A set of fingers as subtle as a bunch of sandpaper bananas jammed themselves under my right ear and stayed there far too long for my taste. My skin burned.

'Oh Christ,' he rumbled, his emotions also gearing up into overdrive. 'Hang on there, love, I'll radio for an ambulance.'

And he was off, clumping down the stairwell, leaving us alone.

The ambulance crew were the first ones to be kind to you. They coaxed you out from underneath me, helped you downstairs and out of the bus. They were even reasonably civilised with me, considering that a few moments' concerted pulse-taking and eyelid-lifting confirmed what I'd known for three-quarters of an hour.

They wrestled me down the narrow stairwell and strapped me to a stretcher laid down in the aisle. I lay there, feeling sorry for myself. They pulled an orange blanket over my face and fixed it there with a strap. So it was official. Then they tipped the contraption on to its end and wriggled it out through the swing-back doors, dropped the wheels and manoeuvred me across the pavement.

The curious were hanging around, all the ones who hadn't lifted a finger to help you, but wanted to make bloody sure they didn't miss a second of any excitement. I could feel the damp little fingers of their prurience fumbling over me: *Was she on drugs? Is that what a dead body looks like? Why aren't we allowed to see her face? Is it horribly mutilated?* Christ, the things the living think about. They should get a life.

I looked at you, pressed against the wall, radiating guilt and nausea. Not a scrap of bereavement or loss, which really got to me. You're *supposed* to be heartbroken, *darling*. We've been together five years, remember? Then it occurred to me that, despite the scratchy blanket belted across my forehead, I could still see you. It was such a surprise I made one of those involuntary movements, like a reflex; raised my hands to my face to check the blanket was really there, and thought, how can I move my arms, they're strapped to the stretcher as well.

I went the whole hog. Sat up. I could see, move, perfectly. After the past hour of being jammed into the most uncomfortable position imaginable, it was wonderful. I jumped off the stretcher and watched it being pushed towards the gaping rear doors of the ambulance, with me swaddled up on it like a luminous orange mummy. No one stopped me. It's a strange sensation, watching your own corpse being trolleyed away. I looked down at myself. I was definitely here. I was definitely there as well. The doors slammed, the engine growled, and they were gone. No sirens, no lights, no hurry, as the contents had nowhere urgent to be.

I turned round and caught you staring at the receding vehicle I'd been carried off in. Your nausea had gone, and it was guilt, guilt, guilt. I walked over, drawn to you like ghostly iron filings to a magnet. You didn't, or couldn't see me. This was really starting to piss me off. What, no sadness? No aching loss? No tears, dammit? I rummaged through the jumble sale of your self-pity, confusion, embarrassment, fear, irritation (good God, I couldn't believe you were *that* fucked off about being held up going to the bank) and guilt, guilt, bloody guilt. I hopped from foot to foot in front of you, waving my arms. See me, damn you, I'm right in front of you. It was enough to make anyone fly off the handle. I was melting inside my clothes. Could I get any hotter? This was ridiculous.

Then I got it, loud and clear, like digging down and finding a rancid old raincoat at the bottom of a smelly pile of clothes. Where you were really going, who you were planning on meeting today. Not a bank manager, you bastard. You were thinking of Marian. Bloody fucking bastarding Marian. I might have known, might have just bloody known it. All the lies you must have told ran through me like formaldehyde. And your thoughts now: *Me; Marian. Me, gone. Marian? Marian?* Still shying away from what I knew you wanted to think about but were too chicken shit scared to get close to. Let me spell it out for you, sweetheart. You were wondering how long you could leave it. How big a gap of politeness before you could go for it openly with her. How long a gap would be acceptable for, go on, say it, *mourning*.

Your thoughts were a beacon, a fire I kept returning to, to singe myself on. I didn't want to know, but it was there anyway, digging its way into my head; how long it had been going on, how good the sex was, how you had only been doing it with me to keep me from suspecting, how you thought of her every time I touched you, how bloody convenient I was, with my house and my car and my sodding nice income.

God forgive me, I wanted to hit you. Very hard. Instead, I clenched my slippery fists and boiled. You looked around nervously as if you could sense yourself being observed. *Well, you are*, I screamed hotly in your ear. I'd swear you winced. Just a tiny twinge, but a twinge. Good. You checked your pockets, got out your gloves and put them on. How could you bear to have them on your hands? I looked at my palms; throbbing, dripping with moisture. Then you were off, through the thinning crowd, down the edge of the tram tracks, dragging me with you, hot under the collar and everywhere else.

Every purposeful step you took, I stumbled after. But I don't want to follow you, I whimpered. I want to stop and think for a bit. I'll catch up with you later when I've worked out how to cool down, how to make you wince a whole lot more. But it seemed I didn't have any choice in the matter. You walked; I followed. It was sodding annoying. I planted my feet firmly on the pavement and folded my arms, ignoring my damp armpits. I might as well not have bothered. My feet followed you doggedly, half a dozen paces behind. I grabbed at a litter bin to slow myself down: my hands slid stickily through it. I tried to hang on to passers-by, and my arms melted through them like ice cream. I was glued to you.

I wanted to walk in the opposite direction. Anything to do that. Sweat was pouring down my back. I took a breath and threw myself to the ground, only to feel myself being dragged along the filthy pavement in your wake. You stopped at the kerb; I stopped. The green man showed it was safe to cross and we were off again. Somehow I got to my feet. *Marian*, you were thinking, *Marian*. Not me at all. I knew, once and for all, just how much I hated you. That's what did it.

It was as though all the hate I'd ever felt in my life had been stacking itself up into a patient bonfire, year after year, waiting for this spark to set it ablaze. The heat, the bloody fucking heat, was enveloping me. As I staggered helplessly behind you, I realised with a certainty that the flame which raged inside me, which burned and burned but did not burn me away, was indeed the fire of my final destination.

Little Ironies
Linda Innes

Little Ironies
Linda Innes

How reassuring is it, to have your lover press her dry lips to your skin? How reassuring, to have her whisper moistly into your ear? How reassuring is her whisper that you are dying? It's dead reassuring.

The papery crispness of her voice was the rustle of dried leaves scratching at my skin, but the feel of those words was fetid and dank, as if bacteria were bubbling away beneath, quickening my decomposition. *There's* an irony: 'quickening', as in 'showing signs of life'. You don't often hear of 'quickening' these days. At least I don't. But then I wouldn't. Not me. Not now. Bad girls don't go to heaven. Or if they do, they certainly don't stay long.

There's a lot of white in my life at the moment. White walls, white sheets, white pillows, white nightgown. I used to joke with Gabbi, 'Life's all white.' Once upon a time, this home we've made together meant serenity for us; I found its pale minimalism cool and relaxing, but now its starkness is eye-achingly bright to me. Even when I close my eyes, startling white after-images sear them, as if I've been staring too long into a naked light bulb. I shield my eyes from the glare, noticing that even the skin of my hand seems a translucent white, the veins pale beneath. Soon I'll fade into my nightgown, dissolve into the bed, evaporate into the walls, and then I'll disappear completely. Much against Gabbi's wishes, I won't 'rage against the dying of the light'. When it comes, I'll be delighted to close my eyes. De-lighted. I like that. It will be delightful to slip gently into the darkness. Good night. Better not tell Gabbi that. She and Dylan Thomas are bosom buddies just now. In fact, in the face of tragedy, she has turned poetical.

'My soul mate,' Gabbi tells me again, 'Don't leave me, Michelle.'

The choice is not mine to make. I lend her a brave smile. Poetry, religion and philosophy seem to be sustaining everyone around me. I have become a philosopher: Live and let die. When you gotta go, you gotta go. My number's up, my cards are marked. Time's winged chariot is about to run me down... Life's a bitch, and then you die. The yarn needles of cliché after cliché skitter and scrape against one another, weaving life and death in and out of my mind, all the time dropping more and more stitches. Clickety-click, I'll never be sixty-six. I'm amusing myself with graveyard humour again. Can't mention that to Gabbi either, because she gets upset too easily, and that's the last thing I need at the moment: having to support her when it's all I can do to support my own head.

Oh, yes. I have a lot of support. You'd think I could support my own partner through this trauma, surely? I watch her struggle, but I can't help her any more. I can't be her crutch while she hobbles through this affair, and she can't be mine. It hurts too much. Still, as they say, at least I have family around me. I am lucky! My parents and grandparents are still around. Anxious, outraged, guilty. Dead at heart. Dead where it matters.

'It's not right that you should go before us! If I could get them to take me instead, pet, you know I would,' Grandma says, patting my pale, perfect hand with her mottled, gnarled one. 'It's a criminal shame.'

Grandad nods his bald head, 'Aye, love, if there's owt we can do...'

Dad frowns, because it's all he can do, his small eyes stricken with fear and impotence. He's as helpless as any of us. He always was a man of few words, and now he's speechless. Helpless, speechless, childless too, before long.

My mother sobs, shouts and appeals with God, argues, begs and prays. But somehow God ain't listening, or else She's arguing back, prolonging the agony. I'd sooner it happen now than watch everyone around me fall to pieces. Take me, I'm yours. I must have been very bad in a former life to deserve this. And as Doris would say, '*Que sera, sera...*' Whatever happens... I'm resigned to it. After all, it's not as if I don't know what to expect. In the face of death, there are those who are devastated and wonder what on earth they'll do. There are those who die suddenly without warning or preparation. But I'm not one of them. Been there, seen it, done it. Lucky, aren't I?

Ah, get it over with, I say. *C'est la vie. C'est la mort.* Or should I say, *'C'est la morte'*? That's the dead woman. That could be the word on the streets. That's what they'd say, if I were up and about in the world. 'Bring out your dead,' they could say, tolling a bell, and there'd be the rumble of a tumbrel and my body lumbered into the cart and tumbled into a mass grave. Arms, legs, bones and rags. I was never fond of my body, anyway, so no loss there.

Gabbi will miss my body, though. The salt taste, silk touch, sheer sensuousness of it. She even misses it now. I know that she longs for our coming together: the physical intimacy, the emotional merging and that spiritual climax in what she used to call 'a communion of souls'. I haven't felt like making passionate love just recently. 'Not sure I feel well enough,' I say, but if I'm truthful I'm distancing myself, making the break now so it's not so painful later. 'Get used to it,' I guess I'm saying, *'I'll* have to.'

Gabbi craves more. I can see it in the starved look in her eyes, the urgent feel of her hand on my arm, on my face, on the crisp cotton of the sheet over my legs. She wants to show me that she still loves me, to prove to me that I'm neither ill nor unattractive, but my disassociation reflects all that back on her. She herself feels sick, unattractive, rejected. I am impassive; I can do nothing for her. I'm on my way now. I'm moving off.

'Moving on up. Moving on out. Nothing can stop me...' M People. Mmmmm... people... I remember them...

'I love you, my angel,' Gabbi murmurs, although she hasn't noticed the irony of that either.

'Well, halo and goodbye!' I taunt her, for sheer devilment. I am too bad for this world.

I suddenly find everything ironic. Life's little ironies are startlingly clear to me, in a way that they never have been before.

Mum brings me some wishy-washy broth to 'build up my strength'. For what? Grandad brings chocolate to 'make me feel better'. I don't think so! I'm not ill, I'm just dying to move on. But I smile and thank them, beautifully and politely and wreak my frustration and cynicism on Gabbi. She can take it – and if she can't, so much the better. Let her make the break before it's too late.

I'm not arrogant, but I do think it's a shame that I'm passing on. Not sure what it is that I am passing on, though. I've passed over already. It's not as if I've done anything – left earth-shattering inventions or ideas or made any life-changing discoveries. But I've learnt a lot one way or another. How to read people, how to work people. What love is, what love is not. What a waste of knowledge and experience! And what on earth was the point of acquiring it when I had to leave? It takes a lack of innocence and a degree of experience to see how ironic life is. I wish I were studying A-level Jane Austen now, instead of when I was sixteen: handsome, clever, poor and unable to recognise irony if it slapped me in the face. It's all so obvious now! Irony is everywhere in existence. I think, therefore I am. Not.

This is my *Book of the Dead*. I don't need anyone whispering instructions and expectations into my ear to prepare me for the transition. I'm no learner, no novice, no initiate. I'll take it as it comes – or as I go. I could tell them a thing or two, if anyone would listen. Gabbi will. She gazes deeply, her damp eyes gleaming with the apparition of me reflected in them. She hangs on my every word for a phrase that will act as a lifeline to her, something she can grab onto to reel herself back in to me. She wants a good thick, reliable rope to drag herself hand over hand to me. Something to stop her going under. I don't give her enough rope to hang herself. I throw her the slenderest of threads that she can barely see, let alone catch hold of. It's tenuous, unlike her – she's tenacious. If she catches a thin strand it will break and leave her struggling to keep her head above water and gargling for breath. Threads as thin as my existence won't keep her afloat.

I feel that I have wise words to say but only I can see the wisdom of them. What a truism – or is it just another cliché? Education is wasted on the young. Sixteen was no age to be struggling with French existentialism, either. Absurdism is here and now, and it is certainly absurd to give school kids all that philosophy to try to understand, when their brains are not completely finished growing, when the cerebral lobes are still developing, when there are neural pathways still to be completed.

Give it me now – existentialism – while my synapses are still sparking, while all my wits are about me and after I've lived a full life! Now. Before it's too late.

L'absurde, c'est l'existence. Give me existence any day. There was so much I wanted to do. Wasted life. Wasted afterlife. Waste.

Gabbi's face has crumpled into sorrow again. She is wracked by grief-stricken sobs. More clichés.

'For fuck's sake!' I lose it with her and she is momentarily transfixed with fear. 'Jesus, Gabbi! You're making me miserable! Get a life!'

Her shoulders heave with the effort of trying not to wail. I've forgotten I'm supposed to be kind to her, eggshell-walking through the remains of our relationship. Her eyes are red-rimmed and glassy, her face is blotchy and beginning to bloat. She has the look of a drowned corpse about her: a soaked, unanchored sponge. Tears mingle with a watery mucus trail that's started from her nose. She turns her quizzical, hurt and swollen face to me. I must keep this image of ugliness in my head, so that it won't be so hard to leave her. I just need to work on making it easier for her to let me go.

'You used to be pretty once, and snot doesn't help.' I don't meet her eyes.

Don't get me wrong. I love her, but you have to be cruel to be kind. When I first came back home to join my family again, Gabbi was the first stranger to make me welcome. Yet 'stranger' is the wrong word because she was never strange to me. We felt as if we'd always known one another: we were immediately intimates. Soul mates, as she says. Love at first sight, a marriage made in heaven, and more clichés. We have been together ever since, although not for much longer. I'm not long for this world.

Don't you just love clichés? 'Ooh – heaven is a place on earth!'

Ironically, and shallow as I am, it was Gabbi's face and body I first fell for. I was blind to her good nature, her spirituality. I went for her corporeal self: her fuckability. Her innocent white shirt and trousers belied the lusciousness of her body beneath: her plump, raspberry-nippled breasts; her slim, easily encircled waist; her ripe-to-be-fucked juiciness. Once tasted, not shy. Gabbi is gorgeous:

shining dark brown curly hair, a cherubic face – what's not to adore? Later, I discovered further depths. In the best fairy-tale tradition, just as she is beautiful, she is thoroughly kind and good. 'A saint,' my mother would say.

You know about saints? Martyrs, most of 'em.

Me? I must confess that I've never been as good as she is and maybe that's my problem. I have been selfish, greedy, jealous with her. Against the law, all that human emotion, they tell me. Can't have that, here. Mortal sins, are they? Punishment, is this? Ah, well – that will change soon enough. Come in, number 69, your time is up. When your number's up... as the cliché goes.

Little shrunken white-haired Grandma with her twisted twig hands and Grandad, his head speckled like a bird's egg– they're the lucky ones. Sturdy, hysterical Mum and silent Dad, too. Steady, mundane. They get to stay together, at least for the foreseeable future. Not Gabbi and me. We thought we had the perfect love – we thought we'd found our paradise. Maybe that's the trouble: we loved one another too much. We thought we were superior, untouchable. I felt all-powerful with her love, and I swaggered with the strength of it. I didn't need God, nor man. Now I discover there's a price to pay for beatitude. And attitude.

'Give me a bucket,' I say.

'Do you feel sick?' Gabbi cries.

'It's time I kicked it.'

Gabbi's mouth twists in anger and upset. I feel a tiny wrench of pain in my stomach, like a memory.

Life goes on. *La dolce vita.* Sweet life. Honey sweet. Life so sweet it cloys in my throat, clogs the roof of my mouth, makes me sick. Pass me the bucket for real. Although I don't know that I could expel anything: my throat is constricted and swollen, as if I've got an allergic reaction to a bee sting, or I'm allergic to the thought of life and all its sweetness. My vocal chords are thickened and choked tight so I can hardly speak. I can't say what I'll miss. Who I'll miss.

We've got it all worked out. Towards the very end, when everything's been said and done, Gabbi will bring over Peter and he'll see me out of here. He's done it before, although no one speaks of it and everyone turns a blind eye, a deaf ear. We are all wise monkeys, but nobody mentions evil, of course. I want this to happen under my own terms, although the very action feeds into everyone's impression of me as wilful and selfish. In readiness I have taken particular care to arrange it all with Peter, because I don't trust Gabbi in this respect. I trust her with my life, but not with my death. It's the best and quickest way, and it's what I want. For myself, I'm ready now and I'd welcome Peter's assistance right away, but Gabbi will cling. She'll cling to what there was, rather than to what there is now. Gabbi would have me hanging on here forever, way past my natural time, way past my usefulness, past my sell-by date. She'd say it was for my sake, but it would be her one small selfishness: keeping me here would make her happy. Happy, is she? With me, here and now? Even I can see that her misery is profound and tangible. In fact I can taste it, like rising bile. I wish she didn't look so bloody miserable all the time.

She brings me white lilies because she knows they're my favourite. I love their architectural grace, their minimalist white simplicity, their art deco grandeur and the fact that they're funeral flowers.

'Ah, funerals – just to get us in the mood!' I breeze. Gabbi stiffens, which makes me laugh. I'm the stiff, after all.

'I could have got you something more gaudy... but I thought you liked them...' Her voice trails off.

'Let me reciprocate! I'll get some flowers for you, Gabs, Michelle-mess daisies! Pushing up daisies for ya – pushing them your way, babe.'

She leaves me to my own devices. Probably gone off to cry somewhere, for a change.

She returns again and again to the same question: 'How long will I have to wait before you come home? Back to me, back to Heaven?'

She says she understands my wickedness, but that doesn't stop her suffering. I've told her it's just another rite of passage, like puberty without the acne. As far as I've been told, and as far as I remember from last time, all that will happen is that I'll say goodbye to my loved ones, move out of the light and down a dark tunnel, experience momentary excruciating pain, and be reborn. I won't remember anything of this. It won't have left a lasting impression on my soul, and it's perhaps this fact which devastates Gabbi most of all. That's life, Soulmate.

'You are an angel, Gabrielle.' I stroke a strand of hair from her eyes. 'I'm dying to see you again.'

Your Ghost
Kim Watson

Your Ghost
Kim Watson

You once told me that houses are sensitive and absorb energy from their inhabitants, which is stored in the walls, the roof and even the foundations. Sometimes this energy is released when someone awakens a component of what has been absorbed. This awakening can be triggered by anything – a familiar song, a fight, an accident, the opening of an old door, and the opening of a closed mind.

I had just moved into my new house after a bit of bad luck. Anna had left me for Cassie, a twenty-one-year-old blonde fitness instructor. I was a twenty-seven-year-old mousy, flabby, new media consultant. No contest, as far as Anna was concerned.

It was my first night in my new home and when I'd unpacked the essentials (and hurriedly eaten a cheese and tomato sandwich) I decided to sit a while in each room and take in my new surroundings. I had moved from a flat, shared with Anna, into a two-bedroom Victorian terrace. The space felt liberating and I breathed a huge sigh of contentment as I went from room to room crooning, 'This is all, this is all, this is all mine.'

I was leaving the bathroom when I noticed the loft door and decided to take a look. 'I'll probably fall off the ladder and break my fucking neck, knowing my luck,' I muttered as I climbed up and hauled myself inside.

It was a large loft and the previous owners appeared to have left some things behind: an old standard lamp with a bent shade that looked like velvet but was given its texture by layers of dust; a big black leather trunk and some wooden packing cases. I trod carefully across the beams, avoiding the hardboard that someone had put down but not fixed. At the back was a cupboard door that turned out to be padlocked. The packing cases were full of china, silverware and crystal glasses – much like the things my grandmother used to bring out for our Sunday evening teas, during which I'd heard many stories about London in World War II.

I flipped open the locks on each side of the trunk and pushed up the lid. The reek of stale dust and mothballs engulfed my nostrils. My throat constricted and then I sneezed all over the contents of the chest – just a black velvet coat with a claret silk lining and a large leather-bound black book. I put the coat aside and picked up the book, scraping dust off the cover with a tissue from my pocket. It was a diary of sorts, belonging to an Evelyn Johns of this address. The first few entries were fairly routine but there were parts that intrigued me.

15 April 1940: 'Went to the Nags with Lily tonight. It was so rare a treat for us to be alone at last. Dorothy and Harry are good kids and I love them like I might one day love my own, but I also love having Lily to myself sometimes.'

Then, about thirty pages on, I reached an entry that grabbed my attention. It was dated 28 October 1940 and read:

'A terrible tragedy has hit us today. Lily was walking home late with the kids along Shernhall Street, when the sirens went off. They were all guided to an Anderson shelter in a garden on Marlowe Road. An hour later three high explosives fell in the area: one on Forest Road by the Technical College, one on the junction of Shernhall Street and The Drive, killing a nun, and at nearly ten o'clock the last landed in Marlowe Road. At first there were no casualties from the Marlowe Road bomb. Lily and the little 'uns left the Anderson shelter unhurt. They were guided to apparent safety across what looked like a shallow crater. They did not see it for what it was – a camouflet. The three of them, plus another woman, were engulfed by the fall of loose earth at the top of the camouflet. The Home Guard and wardens have been digging through the night but bodies still haven't been found. I fear the worst – that I have lost my dear Lily and her two little angels.'

The entries about this incident continued every day for many weeks.

4 November: 'They are still digging and will continue to dig back to the virgin clay if they have to.'

12 November: 'I went back to the site at Marlowe Road. They are still digging and still no sign of the bodies. My poor Lily is still down there.'

Then the entry dated 12 December reported the sad discovery. 'After ten weeks of digging back, down and around the area, the bodies of Lily, Dorothy and the woman have been found. But Harry's body was nowhere to be seen. Digging has now ceased and we will bury the bodies in two days.'

'How do you survive such a thing?' I asked aloud as I read on.

I gathered that Lily had been married to a man who died in the early stages of the war, when she was pregnant with her second child. Evelyn had moved into Lily's home shortly after they met, while both working for the Volunteer Fire Service. After the tragedy, Evelyn continued her moving account, which had me gripped until the abrupt end of the book. The last entry was dated 4 April 1941 and read, 'My heart won't mend and my head has grown muddled. I am so alone in this cruel world and wish one of those flying bombs would hit this house and put me out of my misery. I cannot live like this. I wish to be with Lily, Harry and Dorothy, now.'

It ended there.

'Bloody hell! Did she kill herself?' I exclaimed, as I placed the book back in the trunk. Just as I closed the lid, I felt cold air blow across the back of my neck. Turning with a start, I saw that the light bulb was swaying gently, casting light on the cupboard door. Maybe I'd find more in there? I prised away at the rusty lock until it fell to the floor; the door was stiff but eventually opened out for me.

A blinding light poured out through the door... I saw a huge hole in the roof and then you appeared like a vision of that woman at the beginning of Hollywood movies, minus the torch. A slight wind had caught your hair, the sun gleamed behind you, turning it golden, and your dark brown eyes stared intensely. Your pale skin was flattered by your sleeveless flowery dress and the skirt flapped in the wind.

As I stood staring in amazement, it was you who spoke first.

'You better watch out what you wish for in life, dear... That was the hole left by the nose section of a flying bomb. I was downstairs when it hit, they pulled me out of the kitchen, but I'd been crushed to death by rubble. Still, I look OK for it, don't I? My name's Evelyn, by the way, but seeing as you've set me free, you can call me Eve.'

When I found my voice I rambled nervously. 'Er, I'm Ruth and I live here now. The roof and kitchen are fixed. You look OK to me for a dead person. If that is what you are. Is that your book and your coat in the trunk, then?'

You looked so pained when you replied, 'The journal's mine, the coat was Lily's. It still smelt of her scent. I kept it by me when I wrote about her.'

I had to ask. 'Did they ever find Harry's body?'

'Not in my lifetime, but I heard, through the ghost of the other woman who died that day, that Harry's soul had been released in 1969 when the whole of Marlowe Road was rebuilt.' You wiped a single tear from your cheek.

I didn't know why but I asked, 'Were you and Lily family?'

You replied with indignation, 'Not what most would call family. We were sweethearts.' You blushed as you said it. I felt myself colour too.

'I'm sorry, Eve, I didn't mean to pry. It's not such a taboo today.'

'So, do you have a sweetheart?' you asked.

'No. Did have but she left me for a younger, blonder... oh, never mind.'

'She? Well, that's a bit of luck, I suppose!' You looked me up and down, taking in my jeans and FCUK T-shirt. 'Don't think much of today's fashions... and that embroidery's a bit fresh – and it's spelt wrong too. Don't they teach the three Rs any more? What year is it, anyway?'

'It's a fashion store. It's 2003, more than sixty years since your last diary entry. A lot has changed.'

'Well, you wouldn't have seen the likes of Liberty's selling lewd embroidered clothing in my day.' You smirked and I held back from passing comment on your floral print dress, for now at least.

'Not then, no,' I replied, as I went to close the door to the cupboard. Through the hole in the roof, the view to the back of the house was completely different. No houses by the row on Farnan Avenue, just a big field with a pond, a few houses in the distance and great big gaps of smouldering rubble in between. Then you took my hand and pulled me away.

'Come away from there and shut the door, Ruth. I want to see your world now.' So I did as asked and we descended from the loft together and I gave you a guided tour of your old house/my new house. I tried hard not to laugh at some of your questions and comments like: Was I poor since I didn't have carpets? Where was all the wallpaper? Why were there only two rooms and the bathroom upstairs now? Did I need such a big kitchen if I lived alone? Why did I have so many posters about films, starring a chap called Jodie Foster?

As we toured the house, I took in your features, your eyes and your hands in particular. Brown eyes that, when caught by the light, turned to amber, and your hands neat and yet strong-looking, with tapered thumbs and long fingers. Our eyes met and locked in a gaze, while I was showing you my CDs and DVDs. I blushed but you just smiled, took in my embarrassment and continued asking about the demise of the gramophone.

'We had valve amplifiers in my day,' you said as you traced your thumb around the edge of the CD and studied my reflection in the disc. I guessed that you'd seen me staring at your hands.

When we reached the garden, the first thing I did was look up to check the roof. No gaping hole and no debris, I was in 2003 again. But unlike an hour ago in the loft, it was night-time. We went back into the house and began to compare and contrast 1941 and 2003. You looked through my books. I noticed that you stayed well clear of the computer, stereo and widescreen TV. We sat and talked about our lives, from where we went to school to the Voluntary Fire Service. Briefly, we even discussed what it is that a new media consultant does. We talked until our eyelids grew heavy and the birds had started their morning song. I didn't even question whether ghosts needed to sleep, at that point. I let you back into the loft and returned you to the cupboard, but leaving it slightly ajar, as you had asked. You said you weren't yet ready to spend the night in my world, but promised me you'd return the next day.

I lay awake for a while wondering whether I'd really met you, a ghost in my attic, or whether I was finally going mad after my break-up. When I drifted off to sleep I dreamt about you. You came to my bedside, held my hand and then stroked my hair, your hands smooth and yet firm.

Your eyes held my gaze and you spoke softly: 'It's OK, you don't have to be alone any more.' You bent down and kissed me on the cheek, then moved across to meet my mouth. Your tongue teased my top lip before probing inside to find my tongue. We were held in this kiss for longer than I can ever recall kissing anyone. Your strong, firm hands brushed through my hair then gripped my face. I wanted to laugh, I needed to cry, but more than anything else I wanted you to take me, love me and fcuk me. If that wasn't too forward for you!

Then I woke up. You were there with me and I could see you had been crying. 'I'm sorry I had to stop,' you said. 'It has been a long time and yet I still thought of her. You're the only one I've met since Lily and so I thought you'd do.'

'Well, thanks! At least I find you curiously attractive, when out of that flowery frock. It has been a while for me too, although not sixty-two years.' I got up and told you I had to get ready for work.

'Don't leave me here alone,' you said, scared.

We embraced again and kissed. How easily you persuaded me to stay. An hour later I called work and said I was going down with something. I hung up the phone, went back to bed and did just that.

When we eventually resurfaced it was mid-afternoon. You wanted to go for a walk to the local park and see how the area had changed. I was willing to oblige you anything, after the morning we'd just had.

We walked first to Aveling Park, towards the theatre and gallery. You stopped along the way and said, 'We rescued a Border collie just here. It'd got itself stuck in a huge crater from an explosion. The poor dog had worn itself out trying to scale the sides, it had settled for howling instead. It took five of us volunteers to get the silly mutt out.'

We left the park by the gallery and you pointed over to the Salvation Army building. 'Can't believe that's still here. Twelve people were killed near that corner, from one bomb alone. I'll show you the damage when we go back to my time.'

In the market, you grimaced at all the shops surrounding the stalls: the red-bricked shopping centre, the KFC and Pizza Hut. Only Manzie's Pie 'n' Mash shop remained from your time. 'Oh, to be able to eat pie and mash and liquor,' you remarked.

'Don't ghosts eat, then?' I asked.

'Good Lord, no. We can imagine we're eating and imagine tastes, but that's about it.'

As we wandered through the rest of the market, looking at the vibrant array of tropical fruits, wet fish and fresh vegetables, I wondered if when one died and discovered there was no eating in the afterlife, one regretted that last meal for its ordinariness or hurriedness. 'I must eat better from now on,' I told myself.

On our way back home, we visited the graves of yourself and Lily's family in St Mary's Churchyard. I was touched to see Harry was also named on the grave. You wept and I consoled you by kissing a tear off your cheek, wondering what me kissing a ghost must look like to passers-by, who seemed to ignore me as they walked along Church Path.

Next we went to the local pub – your old local and now my local – the Nag's Head. You told me not to order anything, as you couldn't cope with me drinking while you watched. So we sat in the far corner and you told of how you and Lily used to leave the kids with a neighbour and drink here once a week.

As you were talking, Anna and Cassie walked in from the beer garden and up to the bar. I waved at them, but they seemed to look straight past me.

'Who are you waving at?' you asked, fretful.

'Anna, my ex, and her new partner, Cassie. But I think they're ignoring me.'

'They probably didn't see you. Anyway, where to next?' you asked hurriedly.

'How about we go home and I play you some of my favourite songs. There's this one in particular that I think you'll like. It's by a woman called Kristin Hersh. It's called "Your Ghost".'

We left the pub and headed up through the village, linking arms. It was good to be going home. I hadn't looked forward to going home for a long time and I couldn't remember the last time I had felt so charged, energised and yet relaxed. What had you done to me?

But as we returned to the house, we saw an ambulance and a crowd of people gathering in the street, outside my/our front door. I heard one of my neighbours say to another, 'It's that Ruth. She's fallen from the loft and broken her neck. She's dead, but she looks more peaceful than I've ever seen her. Died smiling, apparently.'

'I'm sorry, Ruth,' you said. 'I wanted to keep you for myself, so I moved the ladder when you went to climb out of the loft last night.'

I was horrified. 'How could you decide my destiny for me? I had a life to live.'

You touched my face. 'No, you had an existence, not a life. Surely you are happy now not to be alone?'

'But I only had a cheese and tomato sandwich for my tea last night!' I exclaimed. Perhaps it was the shock.

After a few days, you started to teach me some ghost skills – like how to make yourself appear as a reflection, how to conjure up a five-course meal (a particular favourite), how to walk through structures and how to visualise what you wanted to see around you that day. I had more control over my destiny as a ghost than as a mortal and was having more fun than ever. At first I struggled with structure penetration, but excelled at scenic visualisations. Things would even out as my powers grew stronger, you told me.

And you were right, I was happier. I was at peace with myself and was able to wander the streets unnoticed and unharmed. We couldn't hurt each other, as we had no feelings other than a rich warm happiness that cocooned us. We had urges to satisfy, memories to share and things to tell and show each other about our two different eras.

I wanted to tell you that I loved you, back then. I should have done, but I was so in awe of your ghost knowledge that I believed you when you said I had no real feelings, just sensations built on memories, wishes, hopes and fears from my mortality. So, I let it lie. I was scared, too.

'When the spirits of Lilian, Dorothy and Harry find me, I will fade away,' you told me once.

I came to realise that my life on earth had been cut so short that I would never experience a depth of passion like the one shared by you and Lilian. Your twenty-five years had amounted to love and loss in wartime and had made you seem in some ways older and wiser, whereas mine had amounted to puberty, university, the start of a promising career and an ill-matched relationship with a materialistic woman. There had been no extremes of joy and devastation, just emotions that crept up on me gradually, pecked at my insides and occasionally got noticed.

That vision of you on the roof with the sun and wind in your hair is the only enduring memory of my life.

They Flee from Me that Sometime Did Me Seek
Cherry Smyth

They Flee from Me that Sometime Did Me Seek
Cherry Smyth

Androula and I will never age. We promised. And we will never moan about ageing and all the things we can no longer do, like a three-mile jog on a sandy beach, or going to work three days running on no sleep. Regret always seems to be full of threes... Mind you, Androula could never run half a kilometre without stopping and if I don't get eight hours' sleep, I can't speak. Even at eighteen, I loved my bed and Androula, her Downward Dog.

We met on the crest of thirty-something in a decade when middle age had been postponed until the distant shore of the late forties. I was at my sexual peak of thirty-two and Androula in its luscious dawn, the discovery of her G-spot still to come. I wouldn't say I'm approaching forty now, rather that it's bearing down on me like the Euro-weight equivalent of Ten-Ton Tessie. When I awoke last Tuesday, my waistband had become a fully inflated rubber ring – overnight. None of my eating or movement patterns had changed. My body was simply being left behind. More and more of it.

Convinced that my boxers had shrunk in a hot wash, I pulled on a pair of my dad's Y-fronts that I'd mistaken for my own the last time I was home and hauled them up over the swollen area. For the first time in my life I looked like a man I didn't want to be, kind of John Major rendered by Steve Bell. I'd gone from James Dean to a withering Tory in a heartbeat. Luckily, Androula had already left for work. The change had no witness.

I slathered my palms in Dax and pushed my hair up into a baby butch thatch, then sandwiched it into the sharp reef of a Hoxton fin. My mouth and chin were still boyish, I told myself. I narrowed my eyes at the mirror and sucked in my cheeks. Not a day over twenty-nine. If I was a girl I would fancy me. I was soon happily flirting with my reflection like a toddler who reaches out to the kid in the mirror. I knew there was something Lacanian about the moment but I couldn't for the life of me remember what it was. Instead, I conjured Denise Lewis and muttering *six pack, six pack*, I resisted breakfast and speed-walked to the bus-stop. The time had come to kick ass, I said to myself. My own. Kick boxing, running, squash, the Marathon. The vest with a number. The Navratilova calf muscles. The snatched cupfuls of water from the sidelines. The finishing line. The TV cameras. The interviews with the fastest woman under thirty-eight. Well, thirty-nine, just. I felt bony at the thought of it. Haggard, even.

The woman next to me on the 73 was gnawing into a Snickers. Weren't they called Marathon before? It was a sign. Someone in my TV memory was overtaking all the others and sprinting out of sight. 'Peanuts keep you going... going... going...' My brain was bouncing between the associations: sweet, unhealthy confectionery and bitter, punishing athleticism. My mouth watered and my stomach squirted and scooped. The bagel at the top of my Diesels rolled over and flopped out. A little triangle of chocolate and toffee stuck to the woman's upper lip. I swallowed and looked away.

Later, on the way home from work, I spied that the hip jean shop on Islington Green was having a sale. Androula once told me that jeans came from Genoa and the word denim came from De Nîmes, where Monsieur Levi Strauss, a French Jew, lived before he sold America its own history. That's the kind of thing she knows. And retains. I tried on a pair of denim baggies and immediately my belly loosened and relaxed out of sight. I bought them and kept them on.

Androula was practising the Shoulder Stand when I arrived home, the room smelling of burnt weeds and Bazooka Joes. And her.

'Hi,' I said. It was one of those days when it felt as though I hadn't seen her for long weeks. The lighting was low. Candles burned around the room. It was home and Androula made it that.

Her legs tilted back and her feet tapped the ground. The Plough.

'Hi,' she said, her voice coming from her chest.

Her legs swung up towards the vertical again like the big hand on a clock at a few minutes after six.

'It's good for the thyroid,' she said breathlessly, as if she could really feel the yogic benefit on her insides.

'So I believe.' I pulled off my boots. You can't tell to look at me, but I know the names of nearly all the poses, the *asanas*, they're called, from years of studying. Studying my beloved executing them, that is. '*Asana*' means 'seat' or 'sitting method', she told me once, and I was tempted to say, '*Asana* right on my face,' but I didn't. My favourite is the one when you lie down perfectly flat and still. The Corpse pose.

Androula flipped down into the Bridge, a movement I hate watching. It looks like her back should snap, crackle or pop at any moment.

'Well done, darling.' She was still breathing. 'You're so brave.'

'It doesn't hurt, you know.' Her teeth were shining. Did yoga even help the teeth? I suddenly wondered if I'd cleaned mine that morning. My routine had been so disrupted by the flab onset that I'd forgotten. I slunk off to the bathroom with my inflexible joints and scuzzy mouth.

I tried taking up yoga to please her, the kind of selfless thing you do in the first couple of years of being together. Androula changed one sparkplug and topped up the clutch fluid and I did yoga – twice.

The first time was on a beach on Naxos, when a fortnight of sun and sea and sex made me believe that some Greek goddess had bestowed suppleness on me along with the golden tan. (Well, the speckled, sunburnt, factor 30 look I achieve on holiday.) Androula showed me the Sun Salutation. I copied my dark-skinned Minerva, bending forward towards the glittering waves, arching back to the hills where the olive groves spread, sliding up into the Cobra… and that's when my lower back had its Waterloo, going into spasm like an almighty, unending period cramp, and I had to be carried back to the hotel. Screaming as if I was in labour. With twins. I'm not good with pain. And there was poor Androula trying to persuade the lifeguards that I didn't need to be airlifted to Athens. At least that's what she told me she was saying.

The second time I was more circumspect. About a year later. After a weekend of such tender, hungry sex that even to let her part from me for an hour to practise yoga hurt. So, Standing Stretches. No harm in that. The Tree pose. Balancing on one leg. A cinch. 'Keep looking at a spot that isn't moving,' ordered Androula in her yoga teacher's voice, her body in perfect poise, her eyes a little crossed. Steady as a stork, I raised one leg up and promptly fell over. I started to laugh. I wasn't damaged. I'd escaped what it has taken most Indians thousands of years to forego. I mean, does every Indian practise yoga? Exactly.

It was only when I came back into the sitting room smelling of Macleans that Androula blinked during her meditation and clocked what I was wearing.

'Not droopies, for heaven's sake!'

'They're longies,' I protested, hoisting up my new jeans and crossing the room as though I was wading through warm honey.

'Your crotch is at your knees. And what's that metal?' Her meditative mood had dispersed with the incense. Her eyebrows met in the middle.

'A key chain.' I fingered my new purchase protectively.

She rolled her eyes.

'They were in the sale.'

'They saw you coming.'

'You have to move with the decades, Androula, otherwise age will creep up on us.'

'Something needs to creep up – like those hems, for instance. They've a tidemark round the bottoms already.'

'You don't get them taken up. Fraying is a statement.'

'Yes, of teenage disenfranchisement.' Her eyes hardened as small and colourless as a shark's. 'How much?'

Not my favourite question. I waded back across the room like a moving target. 'Not as much as those Manoli Blah Blah shoes you bought last summer.'

'*Manolo Blahnik.*'

'Being able to pronounce him is not the same as being able to walk in his shoes.'

'They're exquisite. Classical.' She folded her arms, her face filling with stress.

'They're wardrobe furniture.'

'You're not throwing them out. They're collectibles.'

'Of dust. A middle-age buy and you know it –'

'I'm nowhere near middle –'

'Something you know doesn't suit you but you buy it anyway because you're convinced it takes years off.' I sat down with an anti-authoritative slump. 'Oxfam.'

'Mutton dressed as lamb, you mean,' she said, her voice empty of all combative spirit.

I looked up. Sat upright. She was sad now. Oh God, it was such a tentative balance these days between having a go and having a full-scale depression on your hands.

'I hate that expression. You'll always be lamb-ly. Lamb-like,' I cooed. 'Come on, have a gambol. Hee! Hee!' My atrocious pun made me chuckle.

She put-putted the way she does when she laughs. She didn't bleat or cry. We'd turned a corner, sailed over a green and pleasant hill. I leant down and kissed her. 'Hello,' I said.

'Hello back,' she said. 'So, what you making for dinner?'

Damn, I'd forgotten it was my turn to cook. 'First, tell me one thing. You know about this stuff.' I patted my knee. She obliged, lowering herself on top of me. She smelt faintly of turmeric and skin warmed by the sun. Dabs of sweat darkened on her chest. 'Do anti-ageing creams work?'

I'd only recently tuned into ads for eye-wrinkle cream and had bought a pot from Holloway Road Car Boot Sale – unopened. *Plénitude* it was called. In French. With an accent over the 'e' because the French know how to sell fat of all kinds. It made my eyes water. Andie MacDowell could stuff it. It wasn't worth it. I'd rather wrinkle than weep.

'I mean,' I went on, 'how can something possibly "firm" and "soften" at the same time? It's like saying "bake" and "freeze" in a recipe, isn't it? And another thing – moisturising soap. Which bit knows to stay on the skin? What if the soap sticks and the moisturiser joins the water in the shower? And do you really want grease locked into your skin with yesterday's dirt?'

'Stick to E45 and WD40, honey, and you'll be fine,' she laughed. 'Butches don't have to worry so much.'

'Maybe not, but we do. We do.' My hands gestured emphatically as Graham Norton's towards an unsympathetic guest.

'Listen, swee'art,' she said, 'masculinity grows distinguished with lines and silver hair. Femininity goes dismissed and touched up.'

'Don't ever destroy the nose I love. That chin.' I could feel a Billy Joel moment coming on.

She suddenly stretched her mouth cavernously open, stuck out her tongue and growled.

'I know. The Lion,' I said.

'Try it. It stops wrinkles, improves circulation –'

'Keeps cubs in line too,' I smiled.

'Anyway, your family are long and lean. They age well. Don't forget Gary. He's pretty trim.'

I prefer to forget Gary. 'He's a fitness freak. He hates that I've monopolised all the freak quotient in the family. He makes people look at his calves to compensate for baldness. They're bigger than his thighs, you know. Veined like chandeliers.'

'My family go small and round. Shrink and fatten. Look at my sister.'

I extended my hand. 'Soon I'll be able to carry you in my palm, Thumbelina.' I started to hum Randy Newman.

She placed her hand on mine and our fingers interlaced.

'But I don't think or look middle-aged, do I?' Her tone had that note of disinterest that hides a symphony of deep concern.

'Nothing about you. Except maybe that nightie you wore when you were broody.'

Her elbow delivered a sharp poke. I yelped.

'But my skin. It doesn't come back on its own,' she said plaintively.

'Come again?'

'When I take off my socks there are rubber bands around my ankles. And look –' she squeezed the skin on her forearm. 'It doesn't spring back in the same way any more. See?'

'I know. I know,' I said quietly.

'You mean you've noticed?'

I'd pulled her into my own deep water. 'Only on me, yes. Not you.' I swam ashore fast. 'I thought... oh nothing.'

I wanted to reassure her, not lie exactly, but reverse the inexorable pull of gravity and replace the loss of ping-pong in her skin, but I couldn't. I'd spotted my own ravages and till now had thought Androula impervious to the ill effects of advancing deterioration. Unlike flu, or gloominess or PMT, this wouldn't pass. I thought of all the great lovers who'd killed themselves to win the dignity of exiting at their own pace. No bullying at the hands of nursing staff. No residential care costs. A sweet and timely farewell at a point when your peers are still with it enough to write a touching, trenchant obituary. I felt panic rising. Who would write mine if Androula died first – or with me in a dyke blood pact?

I struggled to recall a Buddhist parable Androula had told me once about waves. We are all different sizes of wave in a vast ocean. High and low. Tsunami and ripple. The wave doesn't need to die to become water. It's water already. No birth, no death as we return to what we always were. Are. In her voice, it sounded sublime, soothing. But serenity had taken a hike. I was drowning in mortal matter.

Age had been eclipsed by anxiety over post... post-humanness... posthumosity. Posterity. That was the word I'd been searching for and into the gap leapt more urgent evidence – encroaching memory loss – Alzheimer's.

'Ginkgo biloba,' I spluttered, leapt up and charged to the kitchen where the white and brown battalions of vitamins stood. 'Vitamin E, quick.'

'What's the matter?' Androula was at my arm.

'I skipped breakfast, didn't clean my teeth and forgot to take my pills!' My heart was galloping. 'I'm going to have an attack.' I kept my options open: heart, brain, lungs, liver, kidney, bladder. They were all vulnerable, invisible. But terribly fragile. Invisibility usually granted magic powers or safety at least. Not with organs.

You had to believe what you were told and couldn't see for yourself.

'Is that what happened to your hair? It stood up in shock?' she asked, trying to suppress an outright guffaw.

I ignored her and angled myself to catch my reflection in the stainless steel sheen of the kettle. I lined up my dolly mixtures in size order on the counter. 'Wouldn't it be great,' I went on, 'if you could peek at your liver everyday and check it was OK?'

'Yours is spotted or rotted by now, sweetheart. You don't wanna see.'

I placed her palm on my heart. I was convinced I was breathy. 'I'm having a palpitation.'

'They don't come singly.'

'Yes, only in gangs. Here come the rest. The Triads. The Yardies of the Internal Blood and Guts World.' My hands shot up in surrender.

'Calm down, baby.' Androula was holding me but I was shaking like I was in leaf. 'You're thirty-nine, not eighty-nine. You've got to keep this in perspective.'

'Oh darling, you're so right,' I sighed. 'But that's what *I* meant to do for you. Bring you back from the edge. I'm useless. I jumped.'

'It's OK. Chill.' Androula stroked my hand. 'And hey, it's still your turn to cook.'

'I know, but listen. Listen.' I looked into her eyes. I held her cheeks in both my hands. 'You are beautiful. It's not to do with your skin – it's your smell, your whistle, your smile, your hum. All things that age will only enhance. And your eyes. Yeah, the pockets might slip a little, the lids loosen, but those eyes of yours are so deep and dark and wise, they carry the world – all its best joy, its worst tragedy. They know it and they're still open and kind. They're all my favourite films. They're poems. Russian poems with apples and cherries and ponies and light in them. I can't wait to watch you ripen, I swear, girl.'

She laughed. She threw back her head and she laughed. Her neck was a beautiful sex organ that only I could see. It made me want to run my fingers down the grooves between the sinews, lick the muscles of her throat – hard.

'How – do – you – do – it?' she asked. 'You only get better.'

She was smiling that 'you have me' smile I love. It melts me every time. And the best, most wonderful thing about saying those words was that they rang with truth and the sound and the depth made me feel young to my feeble but determined little core. Like a bell-ringer who is hoisted up by the swing on the rope of the big bronze bell and hears the peals ring out across the city streets and squares.

I set out an onion and three cloves of garlic on the chopping board and rolled up my sleeves.

She reached to kiss me but I manoeuvred out of her grasp.

I twitched the Kitchen Devil at her. 'Ah ah ah...'

'Your forearms look great,' she whispered.

'It's all the head-scratching I do.'

Her fingernail traced the cord of a vein up my forearm. It reminded me of a game we used to play at the back of the classroom when you closed your eyes and your friend touched the inside of your arm and you had to say stop when she reached the crook of your elbow. Invariably, you guessed too soon, as if the whole arm had become a tingling crease where pleasure could be held.

'Stop,' I said. 'You want dinner or a late supper?'

'Let's skip it.' She led me by the hand.

I put down the knife and followed. She exaggerated the sway of her hips.

There was little I could do. I was like that sculpture on the roof of the Hayward Gallery, the tower of geometric coloured bars that change colour when the wind passes through them. Depending on the weather, it flashes red, then red and yellow, then purple, then blue and red and yellow, then yellow and blue only. At different speeds. She has that effect on me. Makes me produce coloured lights for all to see.

This losing weight thing was going to be easy.

The Auto-cannibal
Kathleen Kiirik Bryson

The Auto-cannibal
Kathleen Kiirik Bryson

The sky is as bright as a watermelon slice outside my closed lids but, if I raised them, the pink hue of flesh would quickly disappear into hot, pale light. It is March, but this means very little. It means only that the skies are becoming brighter; it does not mean that I shall see their summer conclusion. I understand now what 'looking at life through rose-tinted lenses' means. It means you see things through the pink skein of veins and blood-tinted, shuttered flesh.

It means your eyes are closed.

I wait before I open them. I want to remain for several more minutes behind my two overlapping rosy veils, head slumped against the cool glass window, body feeling the movement of the bus. The Number 38 alternately bounces and cruises towards Victoria Station; the other passengers are so accustomed to the uneven rhythm that their bodies anticipate the jerks of the traffic: sliding forward seconds before they have to; bracing their flesh against yet another pothole.

My flesh, on the other hand, is vulnerable. I have lost these city instincts along with three appendages and, simply, the ride hurts. The perfectly healed skin on my stumps still feels raw against the bus seat, and indeed it is.

I open my eyes and dispel the pink.

I see two things almost immediately. One, a huge white retrieval truck, blank as a baby, lumbering past the bus in the opposite lane. Two, several seats ahead in the bus, an off-duty retriever. The retriever sits contentedly under his or her dark shawl, the spidery material preventing recognition. People actively dislike retrievers, a resentment that even overrides their disgust at stumpers. Concealment is necessary; it's not a good thing for retrievers to be easily recognised: not by former family, former friends, former colleagues. They have made their choices. I consider this fact, looking at the dark-clad figure a few feet in front of me. Choices, no choices. The main thing that signifies a retriever, however, is this: they are fat. Gloriously, healthily fat. They are among the few who regularly get food. They get a percentage of meat off stumpers. Off people like me.

The retrieval truck first came for me nine months ago this week. After the first amputation my flesh was good, mouth-watering; I roasted it with chicory, small white pellets of valuable garlic, rehydrated mushrooms – the perks and savouries they allow you for your first time. I've heard of – even seen pictures of – foods like watermelon and goulash and I can imagine their lurid colours, but the truth is I do not know their taste and for obvious reasons my culinary skills are limited. Yet I cooked it myself, propping myself up with both hands and my single leg. It was so good. I ate up my whole limb within two weeks. The second limb was also filling but, as they predict will happen, I grew tired of the oily taste of meat, no matter how well seasoned and prepared. The right arm stuck in my throat. It was only hunger that finally drove it down the hatch; I didn't care for it this time, near raw, the veins too close to the surface, like on my eyelids. I was having problems balancing near the grill this second time and told them so (grumpily) and they had a special cook come to my house to prepare the meal: surly, quick, resentful to be of service to yet another stumper. And after they had taken their cut, the cook and the retriever both, there remained moreover the under-cooked blob of meat for me, duly gagged on, duly swallowed. Still, it was food.

I lean back against the bus seat, pressing my spine hard against the seat cover. The retriever hasn't seen me, but even if it had, I would only be meat to the retriever. Or maybe a constant, niggling, guilty reminder of choices made. A choice to eat rather than to be eaten. No, that's not right. A choice to scavenge, rather than to become one's own parasite.

The bus is drawing close to Angel, Islington. The treble phantom itch is driving me nuts. I can't even concentrate on real pain, like the scraping hunger in my stomach, because my now-invisible limbs are demanding attention. The bus window is dirty, streaked with hand-grease. I can even see fingerprints within the hazy tracks across its glass surface. For a moment, the thought of organic grease makes my stomach revolt in hunger, and I wonder whether I've now acquired a taste for human produce. But then my (non)legs start to itch again, and I realise that I am just hungry, and hunger does strange things to a person.

I make myself see past the window now; through the double-glazing to Essex Road, where from my vantage point I see skeletons walking slowly, just as hungry as me. Some have refused to choose, and these people lie dotted and crumpled through the streets, collapsed. My whole family went this way. My lover went this way too, wasting away until I could count the ribs that pushed through her skin like a series of fossilised parentheses. That's how I often thought they would look beneath. Beneath the dwindling meat of her torso. For those brackets held nothing, really; they were an empty exception: ((((((()))))) Eventually, a retrieval truck will come for these shrinking cadavers who now walk the old Essex Road, too. See, they get you anyway in the end. The least you can do is to enjoy your hangman's meal.

I lied about retrievers being fat. They aren't really, not the way people used to be fifty, even twenty, years ago. Retrievers would have been dangerously thin then, but these days I want them to be obese; I want their relative thickness to be bulging like old-fashioned babies, well-fed, skin tight over all that meat. All that flesh. They are cherubs clad in black, Gothic shawls. They are beautiful. My mouth goes suddenly, embarrassingly, wet and I look down at my hand, curled in my lap. I am trying not to stare at the retriever, but I am not doing very well.

The bus crunches to a halt in Farringdon, but not before I have pulled the special bell with my single hand, the bell they reserve particularly as a privilege for stumpers. Most of the passengers glare at me for the inconvenience, but the retriever in front does not turn around. As I am brusquely lifted from my seat by the skinny 'driver' (all those buses on electric automatic lines, but how we still hold on to ancient titles!), it occurs to me that maybe this person in front of me, still sitting, is *my* retriever. My own pulp having padded out *this* retriever's body. I am part of this retriever.

And I let my anger go.

The bus smells of dread as I am carried like a child down from the top level. I can sense the fear, people now willing themselves not to look at my stumps. People caught up in a weird juxtaposition of thought: that could be me, they think, with three limbs gone and one to go. And: look at that bundle of meat the driver carries; how hungry I am. They turn away, ashamed. They have realised they are animals, and ravenous at that.

Outside, I am dumped – yes, dumped – by the bus stop. The skin on my arm and face is hot, and I stretch out my phantom legs, basking for the moment in the spring sunlight. I am by the old Exmouth Market, and I try to imagine what it once was like here. The sky is bright, too bright across the street, but I conjure up an alley packed with people, healthy people, lively and animated, vibrant. I can almost see them in the brilliant noon haze ahead of me; can almost smell the long-gone scents: leather, cinnamon, honest perspiration, acrid tobacco. I reckon I was ten years old the last time I smelled tobacco, and I am a decade older now. Even when I was ten most standard vegetable produce had disappeared, but sturdy tobacco was surprisingly resistant to GM VeggiePlague Strain IV. Cinnamon is a good memory. When I was a girl people still had dried spices, though the cinnamon tree itself had perished. My nose tingles as I wait, and to casual viewers I am merely a lone stumper by a bus stop. But I am powerful; I can make myself hear an old market clamour: whistles, petrol cars, voices raised in fury or excitement to sell and haggle.

It seems so long ago, this consumerism I'm reviewing with nostalgia. And yet this is why we're starving now. Why the last of the trees died when I was seventeen, why a year later only the extremely rich could eat enough, why now, two years after that, people like me devour ourselves on a short-term contract. I tell myself this, but I feel no bitterness. I feel only sadness as I close my eyes in the heat and dream of a bounty I never knew. I smell and hear and see the market, and then, finally, I allow myself to taste.

I imagine wandering (in my fantasy, I still have legs, of course) through the street, stalls filled with bright crisp peppers, yellow, green and ruby; imagine their clean vegetable taste in my mouth, spiky and fresh. So I've heard. Or stalls full of pastries, breads – thick and chunky with yeast; the taste of flour dry on my palate and only too filling. I've read about these things. I think of sausages, hung in encasements, meat mixed with herbs mixed with bread mixed with meat mixed with meat –

There is a jolting pain in my lower stumps and I open my eyes and look down. There's no explanation for the flash of pain, but a shadow has fallen across my healed stems, and I know the retriever and cook have arrived even before I look up. In my fantasy I had forgotten why I was coming here, making this laborious bus trip, but they have not. They're waiting for me.

As the cook picks me up, I steal a glance at the retriever. I'm reasonably sure that it's the same one as on the bus, but I can't prove it. And then too, perceptions tend to blur these days. All retrievers start to look alike: satiated, covered with a diaphanous shroud of black lace. Still, the retriever shifts suddenly as the cook lifts me up-up-up into the wild blue yonder and I catch a glimpse of eyes beneath the veil. Furtive. Half-ashamed. That's as it should be. But for the moment, I am gripped by a violent jealousy, and I wish nothing more than that, like this retriever, I had chosen to scavenge. But I was full of high-blown morality last year when I chose; I was sure I was making the virtuous choice. I'm not so sure now. It is funny how hunger changes a person. How it makes you realise that the only thing that matters is yourself. I resent retrievers, but I respect them, too.

The great, awkward cook carries me easily through the empty market. In more plentiful times, I am sure he would have been a big man. Now he is folds of skin on a huge bone framework lifting me past the ghost-town of stalls. He gets his scraps too, they all do; just enough to stay alive, like anybody else. The state doles out a stipend of perishables to its people, rationing it out until the day you're told you have to choose. Stumper or retriever or cook. Or nothing at all. There is no surplus of retrievers; everyone is so hungry for a pound of flesh that they'll happily chew off their own feet. Or the hands that feed them. And so on. The state prides itself on being a moral government, dispensing crackers and mush to its dwindling population, all the while waving the promise of real food, bulk food, in front of their noses, if only they become stumped. They must be pleased that most women are amenorrhic now. Fertility is a curse. As they say, another mouth to feed. Though there's some that would eat their own. I'm sorry. It's grim and it's true. There are historical precedents.

More history. The Church of England supported same-sex unions and discouraged het-er-o-sexual ones. I guess they figured fewer parasites on life would then be born. Even then, there were unplanned exceptions: sapphists fucking nancy-boys, ending up with not-so-immaculate conceptions. There were messier methods, too, for those who craved a child despite the anti-reproduction hype – techniques that involved the ungainly manual transfer of spunk from cock to cunt. My lover had often talked of this novel option, and I had listened and smiled, but that was before our blood dried up from hunger, before we both grew as barren as mules. A mule is another noun I've only heard about, like goulash or watermelon. Now I am even nostalgic for nouns you and I have never seen.

Mule. I wonder if it is edible.

I'm sure it is.

Yes, the C of E made breeding anathema. That was just before they merged with the Roman Catholics; joined forces with a religion already dangerously close to cannibalism. The papists, on their part, relaxed their previous insistence on fecundity. These shifts meant less work on propaganda to convince the masses that they truly were not starving; to convince society it had chosen a culture of want, and chosen well. You would think a starving culture would rise up, break down. Any movement at all. That we would hunt each other for meat. That's what you would think would happen. But it didn't. They've even flensed us of our rebellion, along with sinews and marrow. (Crack a shin bone and simmer with garlic pellets for tasty soup with quite a kick!) And so on. That's the history. But history means fuck-all to the living dead of Essex Road, or when your belly is roaring with hunger.

I am borne through Exmouth Market. The retriever hangs back behind the cook and me; under that deep shawl he or she is laden down with the surgery kit. That's one blessing, anyway; I know the operation will not hurt. Retrievers are skilled workers, practised in the art of amputation and healing gels and amazing anaesthetic. Their methods are clean and painless, and when they're done you have only round stumps, smooth and perfect as balls. No trauma here, folks. The only pain is spectral, an apparition in your head.

I know the retriever will be gentle, but it is my last limb and I am suddenly as desperately afraid as when it was my first. It is always the same pattern: right leg, left arm, left leg, right arm. Summer. Autumn. Winter. Spring. I suppose the state feels vindicated in some way by attaching ritual to the process: the ancient flow of seasons, the equinoxes, solstices. It lends authority and credence. It supplants the ceremonies of High Anglican and Catholic. Now the state is Mama: it will give you crackers and benediction; it will give you everything you crave. Soul-food. Or perhaps they feel humane in leaving the right arm to last, bowing to the particulars of a right-handed majority.

But I'm fooling myself… I have no idea what they think. The cook is waiting for the retriever, on the doorstep. I am a moveable feast. I look straight ahead, gripping the cook with my hand.

There is a click as the key enters the lock, and the three of us are inside. It is a different place than for my other stumpings. For the first three, the white luminous electric trucks come for you, gleaming like larvae, and the amputation is done then and there, inside the vehicle, by a silent and perhaps surly retriever – you really can't tell beneath their masks of frail dark cloth. The trucks are generally terrible; I hate the pale sight of them as they come coasting through the streets on powered tracks to pick up the failing almost-corpses of those who refuse to choose. Theirs is not only a retrieval of limbs, but also a retrieval of bodies.

In this new place a damp, almost moist smell fills my nostrils. The odour is familiar. The hallway is dark red; the colour reminds me of the insides of mouths or some people's genital skins. The cook clutches me too tightly as he ascends the stairs, trailing the retriever, and my heart begins to pound in my ribcage.

Don't worry, I hear the cook say softly, it will be OK. Easy for him to say. But he's doomed, too, and so is the retriever, and so are we all; so I let myself take comfort from his words, and I close my eyes again and make myself think of the marketplace, of bright green peppers, as the cook bumps me over several flights of stairs.

There is that scent in the air again as we finally stop before a dark crimson door, and again the retriever digs deep inside its shawls for keys. As the door at last swings open, I recognise the fragrance for what it is. Excitement. A heady, almost sexual excitement, and it is certainly not emanating from me. It's the cook, or the retriever. It doesn't matter. The door clicks shut, and I observe the room quickly from my vantage point of height before the cook sets me down. There is a table, clinical, where the retriever will swiftly operate. There does not appear to be a stove or any cooking facility, and this puzzles me. I was told that was why the cook was here, to transport me, and then to concoct the meal on the spot. Prêt-à-manger, as it were. The walls are made of rust-stained wood. Past the table is another smaller, darker room to which this space is the antechamber. I can see no windows in this room, but perhaps there is a window in the next. I sense again that pervading odour of arousal, or perhaps it is merely hunger. Maybe the smell emits from me, after all.

I shut my eyes and ears to the clicks and twitches as the retriever prepares his or her instruments, clanking, fingering the steel and the miracle anaesthetics. The cook stands silently behind me; I prop myself up on one hand. This will not be a violent act, but I do not want to see its rituals and orchestrations.

It is as quick and painless as the other three. Now I lie here on the table, and I'm completely numb. I feel as if I've been drugged – indeed, I'm sure I have been. As if from a great distance, I can hear them speaking. I imagine I look like some emaciated grub, a torso with a head. And then my stomach starts to rumble like a chorus of raspy-voiced angels. Feed me. I look up at the rust-coloured ceiling, but all I can think about is how my right arm will taste. Feed me.

I'm not sure if the cook and the retriever can hear me pleading, or even if words are exiting from my lips, but I can sense their attention shifting towards me. And then that smell in the air again.

But they are not coming closer; they are not bringing me my last delicious limb. The smell. I can hear them arguing, salivating, and then I smell blood fresher than the dots on my cauterised, former-arm right stump. It's as if I cannot force my eyes down from the ceiling, yet I hear their animalistic fury as their teeth tear at my severed arm, for they are hungry too, and they're sharing this meal between them. I can even feel the brief satiation when at last they've had their fill.

I cannot hate them. I'm still hungry, but I'm floating on some upper level now, up above my body. I could have eaten too, could have filled myself in this great conspiracy of limbs and torsos and broken promises. I chose not to. Yes, I had a choice.

I'm so drugged that I scarcely feel their arms lifting me and tenderly placing me on the floor of the little room beyond. In their arms I can still sense the tremors of their bloodlust, but I realise that they have made the transition; have convinced themselves yet again that they are human. They treat my torso with respect now, and dim the lights in the antechamber before they quietly leave.

I am on my back and once more I stare up at the ceiling. I have no illusions that they haven't pumped me full of poisons or that they won't come back eventually to harvest me. I'm sure they've ascertained that I will not suffer too much. My death will be humane, of course. In the best possible taste.

This room has a window, as I suspected, so the afternoon sunlight comes through. Nevertheless I am aware that there are no light bulbs, not even a light fixture in this room. Why should there be? There is no need. I have no needs now; I should not hunger. I am only a portion of a person, a grave pupa with thoughts above my station. I try to think of a dazzling, noisy market but it's no good; the image grows dim. I try to think of my long-dead lover –

Kathleen Kiirik Bryson

delicate with famine, just a slip of a girl, but she too fades away. My body doesn't need to ponder, but the question of choice is the thought that nags at me: is it better to eat, or to be eaten? I've done both, so perhaps I did well after all. Perhaps we've all done well – the stumpers, the cooks, the retrievers. I try to decide, as the afternoon becomes evening, and as the light in the room becomes bruised and shadowy.

Now it's dusk. To eat. To be eaten. I have still not made a decision. As I lie here, two images bob slowly beneath my lids, from one dulling orb to the other. It occurs to me that it's too late for a fresh conclusion. I am able to dismiss that thought easily. I have all the time in the world to decide. In my left eye, momentarily the blunt white heaviness of a universal blank and trucklike hunger. In my right, first the scaly, butterfly-thin scrapings of a ravenous dark veil, a sexless human shape solidifying slowly, becoming thick crust before my sight, then the pale truck again. Right, left. Back and forth.

Ladies' Fingers
Stella Duffy

Ladies' Fingers
Stella Duffy

She points at me again. The finger is swollen at both joints. She lies
in the bed, cannot move or speak. Points. Just her left hand, heavy
with an unfulfilled engagement ring. Points from me to the bed.
Smooth bed, cool bed, pillow-decked and silent. This room used to
be a whole, now it is the lesser sum of many parts. I cross the room,
twelve halting steps, drawn and unwilling, I pull back the fine
sheet, lift and lay her out. Each limb placed beside the others, all of
them in the correct place, still joined, but as useless as if I had
severed them singly in the night. As if I would sever them singly in
the night.

I take her to the toilet, she shits, pisses, farts. I wipe her like a
baby but nothing like a baby, she is old and her skin smells. Smells
of age and decay. Particular smells. I think some part of her likes
these smells. She would call them human scents, real, truthful. If
she could speak beyond a croak for air. She points to the window.
I gladly let in cool night, take it inside me in thick sips, welcome
the smell of wet vegetation from the unloved garden. And
immediately she points again. More insistent this time, bony finger
grown thinner and longer. I understand (because I am very
understanding) and close the window, close the heavy curtain,
worn and dusty velvet, fully lined, from before the war. She is calm
again, holds the pointing finger at her side, inadequate lungs
shiver her thin frame beneath the sheets, she slips into a place near
sleep. I sit and wait. Watching for the hand to rise, the finger to
point from me to whatever she wants. Age and stupidity and too
much fun and three strokes have done this. Reducing her to an old
woman with spittle at the corner of her mouth and a nicotine-
stained finger.

I dip her into the bath, testing the water first, it is warm and

239

swirls around her, flowing into the crevices left by wrinkled years. The skin folds mark out lines a skilled surgeon might cut along. If she would let them in, let them look at her, let them try. She will not let them in. She believes in time taking its true course. She believes in suffering and in pain. Hers and mine. Her dry dying skin flakes off into the water, she lies in her water, pisses into it, cannot stop herself, does not try. Lies there in her own dead cells and piss. I soap her body, hold her just firm enough, just gentle enough. I am surprisingly considerate for one so angry. Her body teaches me its needs.

In the middle of the night I wake to her pointing. To the finger, ring grown tight around the base, forcing her flesh out and angry dark red against the old gold, rolling in the bed in frustration and impotent fury at my rest. The finger is angry with me. I was meant to be watching. This scene is all for me. I have slept in the old cane chair again and stand, gently sliding muscles against tendon and bone. I stretch my limbs, almost unconscious of her seething jealousy at my abundant mobility. Almost. But as she calms her rage enough to watch me through watery eyes, I choose to stretch just that little more, push my bones against the limits of their skin barriers, to scratch my arse with just that slightly louder sigh of satisfaction. It is better while she sleeps. Easier to study the failing body, easier to sneak in just a little night air. She tries a croaking of saliva in the back of her throat, but in her anger becomes confused and grows silent again while she tries to remember whether to inhale or swallow what is in her decaying mouth. I want her to shut up. I want to shut her up. I want to shut her in. Leave this tight room, walk out into the world. Return to the street with yellow lamplight and cold wind and the possibility of rain showers to wash every piece of her out of my head.

Instead I stand. Stretch. Walk. My movements are as deliberate as her pointing finger. She points at the book. I pick it up, sit closer to the burning light, turn the dry page. In fifty-six minutes she is asleep again and my throat is hoarse. I pick up her water glass, wipe her dark lipstick stain from the edge and sip. The water is warm and smells of her kiss, I gag but force it down. I return to my chair and the list of remembrances. A beach at sunset. A full fridge, every item neatly labelled. Running to catch a bus. Lying awake in a daylight bed and feeling the charge of could-be desire as it lies beside me. Freesias stolen from a neighbour's garden. Cold toast, dry, crisp. A burning hot shower raining down my back, counting each knuckled vertebra as it falls, quickly turning the tap to cold just for the effect it has on my nipples. I think of my sex then and my hand steals to me. From outside my clothes I stroke myself, against the line of this skirt, these stockings, against the grain I stroke myself, come close to me again, my eyelids begin their wanting flutter and I half focus on the bed. She is watching. I start up, a five-year-old caught stealing sweets, and run to slap her face. She still smiles, straining thin muscles to curve her desiccated lips into a half-moon rictus smile with the pointing finger curling towards me, sniffs appreciatively and then, gaping, grins once more. I hit her again. My slapping hand is as much my own as her pointing finger, as ill controlled. She tries to laugh but it comes out in a thin gurgle, catching on her windpipe and throttling her. Laughter choking her laugh.

I should sit her up, help her to breathe. She points at me, she is not laughing now, she is fighting for her breath, fighting me for her breath. Still pointing, the ring heavy, dragging her hand down to the counterpane, the stains dark, the nail overgrown, twisted and yellowing. Her lips are blue. There is no other blue in this room. How interesting I should note the lack of blue. Then. Now. She points again, at the window, the night, the cool wet air, points from me to herself. Again. Bloody pointing finger. I understand, how could I not? But I do not answer. I stand above her wriggling body, watching the spasms jolt around her tired organs. This will not do her any good, she will bruise inside, a brittle egg carton holding cracked goods. There there little heart, hush sweet liver, come now my darling kidney. And then, quite suddenly, the only thing moving is the finger on the end of her hand. She gasps. It is the widest she has opened her mouth in three months. I see her rotting molars. Her involuntary diaphragm snaps itself back again and again, forcing her gaping mouth to suck and gasp, she flares her nostrils, straining to drag in the air she has insisted I shut out. It is no good. The blue stretches from lips to face to eyes, heavenly blue now, and empty.

I breathe then myself. I had not known I was holding my breath, waiting, anticipating. With twelve slow steps I return to my chair. Sit, rest, sleep. Easily and full. This is the first good night's sleep I have had in many months. I am so tired.

It is weeks over. The earth starts to settle over her clean and catalogued body. The morning after I wrenched the curtains from their poles and now I keep the windows open to let in the night until the chill is damp and heavy in the centre of the room. After I had cleaned her, labelled her insides, they took her away in a narrow coffin, lined like the curtains with thin red silk. They dug a deep hole, laid her down and smothered the body, the only gasping against black loam. It was all done. She was all done.

Now, even her finger is still. I know. I kept it. Sitting in the bottom of my carryall. Ring still heavy on the finger, stains still yellow. In the quiet of my wide-windowed night I open the box and take out the pointing finger. I point at things in the room and laugh. It is not so fierce. It is just a finger. Pointing at just a liver. Just a kidney. Just a heart. Just the finger of my lover. The woman I adored. She who I loved and caressed and cared for and hated and allowed to die. The woman who surrendered to her own inner decay. She who schooled me in the individuality of body parts. Who taught me to see a hundred shining units in one composite flesh. I hold her pointing finger. And in a soft box of palest cotton wool the nail still grows, yellow, curled. It points to my heart. And I wait in the night, sit patient in my chair, until the moment it pierces me. Soon.

Dirty Cow
Fi Benson

Dirty Cow
Fi Benson

That's one of her shoes. Her lucky shoes. Miss Hennessey's lucky shoes.

Georgie, Gina, Georgina. Georgina Hennessey. Miss Georgina Hennessey. Miss Georgina Hennessey and her lucky shoes. So, this is where she's been hiding.

I have been looking for her all day and now it's almost night-time. I searched the whole house, just in case, but she wasn't there. Then I searched the lanes, but she wasn't there either. Then I searched the woods. Then the whole damned village. Of course, I couldn't ask anyone if they'd seen her, which made it more difficult. Round and round and round. Looking for her. Round and round and round.

But I've found her now.

I can see your shoe, Miss Georgina Hennessey. I can see your lucky shoe. Lucky me.

Of course, she's *Mrs* Hennessey, to everyone else. But she isn't a proper Mrs, never has been a Mrs, never will be a Mrs. Especially not now. She'll always be a Miss. Very pretty, for her age. Big, brown eyes with really, really long eyelashes. Slim hips, like a teenager, like me. And lovely breasts. Yes, absolutely bloody lovely breasts. Darkest, firmest nipples I'm ever likely to see, ever likely to touch. That's what she told me anyway, when she invited me in. I have the darkest, firmest nipples that you're ever likely to touch, why don't you come in? That's just what she said to me. Would you like to come in? Would you like to come in and stroke them? That's what she said to me. Nobody else around for miles. Would you like to come in?

Standing at her front gate, with her shirt half open, and her lovely breasts, her bloody lovely breasts, pushing against the black wrought iron. Would you like to come in and stroke my breasts?

Yes. Yes, I would.

I'd never stroked a woman's breasts before. I hadn't even thought that I might want to, not until Miss Hennessey at the gate. But then I knew. I knew that it would make me very, very happy to stroke a woman's breasts, and that I desperately, desperately, desperately wanted to stroke Miss Hennessey's.

So I followed her in. I followed her into the house, along the hall and into the front room. And I didn't feel awkward at all. The opposite. I felt very comfortable. Very comfortable with all of it. Comfortable with Miss Hennessey lying on her back across a table. Comfortable with her shirt pulled down around her waist. Comfortable stroking those lovely breasts, those bloody lovely breasts. Very, very comfortable. More comfortable than I could ever have thought possible.

I decided to stay. Stay with Miss Georgina Hennessey and stroke her bloody lovely breasts every day. I would have to go home every night, but I could stay with Miss Hennessey all day, every day. Every day until Laura came back.

Perhaps Miss Hennessey thought that she was safe with me, because when she'd seen me I was always on my own, like her. But she'd only seen me in the past month, only seen me in the lanes since she didn't go far from home herself, only seen me wandering about with nothing to do. She didn't know that I was just waiting for Laura. But I don't think Miss Hennessey knew much about best friends. She knew a lot about something though. She knew a big something about me, and she knew it better than I did myself. But she still didn't know enough.

Now, all of that searching, all of that round and round and round, has me sweating and panting. And it's been raining for most of the afternoon. Still raining now. Heavier then lighter, heavier then lighter. Teasing me. I am soaking wet. And it's all her fault.

I have come back to the house for dry clothes before I start looking again. I have a stitch in my side and I'm out of breath. I have to stop a moment. I've had to stop just as I reach the gate. I can feel sweat running down the insides of my clothes. Down and down and down. This is all her fault.

The rain is easing off again. There is a huge, black puddle outside of the gate. I have a pain in my stomach and I am doubled over. I think I'm going to vomit. Bent over the huge, black puddle, I wait for my insides to empty themselves into the water. I stare down and wait to heave. But, look! Just look at that! I've found her.

I forget to vomit and feel happy that I don't have to go searching again, that I don't need to go very far at all. Because that is definitely one of Mrs Hennessey's shoes. It's one of her best Georgina shoes. Definitely.

It looks like the left one, but I might be wrong because, after all, I'm looking at a reflection, and it's night-time, and my head hurts, and my stomach hurts, and I'm tired. And angry. Very, very angry. Which will make it easier.

You wouldn't think that an earthy sort of woman like Mrs Hennessey, who never ever goes dancing, who rarely even goes into the village, would own a pair of shoes like these, all frills and buckles. But, of course, *I* know that she does, and I know *why* she does, because she has worn them for me.

They're purple, purple like a bruise. But you can't see that they're purple here because of the shadows and because of the water.

She must have thought that she had a chance to get away, but I knew that I'd find her. She has nowhere else to go. And she couldn't go to the village, because nobody would help her. What could she say? She couldn't tell them. She couldn't tell them because if she tried, they would look at *her*, and then they'd look at *me*, and they just wouldn't believe her. They'd think that she'd gone mad. And if they *did* believe her, it would be worse.

Dirty cow! That's what they'd think.

Dirty cow! That's what they'd say to themselves.

Dirty fucking cow! That's what they'd shout.

Soiling our little Abigail! Dirty cow! Putting her hands on Abigail! Dirty fucking cow! That's what they'd shout at her. That's what they'd shout and shout and shout.

Let's have her! Let's kick her head in! That's what they'd do. I know them. And that's what they'd do. They'd kick the dirty cow's head in.

So she's trying to hide, then. Does she think that I'll just give up and go away?

I did try to explain it to her, I really did. I told her. I told her that Laura is due back. I told Georgie, Georgina, Miss Georgina Hennessey, that I had to go. She was sad and cried a lot and wrapped her arms tight around herself. She looked odd like that, very odd. And her face looked really strange. Strange, and old. So then I told her that I couldn't possibly leave her behind and she smiled and started being all happy again and lifting her skirt so that I could put my hand down her pants.

But she didn't understand.

I had to push her away from me to get a good thrust. Only, I must have fallen with the force of it, or maybe she hit me with something, because one minute I was trying to stab her and the next I was opening my eyes and she was gone. I was angry, then. I didn't like her any more after that. I was just angry with her. And my head hurt really, really badly, which made me even more angry. I just wanted it finished with. I knew that I would find her, I just knew.

There is a light in the centre of the water and it is looking at me like an eye. We are staring at each other, me and the eye. I don't like the way it's looking at me. I'm tempted to stamp on the eye and see it break into pieces. But I don't. I look away from the eye at something else.

I can see the plastic butterflies and the wooden squirrels on the wall of the house. I can see the weed sticking out of the guttering. I can see the overhang, the sloping tiles, and the very top of the roof.

The shoe is not moving at all, so she must be standing very still. *I* would stand very still if I was where *she* is. Especially if I was hoping that I wouldn't be seen.

My stomach still hurts and I don't want to look up, but I do want to see the rest of her. I move round the edge of the puddle, to see more of the reflection. The puddle is deep and wide and shines like black glass.

I follow the reflection from the shoe to her ankle to her leg. I move round.

I follow the reflection to the bottom of her dress. I can tell by the shape of it that it is her favourite dress, the one with the layers of silk and gauze and other stuff that I don't know the name of. I move round.

I follow the reflection up her body, to her arms, to her shoulders. I can see that she has left her hair down. I try to see her face, but the reflection stops before reaching it. I move round.

Round and round and round. I still cannot see her face. I am getting dizzy, but something stops me from wanting to turn and look straight at her. I close my eyes for a moment. Open them. She's gone! The reflection shows only the wall of the house and the empty roof.

I turn and run through the gate, round the side of the house, into the back garden. She's lying on her back across the path. There is a large patch of blood spreading out from underneath her head. Her eyes are open. Not blinking.

She doesn't look like Miss Hennessey. She doesn't look like George, or Gina, or Georgina. She just looks like an anyone lying across the path.

I stand and watch her for a little while, just to make sure that she is not going to start breathing.

I am getting cold, shivering. I must go home.

It doesn't seem quite right though. It feels as if there's something else I should do, because I was going to finish her and she's finished herself. I feel odd. Stopped. Stopped in the middle of something. Odd.

Perhaps if I take away her favourite shoes, perhaps that will help. Yes, I'll take her shoes.

But nobody would expect me to wear shoes like these and I might not be able to hide them for very long. If I take them, what will I do with them?

I know! Laura! Laura would wear them! And they'd fit, I know they would.

I'll give them to Laura.

I'll give them to Laura as a coming home present. She'll wear them if I give them to her as a present. She'll love them.

And I can show her the best way to wear them.

That's what I'll do.

Artists' Cemetery
Ann Rower

Artists' Cemetery
Ann Rower

I'm such a fucking ghoul. Now I have added to my collection (which includes [1] a piece of headlight from that time this older woman's foot got stuck on the gas pedal after shopping and doing lunch with her son, ran down thirty people in Washington Square Park, killing five or six (the first time – hard to believe – that I saw that homegrown memorial construct: a wreath, a note, candles, a photo, lasting for days, till the writing ran off the cards from the spring rain. Now they do it all the time. Remember the one on the Mulholland Exit from the 405 for Ennis Cosby, on TV? By now the memorials have morphed from local homegrown to planet-wide, with global 24/7 coverage: Versace, Princess Di, JFK Jr – a particularly scruffy one, I remember thinking, but huge. Now they can be seen at every firehouse and precinct in the city; graffiti autographs scrawled by British royalty on the permanent viewing platforms at what was the Twin Towers. A friend of mine actually snagged – in the early days when Ground Zero was closed off but you could get there from our neighborhood by walking down the East Side Drive and then snaking across Chinatown – some takeout menus with burned edges, a scrap of a 'sell' order from the Coffee Exchange and a shoe – I'd have been right there with her but at the time I couldn't walk because of a herniated disk. But don't you remember when they didn't used to make memorials?); [2] a piece of yellow CAUTION tape from Castelli Gallery in Soho when a huge Richard Serra sculpture that was being loaded in – one that was never supposed to be inside anywhere – crashed down in front of the gallery in Greene Street just as I was walking past on my way to the Angelika Movie Theatre. It fell right in front of me and one of the workers had to have his leg amputated; [3] some concrete, rough on one side and glazed and decorated with little scallops on the other, that I grabbed from the concentration camp (I always call it Birkenstock because I block the real name) that I visited when we were touring in Weimar, a crazy group that included Richard Hell, Kathy Acker, Lynne Tillman, Chris Kraus and Sylvere Lothringer, and was co-sponsored by Semiotext(e) and an East Berlin Press called Galrev, the unofficial backer being a recently exposed Stasi agent named Sascha Alexander who came to every reading smelling of alcohol and his own disgraced unwashed self but treated us to a stay at the Weimar Hilton, from which I still have a bathmat; [4] the pill bottles of dead people – the actor Ron Vawter's last Seconal script, Ralph my ex-student the junkie with AIDS's Marinol bottle, my Aunt Rodie's old Xanaxes) the card from Steve Ross's grave I pinched the first time I took her to Green River Cemetery.

Green River Cemetery, in the back of East Hampton, called Springs Cemetery or the Artists' Cemetery by those in the know, because that's where they all are: Pollock, Lee Krasner, Frank O'Hara, Stuart Davis, Ad Reinhardt, Jimmy Ernst, Alfonso Ossario, Harold Rosenberg, A.J. Liebling, Jean Stafford, James Brooks, Perle Fein and her husband, Henry Geldszahler, Helen Soroff, Stan Vanderbeek, Pierre Franey, Alan Pakula, Elaine de Kooning (but not Bill, because of some scandal about his wife not wanting him to be buried near Elaine, or so the gossip went), as well as many locals, veterans, old families, dogs, odd couples, and my friend Hannah Wilke whose grave I visited right after she died. Because I had printed directions from the funeral, I was able to locate this famous cemetery I'd been searching for for years, waiting to come across, but never found. I should have known it was near Deep Six Road.

If I hadn't visited Hannah, I might never have become so cathected to Steve Ross. At the time of her death, the back part of the cemetery, which is now quite full, was just Hannah; four stacked film reels, anonymous then (now labeled with Vanderbeek's name); Steve Ross, and a bunch of small as yet unmarked boulders for the rest of his family. I didn't really know much about Steve Ross except that he'd been head of Time Warner and died of cancer. For some reason the fact that they called him Steve made me think he was either young or gay. I'd heard that he purchased the land, 111 new plots, himself, when he was dying, perhaps because he wanted the runoff from Pollock's grave to water his own. But later I found out the actual sale was put together by his wife Courtney.

I had no idea how Hannah had wangled herself a spot, especially since she didn't believe she was ever going to die. There too, I later found out it was her husband who bought it, and he must have worked fast 'cos she was in the ground a few days after she died. As I'd known her since high school, when she was Arlene Butter, I visited her a lot, and then discovered my other favourite ghosts. But that first day, it had just been Hannah and Steve that I noticed, so I always thought of them as pioneers – and they had a special place in my heart as well as in that part of the cemetery (then so empty) – especially Steve, who made it all possible. That was three years ago.

'It must be close to the anniversary of his death,' I say, excited, running ahead of her. 'Now I can look up his obituary. I wonder who they're from. There's a card!' I grab it, feeling like a criminal (a familiar feeling). It says: 'Deliver to Steve Ross. Green River Cemetery. Dear Eights, We love you and miss you with all our hearts.' Then a big heart drawn in, then signed 'Quincy'. My heart gets big and crazy.

'Quincy,' I say. 'Maybe it's Quincy Jones,' feeling like a fool. Of course there's a million Quincys but my mind is so pop that the link-up's immediate.

I wonder out loud what the connection is but don't say something really stupid like I'm thinking maybe Steve Ross produced 'We Are the World' – at least not out loud. Maybe Warner Bros is Quincy's label. I even think about when *Quincy* was my favourite TV show, which I haven't thought about in years. Remember *Quincy*? Jack Klugman? That one? Early morgue. I've always loved it.

'You could find out,' she says.

'How?'

We think.

'Yes! Yes! Maybe I could call up Time Warner – no, the Ross family.'

'Keep it simple. Call the florist.'

Why didn't I think of that? 'I'll call the florist,' I say, chagrined. 'But what can I say? This is Courtney Ross and we got these wonderful flowers and the terrible weather washed the card off, or we lost the card and need the address...'

'Keep it simple,' she says. 'I find that when I lie, if it gets too complicated I have trouble keeping it straight in my own head.'

'I know what you mean.'

'And don't say you're Steve Ross's wife. Say you're a personal assistant from the Ross family.'

She's much sharper. Personal assistant is still a relatively new term to me. Later I find out 'keep it simple' is a twelve-step thing.

'Yes, we got these wonderful flowers and the card from Quincy and we know several Quincys and I just wanted to make sure of the last name.'

Even as I'm saying it, it seems pretty stupid, the part about knowing a lot of Quincys. It's never going to work plus I'll be giving myself away and maybe they'd catch me. And then what? But for what? I haven't done anything. Then I slip the card in my pocket and we run away to the next plots.

It was the first time she had been to the cemetery, though she'd been hearing about it from me for a long time, ever since I knew her, when we were writer fans and friends, talking about this book I was writing about the women artists buried in Green River Cemetery. The original conceit of the book was that Lee Krasner and Elaine de Kooning, after all those years of being married to those famous macho art stars, when they come back as ghosts they come back as lesbians and fall in love (something like that had recently happened to me, sort of). The conceit ended up being little more than a one-liner which only lesbians laughed at, but the book developed into a real search to discover what kind of relationship Lee and Elaine did have. I assumed they were friends, having so much in common – their husbands were friends, they hung out at the same bars and went to the same parties and both lived in the city and Springs. How could they not be friends? Mostly this conceit came from my having read, in some introduction to some book, about someone seeing Lee and Elaine bopping down Eighth Street on the late forties, two gorgeous amazon female talents, animated in conversation, bouncing light, as I pictured it. So I interviewed all the survivors, mostly women, to check out my theory, but the real joke was that it turned out they couldn't stand each other. And the real problem was that I hadn't actually been working on the book at all. For months. For six months. Ever since we got together. Longer than I'd ever stopped writing. Because I was in love. And when people would ask us, how is it being two writers, together?, we'd look at each other and laugh.

'We don't write.'

But it wasn't funny. Not anymore. It left me feeling like a ghost myself. So we'd decided that, after that weekend, we wouldn't see each other or call each other, let alone touch each other, for a whole week, because we hadn't been able to write our books since we'd started fucking and after four months it was interfering with everything, even with that, because not writing meant we didn't know who or where we were anymore. But it seemed tragic, like we were breaking up forever, and I was afraid of what would happen when we did see each other.

It was early October but it was very cold. We pulled into the back, like I had the first time I came to Green River, looking for Hannah Wilke's new still-wet grave with the yet-fresh flowers, no headstone yet, just a little placecard made of bronze. I showed her Steve Ross's family plot. I still didn't know much more about Steve except that he was head of Time Warner when he died and I read one article in the business section of the *Times* about what happens when big CEOs get sick in which they said he started out as an undertaker, which struck me as funny. It didn't say that when they get sick they buy cemeteries. Now there are lots more graves quickly filling up Steve's real estate venture. Now it's packed. They had to squeeze Alan Pakula into a corner by the back fence when a pointed steel pole came loose from the truck in front of him on the LIE and rammed his heart as he was making an early getaway from the city right before Thanksgiving. But like I said, when I first saw it, there was only Steve and Hannah and four anonymous empty film reels and somehow I'd communicated my obsession with Steve, as well as all the women artists, to her and she was dying to see them.

'Do you know when Steve died?' she'd been asking, even before we saw the flowers, which I could smell before we saw them, a large slightly wilted bunch of flowers on a stand beside Steve's boulder.

'I don't know.'

We were looking at these two graves en route to the Ross area, graves of, I assume, gay men, one of whom was dead, had died very young, I assume of AIDS, and one of whom just had his name there next to the dead one. I thought it was a little sick and strange. Of course older straight staid couples do this, but they are old people when they make these arrangements and from another time. It seemed strange to me for young gay men, some silly little love song carved in stone that might have to be changed if the live guy finds a new boyfriend.

'Well, probably the other one is very sick too.'

Why didn't I think of that?

I show her the result of the Steve Ross area, all stones, boulders, the Jackson Pollock motif. I wonder if Steve owned any Pollocks and who has them now. One of the kids, probably, the people who have boulders but no names. Maybe some day there'll be a boulder saying Nick and Toni's. Now Mrs Ross, Steve's mother, is there too. It must have been bad. They say losing a child's the worst. But she's here now. Or maybe she was dead already and they moved her here. They do that a lot.

I'm still stuck on the card that's in my pocket. I keep touching it to make sure I haven't lost it or imagined the whole thing.

Why 'Eights'? I wonder why they call him 'Eights'?

We're driving home. Could it be something musical? Well, if it really is Quincy Jones... I could call Quincy up and say I was at Green River Cemetery and I saw the card and was so moved and I'm a big fan of yours and of course of Steve's and I just wondered...

I just wondered... I could talk to Quincy Jones! But I don't know anything about Steve. I should check his obituary first. What if someone notices the card is missing? From the family? I could just say I took it and was going to put it back as soon as I found out. I needed the number.

The first Monday after that visit I decide to dial the florist. First time, I hang up. I've practiced the routine about being the Ross family personal assistant (wonder if I sound too old), but still not quite gotten past the part about finding out the last name of the Quincy person. Finally I call and have the nerve to stay on the line. When I do, I get this young-sounding clerk. I barely get half the sentence out about Steve Ross and the flowers when he burbles out, scarcely able to contain his thrill, 'Yes, yes, they're from Quincy Jones. Quincy Jones. Isn't that fabulous?'

'Quincy Jones, yes, that's what I... I mean –' remembering my role '– I know, thanks, just wanted to check. We know two Quincys.'

'You do?'

'Yes.'

I think now he's excited to have heard from the Ross family. My heart's bumping along and I feel breathless too, then silly, to have been so afraid and to have made up such an elaborate sleuthing strategy. Then I feel guilty to have tricked him. Then relieved, laughing at my fears, my feelings, and thankful. I got lucky. The guy's probably been telling everyone about Quincy. And now he's telling them this, too.

I don't know whose idea it was to fuck in the cemetery. It would be our last night together, at least until we both started working on our books again. We thought it was going to be so cold we spent the afternoon in Revco buying safety pins and improvised a sleeping bag by pinning two shower curtains to a quilt. She had the idea that Revco would sell long underwear. I imagined the kind with little printed animals on it. Wrong. They had nothing thermal. And I could not have imagined how slippery the plastic shower curtain pinned to the outside would make the improvised sleeping bag apparatus. Or how hilarious that part of it would turn out to be, though it didn't feel so cold at all, once we slid inside the bag, once the terror, the fear that this was a terrible error, went away.

At first I felt so scared I thought I was going to pass out. It was only the third time in my life I'd had sex in a cemetery and the other two times I was on chemical drugs. We started to kiss. A car pulled into the back. I thought I was going to faint again. My heart pounded at the thought of getting caught having sex on Hannah Wilke's grave. We kept very still. The car – probably kids looking for a place to park, and not the cemetery police as I'd imagined – made a slow U-turn, crunched over the gravel, pulled out and was gone. Then, soon, the terror slipped away through our warming fingertips and was gone too. We rolled around on top of each other, reversing our positions, laughing, panting, breathing under the covers. Now we were sweating. We lay there for a while to cool down, then flipped over on our backs, and looked at the stars. There wouldn't be that many once I was back in the city. At least, not that I could see.

It was so quiet. We were peaceful. It was beautiful. Romantic. Wild. Daring. But it had to be over. So finally, reluctantly, we slithered out of the bag. We stood up. We folded up the shower-curtain sleeping bag. We tried to be quiet but it was a noisy process. The plastic was crunching too loudly. By now we both felt a little weird. Not bad at all, but it made us very quiet too. What had we done?

Then we got back in the car. I was driving. I turned our car around and shone the headlights on where we'd been. We were already ecstatic. Then suddenly, out of nowhere, we were laughing, hysterical. Marking the place of all this taboo magic, the fabulous secret sex – perhaps desecrating my friend's grave – was this huge shape. Evidence. But of what? You could plainly see it in the headlight beams, the brilliant grass flattened down, this long rectangle of green slippage, at least nine feet long by four feet wide, from the head of the stone where we started sliding downhill to where we stopped afterwards, but so spooky because what it looked like was that some giant long cow, or a herd of cows, had been lying down there. It was hilarious. We couldn't stop howling. That scared me more.

Then I did one more thing. I guess I didn't want the fear to be over. I made her get out of the car again, back into the cemetery blackness, and made her run up in the dark, then dash in the path of the headlights up to Steve Ross's grave and pluck a flower, a big purple lily, wide open, still fresh, fragrant, from Quincy's bouquet, to add, along with the card, to my collection.

The Passing Guest
V.G. Lee

The Passing Guest
V.G. Lee

These are not dreams, they are flashes of memory that bloom like blood-red amaryllis inside my head. I haven't forgotten, only buried them deep, sometimes not deep enough.

I came across the church by accident; a small clearing in woodland, two miles from the unfamiliar town where I was staying. No road passed by, only a footpath, one person wide. A church not meant to be found.

There was nothing frightening in its solitude. The light was bright, the day sunny. Why, there was lawned grass each side of the neat gravel path that led up to the church porch; a pretty boundary wall of painted stone. What is there to fear when you imagine a lawnmower used twice a week at that time of year, when you know that somewhere nearby a tin of white masonry paint is stored, a skin not yet formed across its creamy surface? Someone who mows and paints and stoops to pull weeds from between shiny-leafed rose bushes. What is there to fear?

I wasn't happy. I'd run from a row where all the bitterness and noise had come from me. It had bounced off Monica's indifference like so many blunt knives; the deserted church offered peace. Inside, the silence soothed me, warm as a summer sea. Sun streamed in through the plain high windows, beneath my hands was the comfort of old, smooth wood. On each side of the unadorned altar, a pew stood, each cushioned in velvet, once purple, now almost black with age.

I breathed more easily, my jarring thoughts eased; here was a place and time to move slowly, to rest. I chose the pew in full sunlight, resting my forehead against the palm of my hand. I'm not capable of prayer, I can commune, that's all. If I closed my eyes, I felt I would for once have the space to understand my life; see the wrong turnings taken, the right ones I'd missed. Instead, I was overwhelmed with a sense of complete desolation, as if an ice-cold hand had cupped my heart. Quickly I opened my eyes back into the sunlight. The sensation disappeared, but now I was aware of sounds behind me. I could hear whispering, the rustle of cloth, the crack of dry paper, so faint I realised these sounds must have been with me since entering the church.

I left the warmth of my pew and followed the sound back towards the entrance. There was a narrow wooden door on my left-hand side. In its lock, an old brass key was moving, turning and twisting. I put my hand over it. It continued to turn. I couldn't hold it steady, the whispering grew louder, more insistent, coming from the other side of the door, hissing an eerie, unintelligible entreaty. I put my ear to the wood and felt the press of imprisoned souls. I heard the feeble scratch of nails and saw futile bloodied hands too weak to do more.

'Please, oh please, oh please,' sad clamouring voices rising, finally falling away like a dying wind.

I did nothing. I was frightened, more than frightened. Not running, but walking fast and loudly out of the church, crunching over the gravel, desperate to distance myself from those voices, yet unready to take the dark path back through the trees.

How healing is sun and blue sky, the loud singing of blackbirds. I was safe. Ghosts and voices, the dread of lonely places, we all have our tales to tell. I decided I would take mine back to Monica's flat and we would laugh and shiver and perhaps come back together one day.

For a moment, I sat on the wall looking back at the church. I was smiling, shaky still and for all my apparent ease, ready to run. From behind the church came the benign rattle of a lawnmower being pushed by hand. Before it came into view I could smell and savour the plumes of fresh cut grass tumbling from between the rolling blades. The gardener appeared, moving easily; khaki trousers, shirtsleeves, a lit cigarette. Not a man. A woman.

This is no love story. Any love I was capable of died before this story was born. No, this woman, as pleasant as she looked, as relieved as I was to see her, was a catalyst, no more than that.

Tall, she was my height, hair greying and short like mine. We were of similar age. She nodded an acknowledgement, mowing towards me, head bent as she concentrated on the line she was setting across the grass. When she reached the wall she stopped, turned the mower around and set it in place for the next run.

'Lovely day,' I said.

'Yes, are you all right?'

'Sorry?'

'I saw you rushing out of the church. It's only mice and wind currents in there, at worst, just voices.'

'And the key?'

She shrugged. 'The key is the key. Some things have no explanation.'

'Is the church used?' I asked.

'Well, it's not popular. Too far off the beaten track. But Easter, Harvest Festival, good-weather events, that's about all. I'm paid to keep it tidy. Tuesdays and Saturdays, April to November.'

'Aren't you frightened, out here on your own?'

She smiled, a sweet, surprising smile. 'We're all frightened of something. I'd better get on.'

She stubbed the butt of her cigarette against the wall, then pushed it into the earth.

'What's your name?' I called.

She didn't hear me over the noise of the lawnmower.

I've said that love has no part in this story, that it had died. Not exact enough. Dying suggests a fading away, flame to ember to ash; nothing as abrupt as the reality. My love was licked up, incinerated in just one of the many bonfires Monica lit around her. From a distance I'd loved her – close, and love perished. Subservience, a distorted infatuation was all that was left.

She was attractive, not pretty; clever, not kind; ruthless, not generous – charming when it pleased her to be. Physically, she charmed me. I might be wounded, angry, yet still I remained bewitched by her limbs, her posture, the sounds she made, however ugly – oh, the configuration of her body – lying on the floor, on her bed. 'Love,' you might call it – far too painful for love.

I ran the last half-mile to her flat, polishing and elaborating my story like a stone not quite fine enough for a platinum ring; a story of ghosts and gardeners, or mice and wind currents; humorous, cynical – no mention of my miserable fears. Fast up three flights of uncarpeted stairs, my key twisting easily in her lock, opening the door to high, laughing voices.

Monica and her friends. She had so many. An endless stream of kettle filling and overflowing ashtrays, the telephone ringing late into the night. Only friends, yet they took up all her time, transforming my time to self-pity and destructive jealous anger.

Her friends, her kitchen, their hands half raised in greeting, half-hearted smiles to match. Monica passing me a cup of cold tea, saying, 'Watch out, everybody, I think our Sandra's about to burst. Brought her loved one back a wee scrap of news and can't wait two minutes to let it out.'

The woman on her right began to laugh.

'Fuck off,' I said and walked out of the room.

'Oh dearie, dearie me,' Monica's mocking voice and their laughter.

Later, nice as pie again, rubbing the back of my neck gently, saying, 'Come on, Sandra, a little fun, means nothing, we all tease each other. Sandra, Sandra, tell me a story.'

In the dark I told her, our faces almost touching, duvet pulled up around our ears.

'On Saturday, we'll go together,' she said, 'the two of us. An outing. We'll investigate.'

All was reconciled. She took my face and pressed it into the warm silk of her breasts, wrapped her legs around my waist pulling me into her body. That feeling, when night surrounds you both, blotting out the conflicts of the day and you and she either drown or fly.

I was pushed forward by events. Monica for her part had become careless. It wasn't jealousy on my part – I'm a coward – I know it, so did she. Push a coward, even an inch farther than their fears will sustain them, and be careful. Don't leave your back exposed, don't let your attention wander, not for a minute, not for a split second. Us cowards, we're forever alert, waiting for a chance to escape, to rid ourselves of our persecutors.

At ten o'clock the following Saturday, Monica and I set out. The morning sun was behind us, baking our shoulders and the backs of our heads. We carried small rucksacks containing sandwiches, a can of Coke each, a bottle of mineral water. Over the rusting railway bridge, taking the path that ran up into the woods. On each side we were hemmed in head-high by blackberry bushes, their thorny suckers clutching at our ankles. The blackberries were huge, hanging in lustrous clumps. I pulled several off, they were as sweet as if soaked in sugar.

'Try them, Monica, they're delicious.'

'No thanks.'

'It's such a waste. No one collects blackberries any more,' I said.

Ahead of me, her shoulders twitched irritably.

'We could pick some on our way home,' I persisted.

'I don't think so,' Monica said.

The church was locked.

'I'm sure she won't be long – she said Saturday.'

'Did "she" have a name?'

'I told you, we only spoke for a moment.'

Monica sat down on the grass, pulled her can of Coke from her rucksack, opened it and drank. We waited in silence. Finally I asked, 'What are you thinking?'

'I hate you asking me, "What are you thinking?"'

'Sorry.'

'You do it all the time.'

'Sorry.'

'Sorry's not good enough.'

We heard the hiss of bicycle tyres and the woman's head and shoulders moved lazily towards us on the other side of the wall. She waved, seeming unsurprised at our being there.

'Won't be a minute,' she called as she sped past. I looked at Monica. She was smiling.

Within fifteen minutes Monica had a name and a life history, mutual experiences, a synchronised childhood. I could see they would meet and talk and laugh with all her other friends long after I was gone and well forgotten.

'Sandra says she heard ghostly voices,' Monica said, without looking at me.

The woman shrugged. 'Ghosts. I don't know. I've heard the noises, never seen anything. It's so familiar I hardly notice it any more, they're just the sounds of an old disused building.'

'Will you show me?'

'If you want.'

Monica walked into the church, up to the altar, ran her hands over the backs of the pews as I had done. It was peaceful, no wind today, no voices, no scratching of nails on wood.

The gardener unlocked the side door, leaving the brass key in the lock and went in ahead of us. It was a small, cell-like room, no furniture, nothing. A square box lined with grey stone, two triangular windows set high on the outer wall, the light from them marking the floor like the distorted eyes of a clown. On the floor, in one corner, was a worn engraving:

Hear my prayer Lord,
Listen to my cry,
Do not be deaf to my weeping,
For I find shelter with you;
I am a passing guest.

Monica knelt to read the inscription, tracing the words with her finger, while the gardener stood, arms folded, her calf almost brushing Monica's shoulder. They were a pair, confident equals. I was someone to close doors, to shut up shop.

'I'll wait outside,' I said.

The gardener nodded. Monica didn't look up. I pulled the door gently closed, turned the key, left them to it. Probably, I'd reached the trees before they realised. I hurried. I wanted to be out of range when they started to shout.

I believe we make our own hell. There's no point in believing in celestial punishment, teaching of lessons, all the pain, all the guilt – we cause the situation that brings about its own retribution.

I stayed on in Monica's flat and waited for her to come home. Someone would let them out, I was sure of it. I parried all questions. I said, 'She's gone to London – one week – maybe two – staying with friends.'

After three days I began bolting the door, imagining dragging footsteps on the stairs. Doors frightened me, opened or closed. I was fearful of letting her in, fearful of shutting her out. She'd had water, most of the can of Coke, sandwiches. How long could they survive if no one came? A week? Yes, a week. I couldn't sleep. I fell awake into nightmares. After six days I went back.

In those six days, summer had slipped into autumn. The blackberries hung in desiccated bunches, their leaves beginning to curl. I walked with my head down into driving rain, my thin tweed jacket soaked. The trees creaked and swayed, wind washing through them with huge gusty sighs.

The church door stood open, leaves banked inside the porch. I didn't go in. I stood on the threshold and listened. I could see the narrow door, the key in the lock, unmoving. They wouldn't be dead – not in six days. Frail, mad, surely not dead.

I stepped onto the grass and went silently around to the other side of the church. I found the shed. Its door had broken from its hinges and lay across the path. There was a wooden ladder, old but sturdy, all I needed.

Not a sound except the beat of my heart to alert them. I rested the ladder against the wall. Slowly, stealthily, I climbed up towards one of the triangular windows. In the half-light I could see them, huddled together on the floor of the cell, limbs twined around one another for warmth. I imagined the smell, the horror of that tiny room; not one passing guest, but two.

It wasn't enough for me to see them like that – two heaps of grey clothing, dehumanised. I had to see their faces, their souls. I rapped on the glass; jaunty, just a fellow up a ladder, saying, 'Hey, break it up in there.'

At first nothing, then a slow unwinding of limbs, curled bodies rolling onto their backs, like two worms poked with a stick. I saw no souls, only blurred unrecognisable faces.

'Please, oh please, oh please,' their whisper shivered through the glass.

I went back to the flat and collected my things. Only a small suitcase, not much to show for two years of my life. I disappeared back to Birmingham, did the necessary to avoid being found. Through a friend of a friend of a friend, I heard: two days after my visit to the church, a Mrs Shephard had come in to decorate the church for Harvest Festival – they were both still alive.

Impossible to leave matters quite there. I was uneasy, dissatisfied. I needed something more to close the chapter. Two weeks later, from a kiosk in New Street Station, I rang Monica.

'Hello,' she said. Her voice, yes, but cautious, hesitant – a change had taken place.

'It's me. Sandra,' I said.

A strange sound then; choking that became crying. She didn't put the receiver down on me, she kept on, crying and crying as if her heart and spirit were broken.

Oh yes, my pain was still with me, red-hot in my breast, but those tears, for whatever reason, they did me the world of good.

Justin Thomas Is Dead
Georgina McIntosh

Justin Thomas Is Dead
Georgina McIntosh

It was the same day that my mother went into hospital that the whole Justin Thomas thing started.

I know this because Mary McPherson, the woman who looks as if she's stored a bowl of botulising porridge under her chin, put The Memo into my hand at the same time as the District Nurse rang to inform me that they were taking Ma in, and that:

1. I'd better get more knickers, a hairbrush and let the telly licence folk know; &
2. This was it this time.

My chest opened up and closed in again at what felt like exactly the same time. Big bubbles of air bounced up and down inside me. All the words that I needed to say were inside them but when I opened my mouth none of the buggers would burst. Nothing came out.

I heard one of those screams in my head that I once read about in a book about the Ancient Greeks. It was one of those *Aa-ee-aa-oe-ii-aeeoaeee* numbers that one of their queens used when she'd eaten her next-door neighbour's baby or something, and she didn't have an adequate word around to describe how painful her chest was feeling with the big expanding bubble things inside her. I looked around for some sort of divine saving from all this, but all I could see was Botulised Porridge Lady with a paper in her hand. Somehow the Sword of Protestant Politeness came to my rescue.

'Thank you very much for your kindness to me,' I said, taking the paper and putting the phone down at the same time. Then I read The Memo.

TO ALL STAFF
WE HAVE A GHOST IN THE TEA ROOM
COMMUNICATION WITH ANY DEPARTED LOVED ONES
5.15P.M. TODAY (Wed.)
50p FOR THE TEA FUND
(See Mary McPherson about sandwiches and your car passes)
Crisps 10p extra.

I could tell by the fantastic eye tarantellas that were going on between Lizzie Dalrymple and Isobel Gilfillan that nobody had really expected *me* to be sitting there at five o'clock that night. Probably because I never willingly joined in *anything* with these people because they all had the IQ of a Bingo Book and I couldn't really fathom why I was there myself.

More to the point I had no clean knickers to take to the hospital. None. And if I continued to sit here I didn't know how I was going to get them either. The problem was that I just kept putting all the shitty ones (which Ma thought were hidden under her bed) in the coal cellar, because I couldn't face seeing them all stained after I'd washed them. And please don't tell me to change to Bold Automatic or that Persil is the best, or any of that, because I've done it all, and it's crap. They are all as bad as each other, these washing powders, and when my mother finally gives up the bloody ghost and dies, I'm going to go into that coal cellar and send all her pants to some ombudsman and get those Lever Giants investigated, and we'll see just how damn smart and squeaky clean they are then.

Anyhow, at 5.15 p.m. Mary McPherson came around with her big steel teapot, poured me tea without asking if I wanted it or not, and sat down next to me. 'Custard cream or Jaffa Cake?' she asked pleasantly, opening her mouth up and putting one of each in at the same time. I nodded, without indicating any preference, and certainly without looking directly at her saliva mating with the chocolate, because this is not something that you want to watch without the aid of David Attenborough, trust me.

'Here,' she said, handing me two Jaffa Cakes and some A5 for the Ouija. 'Do "yes/no" papers and numbers as well, will you?'

'I'm not surprised this Justin Thomas keeps coming here,' Fiona Johnstone said, scraping Flora Light onto a newly defrosted Mother's Pride. 'Ma John says this place is built on a cemetery.'

Majohn. That's what I'll call this woman in my head until the day they jail me for her decapitation. I swear, she can't start a day without saying it. And it will be *decapitation* that I'll do to her because every three or four minutes she gets all agitated over absolutely *Nobody-Knows-What* and her head wobbles about like one of those stupid doggie things in the back of a car window. Now if I was Caligula or Zeus made mortal for a short window in the day, I could put every deformed, personality-dead idiot like Majohn Johnstone out of their misery right now and nobody would even bother to clean up *that* mess. They'd all just kiss my toes through my sandals and thank me. And I'd wave back and say, 'It's OK. I did it for you all because I love you. It was nothing.'

'Hey, is banana all right for everybody?' Fiona suddenly said, looking at her creation of bread and fruit. 'Mary, did it not occur to you that not everybody is a bloody monkey like yourself?'

'Banana's *fine*, Fiona,' everybody, including me, seemed to say all at once.

'But I've got *twenty-four* banana pieces here.'

'Nobody's bothered about the stupid pieces, Fiona!' Isobel Gilfillan had organised all the ripped-up letters on the table with the speed of a world champion croupier.

'Come on, come *on*, you lot. I've got a karaoke barbecue to get to after this, and I've got three weans to feed before that.'

I had a vision then of my ethereal mother in the side ward they'd have taken her to. The curtains were closed to keep the sun from disturbing her, but it still overwhelmed its way through them nonetheless. All watered over, her eyes confused and unfocused, her head was making a figure of eight in that delirious Stevie Wonder way she'd been doing for the past week. I was sure she was looking at me when she did that. She wasn't saying anything, not asking for me, or for *anything*, just lost in that stale cloud of hers, emitting the occasional 'oo ee aaeee'.

Nothing concrete or useful came out her mouth, though. No

names or phone numbers so I could phone somebody up and say, 'Excuse me, is this the Fried-Egg Head Helpline? I have a problem – my *mother*, yes. I'd like to reverse the Fried-Egg Head process please. Can you help me? Hello? Can somebody help me, please?'

I felt sick. In my head I was saying, 'Grow up! Get up to that hospital *now*, lady! Let her at least feel your *hand* or *sing* to her or do something that *she* would *like*, you bad, stupid, evil, evil bastard!' But I couldn't move. I'm a terrible weak person, I know it, but I just couldn't help it. I wanted to stay there with the Bingo Book Ladies and have a seance with a ghost I didn't know.

'Oh, a barbecue, that sounds *magic*,' Lizzie Dalrymple chipped in lovingly. 'I'm totally starving, Fiona, honest I am, but there's no way I can have a banana piece right now 'cos me and Jimmy are having a fish supper after this, and I'm on a diet for the wedding.'

I couldn't look at her. Apart from anything else her mouth looked as if her teeth had been extracted at gunpoint and put back in by herself very grudgingly. And Jimmy? No, please don't get me started on Jimmy. Try and imagine Goofy from the Disney cartoons, but thirty years later, wearing overalls and a 'St Francis is my Hero' RSPCA badge, which is very appropriate somehow, I think, considering the Disney connection. Well, that was Jimmy. They were to be married in a fortnight and I'm just glad I didn't have to pay for the photographs.

'I want to ask Justin Thomas if me and Jimmy will get pregnant straight away,' said Lizzie with this beatific look on her face.

Seeing her then, all beautiful in her expectation, I felt the first real happiness that I'd felt in ages come over me. I got this notion to jump up in front of them all, like one of those music hall comedians I loved to watch on old TV shows when I was really young, and shout: 'GOOD EVENING LADIES AND GENTLEMEN!' But instead of 'Ladies and Gentlemen' I'd say, 'Ladles and Jellyspoons,' like I used to say to make Ma laugh when we were watching the shows.

'GOOD EVENING! GOOD EVENING LADLES AND JELLYSPOONS! ROLL UP! UP! UP! FOR THE GREATEST EXTRAVA-GANZA, THE MOST AMAZING, FASCINATING THING YOU WILL

SEE IN THIS AUDITORIUM FOR A LONG LONG TIME TO COME. WHAT IS THIS SHOW? WHAT CAN THIS ASTOUNDING ENTERTAINMENT BE FOR YOU TONIGHT? IT'S THE ONE – drumroll – THE ONLY – more drumroll – NEVER TO BE REPEATED – no more drumroll – big pause – JUSTIN THOMAS IS DEAD SHOW!'

But I didn't get the chance because, as usual, Wing Commander McPherson had taken charge of the whole thing, and before I knew it, my finger was placed on that upturned glass along with everybody else's and we were off.

Was there anybody there?

Y-E-S

Who was it?

J-U-S-T-I-N T-H-O-M-A-S

'Is anybody shoving this?' I asked, then immediately wished I hadn't. They all looked at me as if I'd just asked if they'd flashed their boobs in Mathieson's the Bakers and been oxtered out of the premises by the vanilla slice police to the Extreme Disgrace of their Family Names.

'Look,' said Isobel, 'he won't answer us if we're not all serious about this.'

'For *God's sake!*' I heard myself hiss. 'It's not bloody life or death this, you know!'

'Let's ask him something complicated that nobody here could possibly know the answer to,' Majohn said quickly.

'What? Like does the square root of negative one equal infinity?' I just couldn't help myself. If there's some adolescent smart-arsed thing to say, I'm the total waste of space that's got to do it.

Mary McPherson raised one eyebrow. 'Right,' she started to say to me with just a hint of annoyance, then she stopped herself, and when I looked up, Lizzie Dalrymple was all Bambi-eyed, staring at me as if she was about to burst into tears. Like *I* was the big sad bastard instead of her with her Sunken Garden face and her useless infertile ovaries.

'*What?*' I looked around at them. They all looked as if they were going to blubber. They looked as if it was their fault that I was watching the most decent person imaginable become a half-chewed vegetable in God's diseased casserole of life.

'My mother's dying,' I said to Isobel Gilfillan, 'and you've got a date in your garden to sing "I Will Survive".'

Christ, that Justin Thomas. What a load he had to get off his chest.

Died in Greenock 1912. B-Y M-Y O-W-N H-A-N-D.

We all sat still for a bit, because nobody could really work out which one of us would have the wit to make this up. Frankly my money was on Majohn. She was living her life through somebody else – it had to be her. She was the first to speak, which just proved my point nicely.

She leaned right down to the paper on the table as if speaking to a tiny Tom Thumb-sized ghost.

Why did you kill yourself, Justin?

She spoke slowly and in a very pronounced way because he was obviously deaf and retarded as well as doomed to Eternal Damnation for the Taking of His Own Life thing.

M-Y B-A-B-Y H-A-S G-O-N-E D-O-W-N T-H-E P-L-U-G H-O-L-E.

She sat up.

'What the hell does that mean?' Isobel Gilfillan was not known for her equanimity. 'Fiona, what are you playing at?'

'What do you mean, what am *I* playing at?' Majohn was furious. See, I wasn't the only one who saw her inadequacies. Everybody else thought she was behind this Justin Thomas crap as well.

'My *baby* has gone down the *plug hole?*' Isobel got up with a look of derision on her face that would fry a bigger sausage than Fiona Johnstone.

'"My baby has gone down the plug hole" is one of those old Victorian-type rhymes,' I said. 'It's about people who couldn't afford to feed their children, so their babies died from starvation.'

'So *you're* who's at it.' Isobel Gilfillan turned to me, obviously having forgotten that I'm an emotional mess to be sympathised with at this terrible time.

'I can assure you I am *not*. And don't blame me just because you've never read a book in your life.'

Isobel moved towards me like a sweet cat suddenly wronged. Dying mother or not, I was for it.

'Sit on your arse, Isobel.' Mary McPherson put her crisps back in the bowl. She set her face in a way that said I was a woman on the edge, *remember*. 'It's just a bit of light enter-*tainment*.'

'I am not doing it!' I looked straight at Fiona Johnstone. 'I've got no reason whatsoever to be making up ghosts for your entertainment, I can assure you of that right now!' I wasn't taking the blame for anybody else's emotional mess.

'It is not light enter-*tainment*.' Isobel spat little bits of semi-masticated banana all around her. 'This is precisely the sort of thing the priest has to get out of his bed in the middle of the night to do exorcisms for!'

I wanted to laugh. Mary McPherson's chin was just about curdled in a cartel of chewing and rage, although I wasn't too sure just who or what *she* had to be so mad at. In fact, everybody was all brewed up for no good bloody reason at all that I could see.

Now we were all standing.

There was obviously to be a rammy with the custard creams.

'You either believe in things or you don't,' Lizzie Dalrymple said quietly. 'And I believe this ghost is trying to tell something *very* important to each and every one of us.' Her face was so still, *so* serious, that everybody sat back down again.

Then, out of nowhere conscious, I started to sing:

'My baby has gone down the plug hole
My baby has gone down the plug
The poor little thing was so skinny and thin
He oughter been bathed in a jug...'

Mary McPherson half-screamed and slapped one hand over her mouth, banana piece stiff in the other. This was obviously not my voice they were hearing. I felt like I was two people. One was floating inside me, laughing like the winning baby in a big giggle-fest, whilst the other was howling a howl no one could even hear, not even me. I knew that I was singing: I knew that this was not my voice, but I really couldn't stop it.

Suddenly I was by myself again. It wasn't like some creepy horror show or one of those spoof spooky films or anything. No heads were birling round, no vomit spewing. I was just by myself again, like I said.

'They were obviously quite poor then,' I said.

Nobody spoke.

'I'm definitely not at it, Isobel.'

How did you kill yourself, Justin?

Mary McPherson was still in a state of disablement, so she lost her Wing Commander status to the suddenly animated Lizzie. Our fingers were all back on the glass again.

Nothing.

'See, he's gone now, with all that singing and carrying on.' Isobel didn't know whether to be mad with me still or not. The glass wobbled. Then totally whizzed round the next few letters.

'I-L-A-S-H-E,' read out Majohn. 'Shouldn't somebody write this down?'

We all suddenly got focused on looking for a pen.

'Oh for God's sake! Did nobody think to keep the bloody pen?' Isobel was annoyed but obviously not enough to get off her big short-tempered arse to get it.

'You're a totally crabbit cow, do you know that?' I took my hand off the glass, which had stopped moving anyway. 'I'll write the rest of it down, OK?' I went to the drawer where I'd put the rest of the A5 and sat back down again in a half-huff.

I wouldn't be part of their finger frenzy any more, then.

'How did you die, Justin?' I asked the board.

Slowly, the glass moved.

I-L-A-S-H-E

Then back to the whizzing again.

D-M-Y-S-E-L-F-O-N-A-S-H-I-P-G-O-I-N-G-O-U-T-T-O-S-E-A

I was finding it hard to read the letters out and write them down, the glass was moving so fast.

'What's that about the sea?' Mary frowned, which was not a good idea. It did that chin of hers no favours at all.

'I – Lashed – Myself – On – A – Ship – Going – Out – To – Sea.' It took me ages to work it out.

'I *Lashed* Myself On A Ship Going Out To Sea?' They all repeated it to themselves as if they couldn't quite believe that he hadn't said, 'I Took Thirty-four Anadin Extra And Went Straight To My Bed Like You're Supposed To.'

What do you want from us, Mr Thomas?

Now Isobel was leaning down to the paper on the table.

What is it that is hurting you so much?

Now, I don't know what came over me or why I did it, all I remember were the crisps and sandwiches falling onto Lizzie Dalrymple's knee. As I stood on top of our Ouija board, all the scrappy papers grabbed a burst of air and floated away from me, and I was singing again.

'Do not forsake me, oh my darling,' sang this lovely, perfect, other woman's voice. I was crying. Standing above them all, weeping tears of grief for poor dead Justin Thomas and his starving baby.

As I fell on top of Lizzie and squashed banana into her legs, I was sure I heard a voice. 'Oh that's Ma John's favourite! Was it *High Noon* or *Paint Your Wagon* that was from?'

But it was OK; I didn't have to answer her. I didn't have to clean up slimy, mushed banana or walk over a carpet of crisps, or even hide shitty knickers in the coal cellar any longer, because I was suddenly safe. Lizzie Dalrymple was holding onto me like a baby born that morning.

Touch Pain
Cecilia Tan

Touch Pain
Cecilia Tan

I met Lizette the summer after my mother died. I was doing that thing they call 'keeping busy', working afternoons at the Arts Coop shelving books and doing handiwork. Stuart Green introduced us, actually, ironic as that may seem what with Stuart having been the last man I attempted to date, what, twenty years ago? Maybe he felt like he was making up for it somehow. Anyway, it was Stuart, soft around the middle and gray around the edges, who tugged on my sleeve one late summer day and said, 'There's somebody you should meet.'

I carried my box of used books to a wicker table in the corner and stood there holding them while he introduced Lizette Pierce and then stood there shuffling his feet. Lizette rose after a moment and said, 'Nice to meet you,' and tried to shake my hand, whereupon I put the books down on a chair and Stuart said something about needing to get back to the store. He went to the coffee bar, asked for something to go, and then waved as he crossed the street to his place. Convenient, this little slice of culture in our upstate town. Clustered at one end of Main we've got Earthways (Stuart's new age health food place), a handmade furniture outlet, and the Arts Coop: part bookstore, part art gallery, part café, in what used to be the old post office. The 'new' post office wasn't new anymore, either; they'd built it when I was a child. But the old postwar building still reminded me of riding my father's shoulders to pick up Christmas packages from distant relatives. Whenever I walked into the place, I could almost hear the echoey sound of the clerks bantering and see Mr Grimes, the postmaster, peering at me from under his visor.

I soon figured out why Stuart insisted Lizette and I meet. Stuart was one of the few who knew for sure that she and I did have one significant feature in common, despite the obvious differences – she was ten years younger than me, a well-groomed flowery kind of woman, while I am a denim-jacketed lumberjack type... I didn't ask how he knew about her. He only 'knew' about me as a result of our ill-fated prom date and my radical change in appearance after my first semester of college. It was nosy of him, but, I liked her; she had a nice smile and she liked books. It wasn't long before I had asked her out to the house for dinner.

The house had been empty of my mother for seven months then – eight if you counted the month she spent in the hospital – and now it was mine, really mine. I'd come back to live with her four years ago, to settle down after years in the city with high rent, bad jobs, and fleeting relationships. To keep myself busy, I dabbled in photography, sketching and painting (hence my part in the Arts Coop), did odd jobs and maintenance for neighbors, and now I raised my cats alone in the big old farmhouse where I'd grown up. I could still see my mother, in her home-made apron, cutting up apples from the trees in back to make tarts and rolling out cookie dough – she always made extra so there would be enough for the neighbor kids, too. My cousins visited in the summers, and as a child I'd had friends. The house felt like children belonged here and I wondered what had turned me from such a lively child into such a loner. My parents had never had the son they wanted, a brother I'd imagine would have married and had a bunch of kids to run around the place. I'd never stuck with someone long enough to adopt or conceive. It was getting late for that now, anyway.

But here came Lizette, with a bouquet of flowers to my front door, in a sundress and woven sunhat even though it would be dark in an hour, and suddenly the house didn't seem so empty. The cats, Raven and Bella, took a liking to her immediately. Both of them tried to sit in her lap at once, as we sat on the porch swing and drank hard cider and watched the sky turn purple. We talked about books we'd read and the history of Maple County. And after a dinner of chicken and wild rice, I knew I'd do almost anything to get her to stay.

She was sitting in the living room by the open window, once in a while the night breeze lifting her fine, straight hair from her shoulder, Raven curled up like a black slipper on her feet and Bella a calico pillow in her lap.

'Do you have to go back?' I said, not sure if she had someone expecting her – if, like me, she had come here to be with relatives – or if she lived alone. We hadn't talked about her situation much, or why she'd moved here from the city at age thirty-five.

'Back?' she said, turning a smile on me. 'I can be wherever I want, whenever I want.' Her head rocked slowly from side to side as she looked at me.

Years of being alone had left me rusty and I had never been good at this sort of thing, anyway. 'You're welcome to... I mean, you don't have to, but if you wanted to, you could... stay the night.' There, I'd said it.

She dislodged Bella and stood up, reaching for me with a smooth, tanned hand, to touch my face. Her smile withered a bit. 'There's something I... I should tell you.'

'You can tell me,' I said, trying not to stiffen or bristle, while my mind tried frantically to guess what she might say: she had a lover already, she had AIDS, she would have some reason that would come between us like so many times before.

'I... I have nightmares sometimes. I sleepwalk, see things. Talk in my sleep. Sometimes I scream a lot. It...' She bit her lip and looked off into a corner of the room. 'It's best if you know it now and not later.' I could see pain in her eyes and could imagine lovers abandoning her in the past, almost see their faces turning cold to her as they came to resent her.

'Not a problem, sugar,' I said, pursing my lips. 'I guess I should tell you I snore.'

'We're even, then,' she said, and took the small step forward to close the gap between us and planted a light kiss on my cheek.

The place I see my father most is in the barn. He did woodworking there, some sculpting, some tinkering, just like me, I guess. I'd installed a potter's wheel and built a kiln but hadn't used them much. Otherwise the workshop was mostly the same and when I sat at the wheel I could imagine him shuffling back and forth at the workbench, taking apart an old radio or making a wooden toy for a nephew. I don't doubt where I got my handy streak from, not to mention so many tools.

In the weeks that followed, Lizette spent so many days with me, walking through the woods, weeding the vegetable patch, doing repairs around the house. I had started repainting the third floor when Mom died, and then had abandoned the project, but now I started it again. We did the little corner bedroom powder blue and Lizette stenciled dark blue flowers around the molding. With Dad's pension, the inheritance, and my savings, I didn't have to work for a while, and neither did Lizette. She told me she too had some inheritance; her stepfather had left her a house near the old mill. 'You're so handy,' she said as we worked on resetting the second-floor fireplace. 'I should have you come take a look at my place. It needs a lot of work.' But she never made the invitation specific, and went home every other night to see her dog. In the evenings she devoured my books, everything from feminist theory to tawdry detective novels, and nights when she stayed, we lay like two spoons on the big canopy bed. How I would have liked for it to stay that way for a few years, an almost domestic bliss.

The first night she woke me I clawed my way up out of a dream to find her sitting up in bed next to me, screaming. She put her hands over her face and screamed and screamed like someone was killing her, her body heaving with each exhalation. And then, with a suddenness that made me fear she was dead, she fell onto the pillow, like someone had switched her off. I put my hand on her shoulder and felt her deep, slow breathing. She seemed quite asleep. Adrenaline tides washed through me and I lay back down, but I did not sleep, not for a long while. In my ears the silence seemed to echo her screams, as if somewhere inside her the screaming went on. I felt something come loose in my heart, like there was some emotion knocking around free inside my chest now, something I couldn't quite name or bring to light. But some time before dawn sleep came back up for me.

In the morning Lizette didn't act like anything had happened and I didn't bring it up, but as soon as she went back to her place in her little red hatchback, I took a ride to the county library and did some research. The library was another old building, unchanged since my childhood except for the two glowing computer terminals by the card catalog. My parents used to bring me once a week for a children's story hour, and peruse the stacks while I sat entranced by tales of adventure and fantasy told by gravelly voiced Mrs Mosely.

The computer terminals proved useful and I searched databases for information about night-time disorders. There was a condition called pavor nocturnus, night terrors, that caused people to scream inexplicably during the night. Most people grew out of it, but not all. Lizette was a bit old to grow out of it, I supposed, and there was no known treatment. I read a bunch of stuff about sleepwalking and other disorders too and was disappointed by how little was known.

I was about to leave when I heard someone from behind the stacks, an old woman's voice, intoning a passage I remembered well. The sad, sad, moment from *Charlotte's Web*, describing the end of the county fair, and Charlotte's death. I felt tears come to my eyes, as they had in my childhood, as the chapter ended with the words, almost whispered, 'No one was with her when she died.' I heard the book snap shut.

'Mrs Mosely?' I rounded the shelf, but the tiny chairs were all empty in the children's corner. Some trick of the acoustics? I went up to the desk where a clean-cut young man in an unironed button-down shirt asked if he could help me. 'Is Mrs Sarah Mosely still working here?' I asked, thinking to myself if she was old when I was a child, she must be in her nineties now. The young man looked puzzled and said he didn't know the name. I explained she used to read to the children here every week.

His face lit briefly with recognition and then he shook his head. 'I'm sorry, ma'am,' he said, 'but she passed on quite a few years ago.'

'How do you know?' I demanded, feeling testier than I had a right to.

'There's a plaque dedicated to her outside.' His face darkened, too, reflecting my anger back at me.

'Oh, I... why, thank you.' I tried to smile or say something nicer, but failed. We were both shaking our heads as I left.

Two days went by before I saw Lizette again.

That night we went out for dinner at the fancy candlelit place they've made out of the old mill, Perser's. We could hear the rushing water as we ate, and afterward we sat outside on the stone overlook, listening to the splashing of the old water wheel and looking at the stars. The cobblestone outcrop where we sat was above the mill pond, at the top of worn stone steps leading down to the water. She leaned her head on my shoulder and we talked. I mean Talked. The kinds of talking you do when you really care about someone, when you're getting ready to give your heart to them, all kinds of silly things, like I told her about the first time my cousins and I had come here to catch frogs, and how when I first moved to the city the first thing I'd done was cut my hair. I'd waited until after I left to do it so my father wouldn't be heartbroken over it, and when I came back for Thanksgiving the following year, he never said a word and left me wondering if he really even noticed. Lizette told me about her father's death when she was a small child and her mother's remarriage when Lizette was ten. She'd always wanted a sister and had a pretend sister named Big Beulah who ordered everyone around but only the stuffed animals obeyed her.

Autumn was coming on and it began to get chilly as we sat there, but we didn't care. The restaurateurs closed up and left for the night. The stars shone clear and bright, and Lizette told me the names of some of them, which I forgot. And I wanted to tell her I loved her. But this wasn't the right moment for that, not yet. You only get one time to be the first time, after all, so I settled for hugging her tight.

'Do you think I'm too old for you?' I asked, suddenly needing to know, and knowing that at this moment she'd tell me the truth.

She laughed, a piping, bird-like sound with her mouth closed. 'Mary,' she said, 'too old for what? You're not old enough to be my mother, and that's young enough for me. And look, you've hardly got any gray hair and I've got plenty.'

'That's not true,' I said, but in the moonlight her blonde highlights shone like silver. Now I laughed. For a second she looked to me like a little girl in an old granny wig. 'Did I tell you about how my cousins and I would put on plays for our parents when we were little?'

I was about to tell her how we'd pick an absent family member to ridicule, Uncle Randolph if he wasn't there, usually, when I saw a man walking along the water below us. 'Hey, look down there.'

She squinted and said she didn't see anything. He was limping like he needed a cane but didn't have one, one leg stiff. He was walking toward the mill, along the stone walkway at the pond's edge. He was looking out over the water and not at us, making slow progress with his bad leg. 'Maybe he needs some help,' I said, and stood up, thinking perhaps he was hiking after dark and hurt himself.

'I don't see who you're talking about.'

'Right down there.' I pointed. He wasn't where I expected him to be, though, as if he'd slipped backwards in his progress. I went down the stone steps toward him and by the time I reached the bottom of the stairs, he was all the way back to the path's edge, walking toward me and yet further from me than before. 'Do you need a hand?' I said, but he didn't look up or acknowledge me. I made it halfway down the walk, and yet he remained far away, his feet still treading toward me. I stood still, not daring to breathe somehow, as he took step after step until, at last, he came near. 'Hey.' I reached out to touch his shoulder as he went past me, and I stumbled forward, like when you go down stairs in the dark and forget there's one more.

'Hey, what's going on?' Lizette said, catching me.

It felt like I'd put my hand through a big spider web and I pulled back from her quickly, rubbing my fingers together and dropping the sticky strands as fast as I could. Crazy feelings welled up in me – a surge of depression, failure, hopelessness – and then went away. 'You didn't see him?'

She was shaking her head from side to side, her arms folded over her chest. She was wearing a light knit dress and a matching jacket; she was probably cold.

'Let's get back to the truck.'

She stood firm. 'What did you see?'

'Nothing, I guess. It looked like a man, walking. But he had a limp and it was almost like he went backward.' I shook my head hard.

We walked to the truck and got in.

'Do you think it was a ghost?' I said, once I had the engine started.

She shrugged and looked out into the dark. 'Then why didn't I see it?' She shivered. 'Well, whatever.' I had the feeling she was going to say more, but then didn't. I was not the type to pry.

I had half-planned in my mind to suggest after dinner that we go back to her place since it was so near to here. But when I started to suggest it – 'Do you want to fetch some warmer clothes?' – something in the way Lizette tightened her arms around her chest made me back away from the idea. 'Or... or we could build a fire back at the house,' I finished lamely. Right then I wanted to be home, among familiar things, and so I started the truck and back to the farmhouse we went.

That night, Lizette again woke screaming, only this time she jumped out of the bed and went running through the house, scattering cats and bedclothes as she went. Bathrobe on, I followed as quickly as I could, into the room that had been my mother's study, where most of her books still sat on shelves, waiting to be dusted after years of neglect. Lizette stopped screaming and looked around.

'Liz? Are you awake?'

She didn't answer me. Sleepwalking, I guessed, and tried to lead her back to the bed. 'Come on, honey, it's cold in here.'

She sat down in my mother's old wooden desk chair and said, in a small voice, 'In a minute. I'll be there in a minute.'

'OK, honey, OK.' I looked at her as she sat there, her eyes far away, and she seemed clouded in a nimbus of fog. Or maybe that was my sleep-deprived eyes. I wanted to hug her and make warm milk to put her back to sleep like my mother would when I had a bad dream. But Lizette didn't just get scared of the bogeyman or the big bad wolf. Somehow I knew that now.

The database of sleep disorders had said it was best to wait and not try to wake the person. I sat with my back to the fireplace and watched Lizette, my heart aching.

'It's your fault,' my mother said.

I jumped at the sound. There in the room, my mother's voice. I looked around, and it seemed she was standing by the bookcase, her arms folded over her chest. My hands trembled as I took a step toward her, knowing it couldn't be her, and yet, what else could I do?

'I have only you to blame,' she said.

My father's voice came from behind me, in the doorway. I turned to look at him. He leaned one arm against the open door and said, 'Well, I blame you. You're supposed to be her role model.'

'And when was I ever anything but the perfect wife and mother for you, Tom? I kept your house, cooked your food, and bought your daughter dresses.'

My father's face twisted as he pressed his teeth tightly together. Through his grimace he spoke. 'You encouraged her to go off to school in the city.'

'So it's the city's fault now, is it? Was she supposed to stay here and weed our garden all this time? That didn't stop you.'

'We –' His face turned from anger to sadness. 'Oh, Mandy.'

My mother did not move from where she stood. She unfolded her arms and tossed a piece of paper onto the desk. I knew what it was, it was my coming-out letter to her.

I hadn't known at the time whether she'd tell my father or whether she'd wait. It was many months before I saw them again and things seemed OK then. But last year, when she was near the end, she finally told me they had fought about it and that she thought the fights had taken the life out of him, bit by bit. They never fought in front of me, but perhaps my going away made it easier for them to do it.

I stared at them, younger parents than the ones I remembered, and struggled to understand what I was witnessing. More ghosts?

'You said you'd forgiven me,' he said, his voice almost begging.

Her face heavy with contempt, she turned her back on him.

My brain was abuzz with this-can't-be-happening-this-can't-be-happening, and yet I couldn't let it happen. I jumped up. 'No,

Mom, don't.' I put my hand on her shoulder as if I could turn her around. My hand felt as if it touched insect wings, dry and papery, slick and crumbling. My mother crumbled under my touch, and even as the feel of it sickened me and made me want to run out of the room, wash my hands and spit out what was in my mouth, I kept clutching at her until there was nothing left but smoke-like wisps of dust floating through the air where she had stood. In my stomach I felt pain, the heavy dull pain of grief and blame, of betrayal. I felt everything that the two of them felt, the shock, the unearthed resentment, the longing. I fell to my knees, unable to think, unable to wonder for that moment what was happening, as old pain washed through me like a wave of nausea.

And then it was gone. The relief felt almost like joy to me, except for the heaviness of my thoughts. When I looked up, Lizette was still in the chair, only now it looked like she was dozing. I hardly remembered her being there through the whole thing – maybe she'd already fallen back to sleep. I shepherded her back to bed and installed Raven and Bella on either side of her as guards. And then I slipped on my shoes and went out to the barn. My heart began to hammer and that feeling of something loose in there returned.

The yellowy electric light showed me the wall covered with tools, the jars of ancient nails and screws still as he had left them. I sat at the potter's wheel and tried to picture him, puttering back and forth, taking apart an old chainsaw. One rational part of my brain was trying to guess what was going on – maybe Lizette's screaming woke up my parents' ghosts? But that wouldn't explain Mrs Mosely's voice, or the man by the mill pond. In the non-rational part of my brain, I felt the echoes of the emotions I'd felt upstairs and knew with my heart that he would be here. My vision of him was as solid as the bench in front of him.

'Dad?' I said, but he didn't look up. When he did turn, it was as if he didn't see me. I saw the old screwdriver with its duct-taped handle in his hand, but I could also see it hanging on the wall where I'd left it. He was taking the panels off a sewing machine. 'If you're a ghost, can you hear me?'

He gave me no reaction. I stood up, went nearer to him, but I didn't touch him. Now I could hear what he was muttering. 'As if it would have made a difference. As if I could change something. There's no forgiving, not anymore.' His face crumpled with grief and he looked as if he were about to cry, but then he hardened into anger and grabbed the hammer from the wall and began smashing the machine. Chips of plastic flew off; out of reflex I reached for his arm.

'Dad, no!'

What had looked so solid now collapsed like spun sugar under water. My hands passed through him, destroying him with their solid mass, like a rock tossed through a spider's web. But there was no spider, only me, left flailing with the strands, trying to shake them from my hands, while my father's pain, betrayal, loss, buzzed through me like I was touching a live wire. Somehow, this time, I was ready for that sudden wash of hurt and emotion, and I could see more in it, feel the reasons behind it. My mother, a broken promise... he'd done something she'd promised to forget about, never bring up again, and now, she was not only bringing it up, she was blaming him.

The feelings flared out like a cut gas jet and I stumbled against the workbench. I folded my arms across it and lay my head down, blinking my eyes into the sleeves of my robe. If my insight was correct, and I had trouble believing that it was, my father had once – I didn't have the right words for it – slept with? had a love affair with? fucked? a man. It wasn't like a cheating affair, it wasn't a romance, it wasn't a planned thing, and even though I could feel it in my heart, I could not quite picture how it could happen. But that's every child's blind spot about her parents, isn't it?

When morning came, Lizette was still sleeping and I was still awake. After I'd come in from the shed I took a long shower, as if I could wash away the feelings the way I was washing away the grotesque strands. And then, I couldn't sleep. I wrote Liz a note that I was going into town for fresh rolls and orange juice and would be back with breakfast. But I went straight to Earthways and sat in their parking lot until Stuart pulled in next to me. I got out of the truck and met him at the door.

He laughed when he saw me and said, 'You look like you're here for a hangover remedy.' He had grown his hair hippie-long in the back but he was balding up front.

I didn't want to be rude. But maybe I was. 'You know how you were always telling me about all this spooky stuff and channelling and past lives and all that?'

He held the fat ring of door keys in his hand, his face serious. 'Yes.'

'Is it all true?'

He unlocked the door, we went in, and he locked it again behind us. We went through the store, with its neat shelves of herbal remedies alternating with shelves of crystals and incense, to his office in the back. Stuart cleared the chair behind the desk for me by moving a stack of magazines onto the floor. He sat cross-legged on the floor himself.

I described for him the strange scene at the mill. Then the two scenes with my parents, although I left out what it was they argued about. 'Are they ghosts?'

He frowned in thought, shaking his head and tugging on his silly little beard. 'Ghosts... usually aren't so solid-looking. And they do usually react to people. And the web-like material. I don't know.' He stood up and took his glasses out of the center pocket of his South American sweatshirt. He held them on his face – they were missing one earpiece – while he looked over the books on the shelf. He took a few down and then sat with the books in his lap.

He handed one to me. 'This'll go faster if you look at the same time.'

'What am I looking for?'

'Something about physical manifestation, I would guess. There's an index.' His own head was already buried in the back of the large book in his lap.

The book he handed me was entitled *Through The Door: Paranormal Messengers*. I started flipping through. The first chapter was on seances and Ouija boards. 'I don't know, Stu.'

He looked up and his glasses fell off his face into his lap. He ignored them. 'I need to open the store in a few minutes.'

'And I need to get back to her.'

Stuart folded his glasses and stuffed them back into his pocket. 'Why don't you go on then. I'll keep looking and let you know what I find.' He picked up the stack of books and I followed him out to the counter. He unlocked the door for me and out I went.

In the sunlight I felt ridiculous. Like the day after Lisa Merckle's sleepover birthday party, where we swore we'd contacted her dead grandfather with a Ouija board and he'd told her Brad Frazier was the boy for her. In the morning it seemed silly that the most popular boy in the school would even look at her. They never did go out, I reminded myself.

And yet, I could still feel those sticky strands on my hands, almost. I resolved to let Stuart deal with it and went to pick up rolls and juice.

When I arrived at the house Lizette was making coffee while the cats followed her from one side of the kitchen to the other hoping for a morsel of something good.

I put the still-warm rolls onto the table, got chilled butter from the fridge and sat down. She brought two steaming mugs over and said, 'When I woke up and you were gone this morning I was worried.'

I shrugged. 'I didn't want to wake you.'

'I did it again last night, didn't I?' She stared into her coffee.

'A little,' I said, buttering a roll and breaking it into pieces to eat.

She looked up at me then. 'Your face, you look so tired. I said something, didn't I?'

I shook my head. 'It's not you.'

Her eyes got a little watery and she touched my hand. 'You look so distant. I knew I should have told you sooner.'

'Told me what? You told me about the sleepwalking and screaming way back.'

'I...' she hesitated, her hand rubbing the back of mine. 'But I didn't really tell you what it was like. Couldn't really prepare you, I guess.' Her voice had gone a little flat, like that wasn't what she had meant to say at all.

I ate my roll while I tried to decide what to tell her. 'You really didn't see anything at the mill?'

'No.'

'When you… woke me up last night, I think I saw another ghost.' I closed my hands around the warm coffee mug.

'Your mother?'

'And my father, both. Arguing.' There was no deciding what to tell her – I told her everything, from the letter to my thought that my father had, at some point, done something with another man.

'Does that bother you?' she asked me. 'The thought that he might have had sex with men? How can that bother you – wouldn't that be a little hypocritical?'

'Well, it bothered him that I turned out gay,' I answered without thinking.

'Lots of people have sex in ways they don't expect or don't accept. It sounds to me like your father never accepted it, for himself or for you.' She looked completely calm now, like we were discussing planting peonies instead of petunias.

'I guess it's up to me to accept it,' I said, sighing. Then my heart gave an extra thump as my brain took another leap. 'No, wait, how do I even know that was true? How do I know I'm not just crazy, imagining things? I might be hallucinating it all, for all we know.'

She held up her hands. 'I don't find it so hard to believe. But do you think there's any proof?'

I left my unfinished coffee on the table and climbed the stairs to my mother's study. We hadn't repainted this room yet, with its bookshelves built into the wall and books two deep on each one. Did my mother keep a diary? Lizette helped me search. It was she who found the shoe boxes in the closet.

She put them down on the desk and opened one. I recognized right away what was in it – the letters I had written to my mother from college and over the years. Underneath them were a few I had written to my father specifically, and some others, from my uncle Gerry, uncle Randolph. The other box held two bundles of letters, ones my father and mother had written to each other during the Korean war. He had gone when I was an infant and returned around the time I was learning to talk.

I sat down with the two boxes in front of me and began to read.

Some time later Lizette went to take care of her dog, exchanging a feathery peck on the cheek for my promise not to work too hard.

Nowhere in the letters, of course, was there something as blatant as my father confessing his homosexual love. But I began to piece together a tale that began when he was in the war. He mentioned several times a soldier named Fred Maguire, who I remembered lived in town when I was a child. I always assumed Fred was from here and had known my father all his life, but from the letters it seemed they met in the military, and Fred moved here after they returned from overseas. He didn't come to the house much, not even on Christmas, but we sometimes saw him in town, reading a newspaper at the coffee shop or mailing a letter at the post office. I remembered my father telling me he didn't have to work because he'd lost his leg in the war and the government gave him money.

I could see it then, Fred Maguire with his tell-tale limp as he made his way down Main Street, waving as our truck went by, and the old man on the stones by the mill, also limping. I'd seen the ghost of my father's old... friend, I'd seen my mother and father argue, I'd seen my father angry and unable to forgive himself. What were they trying to tell me?

The phone rang and I jumped in my chair. It was Stuart. He sounded much more chipper than he had this morning. 'Oh, yeah, oh, yeah, there's lots of good possibilities here, Mare. Let me ask you some questions, though.'

'Shoot.'

'Do you ever think you hear voices, or "see" places the way they used to look?'

'I didn't hear voices until recently, but sometimes... does it count when I imagine I can hear or see the old postal clerks at the Coop?'

'It sure does.' He flipped a few pages and I could hear the distant tinkle of the bell on Earthways' door. 'Do you always hear things that are associated with the place you're in, though, or do you ever, say, hear the postal clerks when you're somewhere else?'

'Only in the right places, Stu. I'm not crazy, it's just the way I

Cecilia Tan

remember things.' Raven climbed into my lap and I stroked her slick, black fur.

'I didn't say that,' he said, without venom. 'But it's more than just how you remember things. Mary, I think you're a doleurvoyant.'

'Excuse me?'

'It's like a clairvoyant.'

'Someone who can see spirits?' Raven climbed onto the desk and lay down on top of the pile of letters, twitching her tail and purring at the same time.

'Sort of. Clairvoyant means "clear seer" – clairvoyants in general may be able to see a lot of things, ghosts, footprints, auras...'

'OK, fine. What's a do-lo...'

'Doleurvoyant. It's very rare.'

'And it is –?'

'It means, literally, "pain-seer".'

'I'm not sure what you mean.' Bella took Raven's place in my lap and settled down to poke her claws into my knees.

He took a deep breath, as if the explanation might take a lot of wind. 'The theory is that pain, trauma, certain kinds of psychic damage leave a kind of fallout in the psychic realm. Like footprints, impressions of who was there, but also like... like radiation or residue left behind. The doleurvoyant can sense this residue: hear the voices, see the people, feel the pain. You probably see all kinds of psychic impressions, but the more painful, the more clear or solid it should seem.'

'Shit.' I said it mostly out of surprise. Bella looked back at me in reproach. 'And you think that's what I'm doing?'

'It's the only thing that fits everything you've told me thus far. The residue is tied to specific places, left behind where the argument or fight occurred, for example.'

I chewed the edge of a fingernail. 'Then why don't I see people arguing all over the place? I mean, Jesus, Bobby Gilchrist crashed his car right into my front lawn and his father just about killed him when he came over to look at the wreck. Why don't I see them out there?'

Stuart was quiet a moment. 'Were you close to Bobby Gilchrist?'

302

'No, you know that.'

'If you went out and tried hard, if you learned to focus your talent, maybe you'd pick up that residue there. But chances are it's only the psychic energy of people close to you that you'll sense.'

'But why now, Stu? Why haven't I been able to do it all my life?'

He was silent.

'Tell me.'

'I don't know. Maybe it has something to do with Lizette. Or with the farm. Or with you being ready to finally mature into your crone power. Sometimes people don't "break through" their talent until a particularly strong incident – I just read about a clairvoyant who could see spirits. She could never see them until she visited the site of a battlefield. After that, she could always see spirits who died violently. I mean, your mother did just die, goddess rest her soul. Maybe the pain of it finally awakened your ability. Maybe you picked up something in the hospital, the overload of pain and trauma there?'

'Maybe,' I said, thinking about Lizette. 'But this still doesn't explain the spider webs.'

'Oh, well, it sort of does. The residue, the fallout, can manifest in the physical as well as psychic realm. Could be that's what happens when you reach out to touch them. But they don't last. You may actually be destroying the psychic fallout. There's an island in Indonesia where they believe a shaman has to go through the place where someone died...'

I cut him off before he could give me a lot of information I didn't need. 'You said you had some other theories.'

'Well, none that fit so well. Another one is that you're seeing the psychic residue of your own experiences and subconscious, that instead of leaving your residue behind in the places it happened, it has accrued onto you, and now you're "shedding" it. But that wouldn't explain the guy at the mill, or the fact that you saw a fight your parents had when you weren't even present. So I don't think that's it.' He cleared his throat. 'It's not like they do studies on this at the Mayo Clinic or something,' he said, his voice soft with apology.

'Thanks, Stu. Thanks very much.'

He was quiet a second. 'It was nothing, Mary. I, I worry about you sometimes.'

'One more question then. Is this doleurvoyance dangerous? Should I be worried about it?' Bella, not content with sitting still, batted at Raven's twitching tail.

'That I can't tell you. I guess, I'd give you the advice I give anyone dabbling in the psychic realm.'

'Which is?'

'Don't screw around. Do what is important to you. If you want party tricks or cheap thrills, get David Copperfield.'

'Thanks again, Stuart.' I hung up the phone and put one hand on each cat, stroking them softly.

What he said had made a certain kind of sense. The study seemed quieter now, more peaceful, than it had before. Had I cleansed it of bad juju? If I went through the house, could I find residue of my first splinter or skinned knee? Or the trauma of the moment my father received his draft notice? I was half-tempted to try. But, as Stu had said, I didn't want to screw around. And somehow I was sure that the onset of my 'talent' had to do with Lizette.

It's because you're in love, I chided myself, but that didn't sound right. Love wasn't the same at forty-four as it was at twenty-four, but we didn't make new words for it. Just like I didn't have the right words for whatever it was my father and Fred Maguire had shared.

I didn't know when Lizette would be back, didn't recall her saying, and I wanted to be with her right then. Tell her everything. Ask her everything. Now that I had some kind of explanation for my own phenomenon, my brain was in overdrive trying to explain everything else. This morning, at breakfast, what had she said? She thought she'd told me something, and then, when it turned out she hadn't, she changed the subject.

I was hungry and my eyes were bleary from reading letters all day. In the kitchen cold coffee sat in my mug. I took a crusty roll with me in the truck and drove toward the mill. The setting sun was hidden behind the gloom of a high gray blanket of clouds moving in from the west. In the east the sky glowed deep purple and faint pricks of stars had begun to appear.

I stopped the truck at the front door of Perser's and went in. A young woman (girl? maybe nineteen or twenty years old) with short black hair and a crisp white shirt asked if she could help me. 'Yes,' I said. 'I was looking for the house of Lizette Pierce.'

'I don't think I know her,' she replied. 'Does she work here?'

'No, she's a friend of mine. She told me she moved into a place near the old mill.'

'Oh.' The woman pursed her lips and looked to the side. 'Well, if you keep going up the road you'll come to a fork. On the right fork you'll come to the new development. On the left you'll stay on the old road.'

Lizette had said her place was falling-apart old. 'Thanks.' The hostess smiled perkily at me. 'Another historical question,' I said, turning back to her. 'Did Fred Maguire ever work up here?'

'Who?'

'He was a one-legged war vet, lived in town.'

'Oh my God, you mean there really was a One-leg Fred?' She blushed. 'When I was a kid they used to tell us scary stories about how if we weren't good One-leg Fred would come out of the falls and get us. Supposedly, twenty years ago he committed suicide and all they ever found was his fake leg, floating in the lower pond. Learn something new every day,' she said.

'Sure do,' I replied.

'Near' is a relative term in Maple County. I drove ten, maybe fifteen minutes along the old road before I came to a cluster of mailboxes. One of them said 'Pierce' and the road was packed dirt from that point on. The truck rattled and bounced as I sped on, the sky fully dark now and my headlights showing only trees on either side of the road.

I came to a two-story house, a half-circle of driveway touching the road in two places, and there was Lizette's hatchback by the front door. I parked the truck behind the car, wishing I had thought to get some food at the restaurant, even though I'd used the pretense of bringing her food once already today. I pressed the bell and couldn't hear it ring – probably broken. 'Lizette?' I shouted. No answer. I tried the door.

It was open. I stepped into a foyer with wide pine boards for a floor and woven rugs. To my left was the kitchen, ahead of me stairs to the second floor, to the right, the dining room. I heard a voice in the kitchen, a man's voice.

'Come here, Lizzie.' I stepped into the room and saw a man with his button-down shirt untucked from his pants, his feet bare. I could see the stove as it looked today, unused and unlit, but he leaned down to the burner, lit his cigarette, and repeated his command. 'It's OK, you come here.'

I looked around to see who he was talking to, but there was no one. His hands reached toward someone and he squatted down. 'Come give me a hug.'

His arms closed around nothing but he suddenly stiffened like he held someone tight. 'Listen to me.' It came out lissin-ah-mee. 'I told you what would happen if you didn't keep quiet. You gotta play by the rules, Lizzie, or I won't play nice.'

I could not hear an answer nor see the child I assumed was Lizette. But he held the cigarette threateningly... was he burning her with it? My imagination filled in the searing flesh and I closed my eyes. And then I remembered, if I couldn't erase this trauma from the past I could at least play psychic housekeeper. I waded through him like he was so much thigh-high grass, and papery dust exploded around me, strands of evil stuff sticking to my jeans and wrapping around my midsection. And the pain that went through me hit me first in the gut and then in the heart, his black guilt twisted with his intense love for his stepchild, his desire to protect her strangely mirrored by his desire to defile her, to be her one and only.

Already I could hear more voices, from the dining room – him and Lizette's mother? The dining-room walls were covered with family photos. I stood by one of Lizette in a twirler's uniform. The glass in the frames looked like it had been dusted recently and the chairs and table were stacked together at one end of the room.

'Philip Pierce, I'm talking to you.' I could see the ghost of a pearl necklace around her neck, her hair styled back from her face.

'Yeah, yeah, how am I supposed to know? She stays out till all hours, she hangs around with the wrong crowd. I'm telling you, she should spend more time at home.'

'At home with you?'

He was dressed much as before, but with shoes on this time. A lit cigarette flared in his hand as he waved his arms. 'Oh, Jesus, Melissa, we've been through that. Maybe I was rough on her when she was a kid, but how did I know? I don't know from children...'

The woman's face was ugly with suspicion.

'We've been through that,' he repeated. 'You can ask her. Hell, you, and her school counselor, and her psychiatrist, and just about everybody else in the goddamn world has asked her already, and you know the answer. I never touched her. She said so herself! The real truth is you just can't love me the way you loved him, isn't that it?' He snatched a picture from the wall and smashed it against the dining-room table. 'Melissa, why do you torment me and yourself like this? I've been completely honest with you, I've been to counseling with you, I've paid for the best doctors for you and for her, and still you torture me this way, with distrust, with accusations. It hurts.'

'I did ask her, Philip. I did ask her. Not about before, not about anything but what happened tonight.' Melissa stepped forward, her face haggard but stern.

'If something happened tonight, I don't know about it. I told you, I was down at the bar...' He would not meet her eyes.

'You left her here alone?'

'She's sixteen, for chrissake...'

'And what did you find when you got back?'

He took a long drag off the cigarette and blew the smoke out. 'There was a Jeep coming down the road as I was driving back. So I knew someone was here. I came in, yelled to her "I'm home!" and sat down to watch TV.'

The woman's resolve seemed to be crumbling. She buried her eyes into the heels of her hands and said, quietly, in almost a sob,

'The engine... your car engine was cold when I got home...'

'What is this?' he said, shrugging his shoulders. 'You're spying on me now?'

She lunged at him suddenly, her hands scrabbling at his throat, screaming, 'Lizzie's been raped and all you care about is yourself! Whether you did it yourself or you were responsible, I don't care! It's your fault! It's your fault! I hate you! I hate you!'

Philip had caught her hands so she didn't choke him to death. I swept my arms through them, closed my eyes against their dissolving bodies, and brushed my sleeves as best I could. I was already moving toward the stairs as the feelings surged through me: hate, betrayal, guilt, blame, a tinge of sexual lust that made me nauseous.

I turned into the first room I came to, turned on the light. A teenage girl's bedroom, with a lace bed-cover and stuffed animals on the bed. At first I wondered if the room itself appeared to me as it must have looked years ago, then I realized that nothing in the room had changed in years.

He was here already, whispering something to the stuffed animals. I went closer to hear him say, 'Lizzie, Lizzie, come on, honey, lift up your covers for me.' Again there was no Lizette there. Philip was stepping out of his pants. I'd seen enough and clawed through him.

Lizette's scream from the next room brought me running. I opened the door to find she was sitting up in a double bed in one corner of the room. The room was empty of furniture, not even a dresser, and thickly carpeted. Oriental rugs hung on the walls. She had made herself a padded room, a room safe for a hysterical sleepwalker. I counted eight screams before she stopped and got out of the bed. She looked right through me and then walked to the window. Suddenly she started to talk. What had she been afraid I had overheard last night? They weren't just nightmares, I knew that now.

'No, Daddy, please,' she said in a ten-year-old's voice. 'Please not the big finger.'

She whirled around, her voice older now, as she faced someone with clenched fists. 'I don't understand why you always take his side!'

She ran into one of the carpeted walls and fell, screaming as she went down, 'You'll be sorry! My real daddy will get you for this!'

In that moment I knew the residue of her pain wasn't imprinted to the places it had happened. It was carried with her, always. She thrashed where she had fallen and I was afraid she would hurt herself. 'Lizette, wake up, it's Mary.' I knelt by her. My hand was sticky with the evil gossamer but I reached out for her, wishing I could wake her from the nightmare that was her past.

My hand touched her hair and suddenly I tried to pull away, as the webby stuff on my fingers seemed to merge with her. Pieces of her began coming off in my hands. 'Oh no, Lizette, no...' But there it was, my fingers raking through layer after layer of sticky spidery spew, the horrible stuff not coming off fast enough as I tried to shake my hands free, and as I watched my lover come unraveled, turning to dust under my touch. And her pain, years of psychosexual torture both internal and external, sickened me, blinded me with hot tears and anger, ground my teeth with suffocating frustration, and turned my heart to ice with poisoned love.

But then, something solid and warm met my fingers, something soft and something bony. I tore away the white deathly stuff faster, my breath coming in gasps as I fought to free her of it all, to destroy the pain that had so nearly destroyed her. The pain I felt now was my own rage, the anger that this young woman had, so long ago, been denied any chance to be her own person, to be anything other than a walking cocoon of old pain. And grief, I felt grief, because whatever I had loved about her, surely this too was being destroyed, undone in a whirlwind of my own making.

Then those feelings, too, flared out, as I stared in surprise at what was before me. Lying on the floor amid the insect-wing scraps was a tiny girl, maybe nine or ten years old, curled in a ball and sleeping deeply.

I did not try to wake her up. Not knowing what else to do, I wrapped her in the lace bed-cover and carried her to the truck. Halfway home she rubbed her eyes and looked around. 'Where are we?' her high-pitched voice squeaked.

'I'm taking you home, honey,' I said.

And she answered, 'OK,' before turning over on the wide seat and going back to sleep.

When we got back to the house, I tucked her into bed in the powder-blue room. Raven and Bella sniffed her excitedly as they picked their settling places.

I sat on the windowsill watching her sleep for a few minutes until my stomach, no longer unsettled by horrors of the past, reminded me that I had not eaten all day. I went down to the kitchen for a tart apple and a cup of cold milk. After a while I decided no more surprises were forthcoming that day, and that any new revelations about how I felt or what I knew would have to wait for the dawn. Tomorrow there would be decisions to make. Tonight there would be sleep, peaceful sleep, barely rippled by half a dream.

Switch

Shireen Sharif

Switch
Shireen Sharif

She could hear the voices. Clockwork intervals, regular as London summer rain. But the doctors said she was mad and they locked her up. Section something, they said, ramming the needle into her buttock to make her stop struggling. She went limp. Purple Haze. They called an ambulance and took her to the hospital. From Mayfair W1 to Paddington W2.

Her family had said they would force her to think straight. She was sick. She had caused a scandal in their circles by making a scene at the wedding of her friend Celene. Her family had tried to control her. They let her have her own room but they wouldn't give her money to go out. They punished her because she was lesbian. You can't be, they said. Throughout that summer after graduation and Celene's marriage they persecuted her. The heat was on – it was in the 70s. She rolled up her sleeves and decided to get a job and move out, to make a life for herself.

That's when her family called the doctors in. She was verbally abusive, her language was violent, she didn't want treatment. So they sectioned her for four weeks' close observation in hospital. They treated her like dirt but she was as good as any princess. The voices confirmed it.

Patients at a mental health hospital ward were delighted by a visit from Princess Anne.

She resisted their drugs. She knew she was sane. They were the ones who were mad, for not hearing, for not seeing their own sickness. They wanted her to have a session with a therapist at the hospital, but she said she refused to have anything to do with the rapist. They told her she shouldn't act like a man. She told them she was happy not to be one, that she loved being a woman who loved other women. But her sanity had no sanction in their sickness. When she told them she could suit the action to the word, the word to the action, they told her she had delusions of grandeur. She was mad in their eyes because she wanted a life on her own terms.

Her closest friend had written to her while she was in hospital, saying, 'Madhu, you're the sanest person I know.' Madhu took a lot of strength from that. They had been lovers since their teens. Celene, her first lover, her first love. Celene, goddess of the moon. Madhu worshipped her, she wanted to move mountains for her. They were both Asian and Celene understood her in ways which no other woman ever could. Madhu was emotional, she was intense, and Celene accepted her for what she was. They were good together, walking a wire of in-visibility. And Madhu loved the way Celene mirrored her, reflecting back her own Asianness. It was as if their blood had bonded.

As teenagers they vowed to live together permanently and later chose to go to the same university. Celene was studying art and art history. Madhu was studying English and became obsessed with Shakespeare. How sweetly the moonlight had slept upon them. But things started to change when their families realised the nature of their relationship and exerted a lot of pressure to separate them.

Madhu could have coped with that. But what she hadn't expected was Roger Casaubon, the suave, sophisticated and totally shallow lecturer who swept Celene off her feet. They married in the summer after graduation and Madhu caused a commotion at the wedding ceremony. She was devastated. She knew there'd never be another woman to replace Celene.

After she got out of hospital she broke away from her family, moving from hell to Hammersmith, W6. She got a job as an estate agent and eventually started her own company in property development. She worked hard to get Celene out of her system, but could not give her up. The voices were always there to remind her of Celene's betrayal.

*The wedding of Prince Charles and Lady Diana Spencer
was an electrifying spectacle.*

*

Madhu had started drinking in secret. Of course she could hear the voices. They were speaking to her on the radio, on television, outside on her street.

'You maniacs,' cried the night as brakes squealed outside her open window. She smiled. If only you knew. There was a commotion going on outside. Russell Square, WC1. What a racket, she thought, switching on the television set. The picture flickered into a tennis court. Wimbledon. Martina was serving. Thirty love. She preferred voices to visions. Forty love. She switched channels. Section 28 now law. She switched to the radio, to cap it all they were playing a song that spoke to her.

> *You will find you're out of your mind
> if you don't see
> you can't unwind the ties that bind
> you to me.*

She didn't know why the voices sang such songs. Maybe it was because it passed as romance. She switched off. There was silence. Then sirens. Her blood was boiling with the heat. It was in the 80s. She unbuttoned her top collar and switched on the CD player. Purple Rain.

She knew the voices were real. And part of the reason she loved Celene was that she knew it too – she believed in her. When everyone around them would say Madhu was mad (even as a joke), Celene would trust her judgement.

Madhu had vision, she was ahead of her time. People criticised her for having short hair, for wearing suits and boys' shoes, for drinking, for being an out lesbian – especially as she was an Asian woman. You weren't supposed to behave like that. But Celene had trusted her – which made her treachery more painful.

Madhu was still obsessed with her. Years after they first got together, years after Celene's marriage, Madhu still wanted to live with her. The fixation that fed her was the same: she was going to get Celene back. The voices would tell her when it was a good time to make her move.

*

Buckingham Palace has announced the separation of the Prince and Princess of Wales.

She was in control. She had given up drinking. She could make anything happen. The doctors had said she had fantasies of omnipotence to compensate for her powerlessness. But all that was nonsense. She knew more than they did. She had her switch. From Bellevue Road W13 to Bloomsbury WC1. The heart of the cosmos. She had arrived. She had the power.

They didn't know about the switch. She hadn't ever told anyone, not even Celene. It was between her and her life. The switch of power, never used but always there. Her switch. Her direct line to control.

They'd asked her if she was suicidal. She said no. They didn't ask if she was murderous. They didn't know she had a weapon in her attic.

She was aware of the world's violence. They were destroying the planet. The weather was changing globally. London now had torrential rains in what was sometimes a tropical summer. The earth was in danger because of what men had done to it. They were destroying it as surely as they'd tried to destroy her. But she had her spirit. And she had her switch. She could make mountains move. As it were.

They hadn't made love in months. Although Celene had retained her allegiance to Madhu, it was more as a friend these days and only occasionally as a lover. Now Madhu was looking to change that. She wanted to live with her, she didn't want to be the unacknowledged other woman. And she wanted Celene to embrace her lesbianism.

Celene had flirted with the art school way of life, but had been seduced by middle-class security. She had been unable to resist the supposed safety of having a man who would protect her from the world. Roger was a useful cover: pleasant enough, good looking and solvent. And he was white. The fact that he also had power and status as a lecturer had added a dimension which made the marriage seem inevitable at the time. Celene was genuinely fond of him. She was sorry to have hurt Madhu so badly, but Roger was everything her own family wanted for her, and the pressure they put on her had been the final factor in her decision to marry him.

Madhu had never had a lover who could compare with Celene. She had had occasional partners; she had friends, colleagues, employees, tenants, acquaintances, contacts. But she wanted to put it on record in black ink that her love for Celene still shone bright, as Shakespeare would say. She was caught in a cycle of obsession. She would often implore Celene to leave Roger and come back to London to live with her. But Celene would not endanger her connection with her family, which she knew would be severed if she were out as a lesbian. Celene saw Madhu's obsession as destructive; she said she'd never leave Roger. What she meant was she'd never leave Roger while he was alive. Obviously. She'd said as much when she promised Madhu there would never be anyone else besides her. So Roger had to be removed. It was a simple equation. Love would take Madhu even to the edge of doom.

It was the weekend of another scorching summer. The heat was getting to her, it was in the 90s. As she waited for Celene, each moment seemed a moon. She switched the radio on. The news.

Princess Diana has been hosting a glittering gala of celebrities to raise money for her charitable work.

She switched off. As if by magic the doorbell rang. Trust Celene to be so perfectly on time.

'Hello, love,' Celene said. Madhu felt her pulse race. Celene's words were casual enough, but Madhu understood the intimate feelings behind them. She could tell Celene would be receptive.

She was getting signals already, as their greeting kiss was sweet on her lips.

'I've got something to tell you,' Celene said, 'but not now.'

That night they made love. Touching Celene intimately, kissing her passionately, pleasuring her body, put Madhu in a state of mergence, where the softness of their bodies interlocking made them feel indivisible.

The next morning she made her decision. Roger had to go. She was going to do it, she was going to pull the power switch. While Celene was making their breakfast she went to the hallway, put on the lights, and lowered the ladder from the attic. As she climbed it she could see the colour purple. The switch was in place. Powerful. She put her hand forward, and as she pulled it she felt something imploding in her head. Over the edge.

'You mad woman, what are you doing in the attic?' Celene called up to her, as the sound of the telephone began to ring in the hallway. Roger was dead. A mountain-climbing accident.

They drove down Euston Road and Marylebone Road, past Baker Street W1, through the Westway, and all the way to Wales where Celene identified the body. Then on to the university to organise Roger's affairs. There were no children, a few minor debts, a rented flat with a lease about to run out. And an unfinished thesis on the synchronicity of ideas.

Celene went into shock, sitting passively for days. The inquest returned a verdict of death by misadventure. Madhu made the funeral arrangements.

She never told Celene about the switch. It was better to keep it to herself. They used to say she was mad for thinking things like that – she didn't want all that again. Of course she was sane. Of course the voices were real. They would take her power away if she were to tell people. They would cut her off.

Madhu hoped things would finally work out the way she wanted. But Celene's behaviour changed drastically. She was mourning Roger, but her grief took an obsessive turn, one where she felt personally responsible for his death. When she told Madhu this, Madhu had a sinking feeling and tried to convince her otherwise. Then came the shock revelation: that Celene had decided she was going to leave Roger for Madhu; that she had told him that on the very weekend he died. Celene said Roger had been in a state, that he couldn't really take it in, that he had probably committed suicide and that she had killed him as surely as if she had pulled the power switch on his life-support machine. Madhu felt a chill on hearing this – Celene's guilt was a reflection of her own.

Celene changed from someone who had been alive, productive, fully functioning, to someone now withdrawn, retiring, dysfunctional. She would sit for hours in a state of near catatonia, held there by guilt so as to stay connected to a dead man. Therapy was out, but Madhu managed to persuade her to take up her art again and they fixed the spare room in the flat as her studio. She became more active, producing several portraits, on the condition that Madhu could not see them until Celene felt ready. Madhu agreed, happy to see her taking control of her life.

But she wished she could trust Celene enough to tell her about the switch. While Celene had been able to come out to her about feeling guilty for Roger's death, Madhu had to suppress her impulse to confess that it was she who was responsible. Madhu had her own demons. She went through different states: hoping his death had been an accident, thinking it might have been suicide, knowing it was murder. She felt that Roger would haunt them forever, that his death held their lives in a vice. But then her demons became even more monstrous, when she started thinking he was still alive.

When she went out she felt followed by him. Sometimes she thought she caught glimpses of him among men walking about, getting into taxis, coming out of shops. Once she confronted him, but on close contact she established it was a stranger, a pallid lookalike. She was getting agitated, so she did the thing she knew best: concentrating on her work to keep calm and occupied.

Her company had gone from strength to strength. She first ventured into acquiring flats for a snip in the 1980s: extending or renovating them with a team of experts, keeping some for rental income and selling others to buy larger properties, and so on. In the early 90s property was going for a song, so she had bought into as much as she could, concentrating on flats in Bloomsbury, WC1. It was now 1997 and prices in London were starting to soar. Running her empire helped to keep her functional.

It was the weekend after the August Bank Holiday. Celene had finished the portraits she'd been working on and was going to show them to Madhu. They went out for dinner that Saturday night and after they got back, Madhu eagerly went into Celene's studio to see the work for the first time. Another shock. Celene had been working on copying the Holbein portraits onto canvas. As she unveiled each one, Madhu felt dread and horror. Though each portrait was of a different person, they all resembled Roger. Even *Anne of Cleves* looked like Roger.

The haunting had taken over both of them. Madhu decided that night she had to tell Celene about the switch. It was the only way to put the ghost to rest. She would do it the next day, Sunday 31st. When she awoke that morning, Celene was already up. Madhu switched on the radio.

> *Diana, Princess of Wales, has died as a result of a car crash in Paris last night.*

Oh God, no, Madhu thought, shocked. She hurled herself out of bed to find Celene and rushed into the hallway. The attic ladder had been lowered. Celene was up there.

'Don't pull that switch!' she screamed.

'Which switch?' said Celene, pulling it. The lights went out.

When the Car Slammed into Me
Charlotte Cooper

When the Car Slammed into Me
Charlotte Cooper

When the car slammed into me the first thing I did was laugh. I always thought that I'd die by drowning, not from being run into by a twat in an Audi while I walked home from work. I was already a mass of crumpled limbs and flailing hair as the bonnet scooped me up and threw me high. Broken teeth ricocheted out of my mouth too. But my mode of death seemed funny in a way that I can't describe now, and I laughed and laughed and laughed as people were frozen by the car horn's Doppler effect and necks turned (not mine though, thankfully) to catch me in my moment. Everybody stared at me from far below on the pavement, mouths widened grotesquely; it looked as though they were melting. Some folks were already keying 999 into their mobiles, never taking an eye off me.

I am a hefty girl and the force of the collision gave me enough momentum to shoot up over the city streets, twisting and spinning out like an Olympic diver played backwards in slo-mo, only less pretty.

The view was fantastic at that level. Out past the skyscrapers there were mountains, over them there was the sea, beyond that there were people inhabiting strange architecture in lands far away. Closer to me I saw ant-like trails of commuters marching home. I saw junkies mooching by a needle exchange van. I saw a couple of waiters having a sneaky fag out the back of their restaurant before their shift started. Everyone was getting ready for the night.

I love those warm spring evenings just after the clock has gone forward. Life seems so full of possibility when you leave work and there is still some daylight to be seen. What better time for flying through the air?

Above me there was more sky, all golden and blue where afternoon and evening blended together. Where the sky ended was where outer space began.

There was a hand there too, which grabbed onto mine as I reached the pinnacle of my ascent and kept me there suspended longer than I should have been. The skin was warm and familiar, I knew this hand, the wrist, and I knew the face smiling at me when I followed the arm, the shoulder and the neck to their conclusion. It was my brother.

Georgie looked better than good. He wore the same old things he always wore, fucked-up jeans, his stripy jumper, a necklace with a tiger tooth in it, but he looked – how can I say this without sounding like a dummy? – he shone as though he was golden, kind of holy even. The scars on his temple were deep and ragged but they seemed to glow. His hair stood out like a halo, he had this brightness about him.

Georgie wouldn't let me go. He hung, head down, as though somebody else was holding onto his ankle and I was the last link in the chain. He smiled at me beatifically as I dangled from his grip. I think he wanted me to cling on, he wanted me to stay there in the sky with him. It was a tempting proposition.

Georgie could do anything. He could make friends with anyone, he could dance all night non-stop, he could drive a van, he could score us some righteous acid or some speed at any time of the day or night. He could fuck any of the hundreds of women who fancied him as he pleased. Georgie could call our dad a wanker, he could take the blows dished out. He could take care of his little sister.

Who wouldn't want to stay in the sky with a guy like this?

My hot chubby hand held on as tightly as it could but my sweat became a grease that weakened the hold. The wrist grip loosened until Georgie was clutching onto my fingers, then the end of my thumb, and then nothing at all.

My brother's disappointed face shrank away fast as I fell back down to earth. I mouthed, 'Sorry, Georgie, I love you,' then landed with a deadening thump on the pavement.

Four days later, my girlfriend Karen was lying next to me on my hospital bed, spoon-feeding me raspberry yoghurt. I'd broken three ribs, an obscure bone in my arm and, would you believe, cracked my right big toe. I think being fat protected me from worse injuries although no one admitted it, they just said that I was lucky. I was also deeply bruised and there was talk of concussion.

Karen cried a lot and fussed me relentlessly. I was sick of the way she wanted to hug and kiss me all the time. She'd put her big, gooey, pleading face right in mine and it made me want to scream. Apparently she thought she was contributing to my recovery. Every time a real nurse came to haul me onto a bedpan or give me a shot, Karen would act up and insist on being present as my next of kin.

Being with Karen was often a lonely experience. The showiness of her affection smothered me, I thought it was fake, like a plastic rose squirted with White Musk. I could never shake the feeling that I was invisible to her, that while she was fussing and primping me, she had completely failed to notice that I was a life-size festering, oozing, stinking sore of grief, self-hatred and pain. All she wanted was for me to return her 'I wuv you baby' with a wink and a kiss, to keep it light, keep it frothy. I am not light. I thought about dumping her when all this was over.

I was bored. It was as though I was in a waiting room, just hanging out until I could resume my life again. I was too tired and full of ache to support any kind of activity, including moving or talking for more than a few minutes at a time. There was nothing I could do except lie in my bed, sticking to the plastic mattress cover under my sheet, blinking and staring until my eyes became dry, then nodding off.

I dreamt constantly, in extra-vivid colour, probably a residual effect from knocking my head so sharply when that guy ran me over. And yes, it was Georgie who dominated my sleeping life.

One night I woke up to find all the curtains pulled around my bed. Given the choice I would have kept them closed the whole time I was in hospital, but the doctors and nurses insisted that as part of my recovery I should at least make the pretence of being a sociable member of the ward. Anyway, the curtain was billowing and flapping, like someone was mucking around backstage, checking out the audience.

'Who is it?' I asked. 'Nurse?' My voice sounded uncertain and feeble.

Georgie-boy whipped his head around the curtain, stuck out his tongue and winked at me.

'Georgie!'

My brother's smile was devastating. He put his finger to his lips to quieten me down.

'I've got some microdots,' he whispered enticingly. His eyes were big and they sparkled. 'Do you want some?'

'White Lightnings?' I played along and he rolled his eyes.

'Georgie,' I giggled, 'you know I haven't touched any acid since...' my sentence hung, unfinished for a moment '... you died.'

He waved his finger at me. 'Just wait there a moment.' He vanished.

I stared at the spot where he had been until the light changed and it was morning, but Georgie didn't return. A nurse told me off for having the curtains closed, even though there was no way I could have got out of bed unaided to shut them myself.

I felt broken, cheated that he never came back. I sulked and brooded all morning. Karen rubbed my back when she came to visit at two, she brought me some clean jammies and we watched television together, but all I could do was endure her visit, waiting for her to go so that I could drift back into Georgieland.

Visiting hours ended at eight and Karen gave me a big tonguey kiss goodbye. She made such a show of it for all the other poor folk on the ward, said that she loved me in an over-loud voice, and then left me to it.

I let the act slip as soon as she was gone and invited in the memories, swimming deeper through the past until I found what I was looking for.

Like every other suburban kid in history, the weekend was when it all began for me. Georgie worked in a factory sewing frills onto cushions. It was women's work, but somehow my brother had sneaked in. I'd go and meet him outside the factory entrance at quitting time on a Friday afternoon. I always brought him a can of Special Brew, his favourite, and we'd walk together as he chugged it down, allowing me to brush bits of cushion fluff off his clothes.

We'd hop in his car, a fucked-up Ford, and get on the motorway to Luton, Milton Keynes, Aylesbury, Northampton, any of those shitsville satellite towns where Georgie had friends who would share our drugs or make us laugh or entertain us in some way.

Everyone we knew was dealing, everyone was signing on, everyone was a biker, or had a dog, or had a kid, or had big plans, and everyone was so young. That's what gets me, some of them were not even twenty, not even old enough to know anything.

Bombing down the road at eighty, we would crank up the music as high as it would go and scream along, Georgie and me pounding our feet in time to it all. We loved The Stooges, The Elevators, The Ramones, The Velvets, The Stones too.

That music was like oxygen. I can barely articulate what rock 'n' roll meant to me without sounding like an arsehole, but it was this: it was life then, it still is. It made me wake up and want to live. I wanted to be like a young Mick Jagger, or Joey Ramone, Iggy, or Georgie, that's who I wanted to be. *I'm a street-walkin' cheetah with a heart full of napalm.* I wanted to be a cool motherfucker, a lean, snake-like rock 'n' roll god, a well-respected man of noise with tits and a cunt. And who was I really? A fat white teen virgin from nowhere. I couldn't even say the word 'dyke'.

Here's a memory of me dancing at a party in the woods, oh yes, that was a good night, we did hot-knives. My throat bled.

Here's another one of Georgie flirting with, what was her name, Jill, Joan, something with a J. I watched them secretly the whole time, from the first shared joint to the point at which they trailed blankets behind them as they slipped off to find a quiet place. Neither me nor Georgie could understand why I was so crazy with jealousy the next day when we met up again to go back home. Who was the problem I wanted to erase? Georgie, who could get what I wanted so easily, or the woman, who was clearly unworthy of the man?

That same party was the time I got hit on by Jim, one of the younger ones who was still at school, like me. It was cold, we huddled together under his leather jacket. Jim was so wrecked he could hardly speak, but he managed to stammer: 'Do you like me?' I turned and tried to focus, I was equally mashed. 'No,' I said, 'but your sister's all right.'

I slept with a smile on my face that night in the hospital. Nothing woke me up, not even Georgie, who sat by my bed and stroked my hand, and kissed my cheek as I dreamt of bones breaking and ambulance sirens.

The doctor told me they were satisfied with my progress and that I would be released the following day. Karen came and packed away my belongings and made preparations for my return home. I resolved to be kinder to her.

The last day in hospital was the slowest of all. I drank cup after cup of milky tea, just so that I would have the difficult logistics of a trip to the toilet with which to fill my time afterwards. The nurses thought it was fantastic that I was able to walk. 'You were lucky,' they said, 'you could have died so easily.' I preferred not to think about it. Instead, I went back in time to revisit Georgie.

When I came out to my brother, it was the first time I ever said anything about it out loud to anyone. When I said 'I like girls,' I tried to make it sound as though I was solid and fine about the whole deal. Georgie said it was cool and that's all I cared about.

He never thought I'd be a threat to him.

Not long after that, Georgie started seeing Beck, a student who worked part-time at the cushion factory. Beck was a hippie who eventually dropped out, got into smack, had kids and lost them, got reformed, and now works in the PR department for my local council. In those days she was just this beautiful girl who liked getting stoned.

One time, me, her and Georgie were sitting in the park smoking dope, enjoying the late afternoon sunshine, talking crap. Georgie ran to the offie to get a Brew. My head was spinning in the sun, I was dazed by the warmth of the day, basking like a lizard on a rock.

Beck sat close to me, her tanned shoulders were small and neat and brown. She said: 'Georgie told me that you like girls.' I nodded vaguely, horrified that he had told anyone about this.

'Have you got a girlfriend?' she asked. I shook my head dumbly and Beck looked encouraged.

'Can I kiss you?' she piped. 'I've never kissed a girl, I want to know what it's like.'

I kissed Beck. It was my first kiss and it made me shake. I pretended I was Georgie and kissed her as I thought he would do, like a man. Her lips were softer than I imagined, and her tiny downy moustache tickled. She smelled of soap and of smoke.

Beck told me I was a better kisser than my brother. Beck said maybe she should dump him and start going out with me, although I guessed that was a joke. Beck held my breast as she kissed me. Georgie never knew.

Beck was in the car with him the night that he died. She walked away from the wreck, he didn't. I still don't really understand how a knock on your head can kill you, even if that knock had the force of the road and the entire weight of a fucked-up Ford turning over in a ditch behind it.

Beck, Karen, Karen, Beck. The two bookends holding up my dyke life. What started off so enticingly had ended up so disappointingly. Karen, I thought, is my life now. What would my brother have made of her?

Karen was late getting to the hospital because of the traffic. She let me lean on her as I hobbled to the taxi. It was a beautiful day. She held me and wiped away my tears when we got home and I unlocked my front door for the first time since the accident. Her tenderness surprised me, and I was grateful; it was a hopeful gesture. I didn't know for sure, but I reconsidered the question of whether I would dump her after all. It dawned on me that maybe I needed her. My girlfriend.

Karen gave me some time alone when I was calm and settled, so I crept out to sit in the sunshine on my front step. I sucked in my breath sharply as I moved – everything still hurt, especially my stupid bloody fucking big toe, and Jesus, I was tired. I sat for a while, a long while, simply watching the people going past, minding their own businesses, carrying on with their lives.

I feel lucky, but sad that Georgie died. Even now, so many years later. I feel as though I won some kind of lottery, a big hand came out of the sky and an echoey voice said: 'It's going to be you, you're the one who's going to lose their love.' Then there I was, separated out from the crowd, like an antelope isolated from the herd by a hungry leopard. Being picked to be The One makes me feel special, and losing Georgie allowed me to crystallise him in my memory, like a rare moth trapped in amber, as one who is always loved and always loving.

I try not to be bitter about being chosen, I try and reason that it could have been anyone. Sometimes I even play a game when I'm walking down the road: I look at people going past and try to envision the loss that I experienced happening to them. When I feel too guilty about imagining harm coming to people, I reverse the game, I point an imaginary finger, I say 'You're lucky' in my head, and I pretend that a mystery force of the universe is busy granting these people something good, and they'll get home to find that their lives have been transformed for the better.

I Saw God

Helen Sandler

I Saw God
Helen Sandler

Recently I saw God. I could have kept this to myself. I could have written about a ghost. For instance, when I lived with Frances, we took it for granted that we attracted ghosts or that we would come across them more than other folks. In the flat in Tottenham where I was mostly on the dole and she was mostly worried about negative equity, there was a black cat on the landing that we'd both seen and, more dramatically, there were the night visitations.

Sometimes we would find ectoplasm on our clothes from the visitations. We both thought the same thing – that a ghost had wiped its ghostly fingers across our clothes in the night. Other people thought otherwise, of course, they thought slugs were to blame or talcum powder. But they had not seen and touched the ectoplasm, wiped across a black skirt by those ghost fingers, nor felt the inquisitiveness that hung in the air.

Then there was Mrs W. I don't remember her name now anyway but let's call her Mrs W out of respect. Frances called her Mary. She was dead before we knew her. We bought her house from her after she died.

We were offered the contents, if we would clear out what we didn't want at our own expense. This was foolishness. We would have been better to have made an offer for the green three-piece suite from the mid-twentieth century and the green occasional glasses. I wouldn't usually go for dark green but these were the best pieces in the house. Oh, and the Clarice Cliff. But Frances was sad about Mrs W. She thought she deserved to have her stuff gone through by careful hands. So she took it upon herself to go to Southgate from Tottenham on sorting sorties at weekends in the run-up to the move. She found naked snaps of Mrs W taken lovingly by her husband with his equipment. These she destroyed.

In short, she did the work of a daughter and she was repaid. On her last day of house-clearing, the day when the man was coming with a van for the bulky items we didn't want, Frances found a present from Mrs W in the wardrobe. It was the day before her birthday. It was some writing paper addressed to Frances with love from Mary.

But that's not the story I've chosen to tell in this book.

When I was in infant school, there were two sisters with a rare illness. This affected their skin and one of them looked like she'd been burnt or boiled. I was scared of her and avoided looking at her. I told my mother I was afraid to go in the playground and she arranged with the headmistress Mrs Bannister that I could sit in her room and read a book at playtime. I thought it was a permanent arrangement but it only lasted two days. Those girls were bitter about their illness and they didn't want to hear about anyone else's ailments, least of all my hayfever that kept me indoors with them on summer afternoons. They both died and the library was named after them and their photo was framed on the wall so we could look at them forever.

I had a cleverly constructed story about skin to tell involving those dead girls but I've decided not to tell it after all, nor to tell about the Passover meal when one of the guests, a large Hollywood psychiatrist, had a rather different description of his mother's decline from Alzheimer's than the one his elderly father gave us. The psychiatrist, who is a consultant for the movies, also had a lot to say about a Spanish film where a nurse fucks a patient out of her coma, and even more about the war in Iraq (support it because his brother's in the army; the French are crap) – all of which seemed like material at the time.

I'm not writing about the friend by the sea who's sleeping more and more each day, each week. I'm not writing about being on the beach when everyone starts shouting in different languages and a boat comes across the water from the campsite to the cut-off beach too late and then the air ambulance and then the family walking across the campsite holding each other up.

I thought I might write about when the ghost of my grandma spoke my name at my sister's wedding, 'Heleeenaa,' which is what she sometimes called me (not 'Helin', which is how she said 'Helen'), as I waited for my sister to come down in the lift and walk up the aisle in her blue dress; or about what I've learnt about killing by playing Space Invaders on my mobile phone.

And then I was talking to a friend about God. We discussed our difficulties with the word (God is male, God looks like a man, God is judgemental, etc).

But I realised that since I had my vision, I've been addressing God quite openly, if not in public then in the garden, as God. Not a higher power, a deeper power, the spirit of the universe, not the goddess or the life force or the infinite or the universal love that flows between all beings. Just God.

In the beginning I lay in bed, mindful.

In the middle a vision unfolded itself behind my eyes, a form or a creature of light, shapes, all the colours and none, constantly moving but still, ever changing but constant.

In the end I went to sleep with God.

One of the symptoms of mental illness is having visions of God or hearing the voice of God or believing oneself in direct communication with God. If you are not mad then a vision of God must be explained as one of the following: a dream, a daydream, a vision of something else.

Seeing God is a little like seeing the Loch Ness Monster. In a TV programme debunking the myth of the monster, reasons were given why no such creature can be living in the loch. At the end the presenter became quite insistent, saying that we must desist henceforth from any such nonsense. I said, 'I still believe in it,' as my girlfriend Jane (who prefers to be referred to as my partner) changed the channel.

In Sardinia we saw some wild miniature horses which are not the same as ponies. If you take a certain path through woodland, you might just see them. We took the path until the heat defeated us and as we turned for home a group of seven horses came walking towards us, saw us, considered us, then veered from the path into the woods, through the scrub.

Last night I woke in the heat and sat on the bed to look out of the open window and catch the breeze on my face and there in the lamplight was a large fox, walking stealthily up the road on the opposite pavement, hoping not to be seen.

Deep Night
Tenea D. Johnson

Deep Night
Tenea D. Johnson

Between death and birth lies a deep night. In it, the soul stretches out, comes apart at the seams and disperses, to eventually create itself anew. Evangeline always imagined it to look like multicolored light floating like gossamer or lightning in space. She thought now of her Mama Luella stretched out against the darkness, melding with other lights while she sat stiff-backed and tired in a clearing to pay her respects. She smiled through the distance between them. She did not fear that Mama Luella was lost, only traveling to come back in another face, a deeper dream, a more refined version of her truth. She looked now and again at her father sitting next to her. Only the tendons in his jaw acknowledged the funeral happening around him; they worked diligently, chewing on the pain of death. His round brown face was still but for their movement. The rest of him seemed far away – with her mother, perhaps.

Activity coursed around them. Graceful old mamas crowned in feathered Sunday hats led each other to their seats, spoke and wept quietly in pockets of color – blue, purple, rose. All of Mama Luella's favorite colors were expressed in skirts, homemade blouses, dyed slippers – as per her grandmother's instructions. She didn't wonder when they'd gotten these instructions. Only her father and the Reverend donned the traditional black. She wore the dress she'd found waiting for her in her grandmother's front bedroom, a lush blue wrap with white doves stitched into the hem. Though they hadn't seen each other in ten years, it fit perfectly. Though she'd never worn a wrap in her life, her hands worked outside her conscious mind and cinched it perfectly in a few moments, a deep hum vibrating through her lips as the last fold was tucked in place.

She smiled now at the women she knew had bathed her grandmother at this morning's sunrise. (Carefully dipping swatches

339

of cloth ripped from their own lives into spring water, they wiped off the funeral parlor's makeup and concealer, coaxing Luella out of this impression of her.) They turned the corners of their mouths up, smiling back. They slowly nodded to her, eyes locked on her own. She returned the gesture. It seemed a signal.

The Reverend, who'd been quietly praying in a cluster of oaks, advanced from the trees and walked to the front of the outdoor congregation. He smoothed his thick white mustache and began to collect the spirit.

'Brothers and sisters, we gather today to celebrate the soul of Luella Willet...'

'Mmmm Hmmm,' the mourners sang back to the Reverend.

'... Sister Luella touched all of our lives, but more than that she touched the heart of *God*!'

'*Yes* she did! Yes she *did*,' the older ladies chimed in, fanning the words out of their mouths. Evangeline watched them scoot farther back in their chairs, poised for the next punctuation.

'And for this we KNOW she sits *high* in the kingdom of the Lord!'

'ON HIGH! Yes Lord ON HIGH!' came the crescendo from the audience.

Having released this energy, built up since they learned of her passing, Luella's longtime friends and distant acquaintances settled back in their seats to let the familiar funereal words unfold. Evangeline sat quietly, open, absorbing the Tuscaloosa that had been lost to her since her mother forbade the trip.

'Where do you come from?'

'Long time 'go the way-back folks come from there to here to learn how to be reborn right here on the land. With the trees and all the little animals and everything and they stay alive so there'd come us, and here us is,' the gravel slid from her throat. She said in her own voice, 'Here us is.' Evangeline rocked slightly, small hands cupping the wet bark of the log. As her 'is' flowed out across the water, she looked up to catch Tasha's naked expression. She'd learned to look before Tasha covered up the tense eyebrow, the pinched corners of her mouth. This time, her friend's face was open, the lips parted slightly. She looked ready to ask another question and then nodded to herself, dismissing it. Behind her the water continued to push through the earth, clear water over pastel pebbles. They fell now into one of their silences, the end of a game they played throughout the few weeks Evangeline spent in Tuscaloosa, visiting her Mama Luella.

Nearly every day they would strike out just after lunch and spend whole afternoons lost in the half-acre behind the shed. They were a good pair: Tasha had many questions and Evangeline, answers. Twenty Questions was their favorite game. Though it always had the same theme, they never tired of playing it. No one was better at 'Who Am I?' than Evangeline. They'd walk through the woods, Tasha swatting at dandelions and weeds with the ever-present stick, bringing up the rear to Evangeline's searching eyes. When she'd found something – a little waterfall emptying into a sinkhole, a leaf turned transparent by the sun, a rock whose texture tickled her – she'd hold it, if only with her eyes. Her face would smooth and then Tasha knew she was ready. Tasha would start with simple questions, but had learned not to ask for the name because the answer was always Evangeline. Never mind that, two questions before, she'd said she was six feet tall or, in answer to the one before that, that she made boats for a living. This was the trick in their game: that the answer was never one word or two, but the answers to all the questions stacked up together. It wasn't the 'I' that was important but the 'am'. Tasha found this more interesting than television and spent most of her time with Evangeline. She didn't assume that she knew things, so she wasn't afraid to ask questions, that's what Evangeline liked about her. Most people thought they knew every damn thing, when really what they knew wasn't any deeper than the stream behind her grandmother's house.

'How come your Mama don't like Black people?' Tasha asked into the silence.

Evangeline slid down the log and onto the ground, tucking her long legs beneath her. 'Why do you think that?'

''Cause she don't. You can tell. It's like she don't want to touch us or something. Too good for her own kind, my Mama say.'

Evangeline said, 'That's not true,' and picked up the end of Tasha's stick, dragging it lightly across the grass. She knew what her friend was talking about but she didn't think that was what her mother added up to.

Just before she'd come to Tuscaloosa – she loved saying that word, fast and happy, it sounded like a secret password, *Tuscaloosa* – Marie told Evangeline that her legacy was to struggle and blossom. Evangeline told her that she wasn't delicate enough to blossom, that she'd rather explode like popcorn: 'UH! Here I is!' Marie said all girls were delicate and pointed at the soft blonde woman on the TV screen. After that, she'd thinned herself out, cut back her thoughts, stopped eating butter. Her mother told her they were beyond color, and it was true – if white isn't a color. 'Cause most times, white was the only color Van saw: at school, Brownie meetings, play dates. She went to a private school in a private neighborhood. To Evangeline, private meant white. Except for her private dreams. Not wanting to play Twenty Questions again, she shut down that train of thought and looked up at the lavender sky.

'Come on, it'll be dark soon.' They brushed off their backsides and headed to the shed for jars. Their favorite blue lightning bugs came out earliest of all.

That evening Tasha's parents, the neighbor's family, and Evangeline's got together for a barbeque. Marie and Edward had gotten in earlier that evening to spend the last weekend of Evangeline's visit with Mama Luella. Now they sat outside talking with the other adults. Mama Luella stood over a barrel grill, spraying water onto the meat. In the family room, Tasha and Evangeline played with Marcus, the neighbor's boy.

'You ain't all *that*! You ain't all *that*!' Marcus yelled, his chin pointing upward on the last syllables as he looked down his nose at Tasha. The sound of his voice excited him at this volume. Before, she'd been winning The Dozens, cutting on his brother's too-big nylon jacket and the way it looked on his pointy tall boy body, even noticing that he'd tied his shoes in knots where the laces were broken. He'd lost the rhythm of the contest, could think of no come-backs and so was left listening to a list of his faults. But now he had her – not with wit but with sheer size and volume. She retreated closer to the wall every time he yelled. He liked the power, and bully genius stoked his voice. His hand flashed out, grabbed the doorknob behind her and before she could make real words with her grunts of protest he'd shoved her into the darkened closet. Immediately her voice reached its highest pitch, sirening for someone to get her out.

Of course, it was Evangeline who came to the rescue. Already well over four feet at seven years old, she was a natural protector. Used to plucking the smaller girl out of trouble, she enjoyed this role. This made her walk slowly over to Marcus, preparing her strategy. Before a word came out of her mouth or a hand up to protect herself, he'd grabbed her too and shoved her on top of Tasha whose hysterics bounced off the walls in the small black space. Evangeline knocked the wind out of her. The screaming cut off, lost in the gush of Tasha's breath. In the moment of silence when the other senses faded, her skin took over and told Evangeline that the warm sweat pressed against her was too close, that the hot breath on her neck was fear. Then her skin failed her. It could not tell her that this was not the dream where a box of darkness fell on her as she walked in another life through the abundant plains, the box that blotted out the blue skies and breeze, sealing her away from that happiness. She reacted now as she did then, the last time something tried to take the space out of her soul. When her hands spread out and hit the closet walls, it began: the timbre that got straight to the core of things, a sound beyond sound.

Marcus snapped to attention, his grin breaking apart until the boy looked like he'd been struck in the face. The tendons stood out on his neck. His head vibrated from tension. He looked about to cry.

Conversation on the back porch stopped short. Tasha and Evangeline's mothers wavered in the wind. While Tasha's screams dissipated into the sounds of Earth, Wind & Fire, Evangeline's cut straight through, reaching through the women. Only their eyes shifted – gravitating towards the sound. The men sitting out under the magnolia tree reached for their women's eyes, looking for an explanation. Cans of beer hovered in midair.

Mama Luella moved. Propelled through her family of statues, she ran towards the closet. Evangeline's screaming frightened her, the sound too raw and thick for a child's delicate chords. She tore open the door and went to pick up the girl, but stopped when she saw her eyes. She thought she saw something in them, moving across the whites. She shook her head hard once and took Evangeline in her arms. The sound didn't stop until she pulled her out of the closet. In the light, the child's eyes cleared. She stared out into the distance, pupils straight ahead and expanding. The parents' running feet shook the floorboards. Evangeline hopped a little in the air, but was rooted to the spot. She didn't speak another word all through dinner, only nodding when asked if she was OK. The adults spoke quietly, moved sharply, knocking over a salt shaker and a pitcher of iced tea, slicing through a wishbone. Her father, usually out playing bid whist or pool with the neighborhood men, watched TV all night and stuck close to his daughter. They were unsettled. She spoke only after the visitors had gone and the dinner plates were put away. In the front bedroom, her mother folded her clothes back into a tiny pink suitcase as Mama Luella laid her down for rest.

'Mama Luella, what dreams mean?'

'Dreams are your soul remembering what's been done and what's to come.'

'Mother! I will not have you filling her head with all that foolishness,' her mother interrupted, 'Haven't we had enough for one day?' She turned towards her daughter. 'Dreams are like storybooks, Evangeline. You're just telling stories to yourself.'

She looked steadily into the child's eyes, trying to beam out authority. Evangeline looked at her a moment and then focused on her grandmother with wide eyes and closed mouth. Mama Luella only gazed calmly at the child, then turned and walked out of the bedroom, smoothing the tasseled blanket over Evangeline's feet.

Later, she heard them arguing in whispers out in the kitchen:

'Just 'cause you don't wanna know, don't mean the child don't.'

'Gracious! And you wonder why I left Tuscaloosa. Too many backward people and their backward ideas.'

'You can be as saditty as you want, Marie Mae, but don't sass me like you didn't come out me, ya hear.'

'Now Mama...'

'*Now Mama,*' and then the screen door banging shut, feet following after.

That night Evangeline dreamed of her Mama Luella, shrunk down to her size, with a little girl's face and strong hands. The Girl Mama Luella carried a bucket across a dusty patch of land, her eyes brushing the grass. Evangeline couldn't see her own whole dream self, only its hand – large, brown, and mottled with scars – which took the burden out of the other's small hands and grasped it. The Girl Mama Luella looked up and smiled. A beautiful brown girl who'd been waiting to smile. Its flash faded slowly from Evangeline's unconscious eye, first the color, then the presence. The last remnants of floating light melded into the golden sun splashed across her face when she awoke.

The next morning she repeated the action, taking her grandmother's hand after breakfast.

Rubbing the child's smooth supple knuckles, a tear slid down Mama Luella's cheek. She gathered the girl in her arms and placed her in her lap. 'I just want you to be safe.' She kissed Evangeline's forehead and rested against her rock. Through morning's first shy rays towards the full beams of early afternoon, they sat that way, not moving until the car was packed and Ed came to say goodbye, collecting Evangeline. Marie sat in the front seat of the Volvo, reading a magazine. As the car pulled away, Evangeline smiled big for her Mama Luella.

When Marie Brown read one of the child's letters to her grandmother the following autumn, she decided she didn't like what came out of her daughter in the backwoods of her childhood, and Tuscaloosa became a memory to Evangeline.

But Evangeline remembered more than her mother could fathom. That much was evident even in the seven-year-old's scribblings, which changed everything. Marie had been cleaning

Evangeline's room, looking for any loose ends that could be sent down to their new home in Savannah. Edward stood in the doorway again asking why they couldn't just wait and do everything at once when Evangeline was done with the school year. She turned and leveled her eyes upon him.

'Edward, the sooner we start, the sooner we finish.'

'But we still have lives here, Marie, things that have to get done before the move. I've got two projects to finish at the firm. Van's got her million and one classes and clubs, and you –'

'And I am keeping this family in order, moving us on to new things. Don't you want to take the next step, Edward? Or do you want to stay at a mediocre firm where they don't appreciate you? Or maybe you want our daughter to have to grow up around this mess like we did?'

'What mess, Marie? I've been listening to you talk about "this mess" for months. I don't see any mess, except for the one we're making trying to hurry this move.'

'Oh, don't lose your reason now and don't take that tone with me. Don't you trust my judgment?'

'Of course I trust your judgment, Marie. That's not the point. It's just that these last couple of months, you've been... agitated or something, I don't know.'

'And this move is just what I need – what we all need. To settle down somewhere safe. That's all, Edward. The thought of it just... excites me.' She moved in close, putting her arms around his neck and looking up into his nutty brown face, reassuring herself that yes, she had married the right man for the job. Nothing to worry about. Soon there won't be anything to worry about. She kissed him, letting just enough warmth out to calm his fears. 'Savannah's going to be great, hon. *We're* going to be great in Savannah.'

He looked down and saw his Marie, bit the side of his mouth and nodded in agreement. He held her for a moment, bringing her close to him and then backed away.

'I have to get back to work,' he said and turned down the hallway.

She watched him round the corner and then returned to her work. Packing away some of Evangeline's books, she came across the letter sticking out of an old *National Geographic*. She unfolded and read:

Mama Lu. How are you? I miss you. Did you eat all the tomatoes in the garden? Will you send me some, Mama never buys them. She cooks little green pencils. They tast like yuck. We are moving soon. Their will be a grate school. I can take better clases. Mama say she sick of the fokes here. Say they a bad enflunce. I had a dream with the hurt lady. I have a lot. She still says no thing. She looks at me. She smiles and tuches my face. I know she will say sum thing soon. I want her to talk. Are dreams what you say or what Mama say? The hurt lady is not like a dream. I play kick ball and go to the beech when I dream. Not like when I see her.

I love you.

Love

Evangeline

This was the last letter never sent from Evangeline to Mama Luella. When they moved to Savannah, Marie redoubled her efforts to fill up her daughter's mind: with activities and near constant instruction on how to act. She spent every waking moment standing over her, whether she was physically there or not. At night she took two prescriptions so she could do it all again in the morning. She meant to make Evangeline cultured by her definition, to follow in her footsteps and beyond – but most of all she meant to leave no room for the hurt ladies in Evangeline's dreams. The girl was a fledgling ballerina by eight, a Girl Scout with every badge by eleven, and a formidable chess opponent by thirteen. Amongst her mother's perfumed and perfectly coiffed crowd of pale friends, there was talk of geniushood. As the martini glasses clinked in the parlor, the subtle tones of jealousy could be heard between the congratulatory words, the exclamations of great mothering. Marie accepted these compliments with a chiseled smile. Her eyes stayed cast in front of her, darting towards the clock on the mantel, counting the minutes until it was time to shuttle Evangeline from French tutoring to gymnastics.

Mama Luella wrote over the years, first demanding then

begging that she be allowed to see her grandchild. She called Marie out for severing the connection and trying to hide her own dreams. She told her that no good would come of it – and she was right. 'It won't stop just because you want it to, Marie. You can't run from it. You should be running *to* it.' Marie scoffed at this last, but it came back to her many times over the years: as she sat in PTA meetings, a little brown dot in a sea of white; once as she watched the waves rippling up the shore on a vacation to Virginia Beach with Edward's friends; that time the butcher mistook her for Evangeline and called her 'girl'; every night as the chalk of the little blue pills melted onto her tongue, she thought of her mother's words, blurring on the page that she still kept in her night-stand drawer. When it came time for Evangeline to graduate high school, she wrote her mother back. '*Mama please come,*' she wrote. The pills weren't working.

There were signs of course, but, like most, her family didn't see them until after: little things could be found out of place in the fastidiously clean bedroom that she and Edward shared; twice when she was supposed to pick her daughter up she found herself out by a lake staring deep into the water, looking at it as if there were no bottom at all. She started to avoid her friends. Their crumbling pale faces vaguely nauseated her. She found herself staring at the way this one's mouth was drooping into a tight frown or that one's chin expanded, grew ruddy and flaccid connecting to the neck. They looked alien to her, these proper white women she'd spent formal brunches and dinners with. She could no longer stand to be around those who had once been so valuable to her and, more importantly, her daughter's opportunities. She declined invitations to galas and golf tournaments. After the incident at a dinner party for Edward's company, Marie could no longer control the remembering and it came back to her in a whirlwind.

Edward had been off mingling with clients, buttering up his boss for a promotion. She could hear his clear baritone ringing out among the other voices. The glass of champagne in her hand kept her connected to the room. She concentrated on its cold mingling with her skin. She didn't see the man approach her from behind.

'Mrs Brown,' his voice slithered. She turned abruptly to find Matthew Leonard, one of Edward's associates – by far her least favorite – standing before her in a crowded brown three-piece suit. A dim red rose stuck out of the lapel.

'How *lovely* to see you again.' All the time he spoke, his eyes moved up her body, noting the ample curves and muscles shrouded in the purple wrap she'd bought that very evening.

'Mr Leonard,' she replied.

'You're looking fabulous – but then again you always do.' He did not wait for a reply before continuing. 'Catherine and I are having a little affair next weekend. You know, just a little something in celebration of the upcoming commencement, a bit of a celebration for the ones who've been paying those exorbitant private school fees all these years.' He laughed at his own joke. 'We were really hoping you and Edward could stop by. After all, Evangeline is the valedictorian, and the four of us should have been coupling up a long time ago.'

She looked at him sharply at this last comment. Immediately, she knew it was a mistake to look him in the eye. His face was poised in a lascivious sneer.

'I'll really have to ask Edward about that,' she said, looking over his head for her husband. She'd lost his laughter in the crowd. 'Evangeline's speech at the NAACP Youth Scholars is coming up, and we still have to prepare for graduation. So we've made quite a few commitments already.'

'Not too many, I hope. They have a way of dictating our lives, don't they?' he said, taking a step closer. 'I, myself, try to stay open to the possibilities.' As he spoke, his hand crossed the threshold of insinuation and rested on her hip. 'Would you care to dance, Marie?' he asked, his hand moving towards her ass.

In one motion she moved close to his ear, broke her glass on the side of the table, brought it against his thigh and whispered, 'Would you care to bleed, Matthew?' The sharded glass shook in her hand. Slowly she moved her head around his and looked him in the eye.

He saw something moving across the whites of her eyes and took two quick steps away from her.

'Marie! I see we've had a little accident,' her husband intoned, moving up briskly from the other side of the room. 'Let me get someone.' He called out to a waiter and then turned back to his wife. For a moment she kept her back to him. Then she took a deep breath, making sure to look at the floor first, and replied, 'Yes, it seems so,' handing him the broken glass. 'I'm afraid I don't feel very well, Edward. Can we go?'

'Of course.' They left Leonard staring at the spot they'd been standing in.

That night, dreams came back to Marie – through the veil of sedatives and the wall of her stalwart restraint, Marie's woman came back to her.

'WHY YOU HIDIN'? YOU CAN'T HIDE, GIRL, YOU CAN'T HIDE!'

She could see the white face clearly in the blackness of the hold. She tried to breathe only when water lapped against the hull. She wanted to close her eyes and fade completely into the safe blackness, but she was afraid of not seeing the white man who searched her out, stepping on people, feces and rats to find her. She scooted closer to the wall, balancing herself on the dead man beneath her. She tried not to recognize his marks, the same etched across her own face. The sleeping Marie knew this memory and didn't want to see its end. She steeled herself against what was coming. Before his hand grabbed her arm, she blinked out and turned her inner eye to imagining the stars outside were familiar. He slapped her hard across the face, bringing her back. Her eyes reacted and opened. The white man was gone.

'Why you hiding?' the woman asked, her face floating warmly inches from Marie's. 'You can't hide, child. We belong to each other. You can't deny me. Don't you see that?'

The next morning she wrote the message to her mother and began counting the days until her arrival. She threw away the pills when she got back from her morning errands. When Evangeline pulled into the driveway, she saw a sight: Marie digging up the side of the yard, planting yams in place of the stone garden she'd laid out piece by piece the spring before.

Marie came in while Evangeline was sitting at the table poring over a thick volume of Lacan.

'Why don't you stop straining your eyes and call your grandmother? Tell her about the NAACP ceremony,' she said and walked out of the room.

At first, the girl was perplexed, but she quickly recovered and picked up the phone. Mama Luella said she would be there in two days.

The next day the neighbor's septic tank backed up and exploded all over his yard. The smell was horrific. Edward suggested that they stay at a hotel for a night or two.

'There's too much left to do. I don't want to celebrate Van's graduation in a hotel,' Marie said. 'Besides, Mama's coming tomorrow and I want her to be in our home. Not some strange bed in a strange place. We'll just close the windows, burn some potpourri. It can't last long. Remember, they're the ones without a toilet. I'm sure it'll be fixed soon.'

And it was: two days after they took Marie away, as Edward and Evangeline climbed into a cab to the airport, workmen packed away their tools and prepared the broken valve for its final resting home at the Savannah City Dump.

You might say it was the smell that pushed her over the edge, or the possibility of finally talking to her mother about the dreams, or maybe even the thought of letting Evangeline go off into the world. You might say this and you might be right, but let me tell you what happened.

On May 22, 1999, the day before darling Evangeline's graduation, the Browns received one phone call and one package. The call came just before they were about to leave for the airport. Marie and Evangeline, focused on picking up Mama Luella, ignored the ringing. Edward picked up the receiver, expecting a call from work. He was on the phone for approximately thirty seconds. In that time his face flowed from easy expectation to stoic gravity. He sat his women down in their impatience and spoke the words he wanted to bottle up and save for another day.

'Mama Luella...' he began.

The story was simple: the rain, the cars, the crash. Its meaning was profound. Light turned to darkness, expectation turned to grief, joy to sorrow. Evangeline's day turned into Mama Luella's life. The house was silent; shadows hung in the room. Evangeline began to cry, first quietly then in long ragged breaths. Edward tried to comfort her, smoothing the hair away from her face. He looked at his wife; she was not there. A woman made of stone stared back at him.

She stood up and walked out of the room. He heard her mount the stairs and close the bedroom door behind her.

Sometime later the doorbell rang... and rang... and rang. Finally, Edward answered it and the house returned to silence. It was a package with two names written on the front:

To: Evangeline Brown
From: Luella Price

He stood there trying to decide. In the end, he walked past his own closed bedroom door and into his daughter's room.

'It's from your Mama Lu,' he whispered, leaving the package in her trembling hands.

She didn't know what to do with it, at first, that thing her grandmother had brought her even after she was gone. She opened it though and found her Mama Lu's love for her wrapped up tidy in Fed Ex cardboard. She read the letter first.

I write these words the night before my death. It was foretold to me in a dream.

Do not grieve too harshly. Accidents don't happen at my age, Angel. You, my child, must prepare yourself. The time has come for sumthin that shoulda come a long time ago. But your mama wouldn't have it, nor your father. And livin in the white folks' world has left you unprotected. I cannot leave this place with you so vulnerable, but by will alone I cannot stay. Do not be afraid, Angel. You cannot fear yourself, and that, child, is what's coming. You're catching up with yourself. Don't try to fit, just be. Not the Middle Passage, but a clear path. I can't tell you every detail 'cause I don't know. You children are made from different things

than me and mine – our time, I mean. And you, Angel, are made up of
something different altogether, I spect. Just try to remember you're
becoming what you are.
   Luella

Evangeline ran to tell her mother, finally to tell her mother about the woman in her dreams. She wanted to tell her all about herself, 'cause maybe she didn't know dreams weren't storybooks. The door was locked. She yelled for the first time in her house: 'Mama! Mama open the door! Mama I want to see you! Mama!

'I want you to see me! Don't hide!'

Her voice cut through the darkness in the room. It cut through Marie's darkness. She could not respond. They were coming too fast on her, the colors and sounds from all her lost souls. But mostly from the first, from the one who traveled the waters.

She saw her mother, a young giant with wings enough to protect Marie from the waiting world. She saw the day that she closed the door between her selves, heard the reverberation of silence all over again. She saw her woman for the first time again: the strongest part of her spirit reaching out to touch her face when she was just a girl, five years old, picking blueberries in Mr Jackson's patch. She saw the splotches of blood on the tablecloth where she was born. The man in New Orleans who reached out to her then pale-lemon hand: 'Hey girl, you want a daddy?' The Minstrel show that played out in the clearing. Choked on her first swig of whiskey that signaled her manhood in a remote village where green rolled strong and proud ever towards Ballyheige Bay. The little girl she'd seen die cut in two by a train when the hulking monsters were still new to the world. Felt the heat of the brick oven the master's food simmered in. Tasted the sweat on her mother's breast when she came to her a few precious moments between sunset and rise. And yes, she even reached back and saw the water before the darkness that was her only ally when the hold doors closed, sealing the tomb of living bodies.

She tried to clear her mind, regain control. She took a deep breath and the reek of human waste filled her nostrils. She closed her eyes and there were the bodies. She started to hyperventilate and each breath was another face. She reached out to grab hold of something and the curd of excrement was pasted across her hand. Marie could not hide. She reached her depth. Compelled by *all* that lay inside her, she began to remove her illusions.

Outside the door, time continued to slip into the past. Evangeline gave up her hoarse words at the door. Edward paced back and forth downstairs, eventually coming to rest on the other side of the bedroom door, his legs tucked under him, the right side of his body against the door. He slowly sang a song he thought he'd forgotten the words to, his cheek brushing the wood: 'Marie... Mae... Marie... Mae... Marie May I Come In? Marie... I... Marie... I... Marie I'll soothe your skin... Marie... Mae –'

The door to Evangeline's room swung open. She stood in the backlight bright as an angel; she wore a quilted robe of white. He recognized a piece of linen napkin at the hem. It was from his wedding.

'Mama Lu's graduation gift,' she said reaching down to help her father up. She pointed at the collar: 'From her favorite dress, the one she was baptized in... and I think this pink piece is from Mama's birth. I don't know about the rest, but I will.'

He kept staring at her face; it brought him peace.

'Daddy, I've got to go give this speech. I've got something to say. I want you to be there. Mama won't come out till she comes out,' she added, matter-of-factly.

He turned back towards the wood that stood between him and his Marie, laying his palm flat against it.

'Daddy, I need you.' The words were like magic. He stood up tall, brushed off his clothes and walked down the stairs.

'Mama,' she whispered, leaning into the door, 'don't be afraid. Bring them together. We'll be waiting for you, Mama.'

Inside the dark room, Marie stopped her scissors in midair and smiled. When she heard the door close behind her she continued to remove all the soul-less things from her; later she moved on the rest of the house.

*

While her mother stacked dishes, clothes and furniture into a neat pile in the backyard, Evangeline walked up to a podium, exuding a confidence that flowed over the sea of brown faces stretched out before her.

'I had a speech prepared for tonight, but I won't be reading it. The world has changed since then. Today Luella Rivers Price died; she was my grandmother. But that's not why I'm telling you. She gave me a message, one so important that she could not go without passing it on to me. *This* is purpose and devotion. Tonight I operate in her honor, in the service of purpose and devotion, to deliver my own message. And that is simply this: integrate your spirits. We who are so wrapped up in the concept of integration in the schools, in the workforce, even in families. We who need it the most, not to better, but to survive *whole*, speak no words and make no effort to integrate our spirits. I'm here to tell you that you have more than one. I'm here to tell you that every voice inside you must be given a chance to speak. I'm here to tell you that there is no greater gift or accomplishment or reward than a soul that is strong, coherent and free. Each one of you has been here before and will be again.'

With this she walked off the stage and to her father. Edward put his arms around her, squeezed her closer to himself and kissed her forehead. The two walked out of the darkened room, not hearing the applause or pausing between their strides. They took one step after another into the evening.

When they took Marie away she was a different woman: her hair hacked off, nails broken off to jagged weapons, blood running down her face, her finery laid to waste in the bonfire only now cooling in the backyard. Walking between two men in white, she was dressed simply in a brown dress with no shoes upon her feet. She hummed a low song to herself and intermittently spoke what the attendants thought was gibberish, but was actually Wolof, one of her first languages (the others being English, French, and more Creoles than it makes sense to mention). One of the last things she did before getting into the back seat of the van was reach down, grab a handful of dirt and put it in her pocket. Then she turned, pushed her palm high towards her family and got in with the brown man idling the engine. For a moment the white and orange lights lit up the yard and then there was only darkness surrounding the two figures standing in the front lawn.

'You know what medium mean, Mama? Medium mean halfway through. That's you and me – mediums. You went too far one way, and I thought you were too far in another, but the woman come to me again last night. She said you be all right soon, she say you shouldn't delayed it so long, that it'll leave its mark, but you be all right. And I'll be here with you, Mama... my child's child. We'll walk back into the world together. Go anywhere you want. This is a hard thing, but I'm with you. Daddy'd like to see you... Well, when you're ready, if you want. Later, I dreamed you someplace beautiful, Mama. There were houses made out of wood and mud, painted yellow and red and white. Even the ground was painted beautiful. You sat outside next to a river staring into such blue waters. You were smiling. Then a woman called you and you came running, so happy. I've never seen you smile like that. I hope you're there now. I hope you're there right now.'

Marie's lips moved a bit and then were still again. As she looked up at her daughter for the first time in months, her eyes were clear and smiling.

Contributors

Contributors

Caril Behr was born and grew up in Cape Town, South Africa. She moved to the UK in the early 70s and lived in north London for many years. She now lives in Stockholm, where she teaches English and translates for a living. Caril has had stories published in anthologies and journals and has twice been a winner in the Queer Words Annual Short Story Writing Competition. She has always written short stories, many of which turn out to be long stories. Caril has several projects on the go and hopes to finish them some day.

Fi Benson's career as a freelance writer began with the publishing of her short story 'A Fable' in *Diva* magazine in 1998. Since then, Fi has had short stories, poems, articles and book reviews published in *Diva, Buzzwords, Roadworks* and *QWF* magazine. She has also had poetry, prose and short plays broadcast within the regular writers' slot which she hosts on local Forest Radio. Fi is currently writing a play called 'Rosa-goccy' for The Other Space theatre in Cheltenham and is completing the first draft of a novel as part of her MA with Lancaster University.

Frances Bingham has contributed stories to anthologies including *The Diva Book of Short Stories* and *Long Journey Home*. Her long poem 'Mothertongue' was published in 1999, and she has performed her work at various literary festivals and won a York Poetry Prize. Also a writer of non-fiction, she regularly contributes articles to *Diva* on artists and writers in lesbian history. Currently she's writing a literary biography, *This Wild Solitary Heart: The Poetic Life of Valentine Ackland*, commissioned for publication in 2006. She lives in London with Liz Mathews, the studio potter, and they work together at the Whitechapel Pottery.

Cara Bruce is the editor of *Best Fetish Erotica, Best Bisexual Erotica, Viscera* and *Horny? San Francisco.* She is the editor-in-chief of Eros Guide (www.eros-guide.com), Eros London (www.eros-london.com) and Eros Noir (www.eros-noir.com), as well as running the award-winning ezine and publishing company, Venus or Vixen (www.venusorvixen.com). Her short fiction has been published in dozens of anthologies, including *The Mammoth Book of Best Erotica* and *Best American Erotica.* You can visit her at www.CaraBruce.com.

Kathleen Kiirik Bryson is a novelist/actor/painter who was born and raised in Alaska. Her first novel *Mush* was published by Diva Books in 2001. Current novel projects include *Girl on a Stick* – a pitch-black comedy about rebus puzzles, Catholicism and Americans – and *He's Lucid*, reminiscent of *Slaughterhouse* 5 and set in Alaska in the year 2131. She is also writing and directing two low-budget digital feature projects: *The Viva Voce Virus* (fiction) and *Glamorous Life* (documentary).

Rose Collis is the critically acclaimed author of *Portraits To The Wall: Historic Lesbian Lives Unveiled* (Cassell, 1994); *A Trouser-Wearing Character: The Life and Times of Nancy Spain* (Cassell, 1997); *Outlines: kd lang* (Absolute Press, 1999) and *Colonel Barker's Monstrous Regiment: A Tale of Female Husbandry* (Virago, 2001). She was commissioning editor of *The Mammoth Book of Lesbian Erotica* (Constable Robinson, 2000). Her journalism has appeared in more than thirty publications, including the *Independent, The Times, Time Out, City Limits, Tribune,* the *Bookseller, Diva* and *Gay Times.* Born in Wimbledon in 1959, she now lives in Sussex. No A levels, no degree – but she is a recent City & Guilds qualified gardener, which has been of infinitely more use. She still believes truth is stranger than fiction.

Charlotte Cooper wrote a dirty novel called *Cherry* that was seized by Canada Customs for its obscene fisting content. She writes things for a living and is also the boss of www.CharlotteCooper.net.

Her beautiful older brother Paul died in a car crash in 1988 when he was twenty-four. She's still here so don't be a stranger, OK?

Stella Duffy has written three novels published by Sceptre – *Singling Out the Couples*, *Eating Cake* and *Immaculate Conceit*; and four crime novels – *Calendar Girl*, *Wavewalker*, *Beneath the Blonde* and *Fresh Flesh*, published by Serpent's Tail. Her next two, *State of Happiness* and *Parallel Lies*, will be published by Virago in 2004. She has written many feature articles and more than twenty short stories. With Lauren Henderson she is the co-editor of the crime anthology *Tart Noir*. In 2002 her story 'Martha Grace' won the CWA Short Story Dagger Award. With the National Youth Theatre, she has adapted *Immaculate Conceit* for theatre. Stella writes for radio and theatre, and is also an actor and improviser.

Susan Em has been writing prose, poetry and screenplays for many years. She has won the Smirnoff GCN/Queer Writes award and has had both stories and poetry published in magazines and anthologies. Much of her writing explores a character's recognition of the disjunction between their subjective perception and objective reality. She is currently completing a novel and a research degree in medieval history. She works as an archivist and records manager and lives in south London.

Carolyn Finlay spent her childhood in Tasmania and New Guinea, and moved to England in 1969. She has published two collections of poetry, *Giveaway* (Stride, 1997) and *Foreigner* (Waterdog, 2001). Following are some of the things she's loved / been / lost / had / remembered: a child on a beach / three children / an only child / a tall house / a mother with a dog / invisible / the scent of eucalyptus / two men and three women / beechwoods / four children / fifteen single earrings / Alaska. She now lives in Cheltenham.

Ellen Galford is the author of four novels: *Moll Cutpurse – Her True History*, *The Fires of Bride*, *Queendom Come* and *The Dyke and the Dybbuk*, which won an American Publishers Association Lambda award in 1994. She's also written short fiction and non-fiction pieces for various lesbian/gay and Jewish anthologies. Although she was born in New Jersey, she emigrated across the Atlantic in 1971, and since then has lived in Glasgow, London, Edinburgh, and Pittenweem, a fishing village on the Firth of Forth.

Frances Gapper's story collection *Absent Kisses* was published by Diva Books in 2002. Her story 'Pink and Blue' appeared in *Pretext 5*. She interviewed Ali Smith for the summer 2003 issue of *Mslexia* magazine. She wrote a novel fifteen years ago and is now writing another.

Linda Innes lives on the north-east coast, with her partner and teenaged daughter. She has been a teacher, creative writing tutor, performance poet, silver polish demonstrator, stand-up comedian and arts administrator. She has had short stories in both *The Diva Book of Short Stories* and *Diva* magazine. In her first novel, *Smother*, published by Diva Books, comedy is woven with destructive passion, obsession, betrayal, revenge and death. In fact, it's a story of everyday lesbian life. Linda is currently working on her second novel. Always slow on the uptake, she accidentally fell into lesbianism at the age of thirty, but can highly recommend it. Of death and dying, she is less confident.

Tenea D. Johnson is a writer, scholar and musician living in New York City. She was blessed to be born a Johnson, 'the latest survivors in a long line of the constantly strong'. Raised in Kentucky, she attended New College of Florida (BA) and New York University (MA). Between classes, she learned to coax the stories from djembes, dumbeks, and jazz guitars. Various venues around NYC, including the Knitting Factory and The Public Theater, have opened their doors to their collaborations. Her fiction, poetry, essays and interviews have appeared in *African Voices*, *Arise*, and *Humanities in the South*, among others. You can reach her at latestsurvivor@hotmail.com.

Kathi Kosmider has been in love with the dead for centuries. She was haunted at a young age: the Virgin Mary made many visitations, along with Felix the Cat and Speed Racer, Kimba the White Lion and various other dead comic-book characters. From that point it was up, up and away. She's been time-travelling on various 'planes' ever since. Along with many short stories and short films, she's written a lesbian *Sex and the City* called *The Knitters* and is in quest of an agent who isn't as haunted as she is. She would like to move to Berlin in the hope of finding her dead mother.

V.G. Lee lives in Hastings. She rises as the sun sets to write her horrid stories with a plumed pen dipped in the blood of hamsters, voles and other small mammals found on her sinister rambles o'er the cliff tops. It is rumoured that she has the ability to turn into a vampire bat and bite the throats of innocent women as they leave the local pub. She is also the author of two diabolical novels, *The Comedienne* and *The Woman in Beige*, both from Diva Books. Her doings are further documented on the worldwide web at www.vglee.co.uk.

Rosie Lugosi has been tantalising audiences with her unique blend of poetic perversion, humour and song for years, at events as diverse as the Cheltenham Literature Festival and SM Pride. She has an eclectic history, from singing in 80s Goth band The March Violets to her current incarnation as Rosie Lugosi the Vampire Queen, performance poet and organisatrix of the infamous Club Lash. As well as two solo collections of poetry (*Hell and Eden* and *Coming Out at Night*), her stories, poems and essays have been widely anthologised. 'You'll Do' appeared in *The Diva Book of Short Stories* and 'The Purple Wallpaper' in *Groundswell*. She won the Erotic Oscar Award for Performance Artist of the Year 2001, and was runner-up for the Diva Award for Solo Performer 2002.

Georgina McIntosh was born in Falkirk in 1965. She writes sporadically, having had several stories published in *Chapman*,

West Coast, Edinburgh Review and various travel magazines. She is a winner of the Scottish Young Playwrights award and has written *Someone in My Corner* for BBC Scotland's Education Department. She currently works as an administrator for local government.

Ann Rower has mostly lived in and around New York City and the surrounding beaches. At the moment she lives in the East Village. She has published three books: a collection of stories called *If You're a Girl* (Semiotexte), and two novels from High Risk/ Serpent's Tail – *Armed Response* and the recent *Lee & Elaine*. Her work has also been widely anthologised, stories appearing in *Bomb Magazine, Journal of Contemporary Fiction*, and anthologies like *Living with the Animals* (Faber and Faber), *Hatred of Capitalism* (MIT), *Cooking with Honey* (Firebrand) and *High Risk 2*.

Helen Sandler is the author of two novels, *Big Deal* (rude) and *The Touch Typist* (proper), and the editor of two previous anthologies, *The Diva Book of Short Stories* (winner of a Lambda Literary Award) and *Groundswell*. After four years at Diva Books, Helen recently gave up her job to slow down, write more and work freelance. She lives with her lover in north London but has a dimming memory of growing up in Manchester.

Shireen Sharif is a pseudonym. She wrote 'Switch', subsequently re-edited, in 1988, inspired by the central motif of *Necessary Doubt* by Colin Wilson. Shireen deliberately developed an unreliable narrator, with literary devices from the opening voices to the metaphor of power as a switch. The story's references include: Shakespeare; George Eliot's *Middlemarch; The Mad Woman in the Attic* referencing Bertha Rochester in *Jane Eyre*; Émile Zola's *Thérèse Raquin*; Alice Walker's *The Color Purple*; 'Purple Haze' (Jimi Hendrix) and 'Purple Rain' (Prince). She has worked in television and, under her own name of Shameem Kabir, is the author of *Daughters of Desire: Lesbian Representations in Film*.

Ali Smith was born in Inverness in 1962 and lives in Cambridge. Her second novel, *Hotel World*, was shortlisted for both the Orange Prize and the Booker Prize in 2001 and won the Encore Award and the Scottish Arts Council Book of the Year Award in 2002. Her third collection of short fiction, *The Whole Story and Other Stories*, was published by Hamish Hamilton in 2003.

Cherry Smyth is Irish and lives in London. Her collection of poetry, *When the Lights Go Up*, was published by Lagan Press in 2001. *Damn Fine Art by New Lesbian Artists* appeared in 1996 from Cassell. She is also the author of *Queer Notions* (Scarlet Press, 1992). She has just completed a novel called *Cut Stars* about a teenage butch growing up in Northern Ireland in the 70s at a time before there were any Androulas to save her. It is not a comedy.

Cecilia Tan is known for mixing the erotic and the fantastic. Her short fiction has appeared in *Penthouse, Ms., Best American Erotica, Best Lesbian Erotica*, and *Asimov's*, among other places. She is the editor of over forty anthologies of erotic science fiction for Circlet Press and the author of the books *Black Feathers, The Velderet*, and *Telepaths Don't Need Safewords*. She welcomes visitors at www.ceciliatan.com.

Julie Travis was born in London in 1967. She played in various punk-rock bands and wrote political and music fanzines until her mid-twenties, when she began writing horror/dark fantasy short stories. Her work has appeared widely in the British science fiction small press, including *Kimota, REM, Psychotrope* and The Third Alternative's award-winning first anthology, *Last Rites and Resurrections*. As well as working on her first novel, Julie is now painting and studying chaos and runic magic from her new home in West Cornwall.

Robyn Vinten came to England from New Zealand in the mid-80s and forgot to leave. She lives in an unfashionable part of north

London with the neediest cat in the world. She plays football, tennis and, despite her advancing years, has taken to doing triathlons. She has three stories in various Women's Press anthologies and this is her third story in a Diva anthology. She is working on several novels that could be published without having to resort to a pseudonym. This story is of course dedicated to her mother, who died in December 2002.

Kim Watson was born in Hampton in 1964 and grew up in West Sussex. She has worked in publishing and marketing since graduating from business school and now lives in Walthamstow, north-east London, with her partner Angie and their daughter Ruby. Apart from marketing plans and press packs, she has written occasional interviews and features for the *Pink Paper*, *Shebang*, *Gay Times* and *Diva*. 'Your Ghost' is her first short story.

Bryony Weaver first caught the writing bug in Year 5, when a poem about the sun won her a Biro. Boldly going in search of other glittering prizes, she joined a lesbian *Star Trek* group, where a chance remark on a day trip to Dungeness led to her writing sci-fi and erotic stories and becoming a channel editor for RainbowNetwork.com. Her defining moment there came when she made it into the Guardian Online's 'Monkey' column, when Channel 4 got miffed that she'd returned the Size XXS Xena Warrior Princess T-shirts they'd offered for a competition. Bryony is currently the sub-editor for *Diva* and *Gay Times* magazines, and lives in Peckham with no cats.

Elizabeth Woodcraft was born in Essex and went to Birmingham University. She taught English in Leicestershire and France; then, after working for the National Women's Aid Federation, became a lawyer. She has practised as a barrister in London since 1980, representing Greenham Common peace women, striking miners, Clause 28 demonstrators and victims of domestic violence and sexual abuse. Elizabeth has written three novels, all featuring barrister Frankie Richmond. They are: *Good*

Bad Woman (which won a Lambda Literary Award), *Babyface* and *Crazy Arms*.

Fiona Zedde is a transplanted Jamaican lesbian currently living and working in Atlanta, Georgia. She spends half her days as a starving artist in the city's fabulous feminist bookstore (Charis Books and More) and the other half chained to her computer working on her first novel and on an endless collection of dark and dirty stories that she hopes to get published some day. If you see her, please don't make jokes about her getting a life. She might bite. Those starving artist types tend to do that.

The first two fabulous Diva anthologies

The Diva Book of Short Stories
edited by Helen Sandler

Winner of a Lambda Literary Award

"This wonderful collection presents fresh work from familiar names –
including Emma Donoghue, Stella Duffy and Jackie Kay – alongside
the best from a new generation of British talent... The selection and
originality of the work makes a refreshing change... Recommended!"
Gay's The Word website

"Look out for *The Diva Book of Short Stories*" *Observer Magazine*

"A brilliant collection of stories" *Rainbow Network*

"Audience participation opportunities, as well as twenty-eight stories,
make it good value" *Time Out*

"Helen Sandler merits high praise for her intelligent and resonant
arrangement of this cabaret of short fiction" *Lambda Book Report*

"Many [of the stories] are good and some have universal appeal"
Guardian

"Introducing fresh voices alongside established names, Sandler has
gathered together an indispensable collection of contemporary
lesbian fiction" *City Life*

"Britain's best-selling lesbian anthology, full of exciting new work"
Libertas! website

RRP £8.95 ISBN 1-873741-47-2

Groundswell: The Diva Book of Short Stories 2
edited by Helen Sandler

Even better than the first time...

"Helen Sandler has excelled herself with *Groundswell*... The stories are idiosyncratic, often throwing light on intimate lesbian lives where we least expect them" ★★★★★ *The List*

"This grown-up sister of the first Diva collection boasts a more daring range of writing styles and subject matter, from the usual suspects of school, crushes on older women, mothers and mental instability (sometimes all at once), to the thankless life of a sex toy" *Time Out*

"Plenty of good stuff" *Guardian*

"Helen Sandler has outdone herself with a wonderful mix of short stories by British, American and Canadian lesbian authors" *Gay City News*

"These authors show us that lesbians are wild, vibrant, introverted, diverse and occasionally (very) fucked up. It's all here" *Gay Times*

"From lightweight to luscious and all things in between... *Groundswell* will hopefully appeal to more than just its target audience"
★★★★ *Big Issue*

"There's a lot of heartbreak, extreme passion and a healthy dollop of insanity; but this is interspersed with a great deal of warmth, humour and self-assurance. You will want to re-read this collection and give it to your friends" *3Sixty*

"*Groundswell* has definitely taken its place among the best of Diva"
★★★★★ *Out in Greater Manchester*

"Proof that new lesbian fiction is alive and kicking... A real accomplishment" ★★★★ *Rainbow Network*

RRP £9.99 ISBN 1-873741-77-4

How to order your new Diva Books

Diva Books are available from bookshops including Libertas!, Silver Moon at Foyles, Gay's the Word, Prowler Stores and Borders, or direct from Diva's mail order service:
www.divamag.co.uk or freephone 0800 45 45 66
(international: +44 20 7739 4646).

When ordering direct, please add P&P (single item £1.75, two or more £3.45, all overseas £5) and quote the following codes: Diva Book of Short Stories DVB472, Groundswell GRO774, Necrologue NEC871.